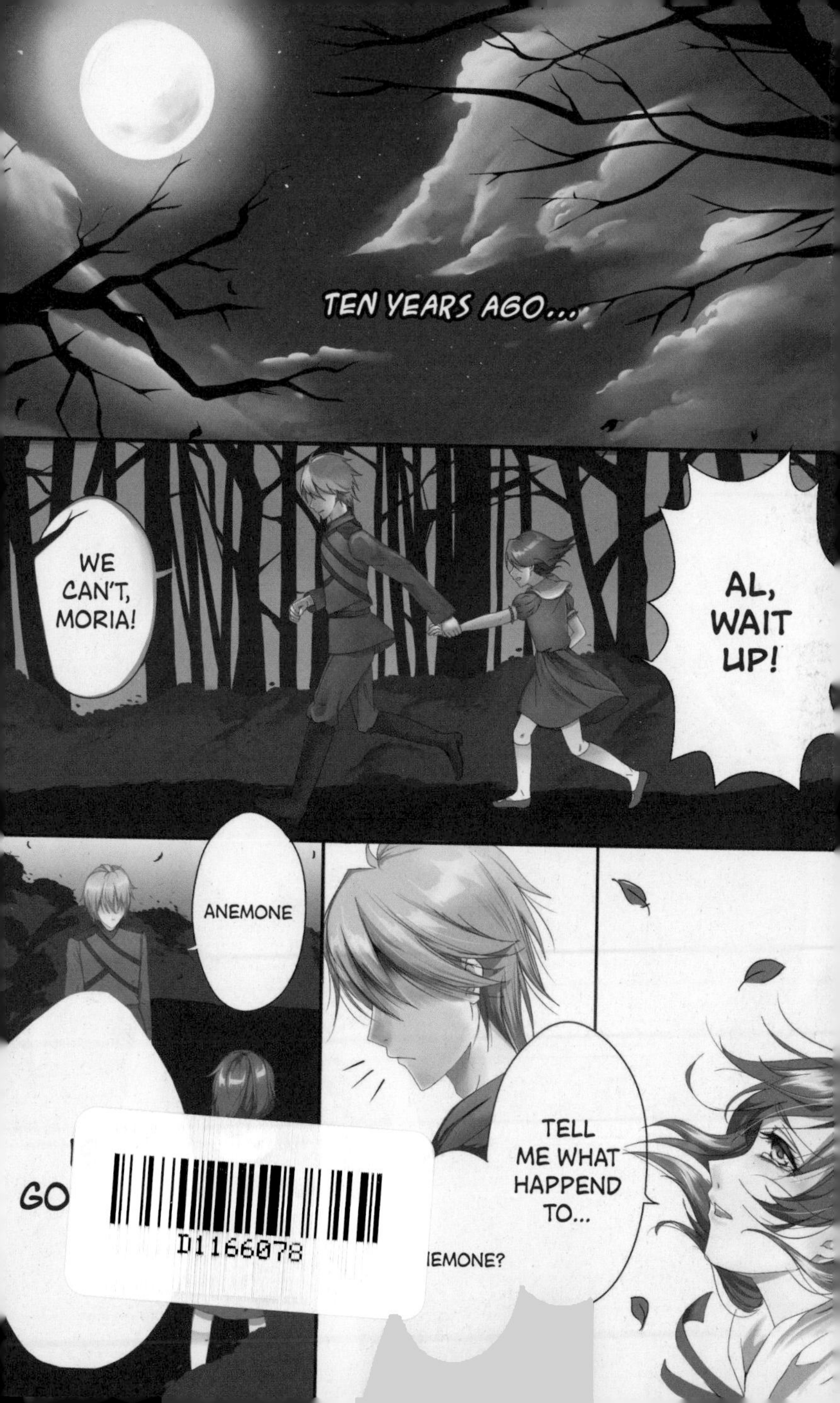

TEN YEARS AGO...
AL, WAIT UP!
WE CAN'T, MORIA!
TELL ME WHAT HAPPEND TO...
ANEMONE

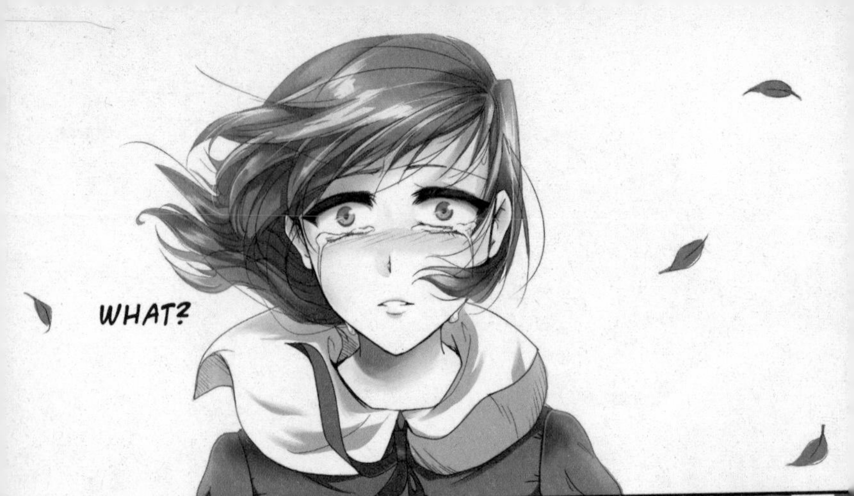
WHAT?

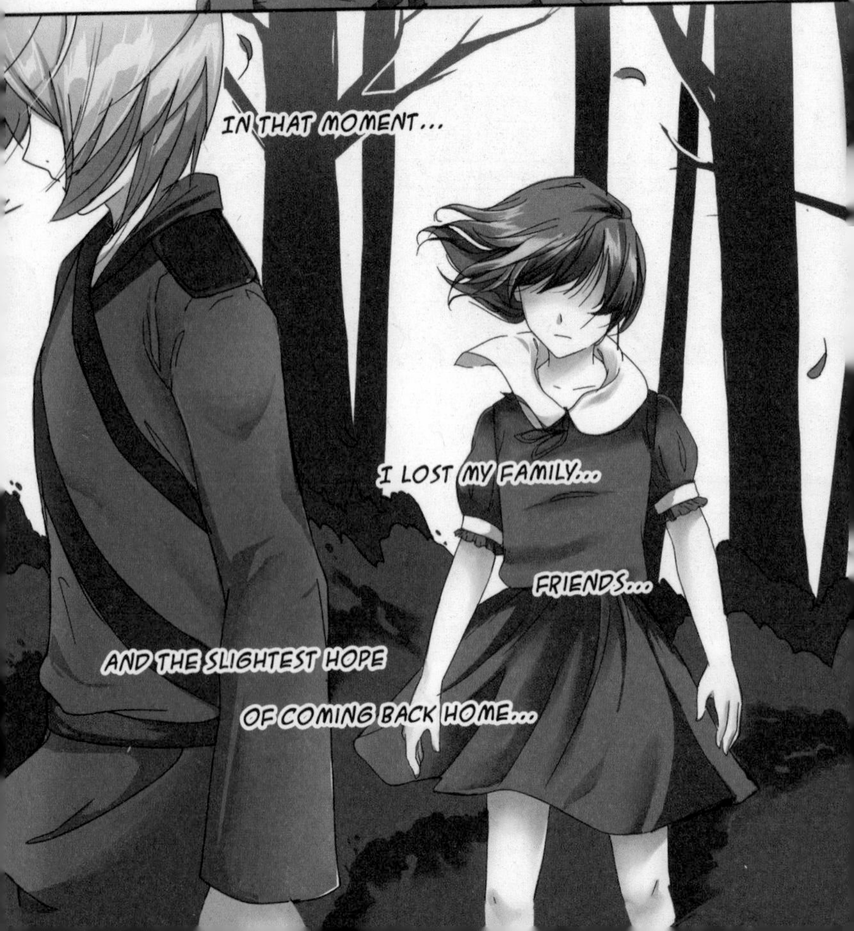
IN THAT MOMENT...
I LOST MY FAMILY...
FRIENDS...
AND THE SLIGHTEST HOPE
OF COMING BACK HOME...

A message to my readers

Hey there!

Thank you for picking up *Ocean of Secrets* - a story that I have put my heart and soul into!

I hope the book you're holding becomes a sweet reminder that you can reach your goals even when you're sailing against the wind. We all have magic powers within ourselves that turn these far-fetched dreams into realities; these powers include hard work and determination. I couldn't have done this without the support of my family, friends and fans.

I dedicate this manga to each and every person who believed in me and made me the artist I am today. I hope you find *Ocean of Secrets* as enjoyable and inspiring as I felt when creating it.

Love,
Sophie

Ocean of Secrets

CHAPTER 1

DESTINED TO LIVE

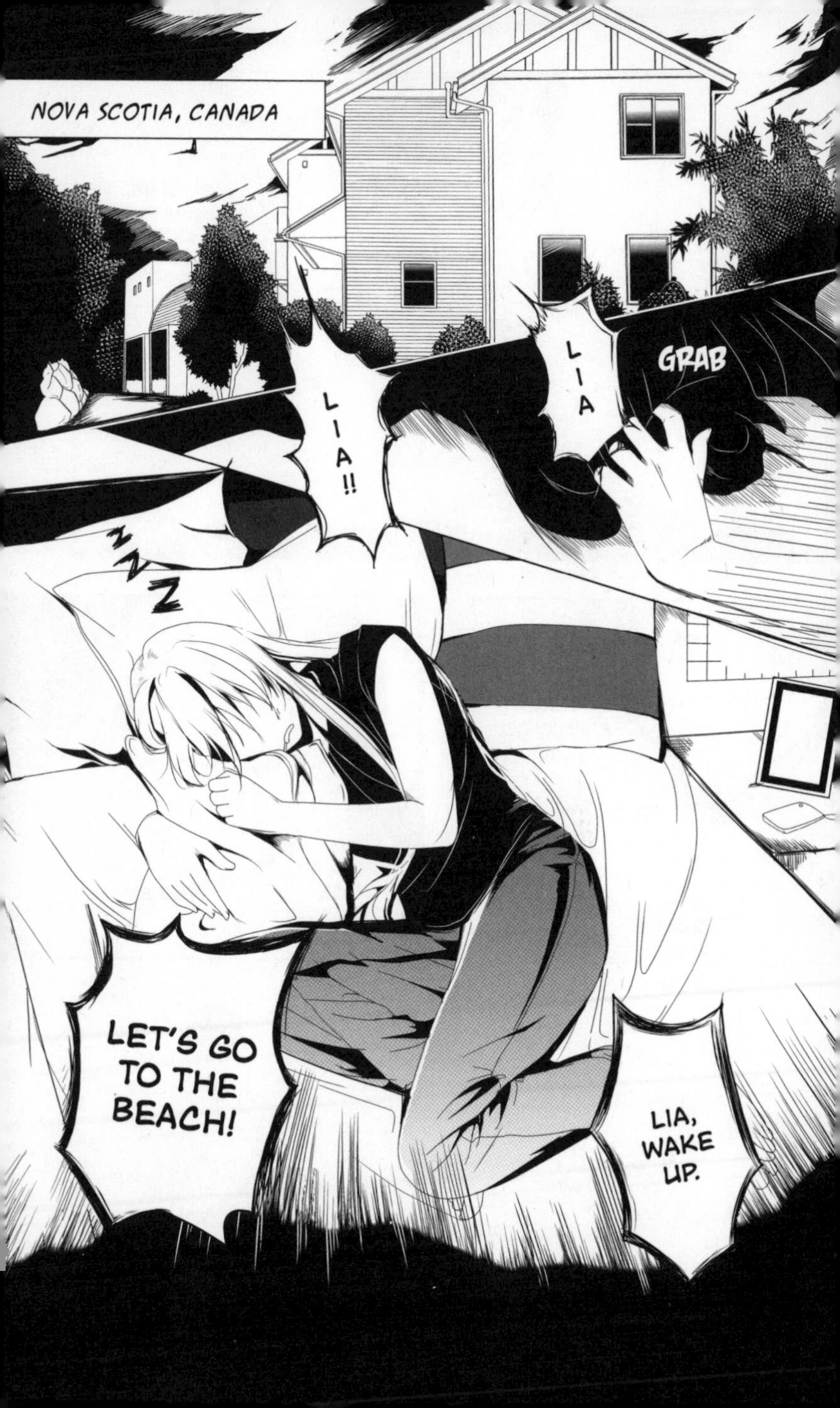

NOVA SCOTIA, CANADA
LIA
GRAB
LIA!!
ZZZ
LIA, WAKE UP.
LET'S GO TO THE BEACH!

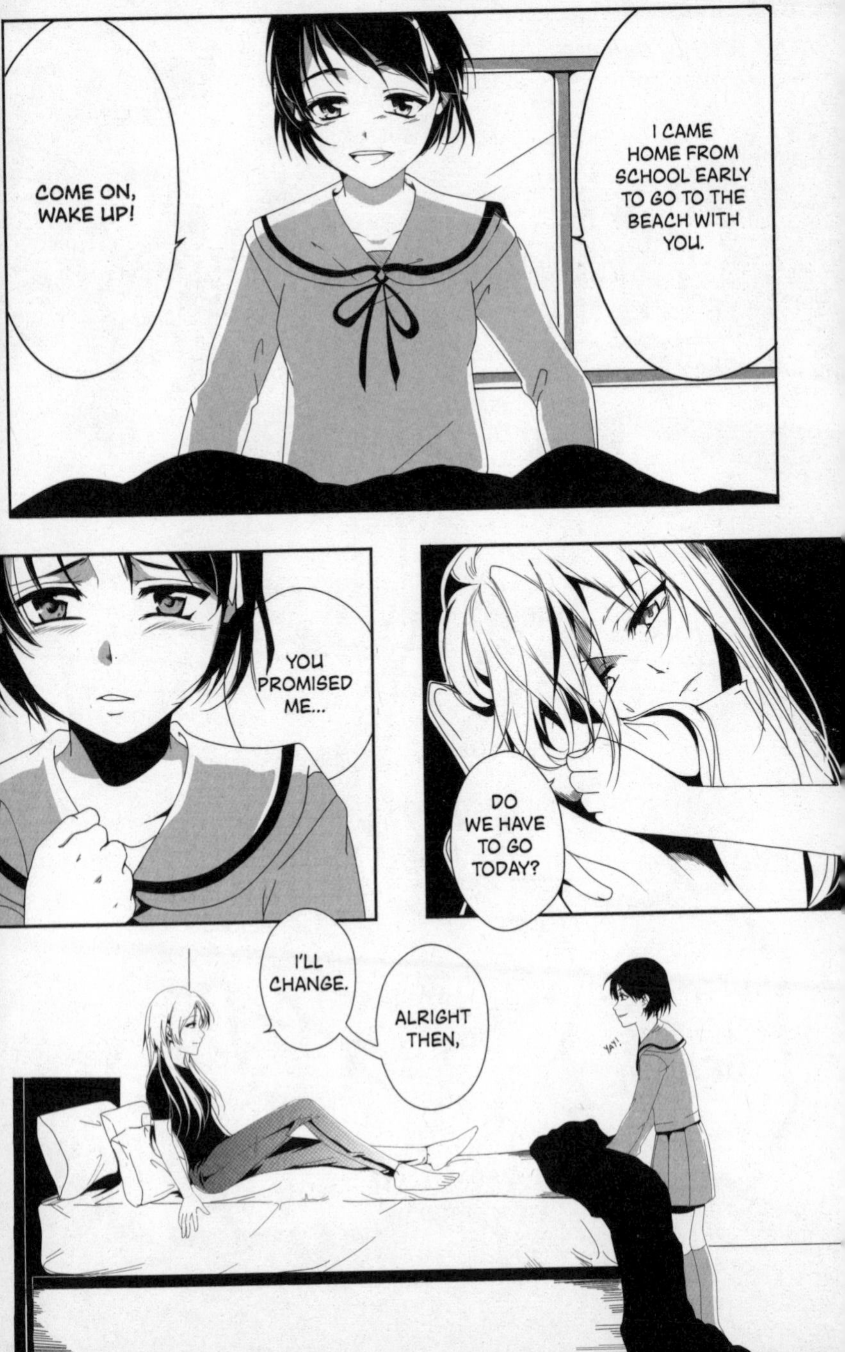
I CAME HOME FROM SCHOOL EARLY TO GO TO THE BEACH WITH YOU.
COME ON, WAKE UP!
DO WE HAVE TO GO TODAY?
YOU PROMISED ME...
ALRIGHT THEN,
I'LL CHANGE.
YAY!

READ THIS WAY

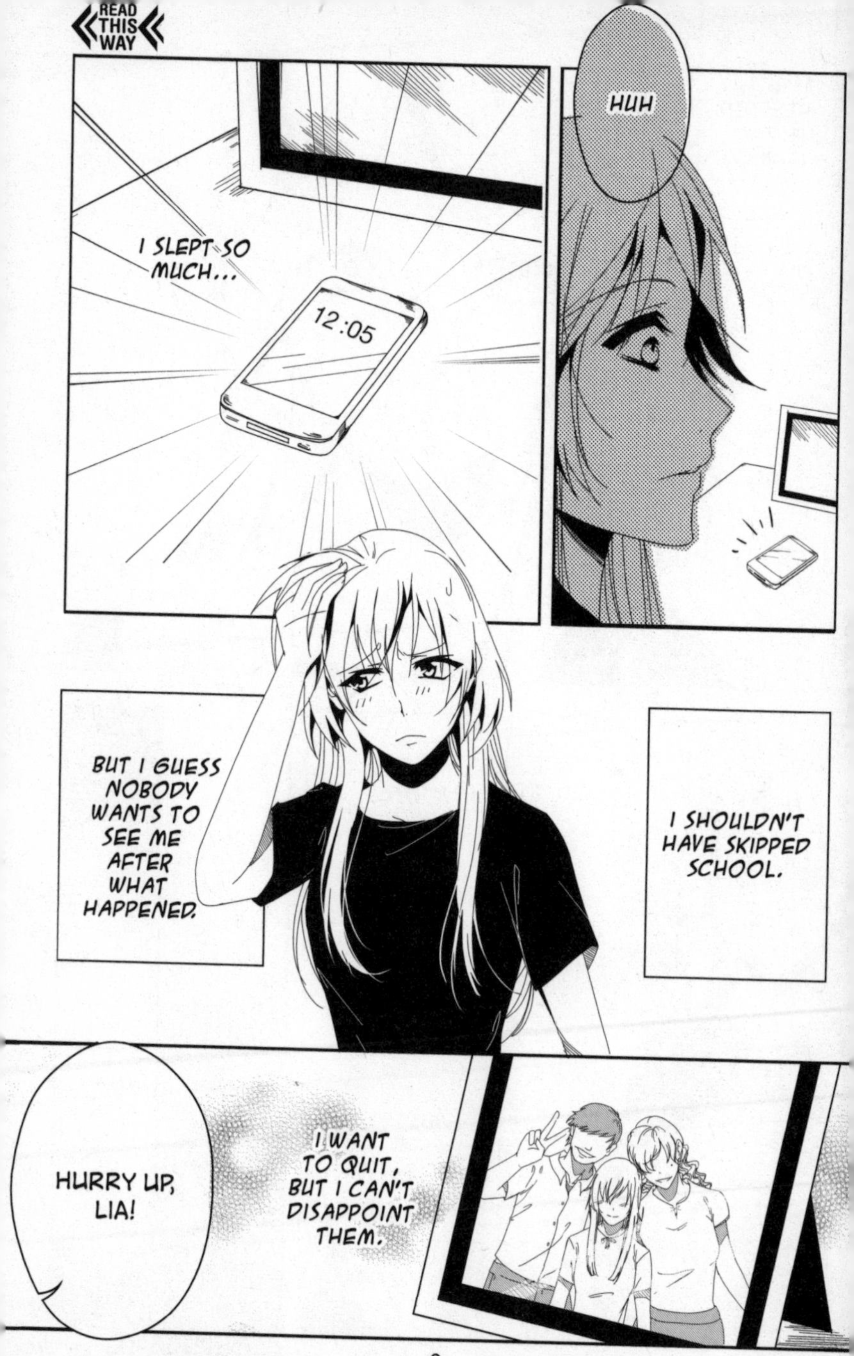
HUH
I SLEPT SO MUCH...
12:05
I SHOULDN'T HAVE SKIPPED SCHOOL.
BUT I GUESS NOBODY WANTS TO SEE ME AFTER WHAT HAPPENED.
I WANT TO QUIT, BUT I CAN'T DISAPPOINT THEM.
HURRY UP, LIA!

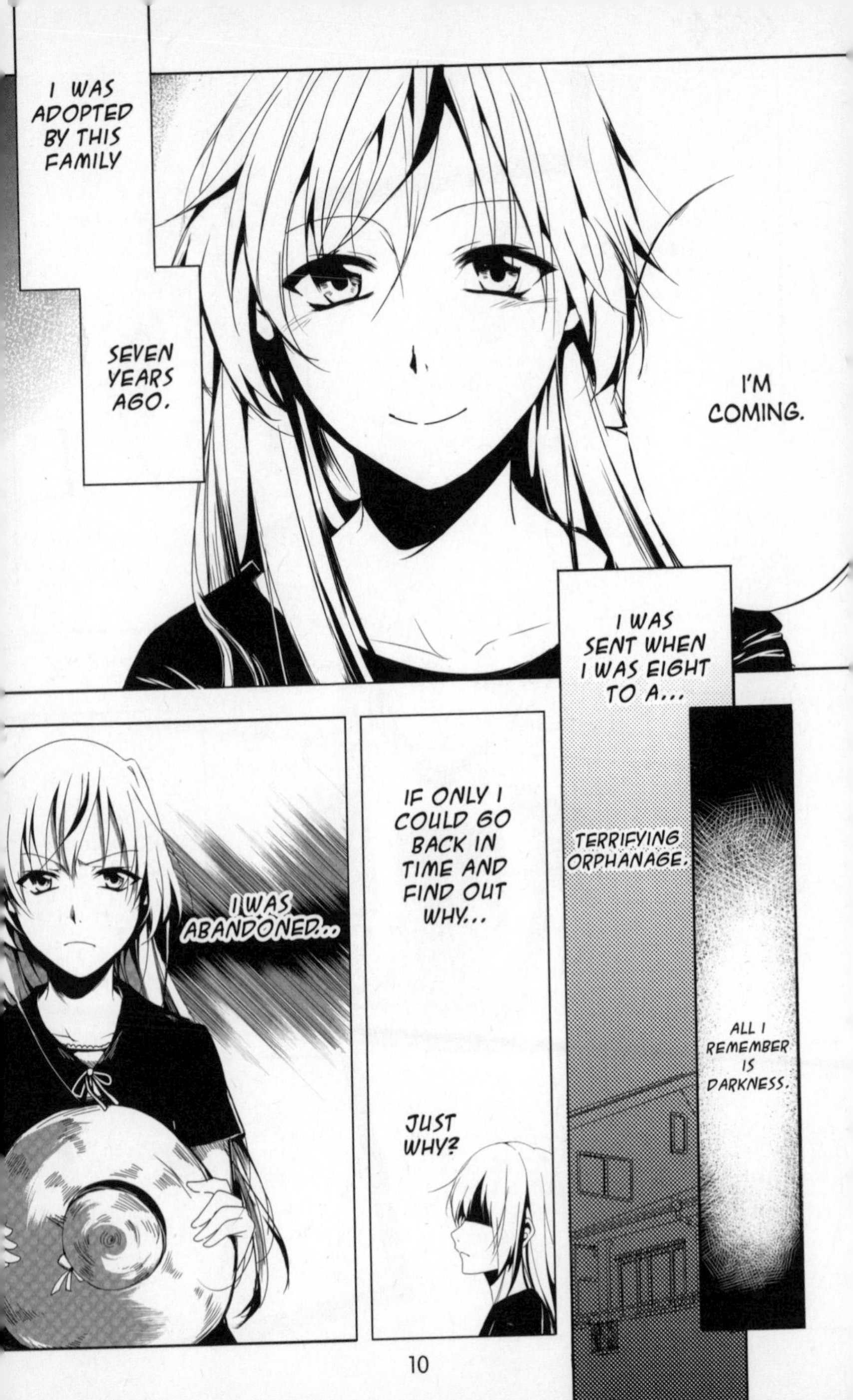
I'M COMING.
I WAS ADOPTED BY THIS FAMILY
SEVEN YEARS AGO.
I WAS SENT WHEN I WAS EIGHT TO A...
TERRIFYING ORPHANAGE.
ALL I REMEMBER IS DARKNESS.
IF ONLY I COULD GO BACK IN TIME AND FIND OUT WHY...
JUST WHY?
I WAS ABANDONED...

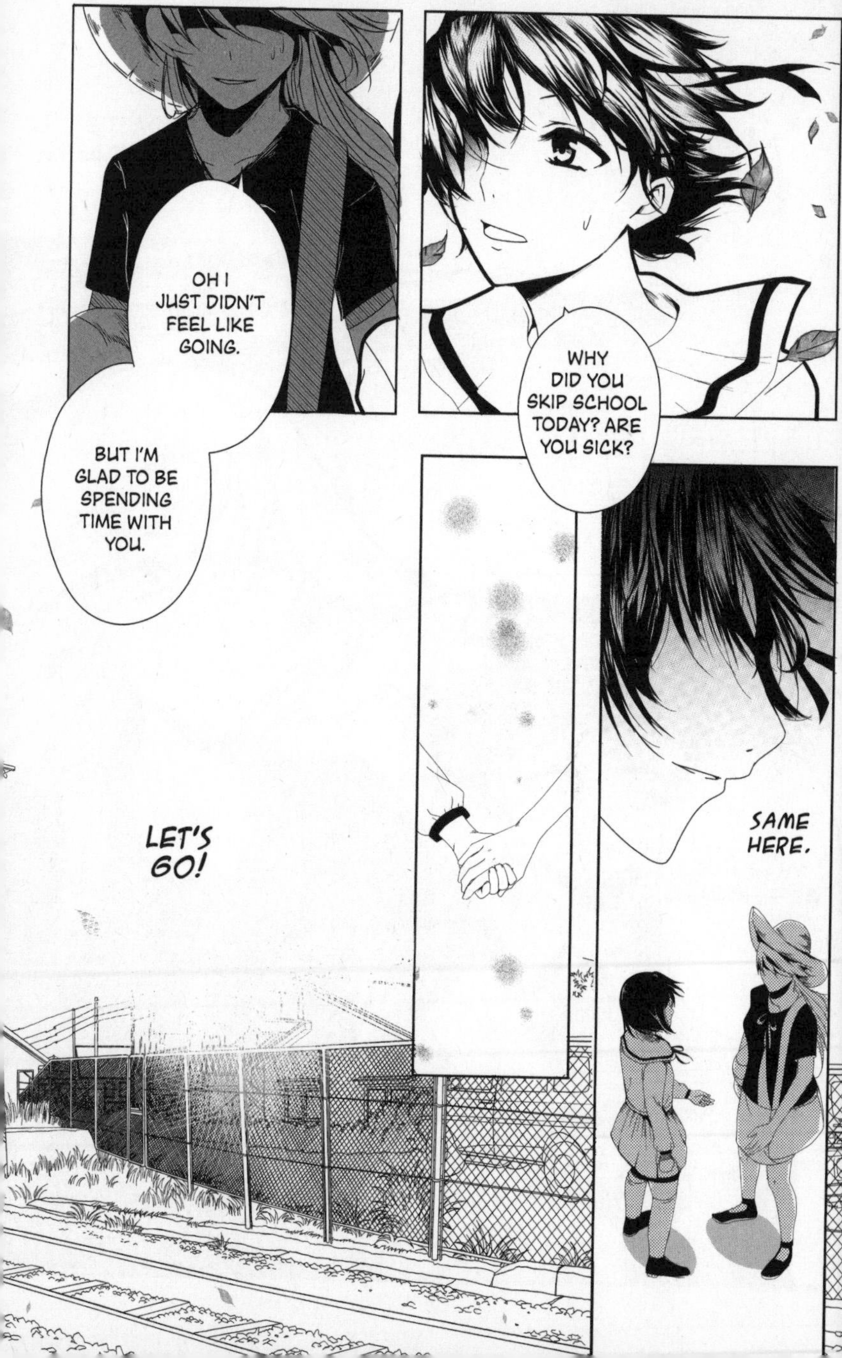
WHY DID YOU SKIP SCHOOL TODAY? ARE YOU SICK?
OH I JUST DIDN'T FEEL LIKE GOING.
BUT I'M GLAD TO BE SPENDING TIME WITH YOU.
SAME HERE.
LET'S GO!

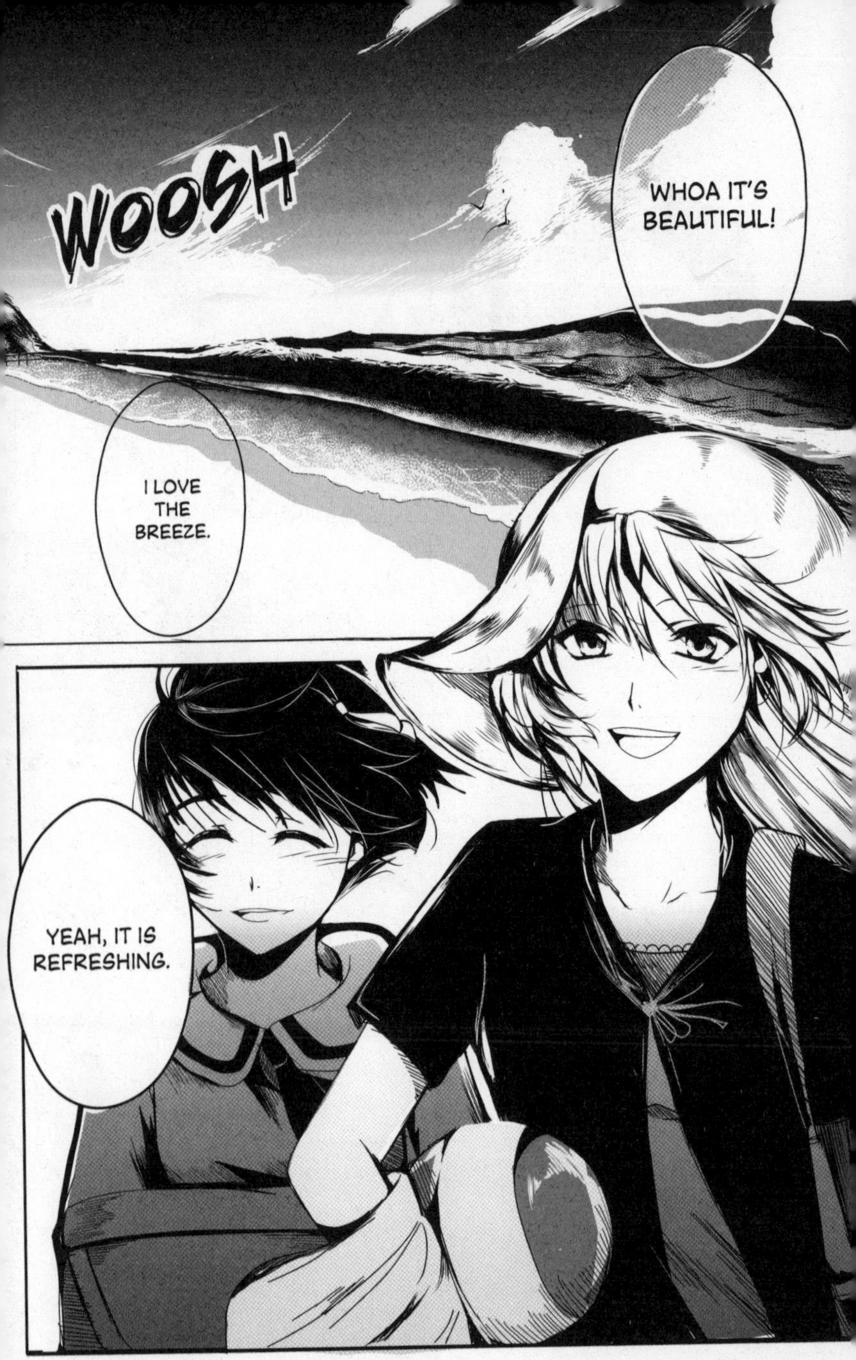
WHOA IT'S BEAUTIFUL!
WOOSH
I LOVE THE BREEZE.
YEAH, IT IS REFRESHING.

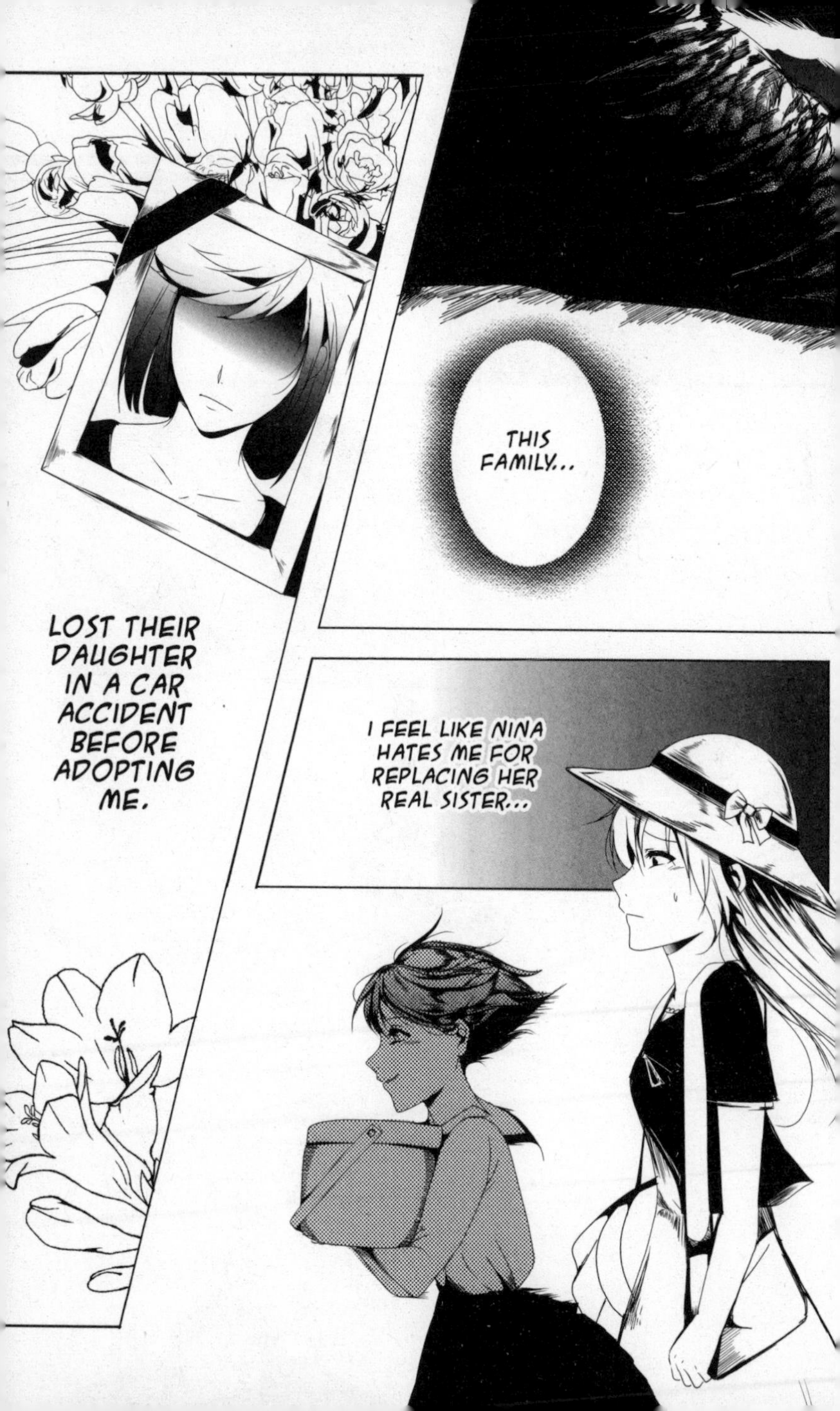
THIS FAMILY...
LOST THEIR DAUGHTER IN A CAR ACCIDENT BEFORE ADOPTING ME.
I FEEL LIKE NINA HATES ME FOR REPLACING HER REAL SISTER...

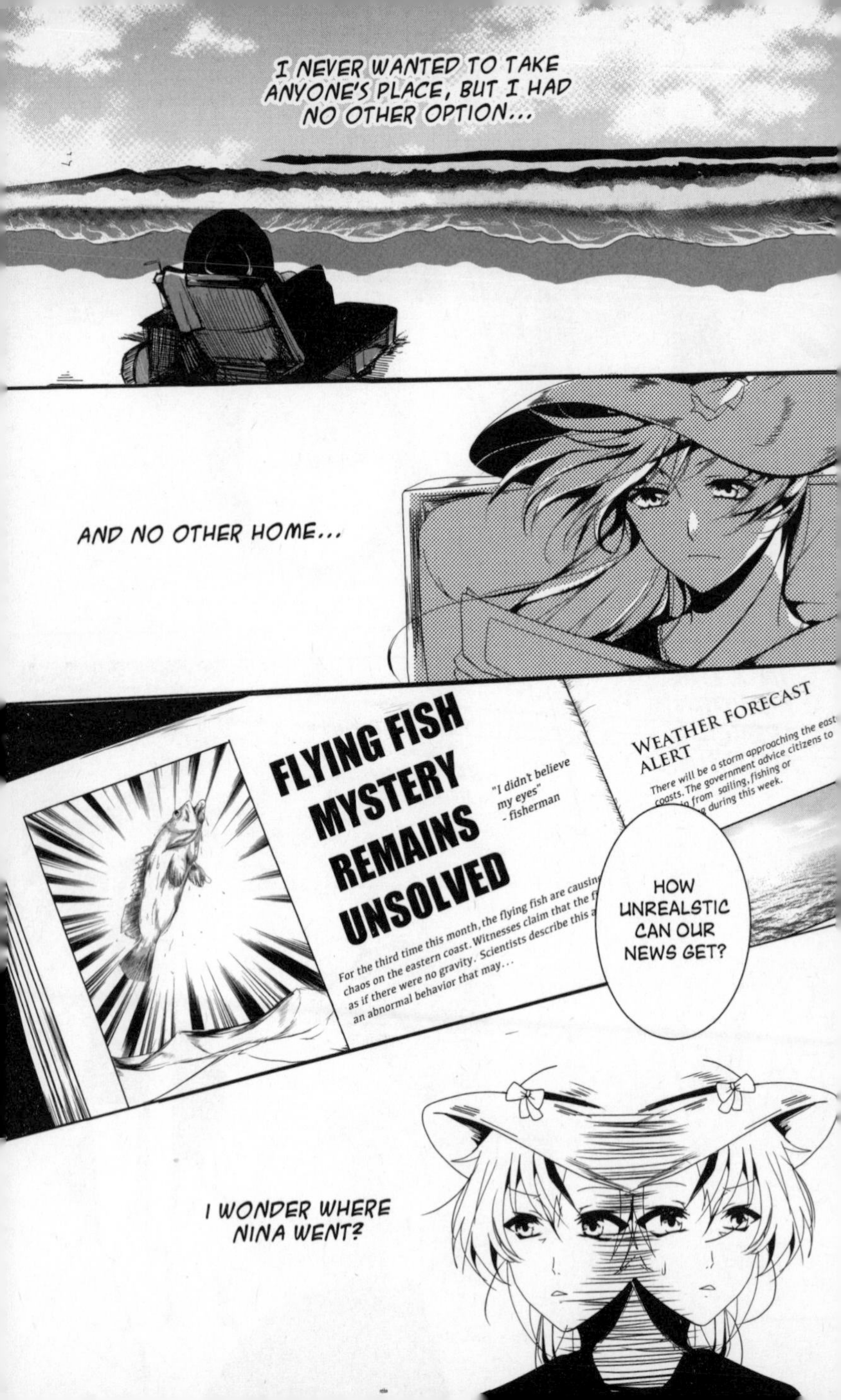
I NEVER WANTED TO TAKE ANYONE'S PLACE, BUT I HAD NO OTHER OPTION...
AND NO OTHER HOME...
WEATHER FORECAST ALERT
There will be a storm approaching the east
coasts. The government advice citizens to
from sailing, fishing or
during this week.
FLYING FISH MYSTERY REMAINS UNSOLVED
"I didn't believe my eyes" - fisherman
For the third time this month, the flying fish are
chaos on the eastern coast. Witnesses claim that the
as if there were no gravity. Scientists describe this
an abnormal behavior that may...
HOW UNREALSTIC CAN OUR NEWS GET?
I WONDER WHERE NINA WENT?

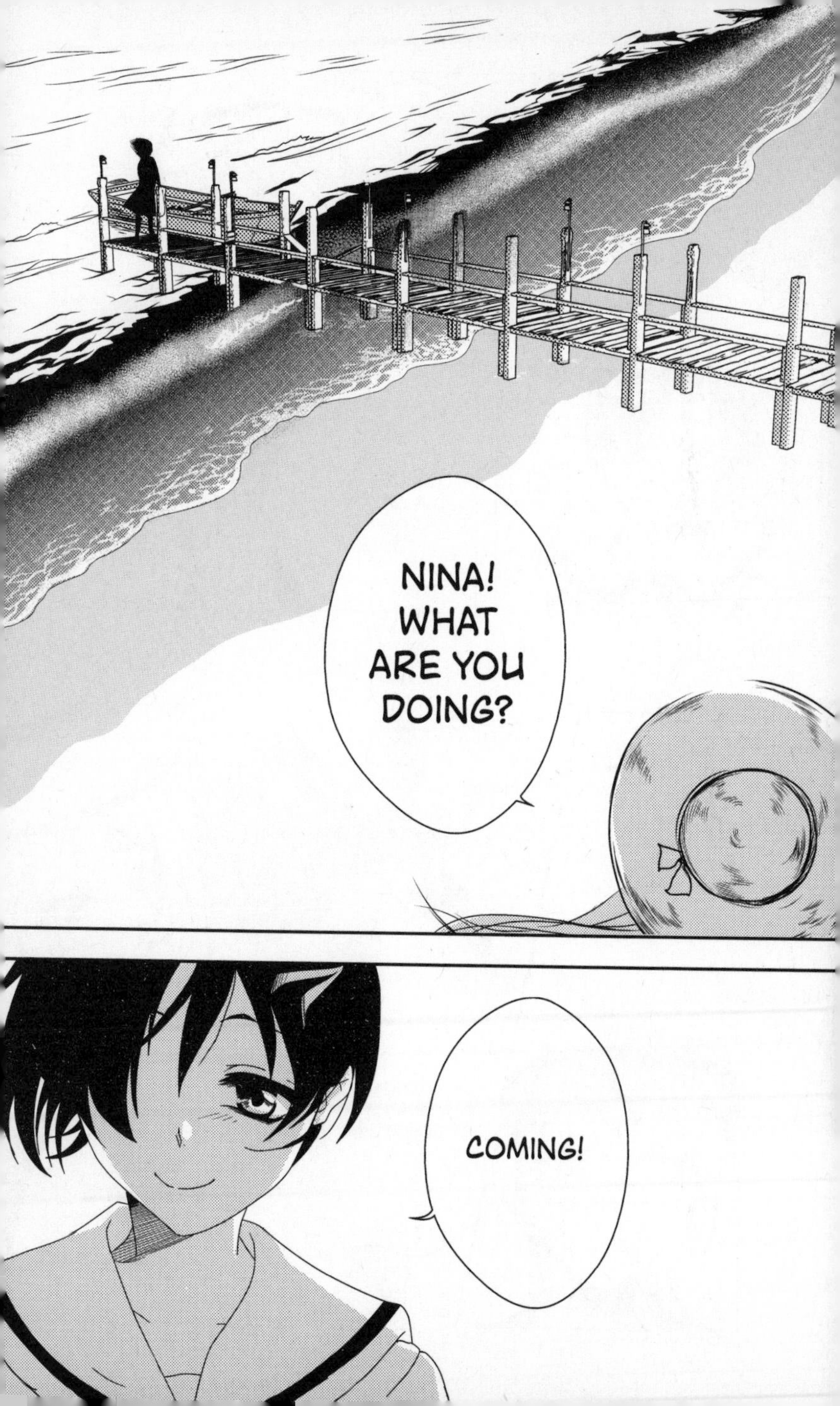
NINA! WHAT ARE YOU DOING?
COMING!

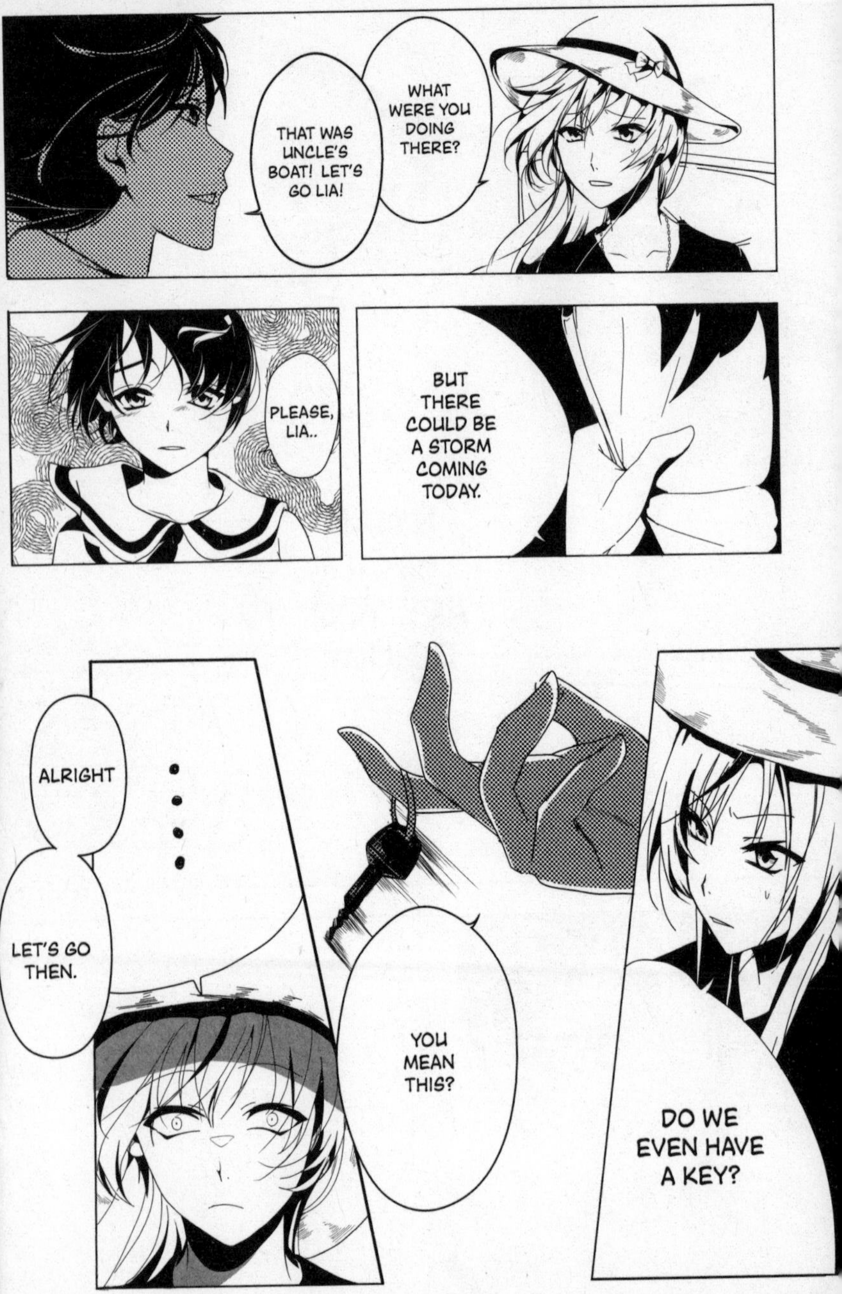
WHAT WERE YOU DOING THERE?
THAT WAS UNCLE'S BOAT! LET'S GO LIA!
BUT THERE COULD BE A STORM COMING TODAY.
PLEASE, LIA..
DO WE EVEN HAVE A KEY?
YOU MEAN THIS?
• • • •
ALRIGHT
LET'S GO THEN.

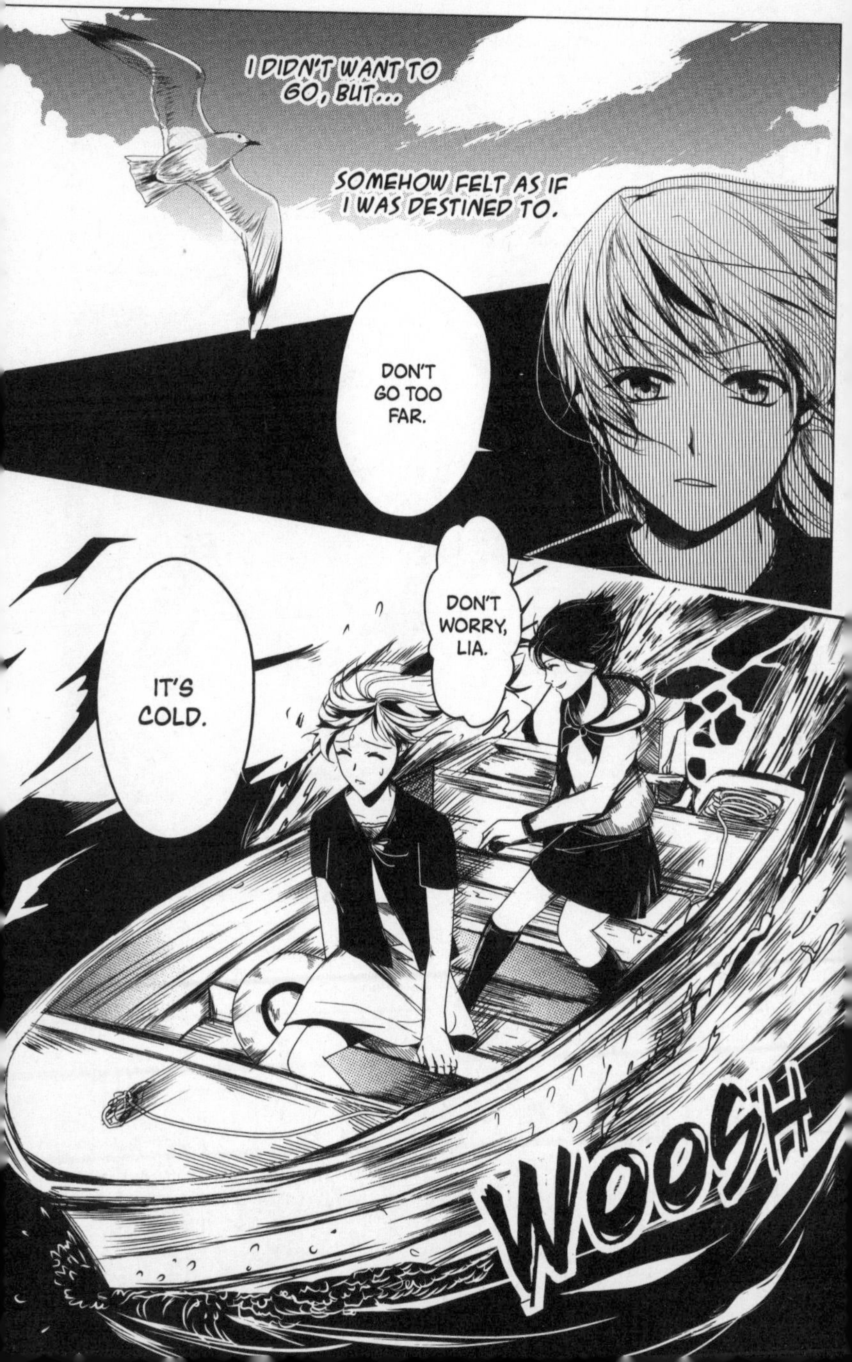
I DIDN'T WANT TO GO, BUT...
SOMEHOW FELT AS IF I WAS DESTINED TO.
DON'T GO TOO FAR.
DON'T WORRY, LIA.
IT'S COLD.
WOOSH

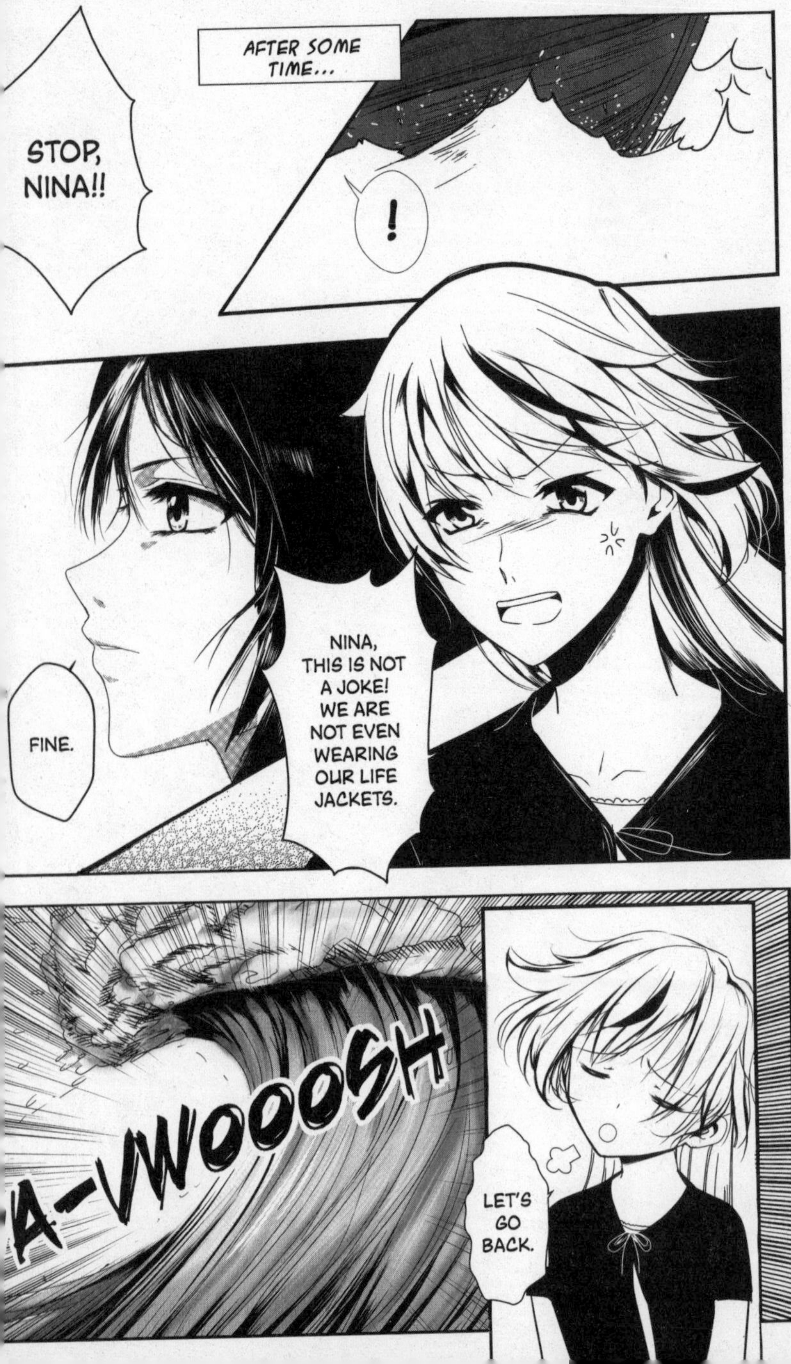
AFTER SOME TIME...
!
STOP, NINA!!
NINA, THIS IS NOT A JOKE! WE ARE NOT EVEN WEARING OUR LIFE JACKETS.
FINE.
LET'S GO BACK.
A-VWOOOSH

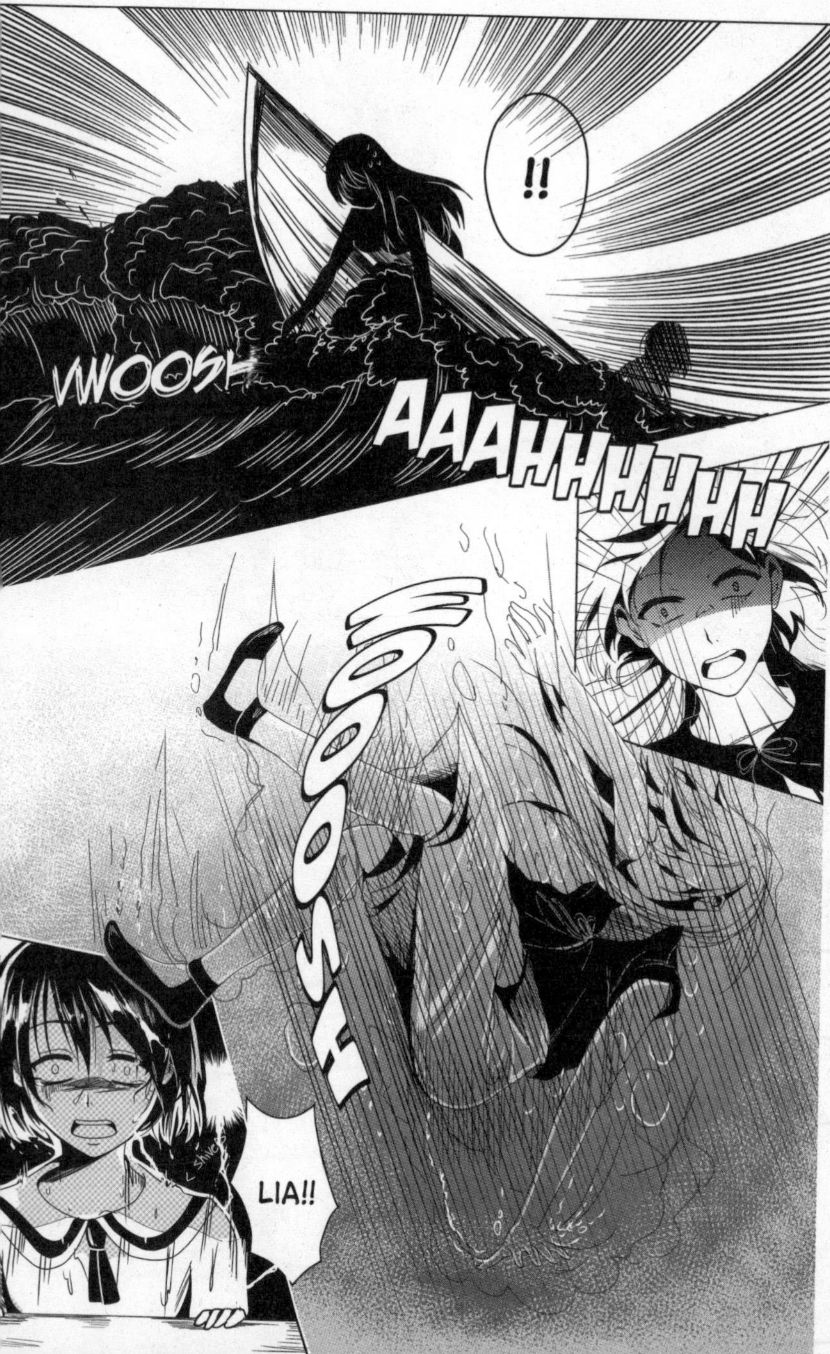
!!
AAAHHHHHHH
VWOOSH
WOOOOOSH
shiver
LIA!!

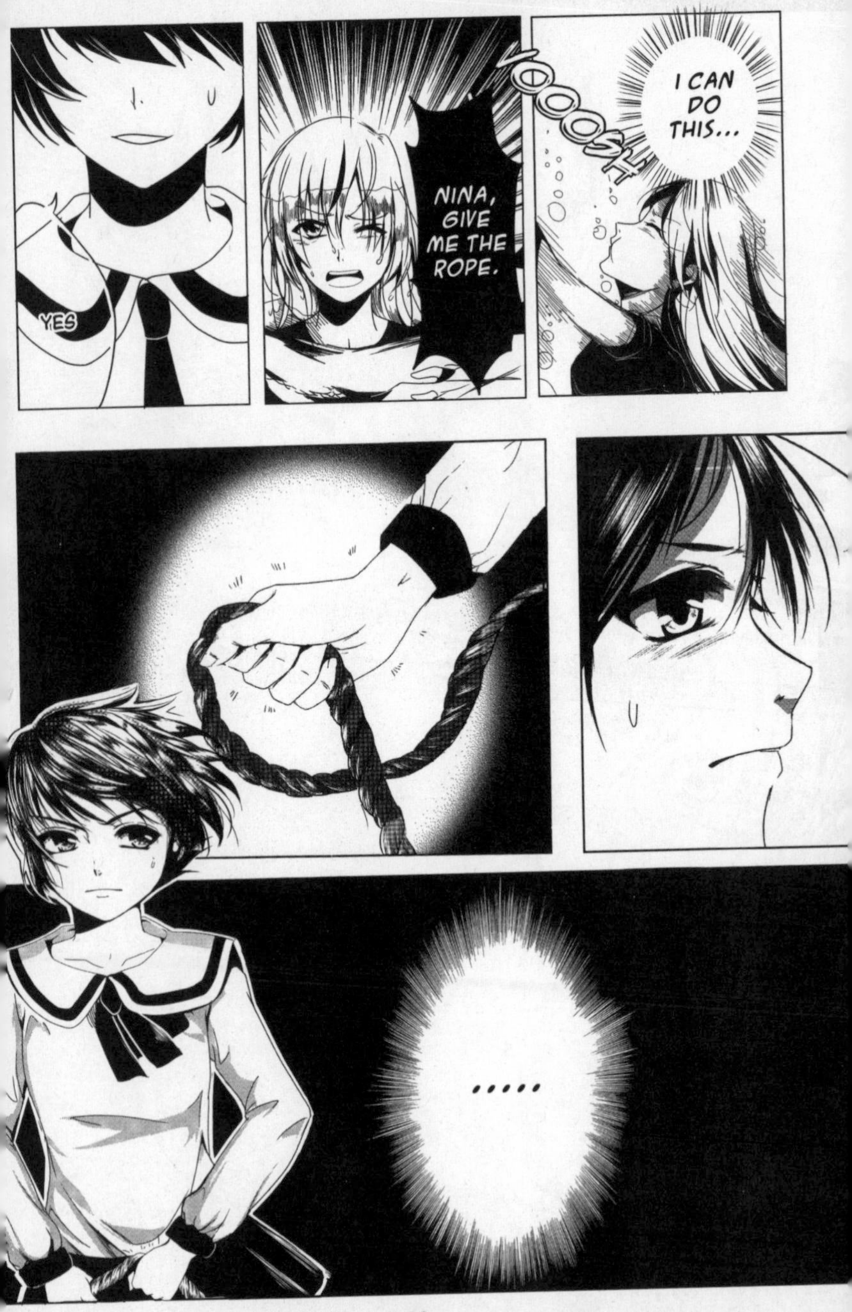
I CAN DO THIS...
VOOOSH
NINA, GIVE ME THE ROPE.
YES
.....

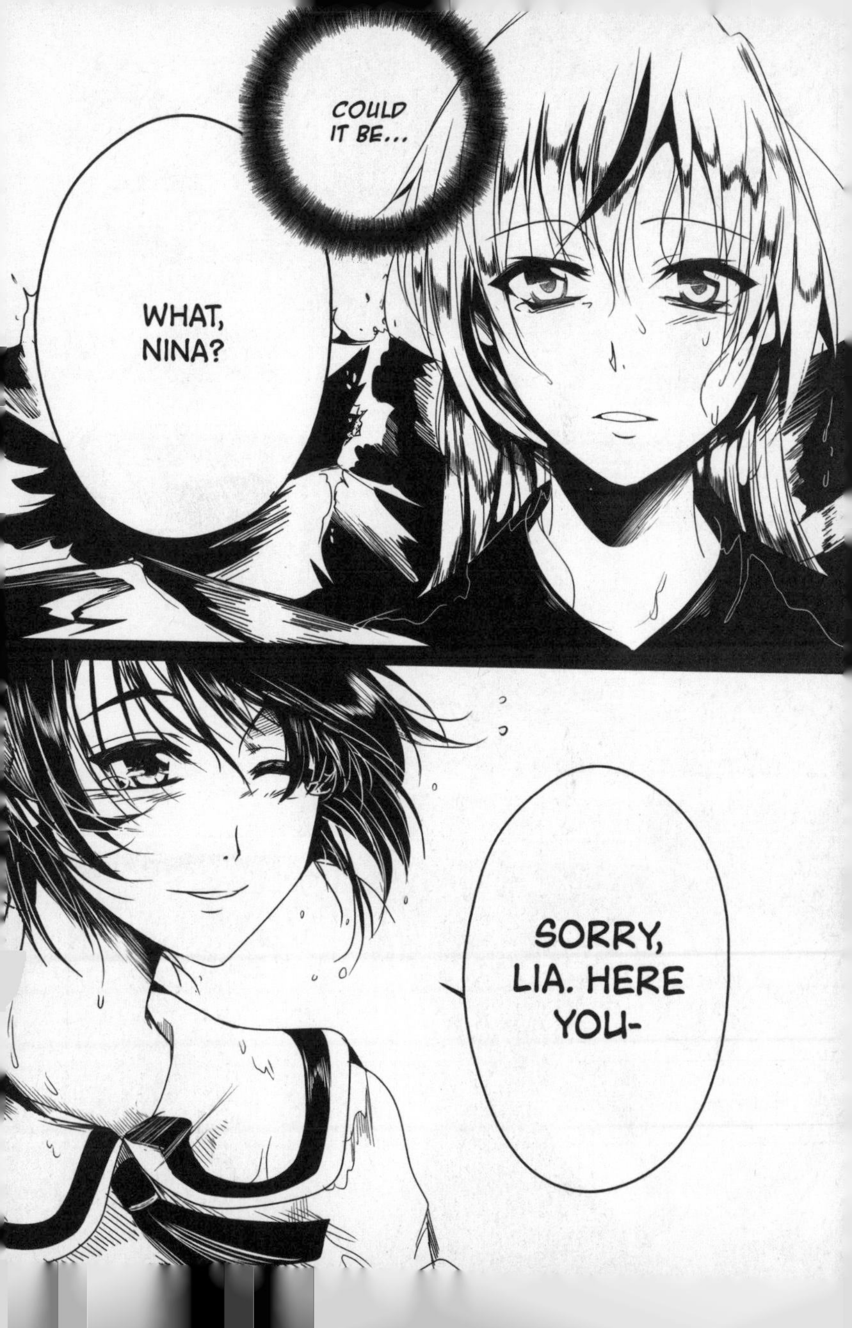
COULD IT BE...
WHAT, NINA?
SORRY, LIA. HERE YOU-

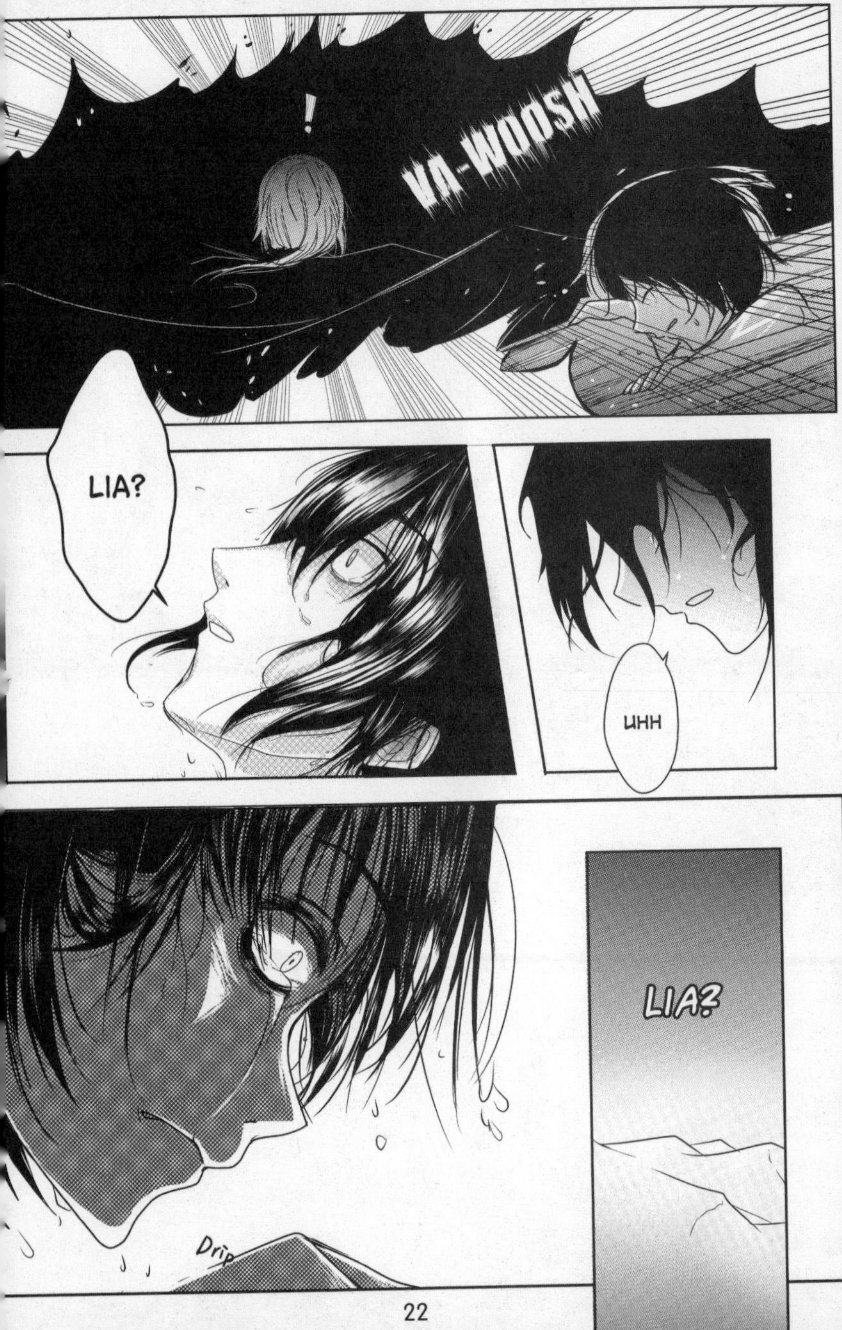
!
VA-WOOSH
UHH
LIA?
LIA?
Drip

READ THIS WAY

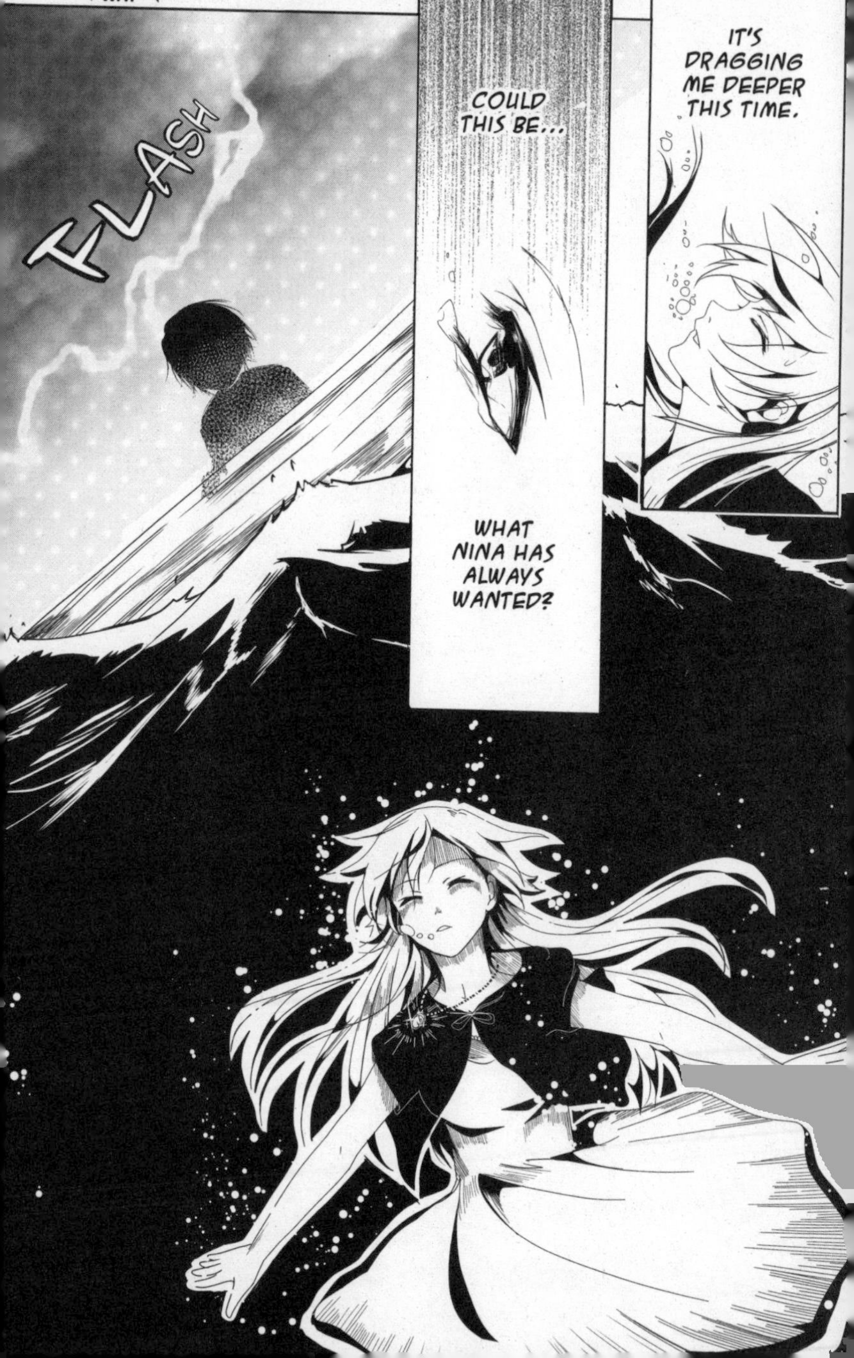
IT'S DRAGGING ME DEEPER THIS TIME.
COULD THIS BE...
WHAT NINA HAS ALWAYS WANTED?
FLASH

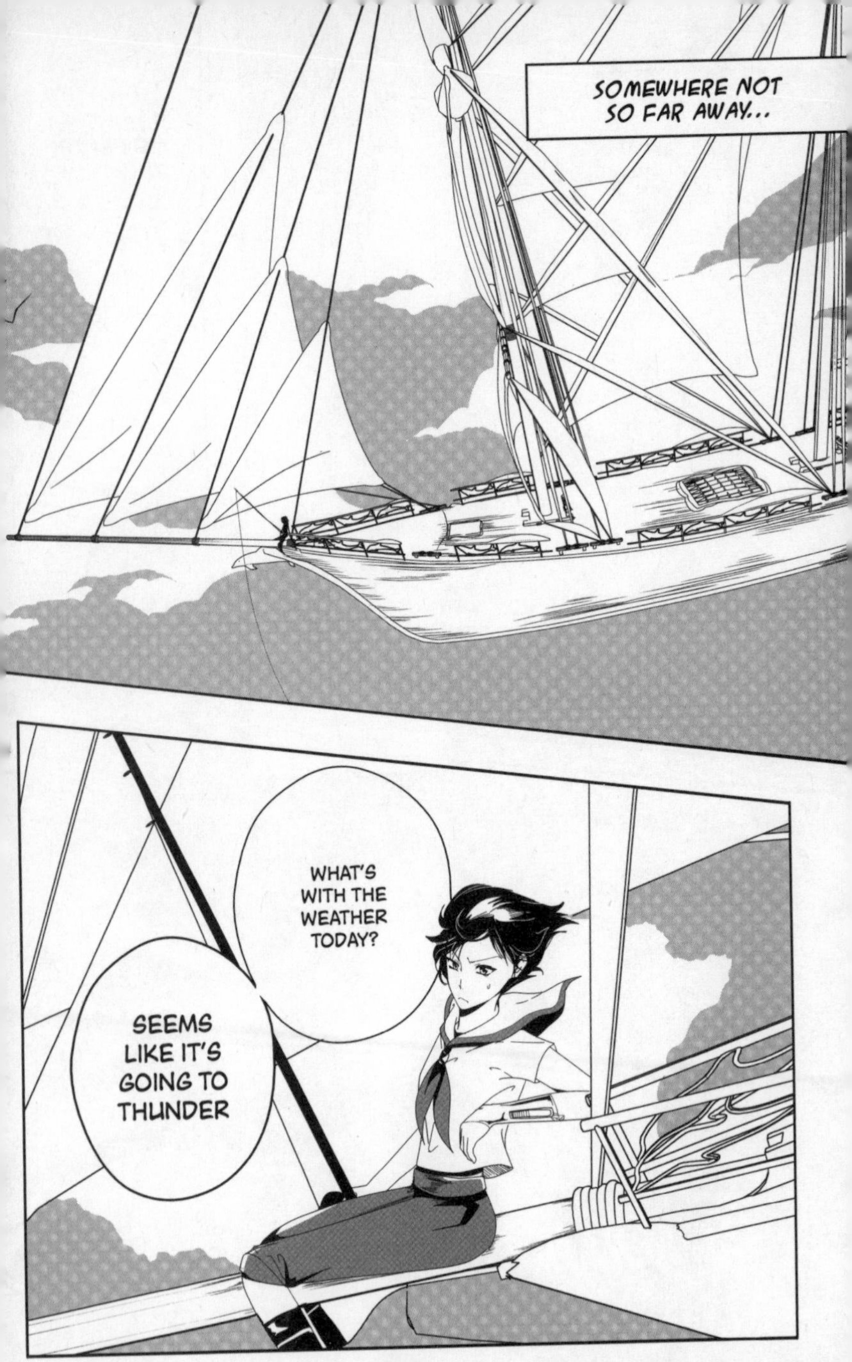
SOMEWHERE NOT SO FAR AWAY...
WHAT'S WITH THE WEATHER TODAY?
SEEMS LIKE IT'S GOING TO THUNDER

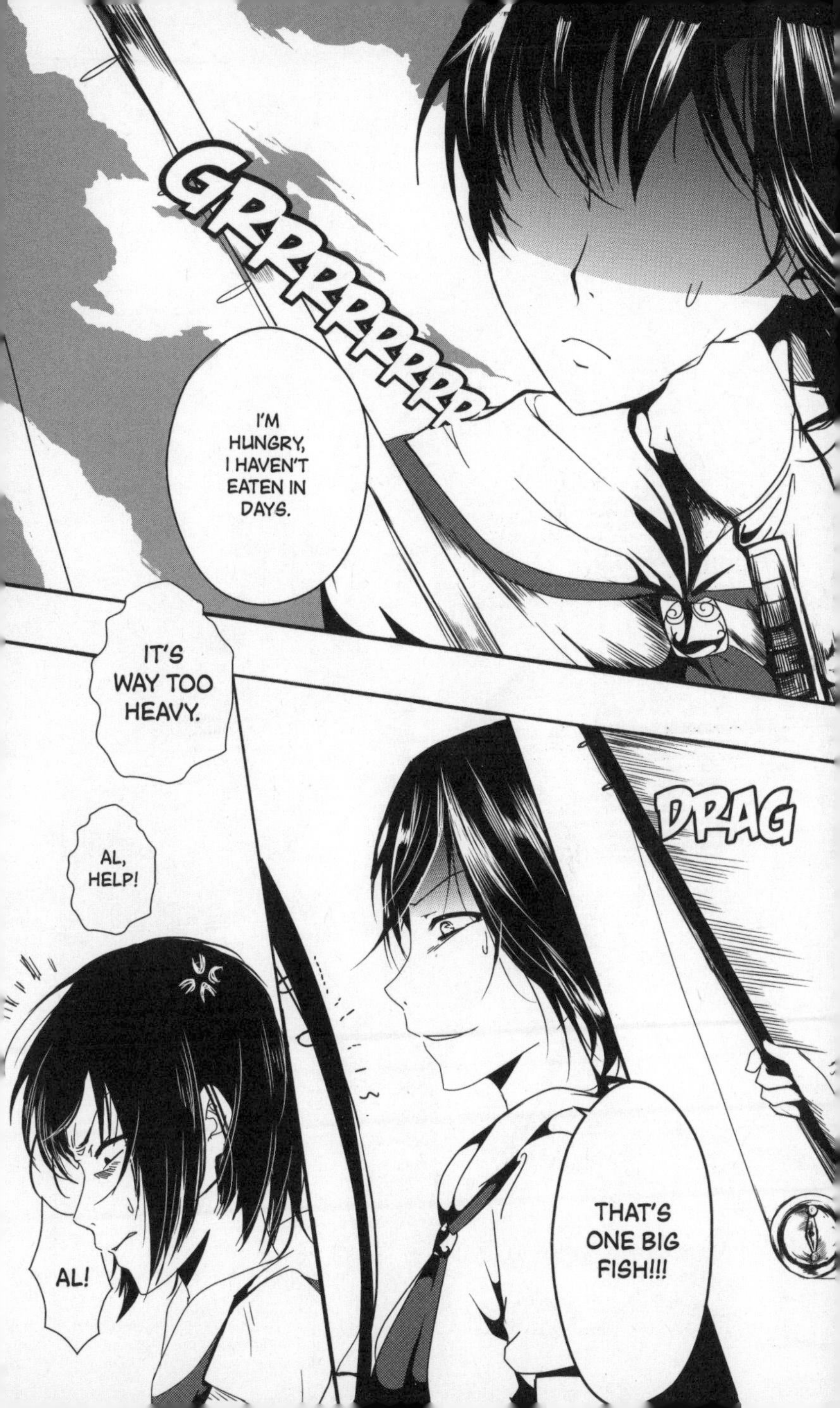
GRRRRRRRR
I'M HUNGRY, I HAVEN'T EATEN IN DAYS.
DRAG
THAT'S ONE BIG FISH!!!
IT'S WAY TOO HEAVY.
AL, HELP!
AL!

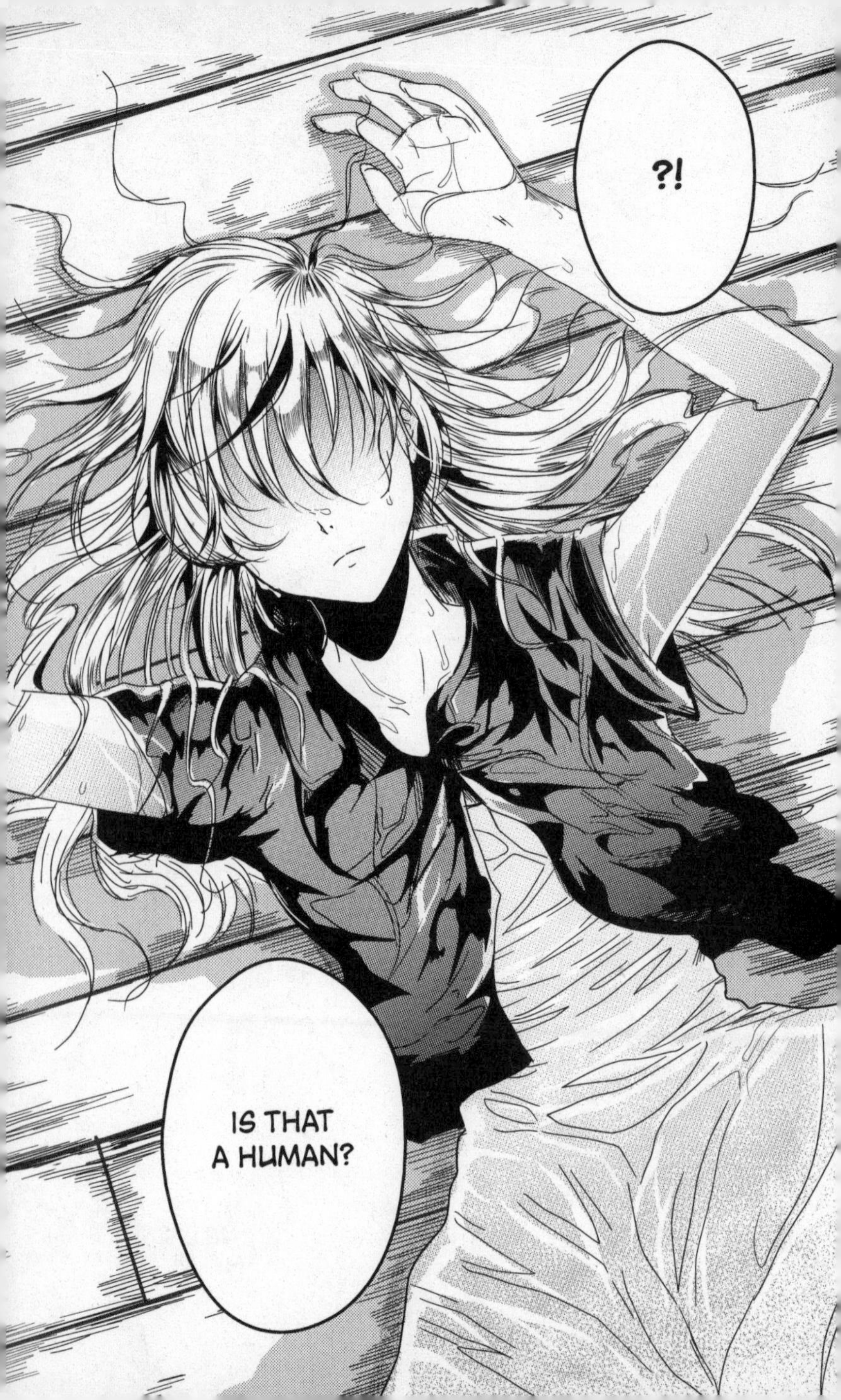
?!
IS THAT A HUMAN?

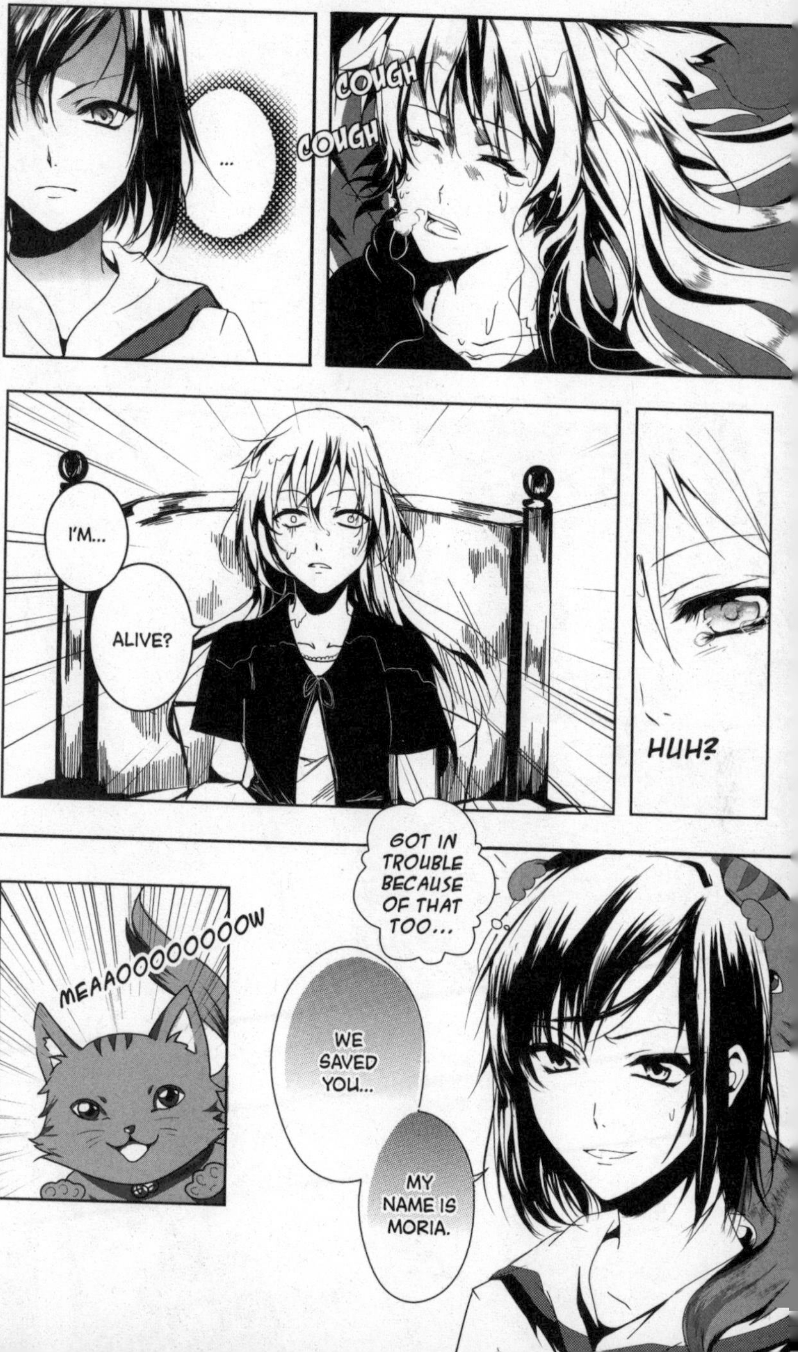
COUGH
COUGH
...
HUH?
I'M...
ALIVE?
GOT IN TROUBLE BECAUSE OF THAT TOO...
WE SAVED YOU...
MY NAME IS MORIA.
MEAAOOOOOOOOOW

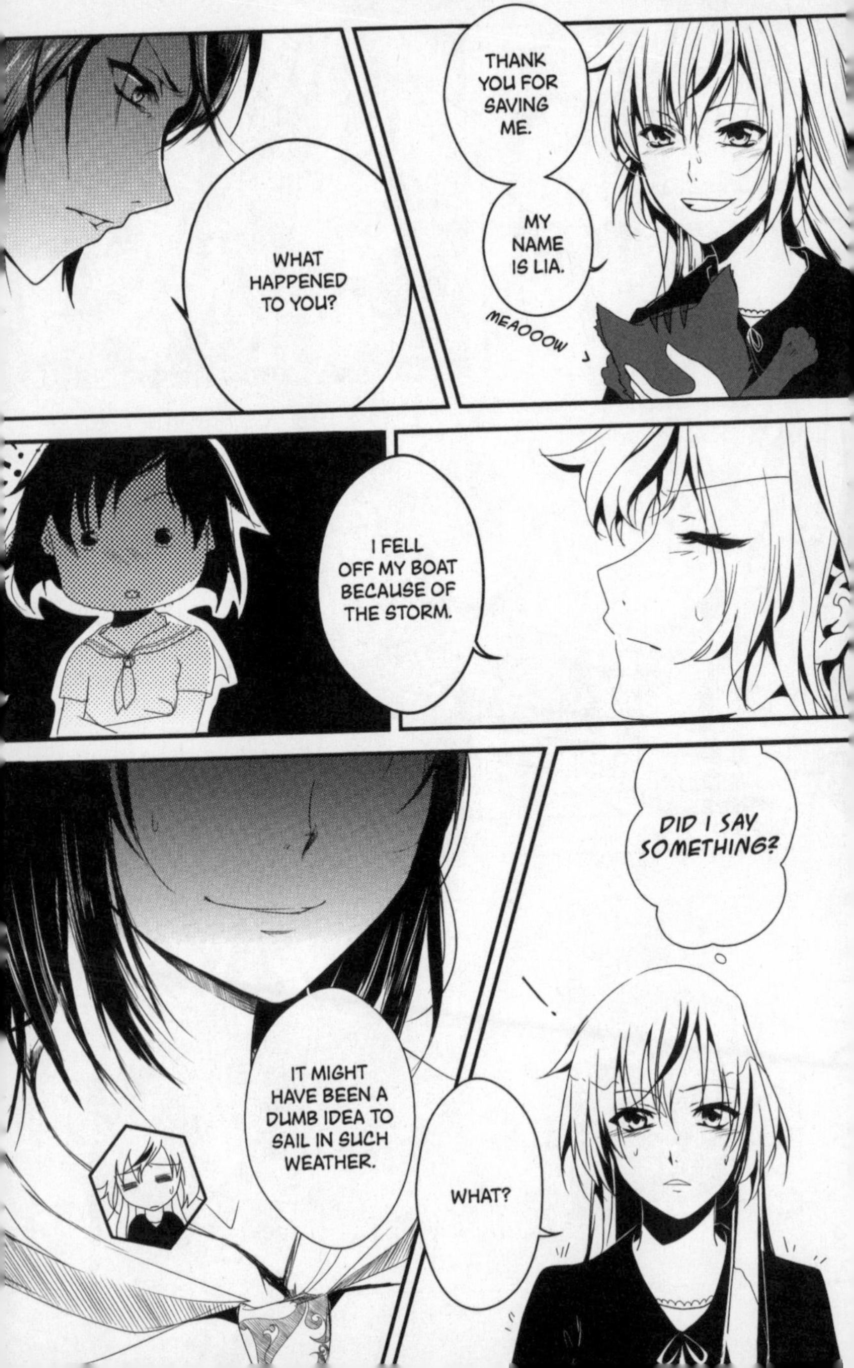
THANK YOU FOR SAVING ME.
MY NAME IS LIA.
MEAOOOW
WHAT HAPPENED TO YOU?
I FELL OFF MY BOAT BECAUSE OF THE STORM.
DID I SAY SOMETHING?
WHAT?
IT MIGHT HAVE BEEN A DUMB IDEA TO SAIL IN SUCH WEATHER.

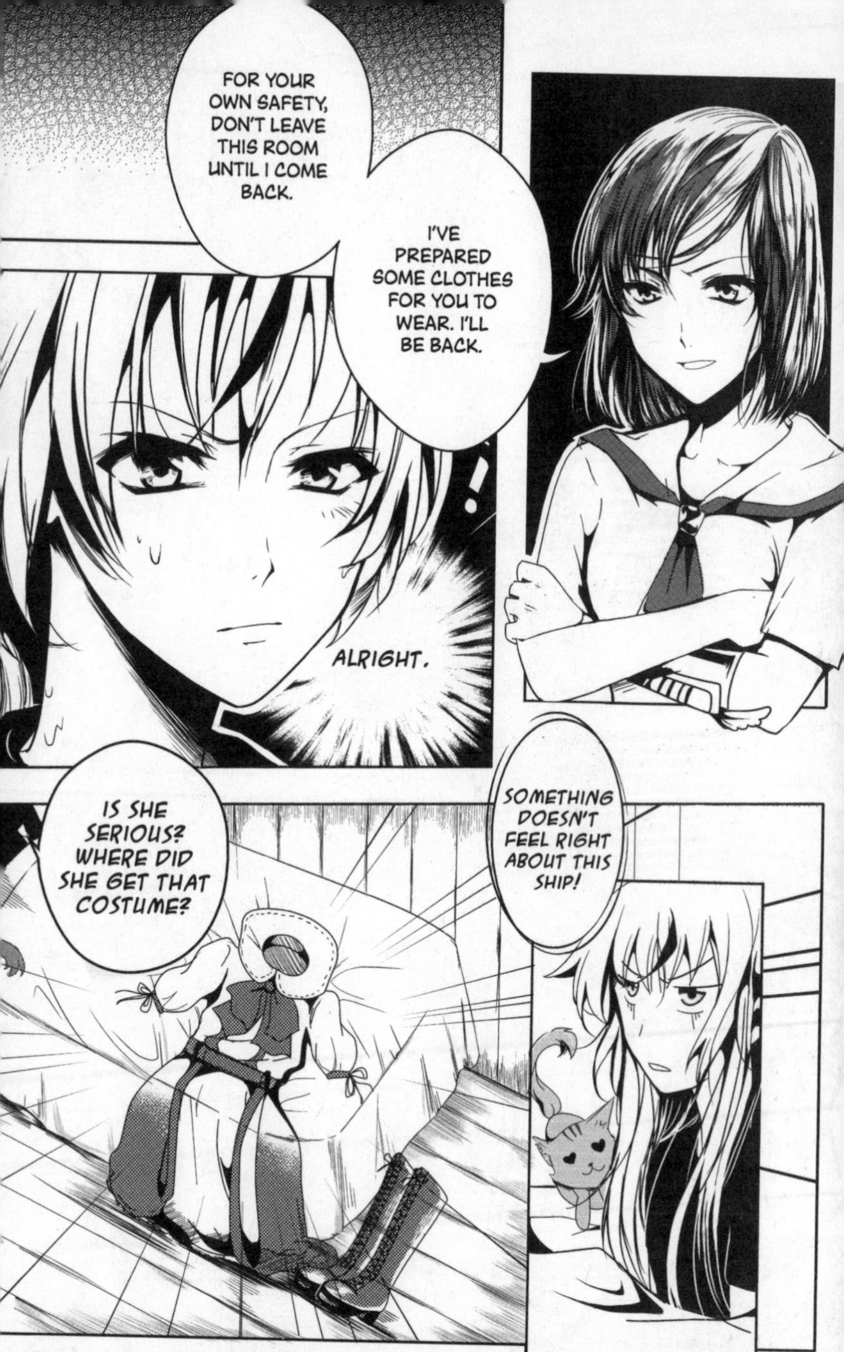
FOR YOUR OWN SAFETY, DON'T LEAVE THIS ROOM UNTIL I COME BACK.
I'VE PREPARED SOME CLOTHES FOR YOU TO WEAR. I'LL BE BACK.
!
ALRIGHT.
SOMETHING DOESN'T FEEL RIGHT ABOUT THIS SHIP!
IS SHE SERIOUS? WHERE DID SHE GET THAT COSTUME?

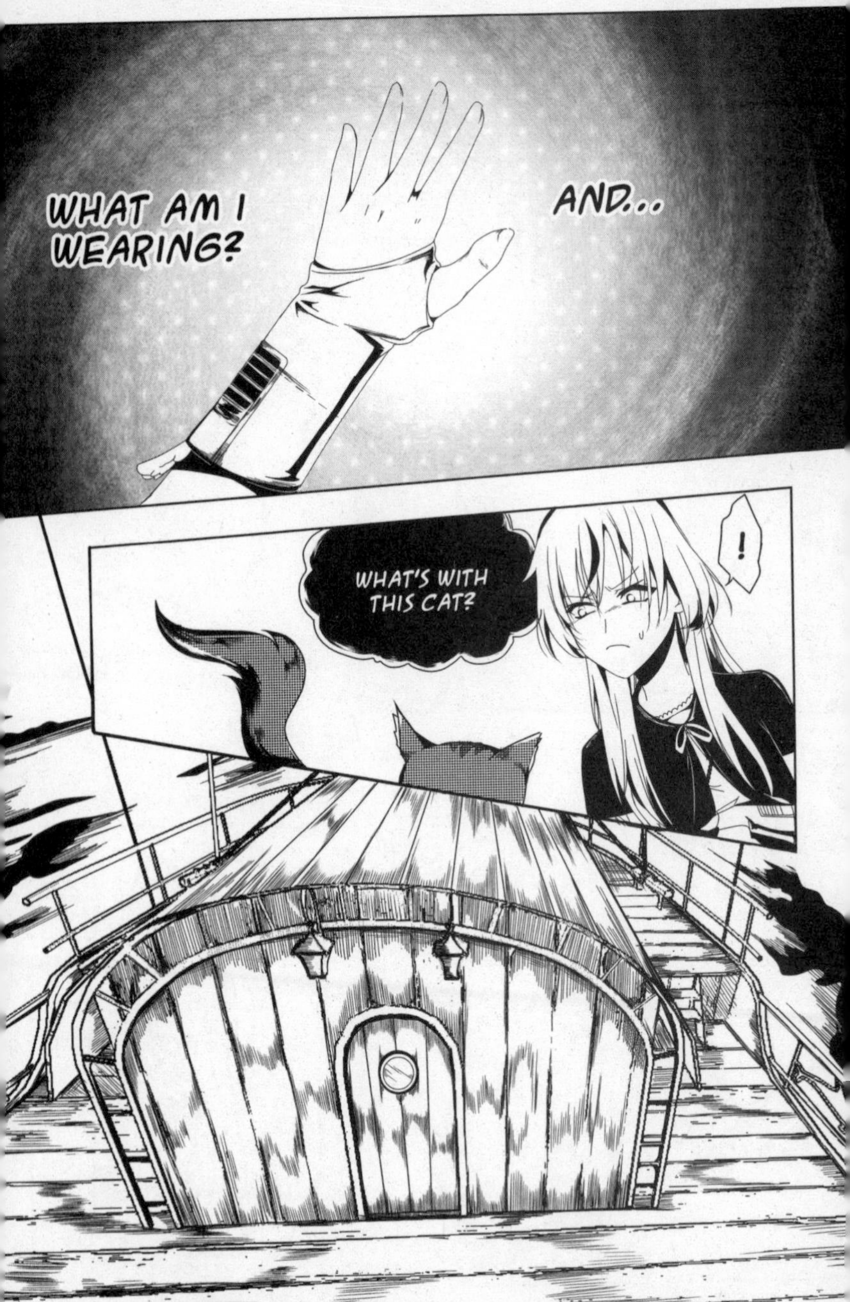
WHAT AM I WEARING?
AND...
!
WHAT'S WITH THIS CAT?

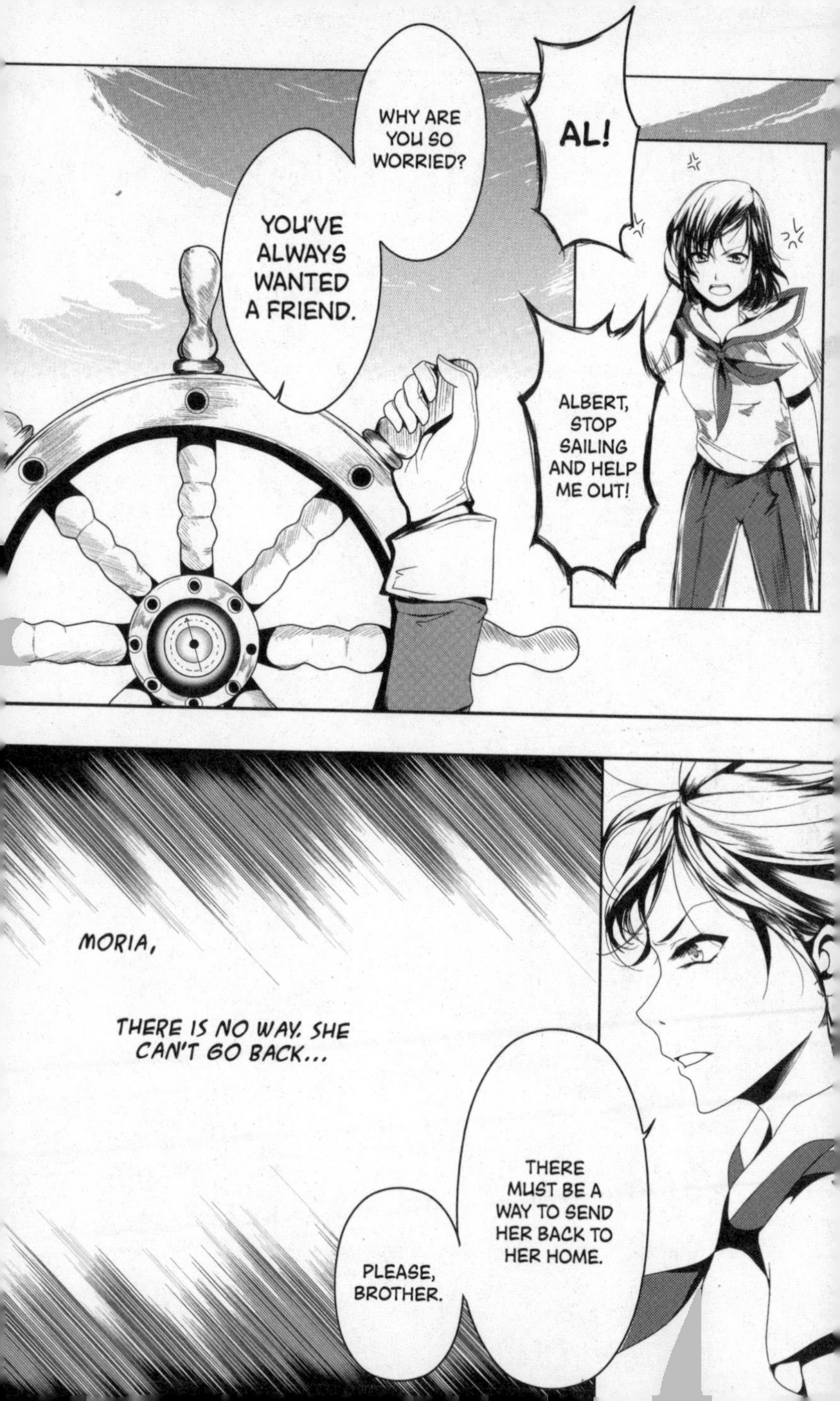
AL!
ALBERT, STOP SAILING AND HELP ME OUT!
WHY ARE YOU SO WORRIED?
YOU'VE ALWAYS WANTED A FRIEND.
THERE MUST BE A WAY TO SEND HER BACK TO HER HOME.
PLEASE, BROTHER.
MORIA,
THERE IS NO WAY. SHE CAN'T GO BACK...

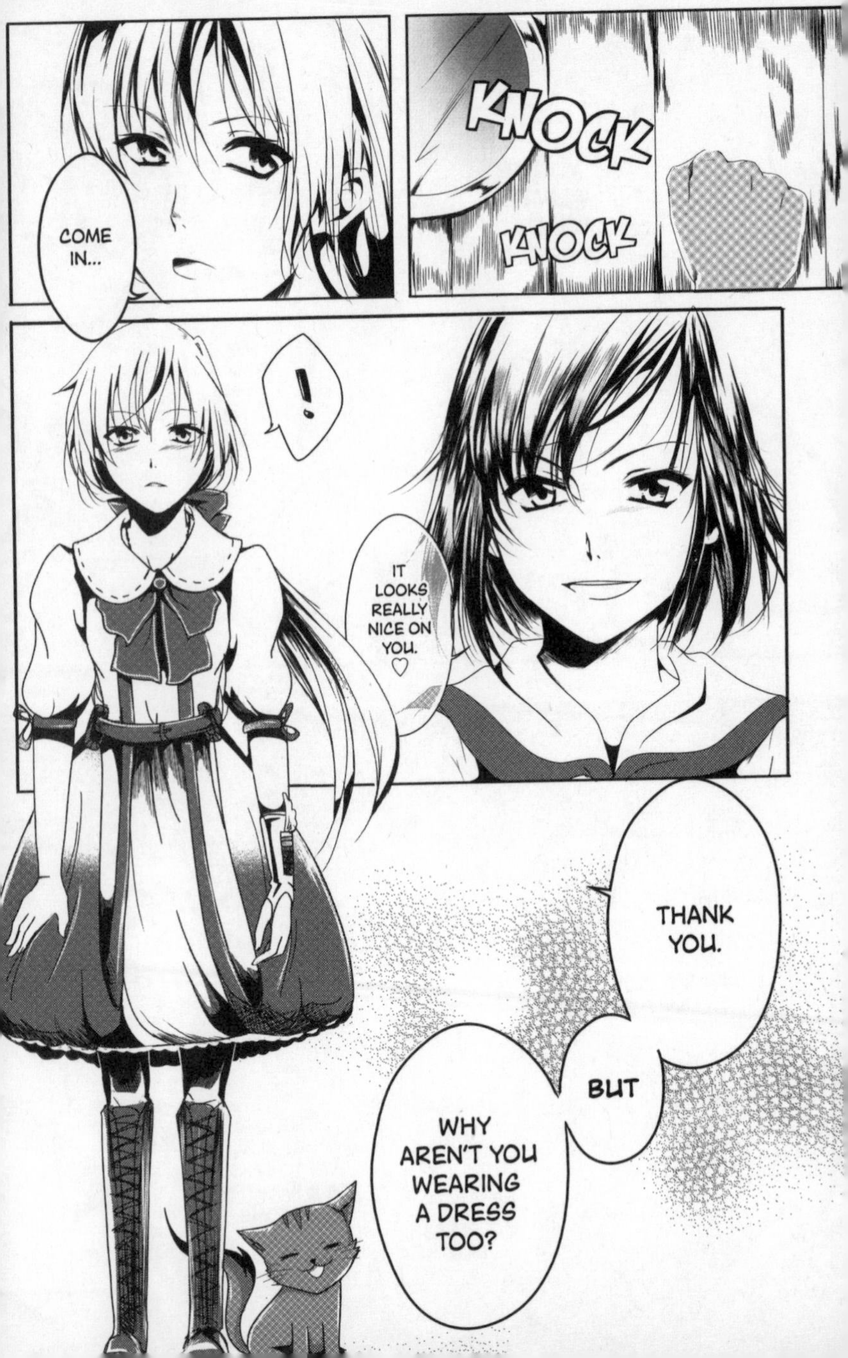
KNOCK
KNOCK
COME IN...
IT LOOKS REALLY NICE ON YOU. ♡
!
THANK YOU.
BUT
WHY AREN'T YOU WEARING A DRESS TOO?

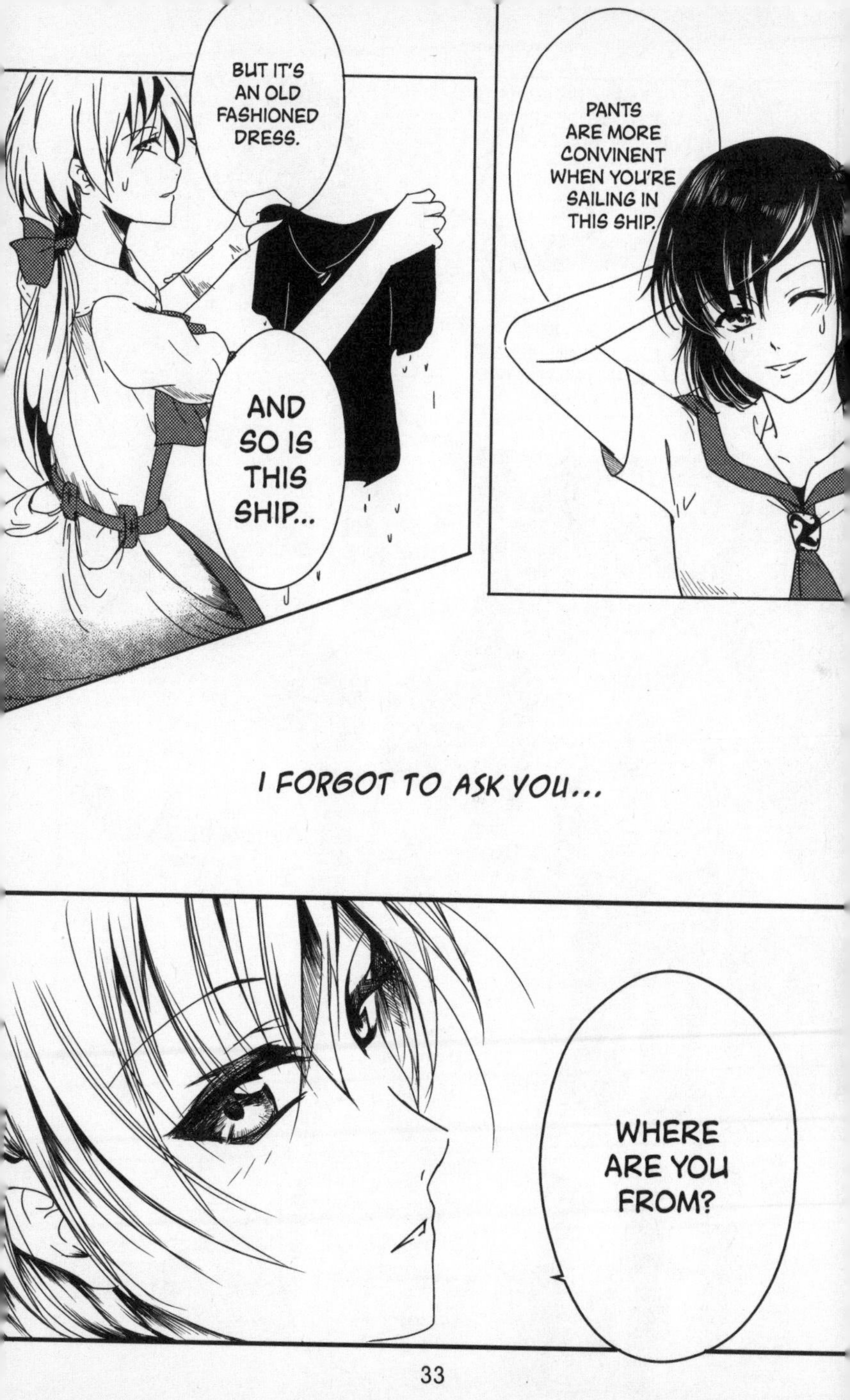
PANTS ARE MORE CONVINENT WHEN YOU'RE SAILING IN THIS SHIP.
BUT IT'S AN OLD FASHIONED DRESS.
AND SO IS THIS SHIP...
I FORGOT TO ASK YOU...
WHERE ARE YOU FROM?

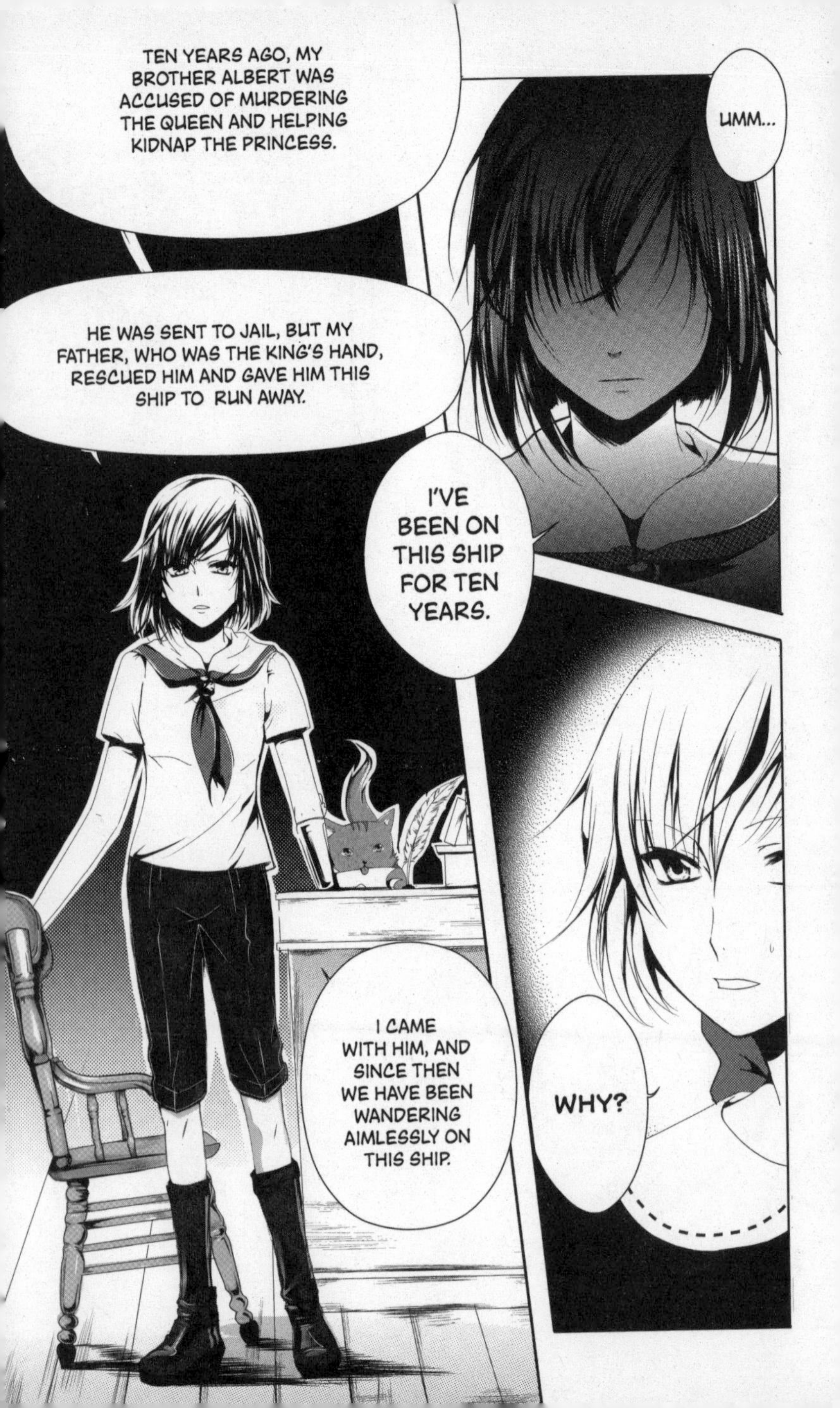
UMM...
WHY?
TEN YEARS AGO, MY BROTHER ALBERT WAS ACCUSED OF MURDERING THE QUEEN AND HELPING KIDNAP THE PRINCESS.
HE WAS SENT TO JAIL, BUT MY FATHER, WHO WAS THE KING'S HAND, RESCUED HIM AND GAVE HIM THIS SHIP TO RUN AWAY.
I'VE BEEN ON THIS SHIP FOR TEN YEARS.
I CAME WITH HIM, AND SINCE THEN WE HAVE BEEN WANDERING AIMLESSLY ON THIS SHIP.

READ THIS WAY

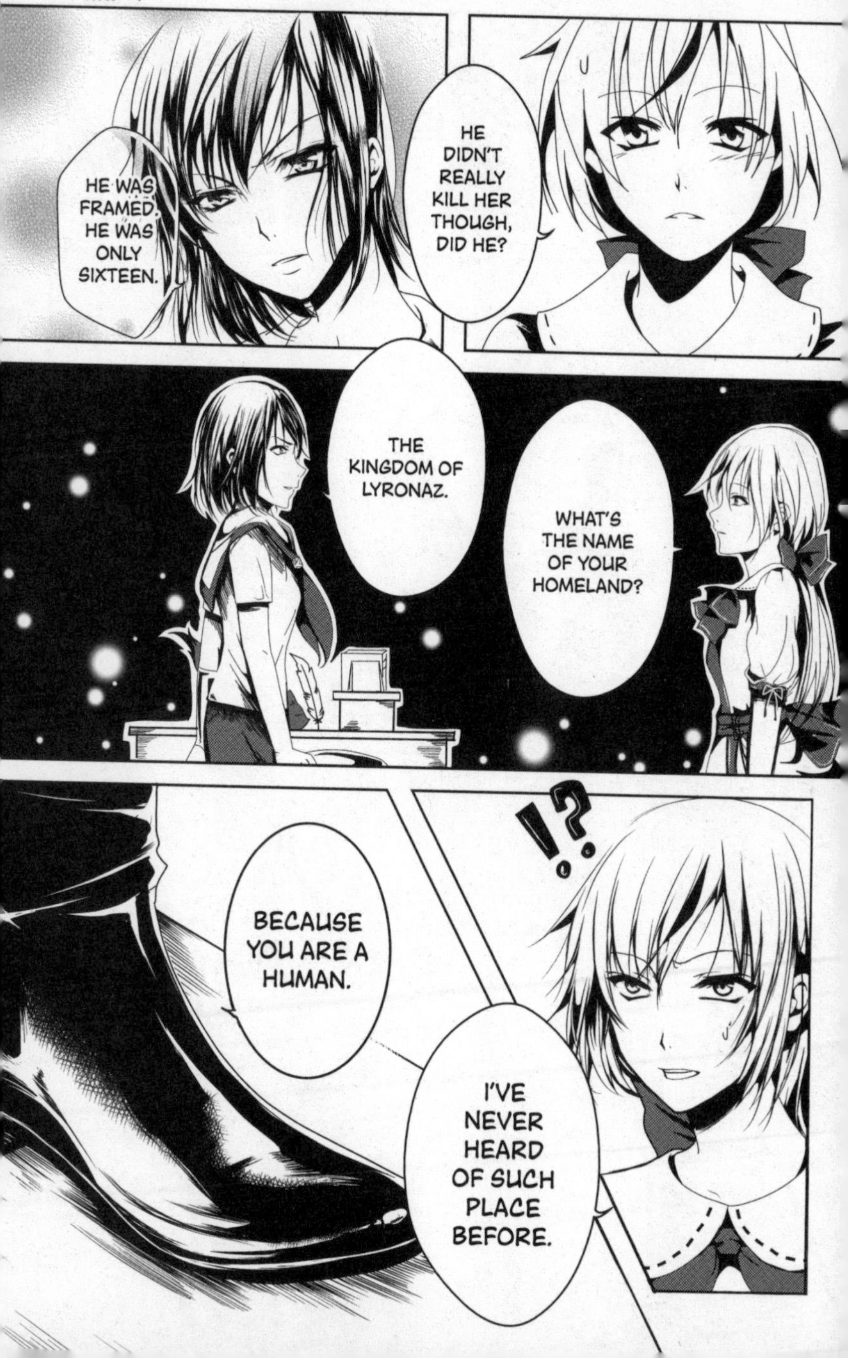
HE DIDN'T REALLY KILL HER THOUGH, DID HE?
HE WAS FRAMED. HE WAS ONLY SIXTEEN.
WHAT'S THE NAME OF YOUR HOMELAND?
THE KINGDOM OF LYRONAZ.
!?
I'VE NEVER HEARD OF SUCH PLACE BEFORE.
BECAUSE YOU ARE A HUMAN.

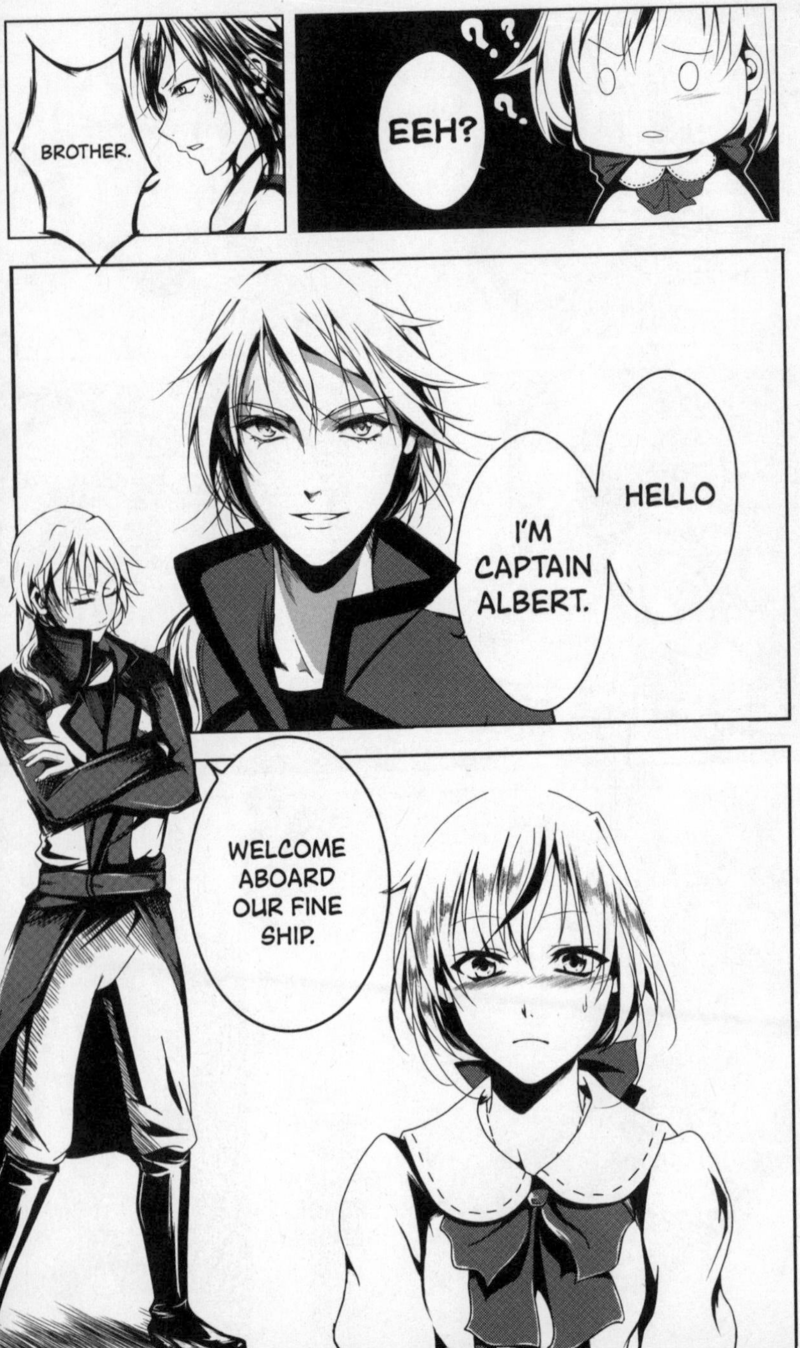
EEH?
BROTHER.
HELLO
I'M CAPTAIN ALBERT.
WELCOME ABOARD OUR FINE SHIP.

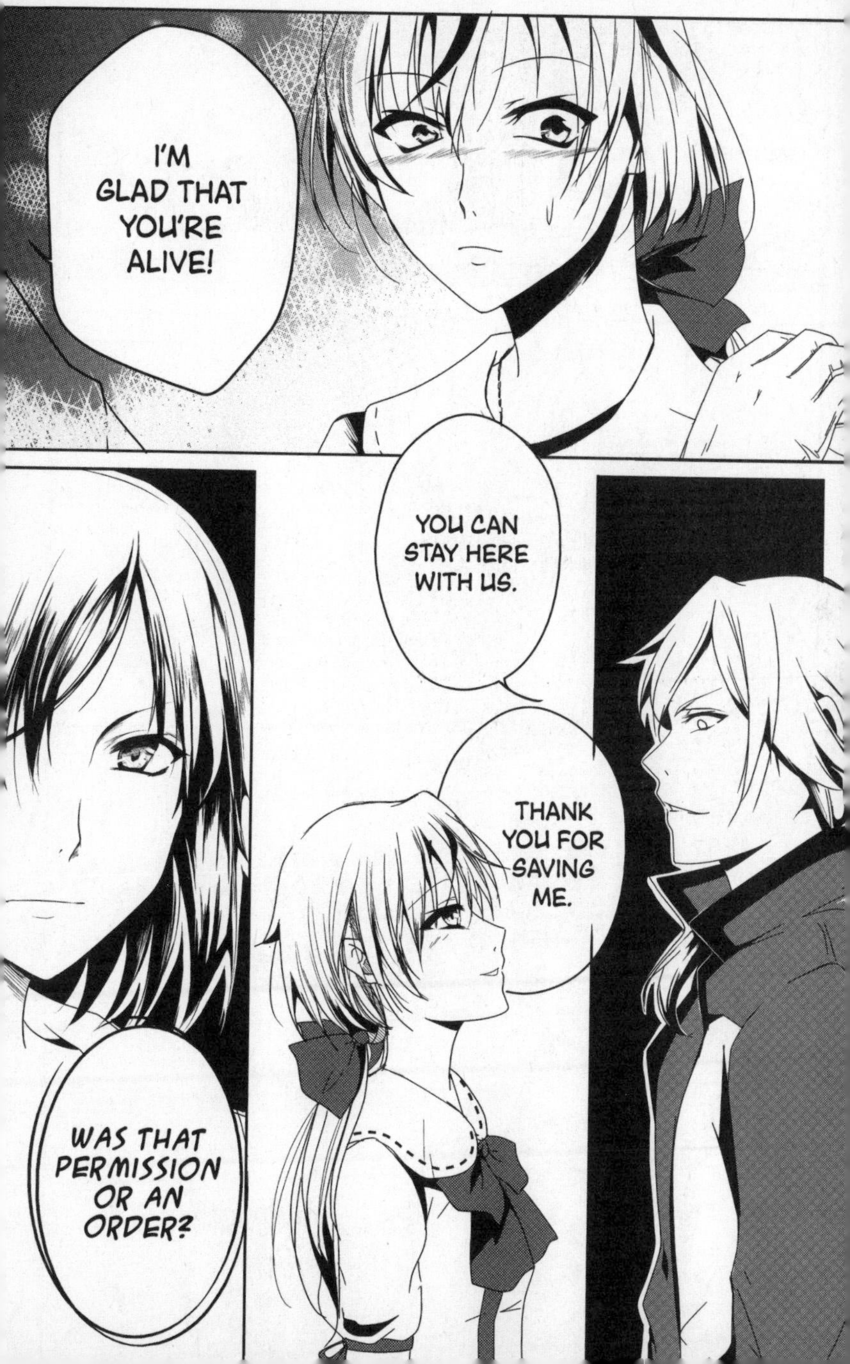
I'M GLAD THAT YOU'RE ALIVE!
YOU CAN STAY HERE WITH US.
THANK YOU FOR SAVING ME.
WAS THAT PERMISSION OR AN ORDER?

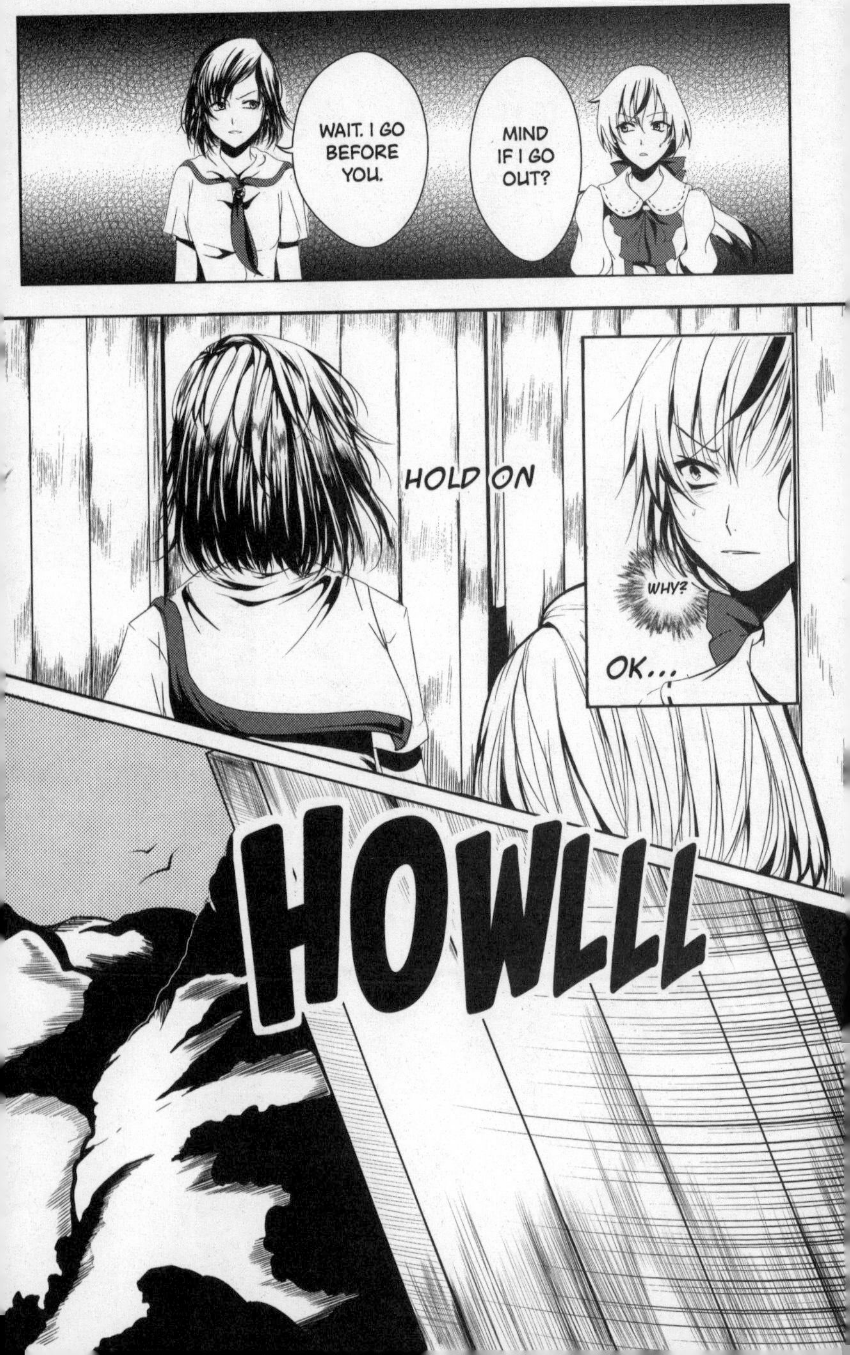
MIND IF I GO OUT?
WAIT. I GO BEFORE YOU.
WHY?
OK...
HOLD ON
HOWLLL

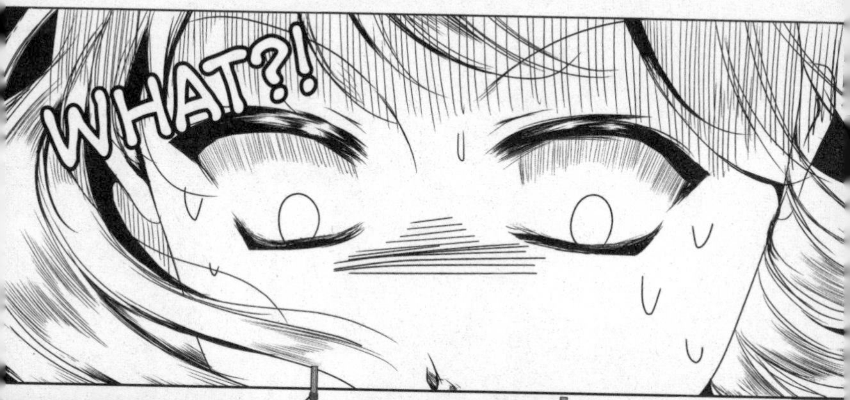
WHAT?!
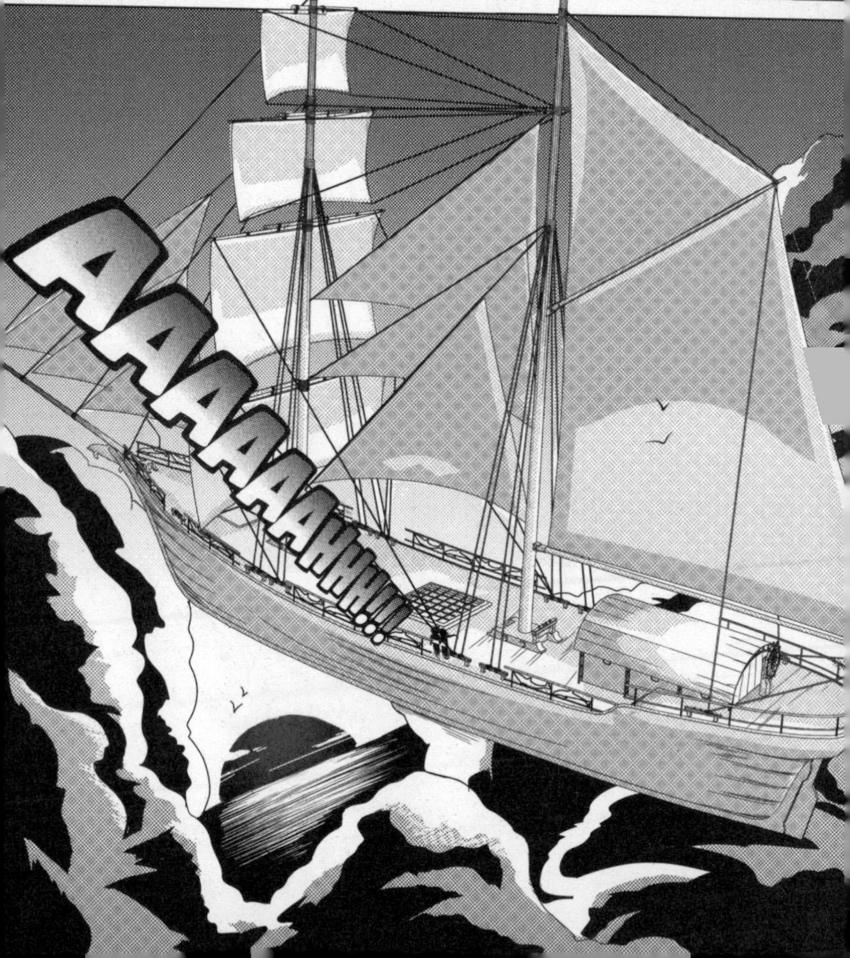
AAAAAAHHH!!!

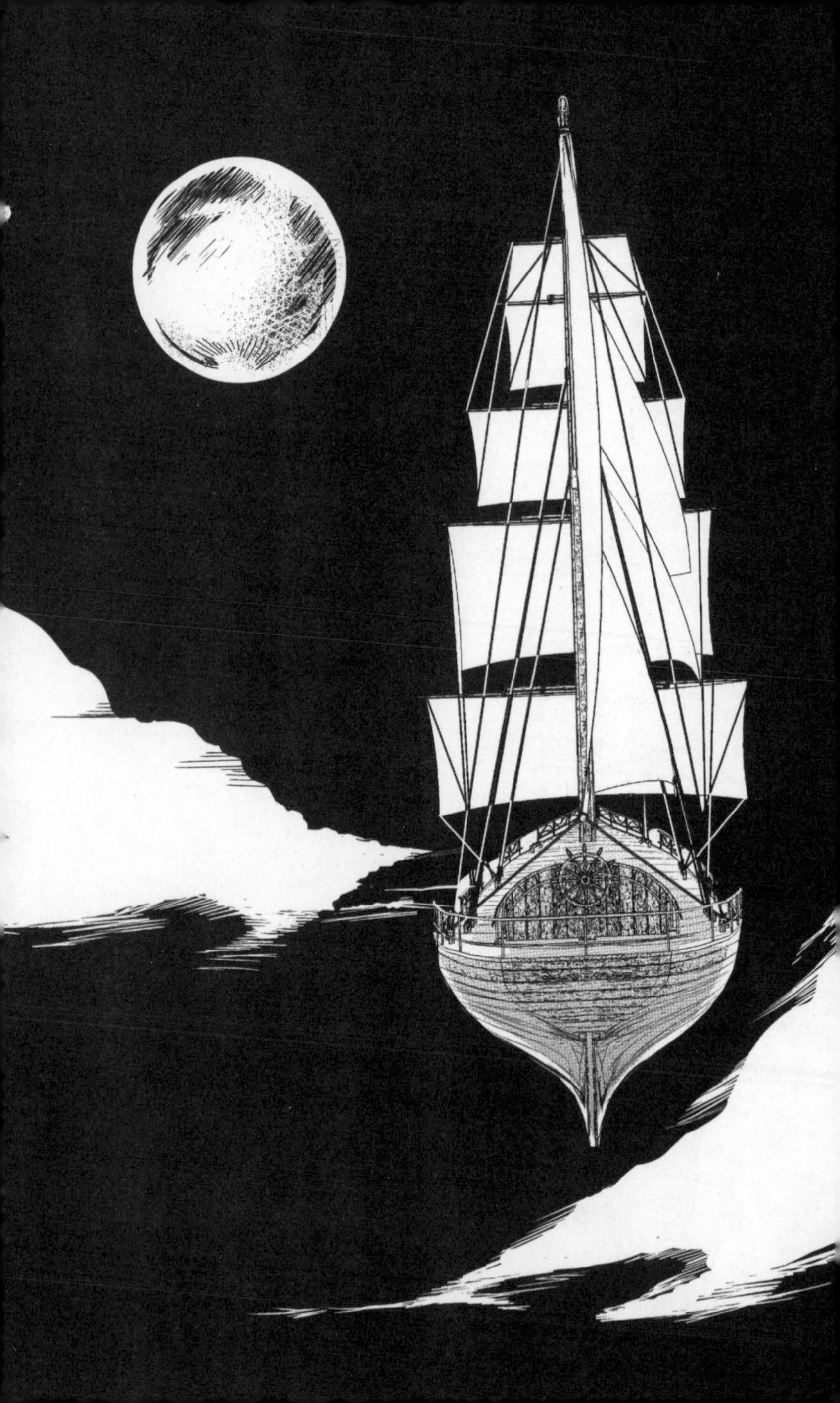

Ocean of Secrets

CHAPTER 2
NEW FAMILY

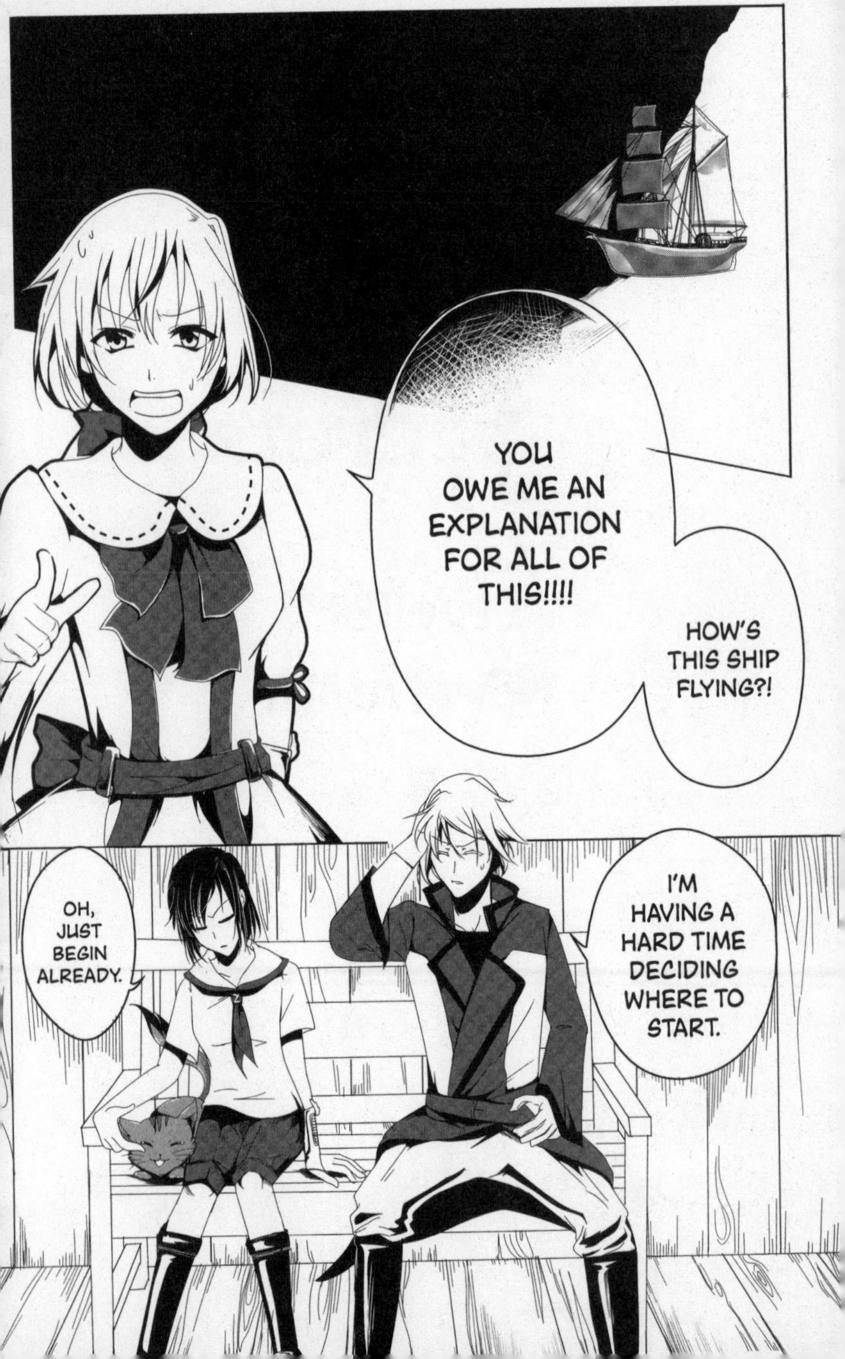
YOU OWE ME AN EXPLANATION FOR ALL OF THIS!!!!
HOW'S THIS SHIP FLYING?!
I'M HAVING A HARD TIME DECIDING WHERE TO START.
OH, JUST BEGIN ALREADY.

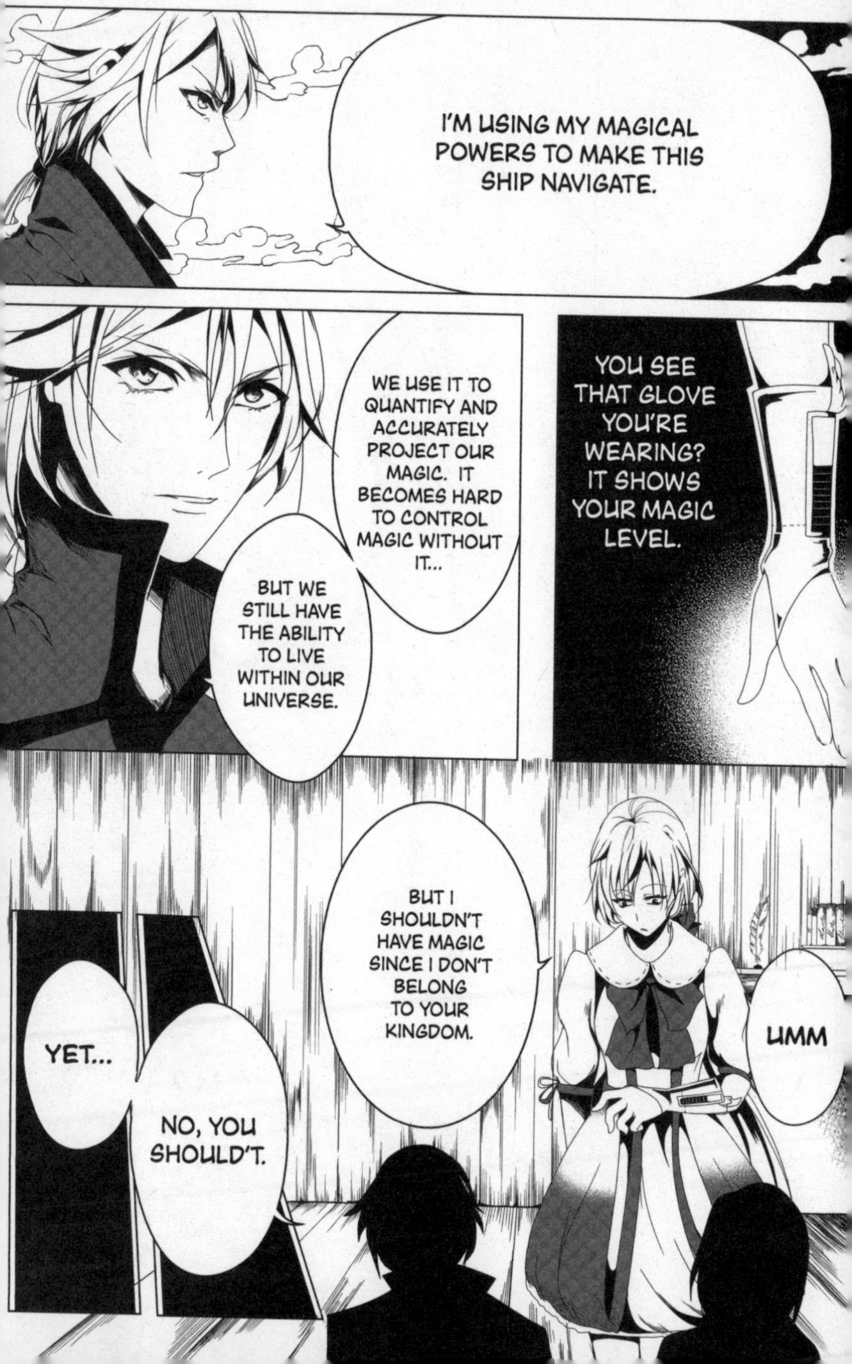
I'M USING MY MAGICAL POWERS TO MAKE THIS SHIP NAVIGATE.
YOU SEE THAT GLOVE YOU'RE WEARING? IT SHOWS YOUR MAGIC LEVEL.
WE USE IT TO QUANTIFY AND ACCURATELY PROJECT OUR MAGIC. IT BECOMES HARD TO CONTROL MAGIC WITHOUT IT...
BUT WE STILL HAVE THE ABILITY TO LIVE WITHIN OUR UNIVERSE.
UMM
BUT I SHOULDN'T HAVE MAGIC SINCE I DON'T BELONG TO YOUR KINGDOM.
NO, YOU SHOULD'T.
YET...

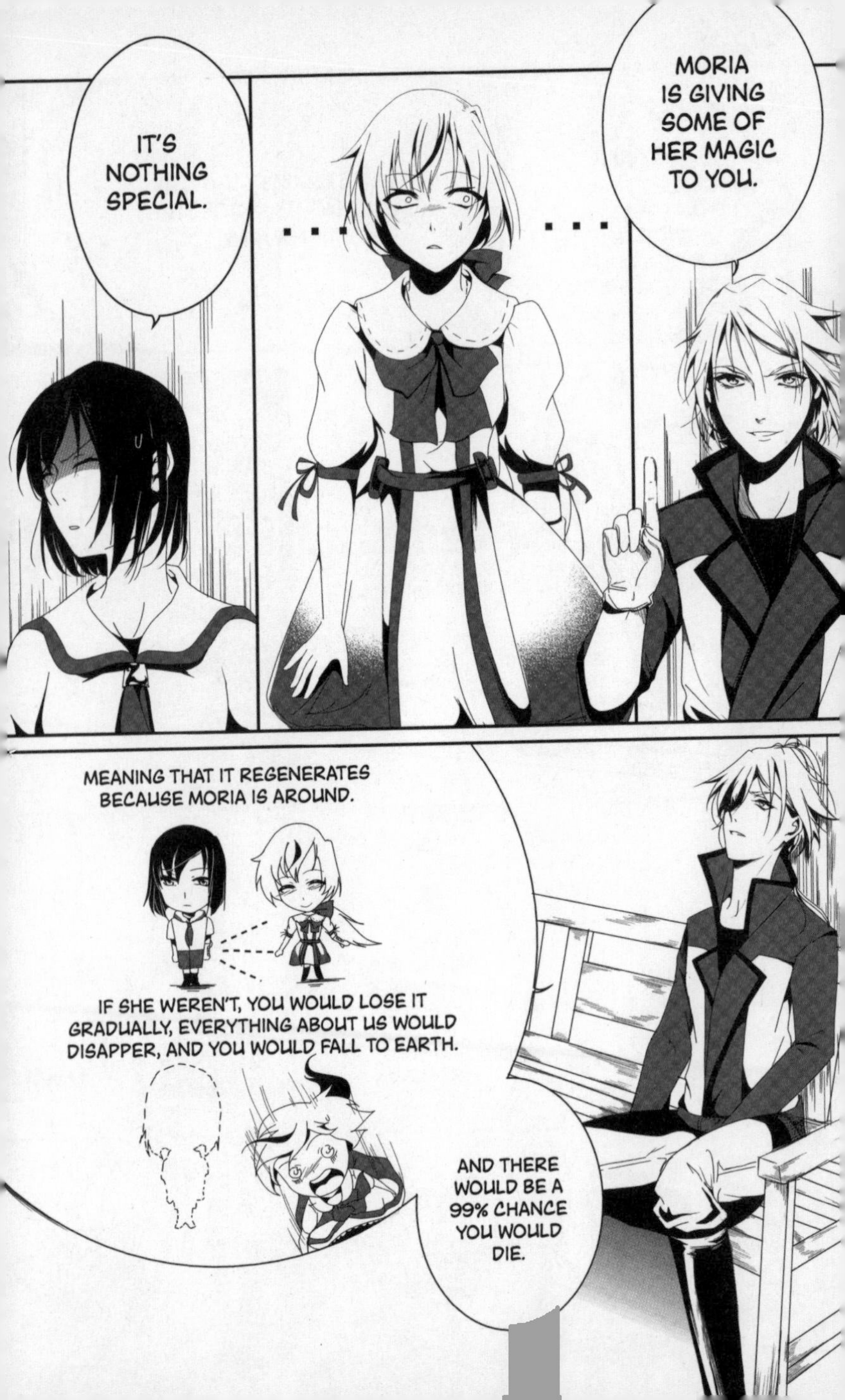
MORIA IS GIVING SOME OF HER MAGIC TO YOU.
. . .
. . .
IT'S NOTHING SPECIAL.
MEANING THAT IT REGENERATES BECAUSE MORIA IS AROUND.
IF SHE WEREN'T, YOU WOULD LOSE IT GRADUALLY, EVERYTHING ABOUT US WOULD DISAPPER, AND YOU WOULD FALL TO EARTH.
AND THERE WOULD BE A 99% CHANCE YOU WOULD DIE.

READ THIS WAY

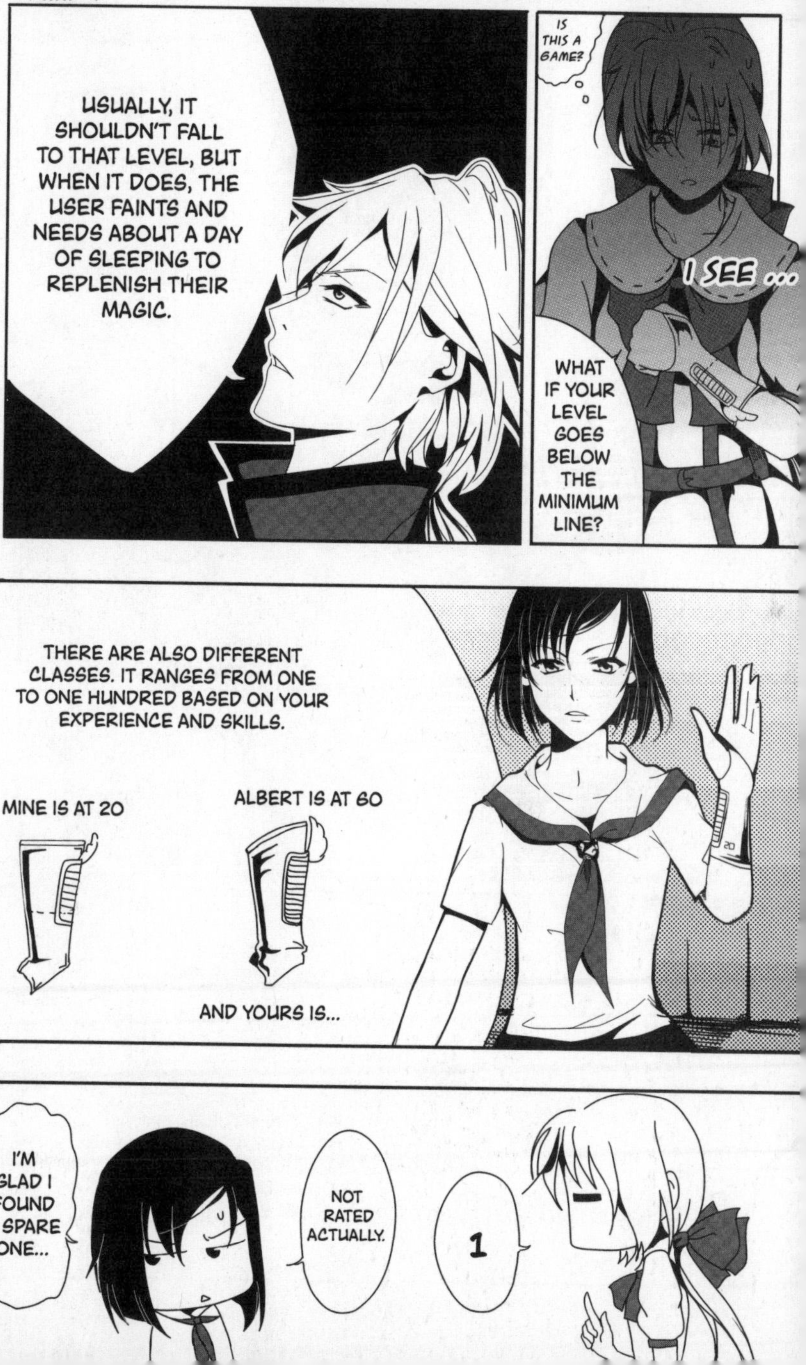

IS THIS A GAME?
I SEE ...
WHAT IF YOUR LEVEL GOES BELOW THE MINIMUM LINE?
USUALLY, IT SHOULDN'T FALL TO THAT LEVEL, BUT WHEN IT DOES, THE USER FAINTS AND NEEDS ABOUT A DAY OF SLEEPING TO REPLENISH THEIR MAGIC.
THERE ARE ALSO DIFFERENT CLASSES. IT RANGES FROM ONE TO ONE HUNDRED BASED ON YOUR EXPERIENCE AND SKILLS.
20
ALBERT IS AT 60
MINE IS AT 20
AND YOURS IS...
1
NOT RATED ACTUALLY.
I'M GLAD I FOUND A SPARE ONE...

ALRIGHT.

I NEED TO CHECK THE NAVIGATION. MORIA, CONTINUE.

COME HERE.

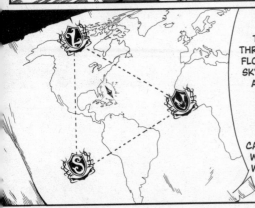

THERE ARE THREE KINGDOMS FLOATING IN THE SKY. THEY MAKE A TRIANGLE.

THE NORTHERN KINGDOM IS CALLED "LYRONAZ" WHICH IS WHERE WE COME FROM.

LOOK HERE.

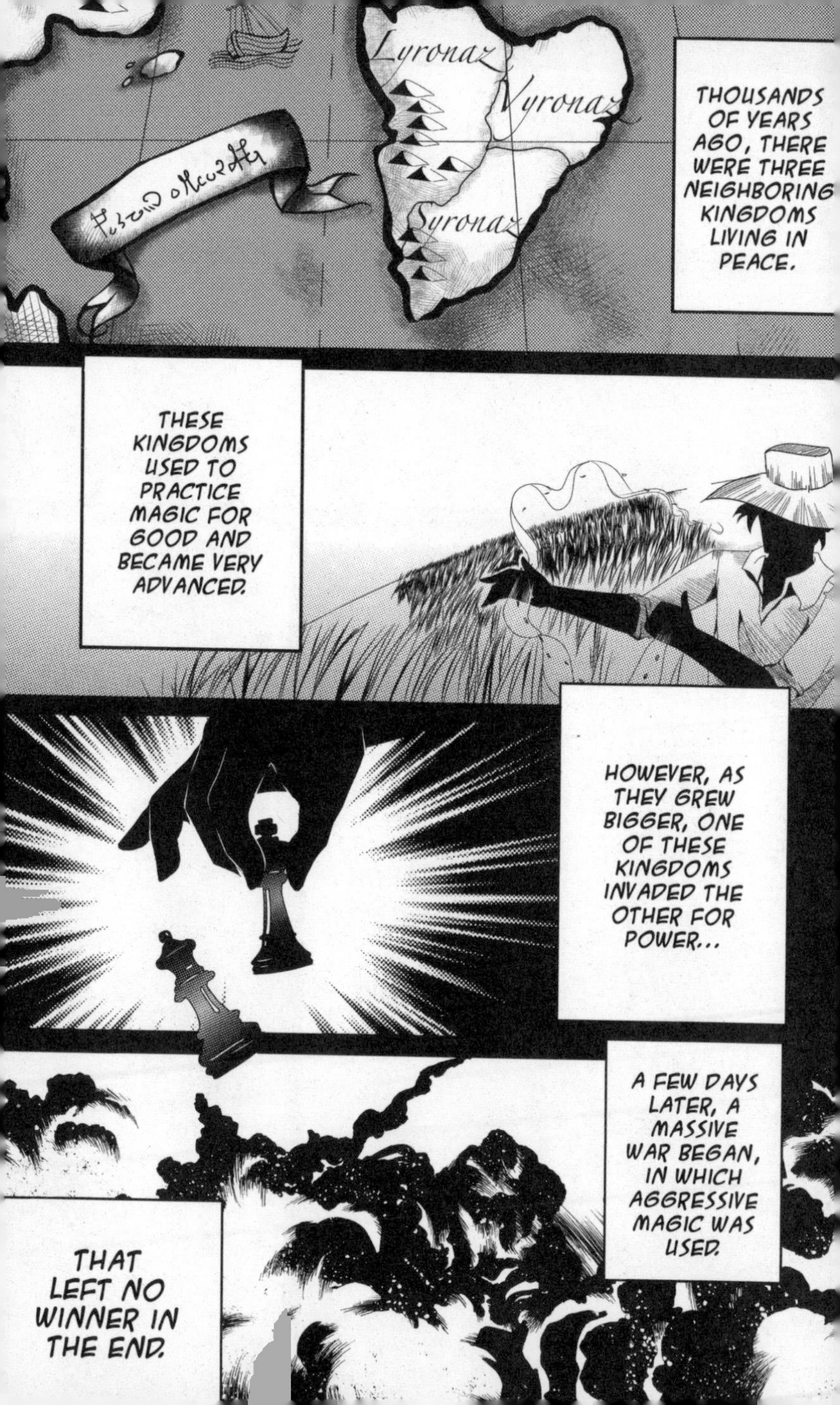
THOUSANDS OF YEARS AGO, THERE WERE THREE NEIGHBORING KINGDOMS LIVING IN PEACE.
Lyronaz
Vyronaz
Syronaz
THESE KINGDOMS USED TO PRACTICE MAGIC FOR GOOD AND BECAME VERY ADVANCED.
HOWEVER, AS THEY GREW BIGGER, ONE OF THESE KINGDOMS INVADED THE OTHER FOR POWER...
A FEW DAYS LATER, A MASSIVE WAR BEGAN, IN WHICH AGGRESSIVE MAGIC WAS USED.
THAT LEFT NO WINNER IN THE END.

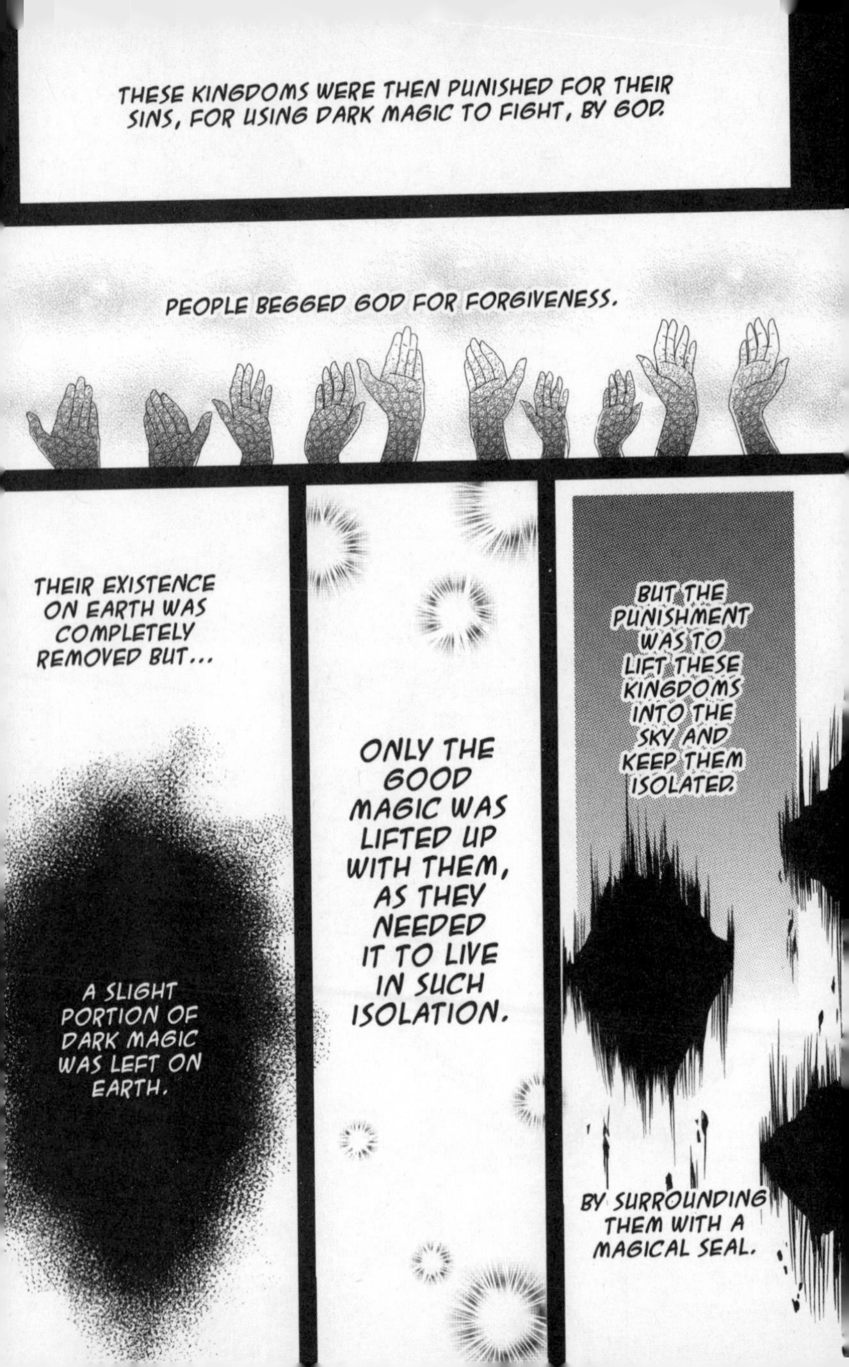
THESE KINGDOMS WERE THEN PUNISHED FOR THEIR SINS, FOR USING DARK MAGIC TO FIGHT, BY GOD.
PEOPLE BEGGED GOD FOR FORGIVENESS.
BUT THE PUNISHMENT WAS TO LIFT THESE KINGDOMS INTO THE SKY AND KEEP THEM ISOLATED.
BY SURROUNDING THEM WITH A MAGICAL SEAL.
ONLY THE GOOD MAGIC WAS LIFTED UP WITH THEM, AS THEY NEEDED IT TO LIVE IN SUCH ISOLATION.
THEIR EXISTENCE ON EARTH WAS COMPLETELY REMOVED BUT...
A SLIGHT PORTION OF DARK MAGIC WAS LEFT ON EARTH.

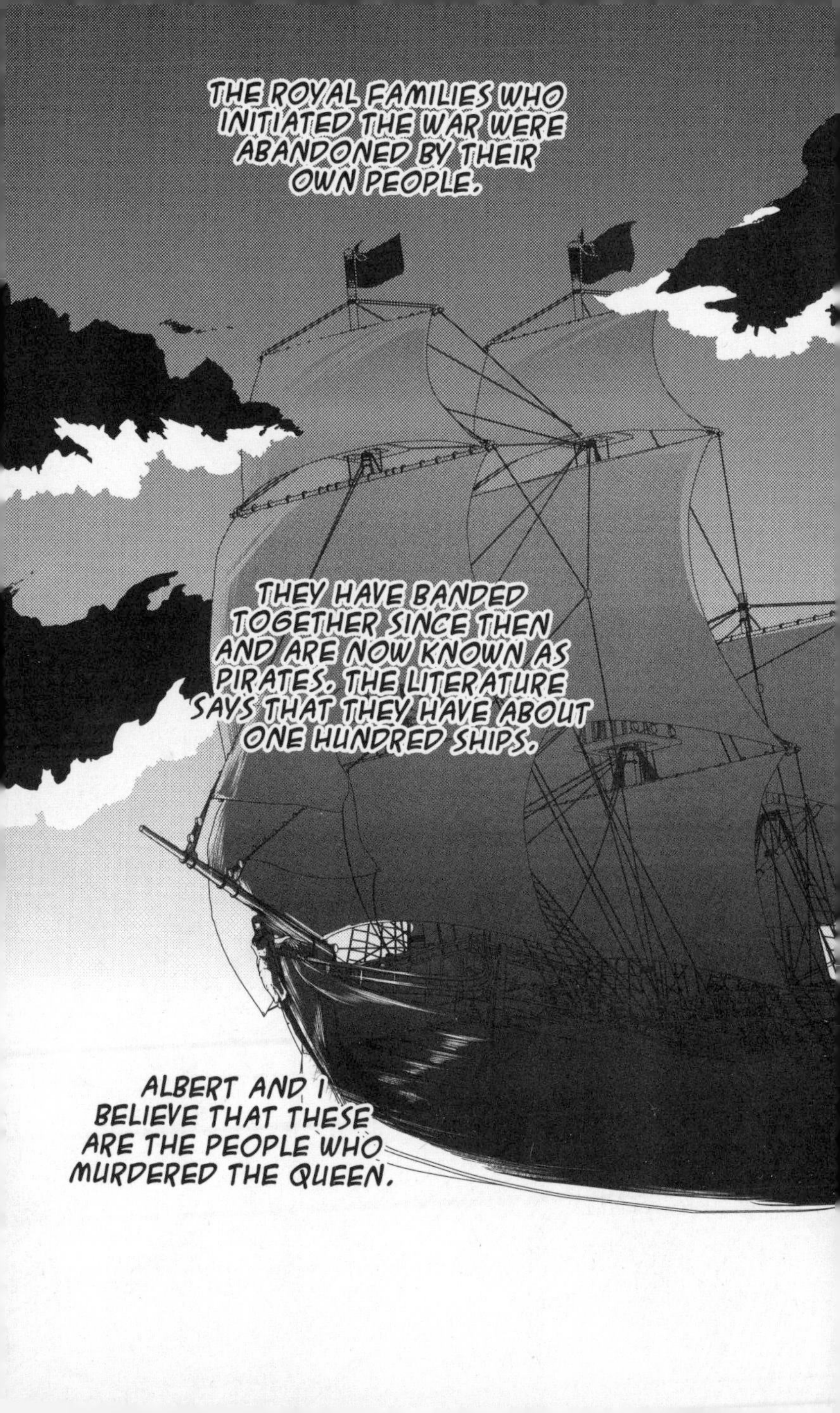
THE ROYAL FAMILIES WHO INITIATED THE WAR WERE ABANDONED BY THEIR OWN PEOPLE.
THEY HAVE BANDED TOGETHER SINCE THEN AND ARE NOW KNOWN AS PIRATES. THE LITERATURE SAYS THAT THEY HAVE ABOUT ONE HUNDRED SHIPS.
ALBERT AND I BELIEVE THAT THESE ARE THE PEOPLE WHO MURDERED THE QUEEN.

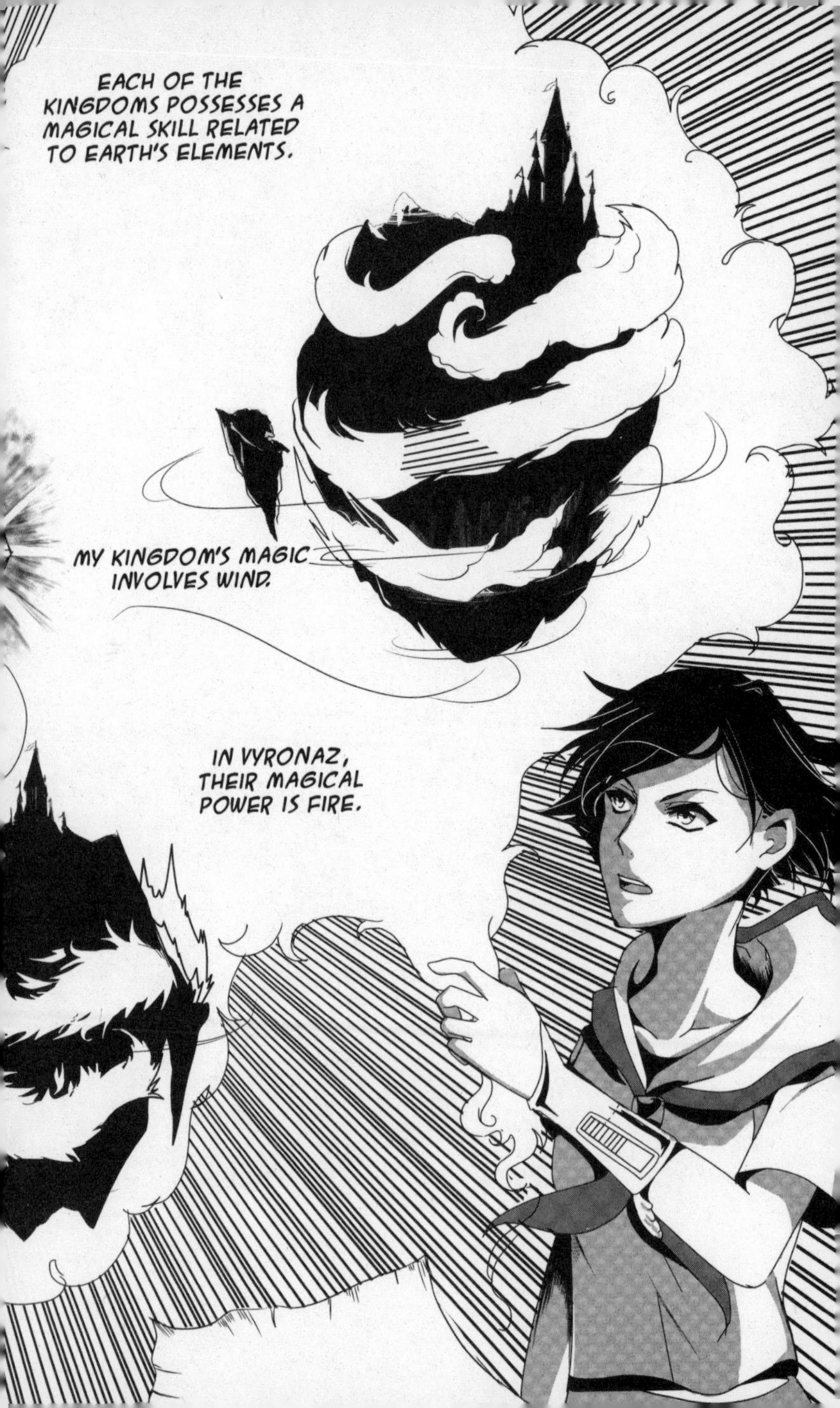
EACH OF THE KINGDOMS POSSESSES A MAGICAL SKILL RELATED TO EARTH'S ELEMENTS.
MY KINGDOM'S MAGIC INVOLVES WIND.
IN VYRONAZ, THEIR MAGICAL POWER IS FIRE.

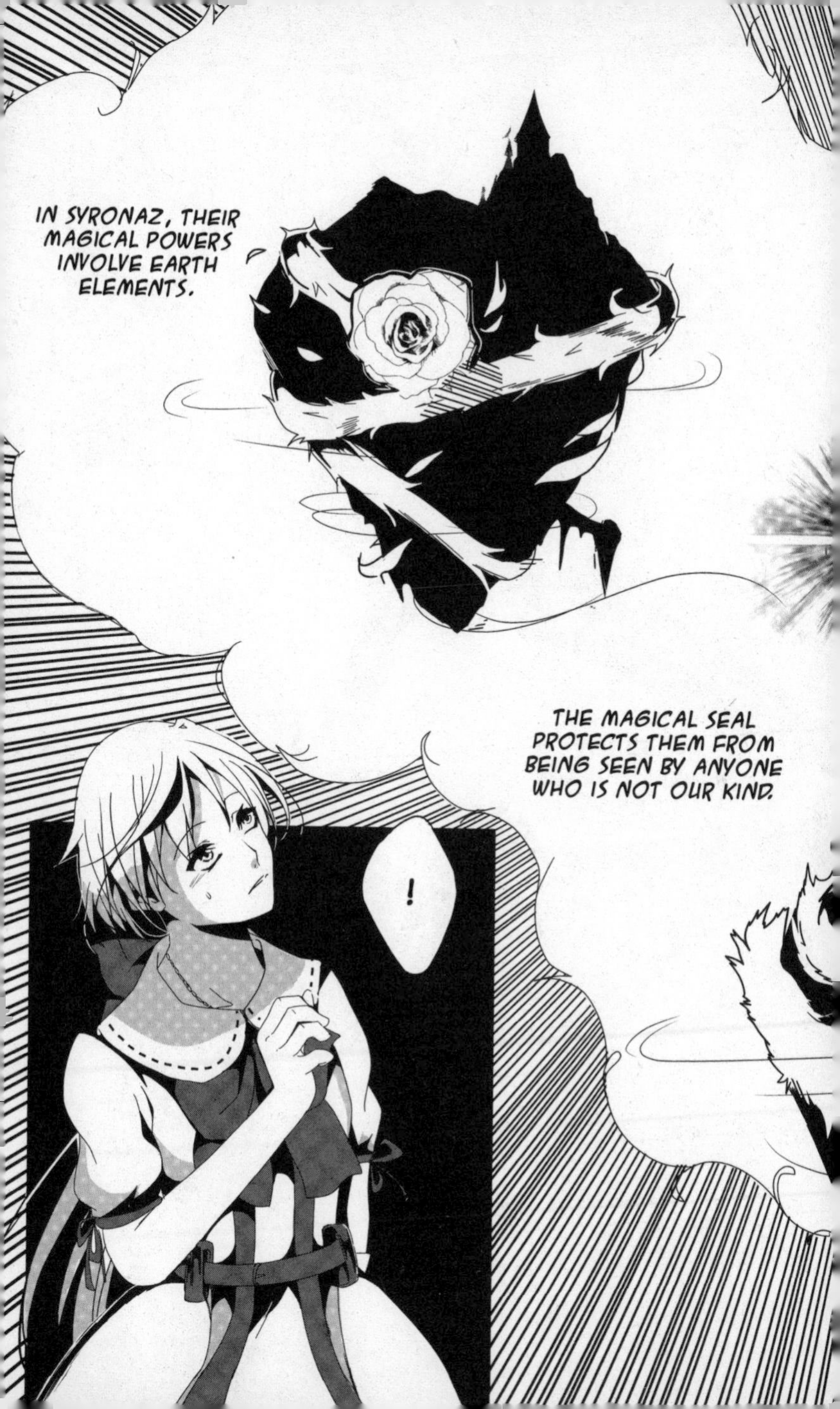
IN SYRONAZ, THEIR MAGICAL POWERS INVOLVE EARTH ELEMENTS.
THE MAGICAL SEAL PROTECTS THEM FROM BEING SEEN BY ANYONE WHO IS NOT OUR KIND.
!

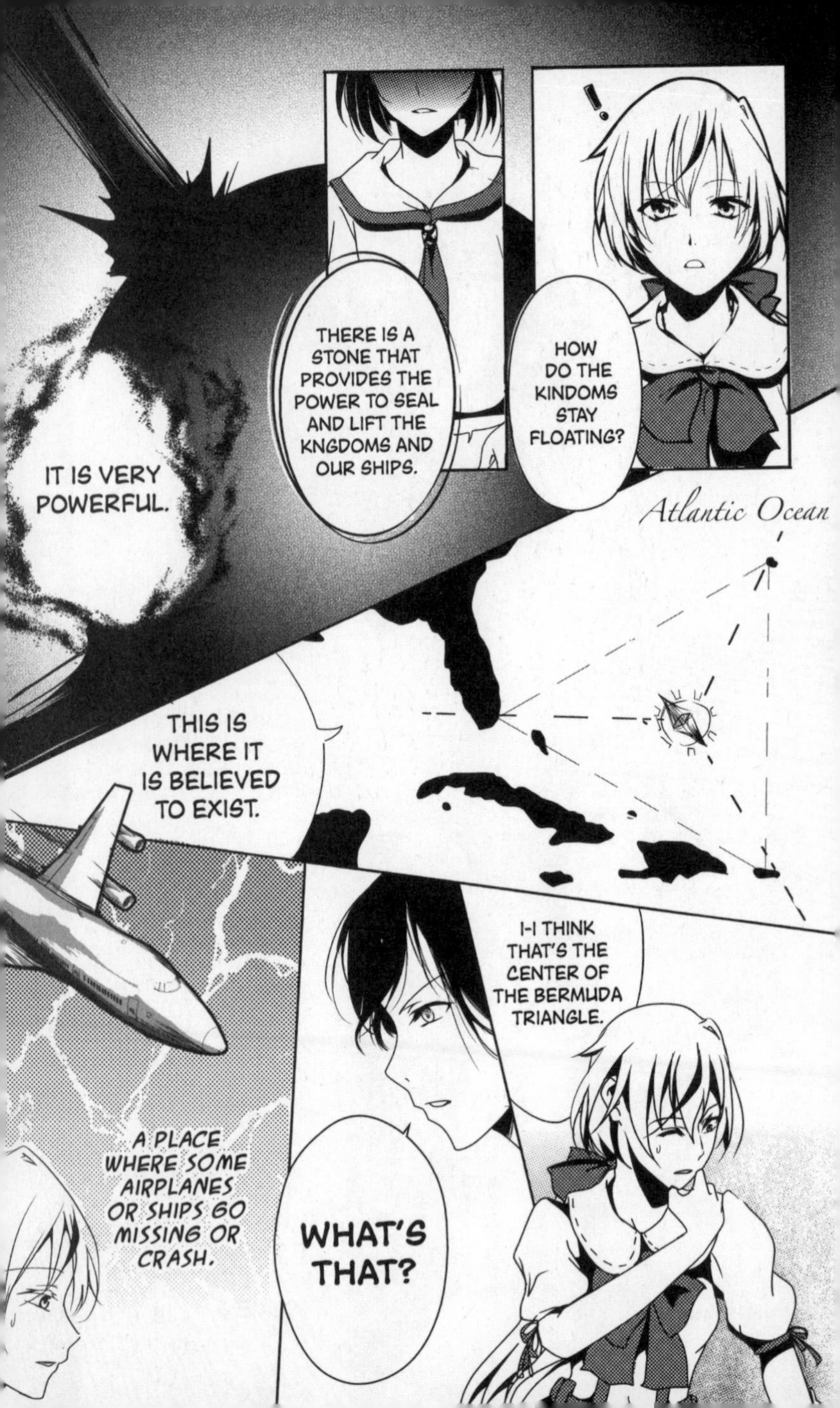
!
HOW DO THE KINDOMS STAY FLOATING?
THERE IS A STONE THAT PROVIDES THE POWER TO SEAL AND LIFT THE KNGDOMS AND OUR SHIPS.
IT IS VERY POWERFUL.
Atlantic Ocean
THIS IS WHERE IT IS BELIEVED TO EXIST.
I-I THINK THAT'S THE CENTER OF THE BERMUDA TRIANGLE.
WHAT'S THAT?
A PLACE WHERE SOME AIRPLANES OR SHIPS GO MISSING OR CRASH.

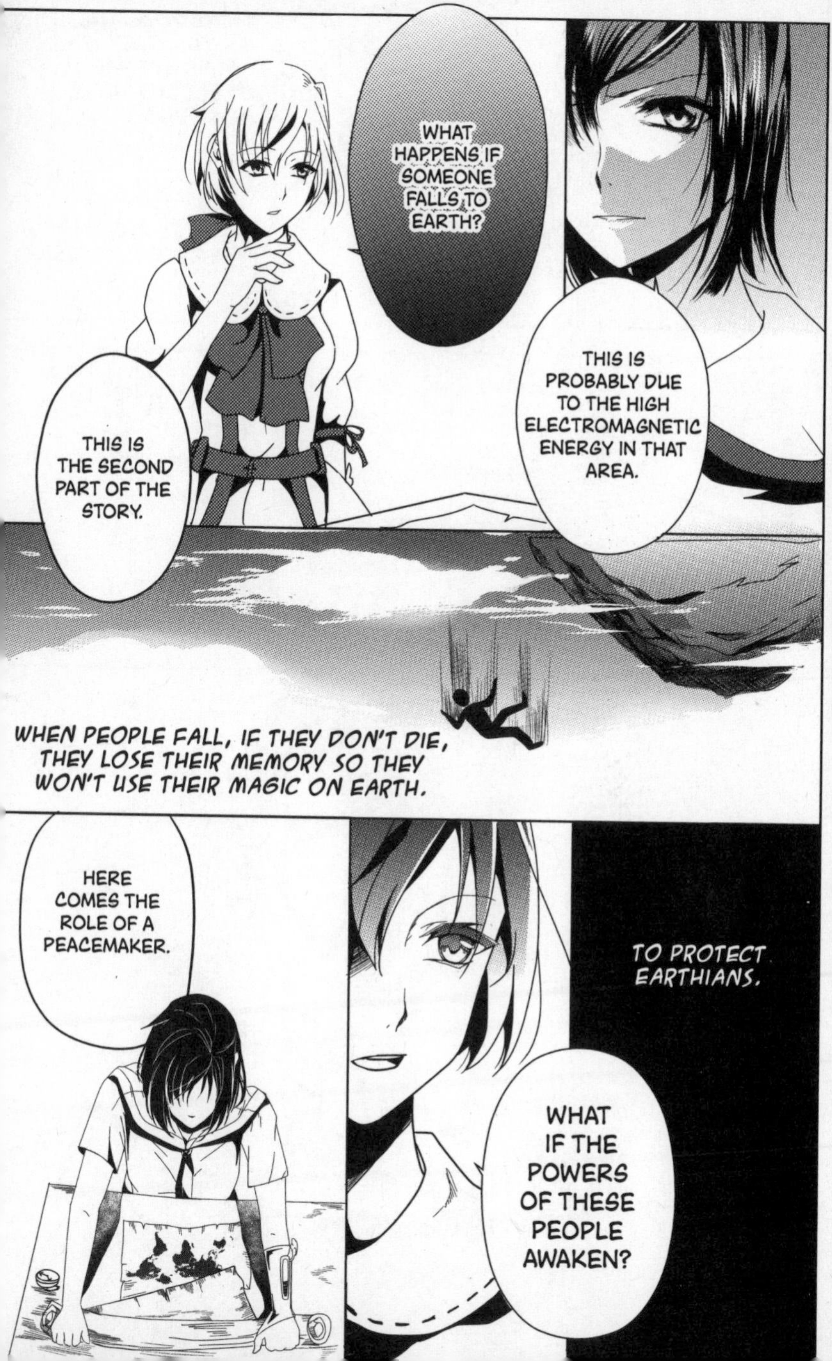
WHAT HAPPENS IF SOMEONE FALLS TO EARTH?
THIS IS PROBABLY DUE TO THE HIGH ELECTROMAGNETIC ENERGY IN THAT AREA.
THIS IS THE SECOND PART OF THE STORY.
WHEN PEOPLE FALL, IF THEY DON'T DIE, THEY LOSE THEIR MEMORY SO THEY WON'T USE THEIR MAGIC ON EARTH.
TO PROTECT EARTHIANS.
WHAT IF THE POWERS OF THESE PEOPLE AWAKEN?
HERE COMES THE ROLE OF A PEACEMAKER.

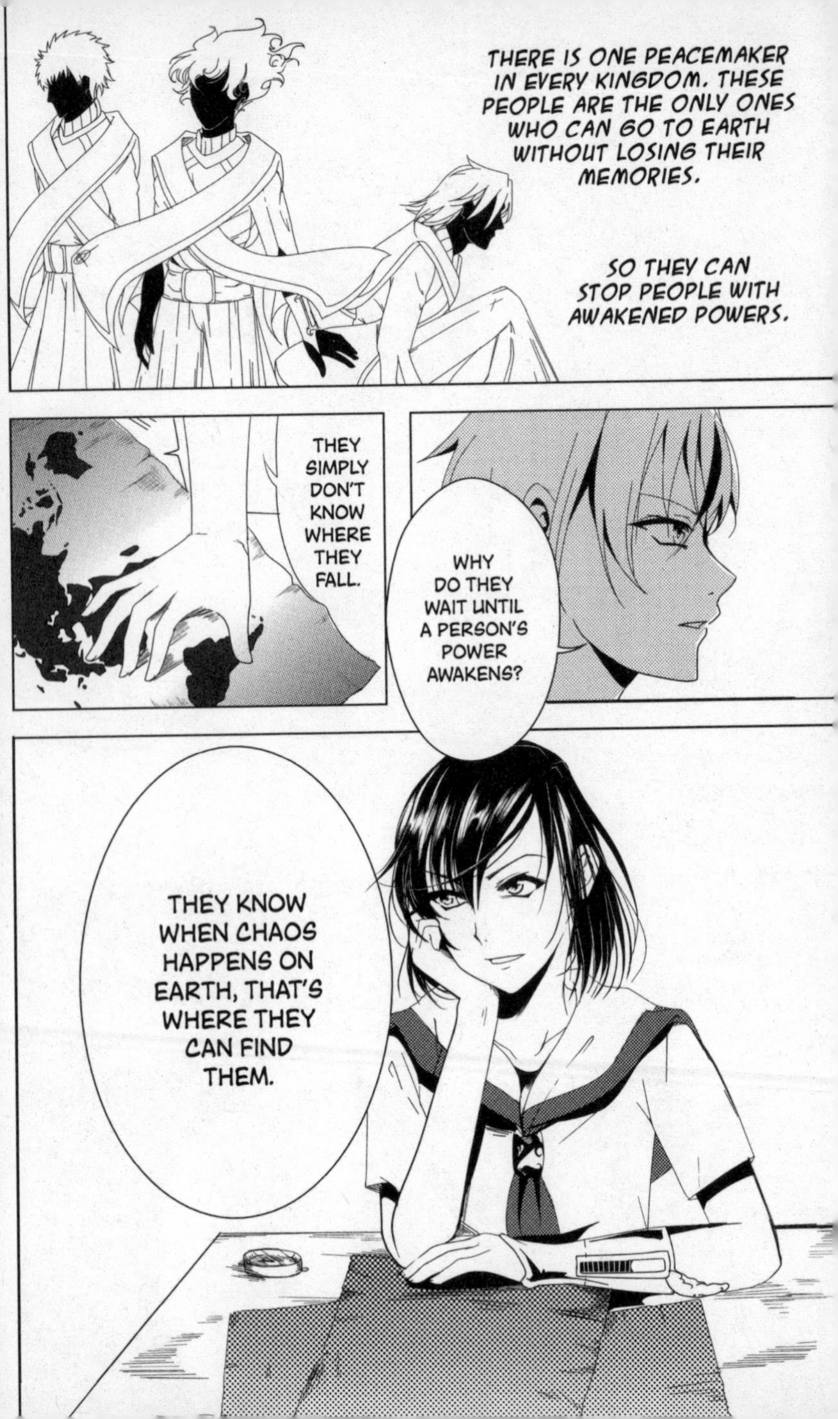
THERE IS ONE PEACEMAKER IN EVERY KINGDOM. THESE PEOPLE ARE THE ONLY ONES WHO CAN GO TO EARTH WITHOUT LOSING THEIR MEMORIES.
SO THEY CAN STOP PEOPLE WITH AWAKENED POWERS.
WHY DO THEY WAIT UNTIL A PERSON'S POWER AWAKENS?
THEY SIMPLY DON'T KNOW WHERE THEY FALL.
THEY KNOW WHEN CHAOS HAPPENS ON EARTH, THAT'S WHERE THEY CAN FIND THEM.

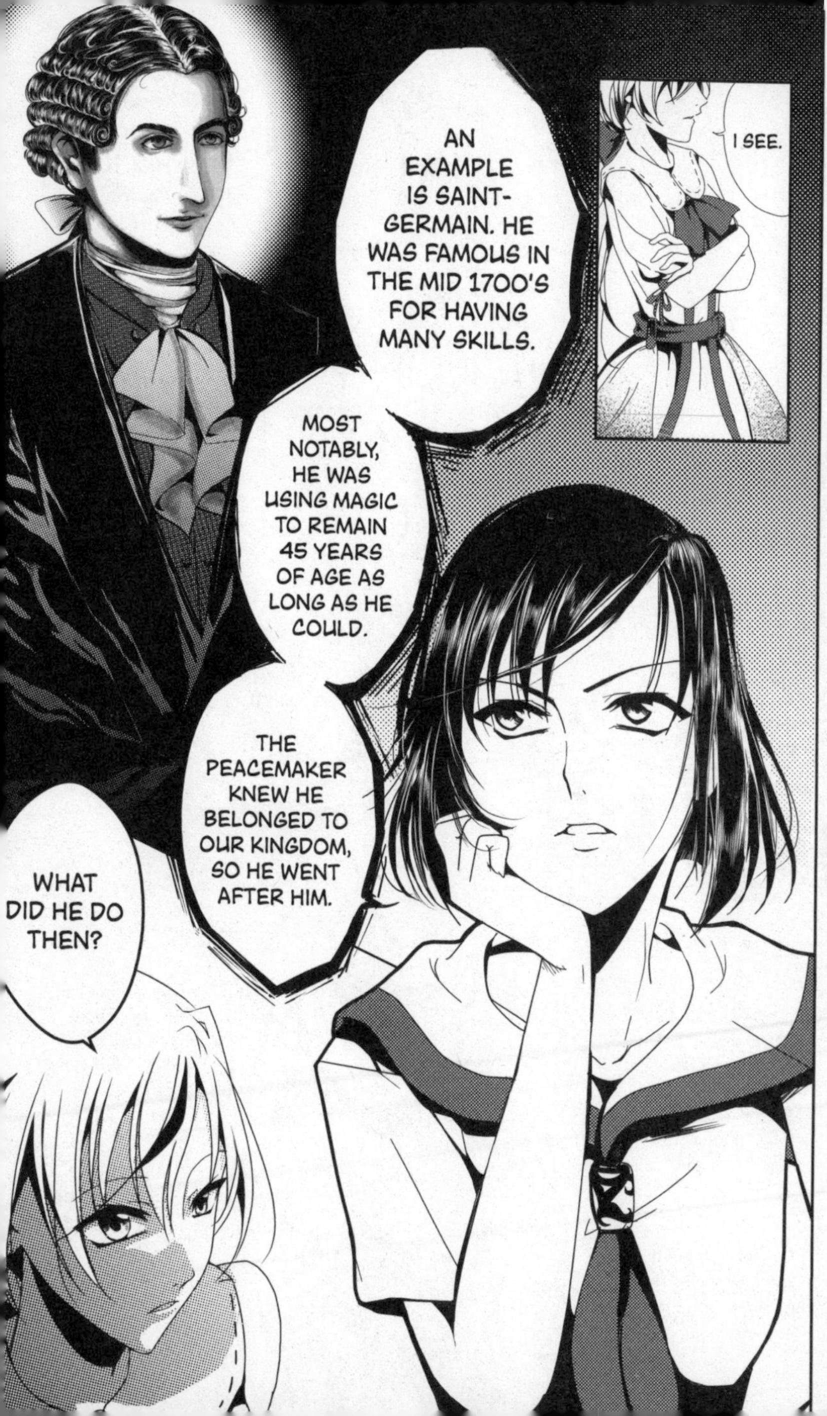
I SEE.
AN EXAMPLE IS SAINT-GERMAIN. HE WAS FAMOUS IN THE MID 1700'S FOR HAVING MANY SKILLS.
MOST NOTABLY, HE WAS USING MAGIC TO REMAIN 45 YEARS OF AGE AS LONG AS HE COULD.
THE PEACEMAKER KNEW HE BELONGED TO OUR KINGDOM, SO HE WENT AFTER HIM.
WHAT DID HE DO THEN?

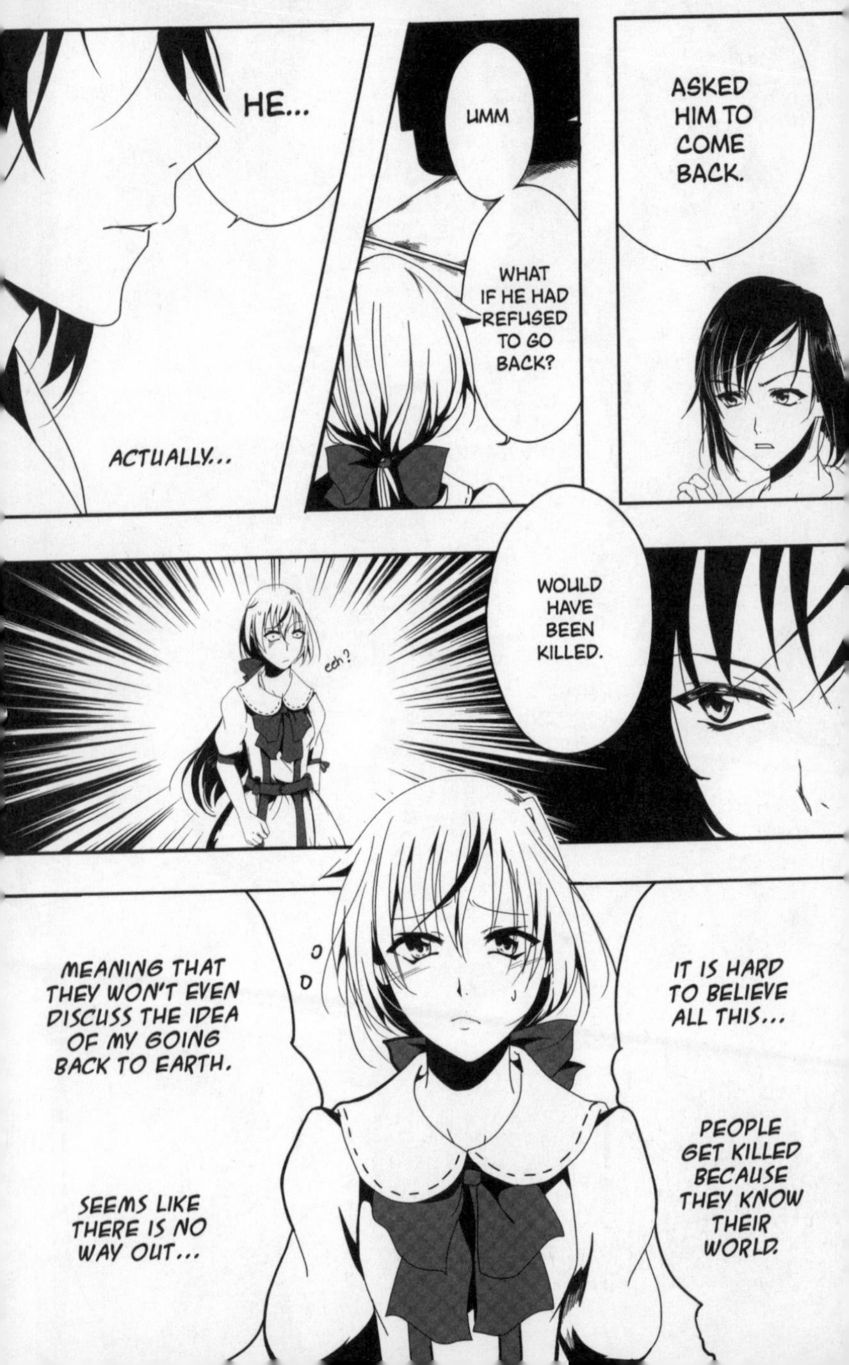
ASKED HIM TO COME BACK.
UMM
WHAT IF HE HAD REFUSED TO GO BACK?
HE...
ACTUALLY...
WOULD HAVE BEEN KILLED.
eeh?
IT IS HARD TO BELIEVE ALL THIS...
MEANING THAT THEY WON'T EVEN DISCUSS THE IDEA OF MY GOING BACK TO EARTH.
PEOPLE GET KILLED BECAUSE THEY KNOW THEIR WORLD.
SEEMS LIKE THERE IS NO WAY OUT...

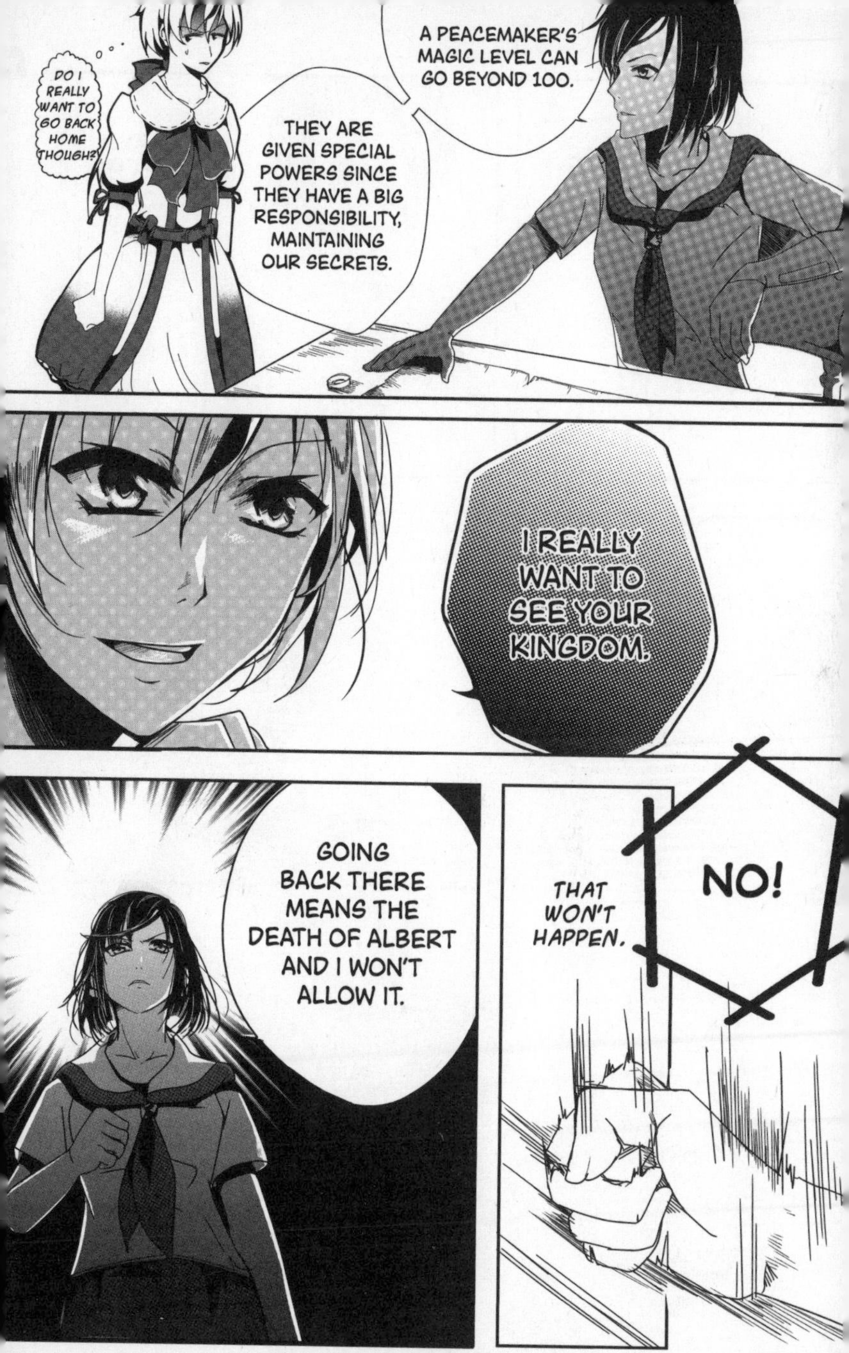
A PEACEMAKER'S MAGIC LEVEL CAN GO BEYOND 100.
THEY ARE GIVEN SPECIAL POWERS SINCE THEY HAVE A BIG RESPONSIBILITY, MAINTAINING OUR SECRETS.
DO I REALLY WANT TO GO BACK HOME THOUGH?
I REALLY WANT TO SEE YOUR KINGDOM.
NO!
THAT WON'T HAPPEN.
GOING BACK THERE MEANS THE DEATH OF ALBERT AND I WON'T ALLOW IT.

I WISH I HAD A BROTHER.

I'M SORRY.

OH...

I'M AN ORPHAN.

WHY?

SORRY. I DIDN'T KNOW.

OH...

DON'T APOLOGIZE.

I'M FINE WITH IT.

WE WILL BE YOUR FAMILY. WE WON'T LET YOU GO...

THANK YOU.

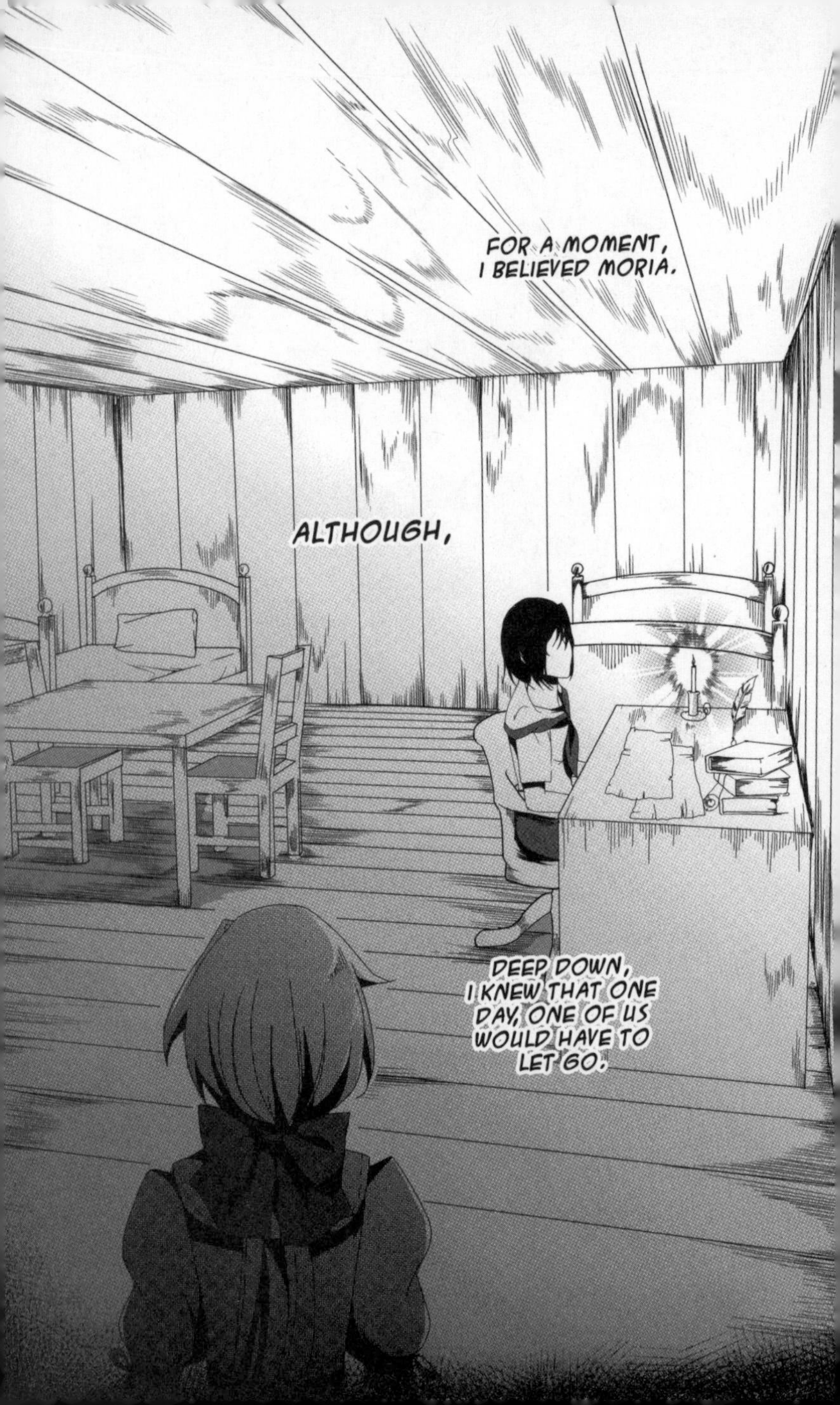
FOR A MOMENT, I BELIEVED MORIA.
ALTHOUGH,
DEEP DOWN, I KNEW THAT ONE DAY, ONE OF US WOULD HAVE TO LET GO.

Ocean of Secrets

CHAPTER 3

WE ARE IN DANGER!

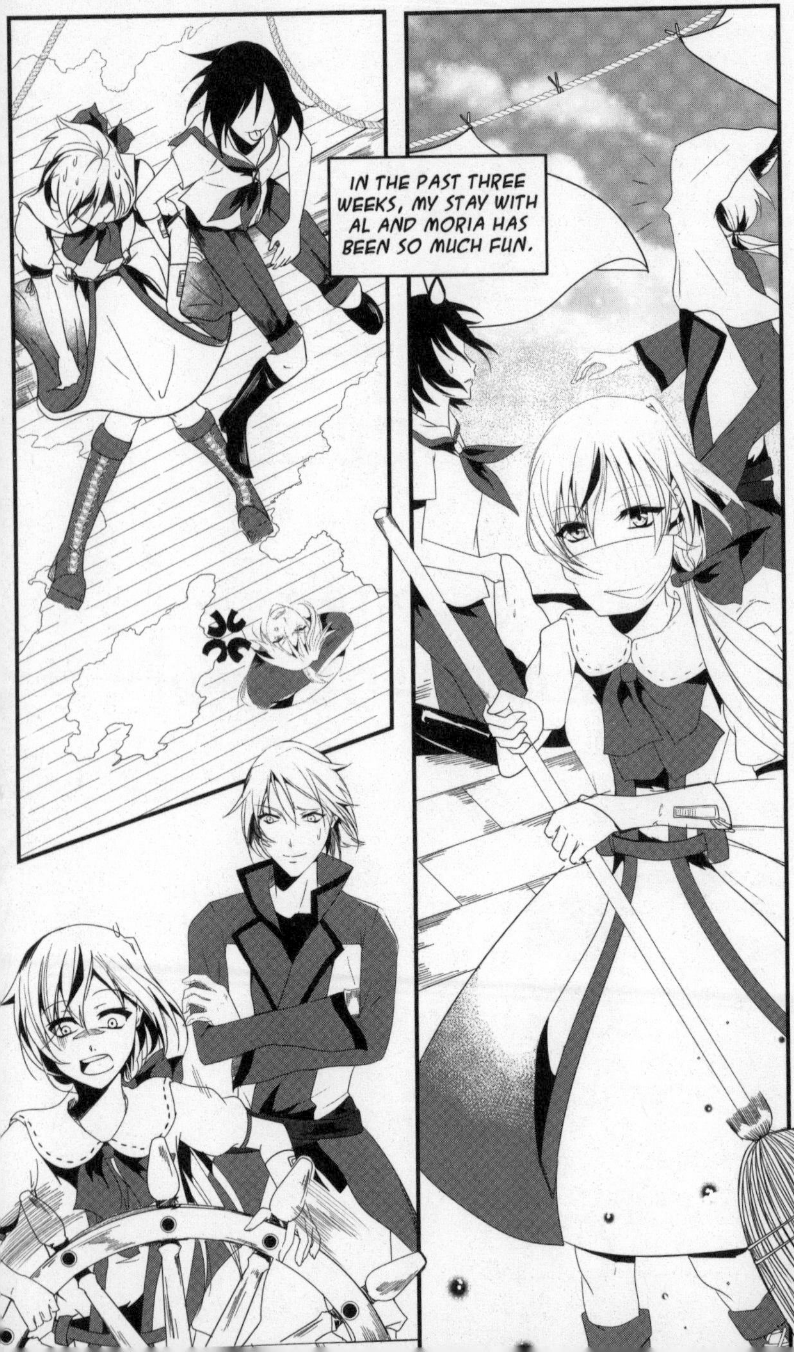
IN THE PAST THREE WEEKS, MY STAY WITH AL AND MORIA HAS BEEN SO MUCH FUN.

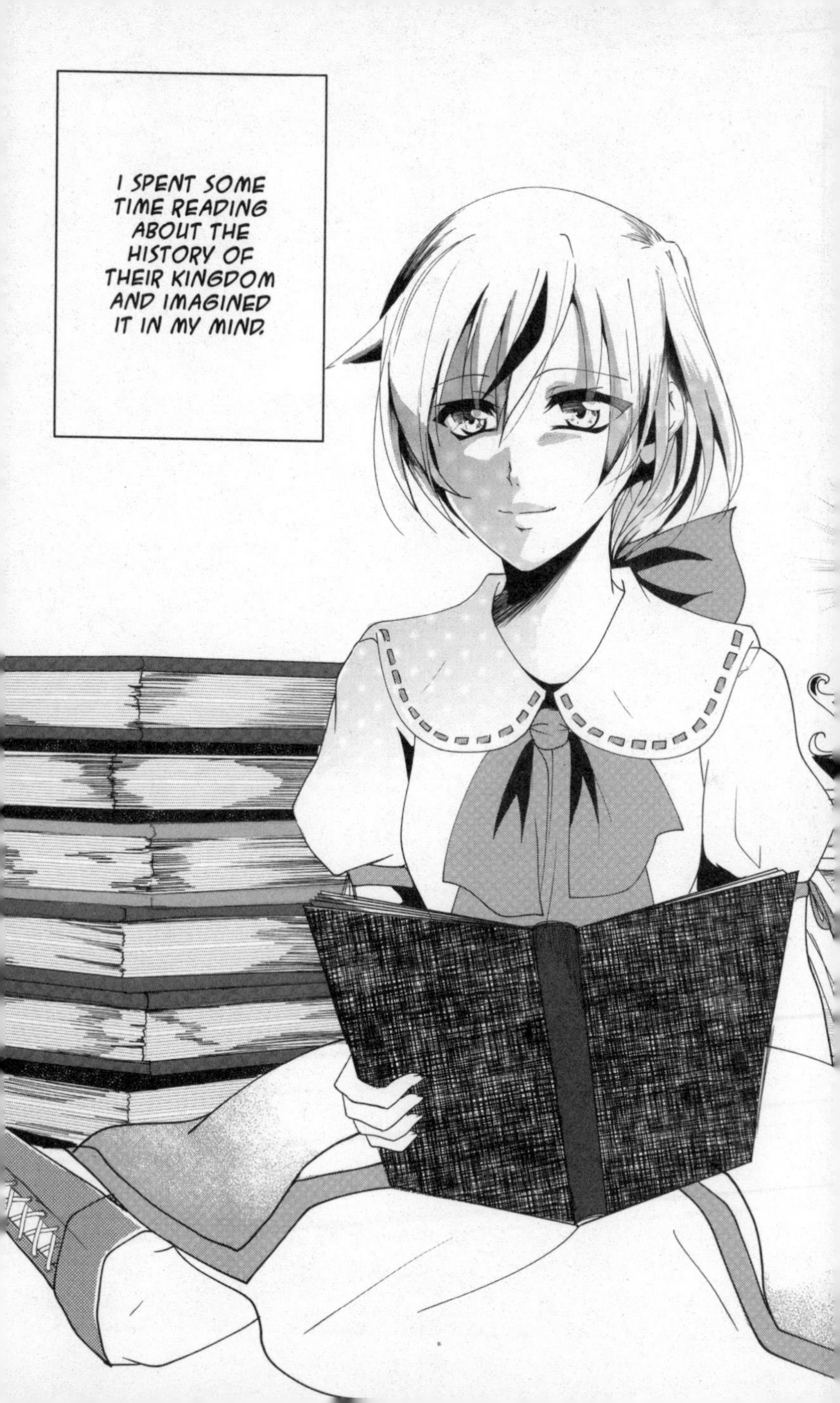
I SPENT SOME TIME READING ABOUT THE HISTORY OF THEIR KINGDOM AND IMAGINED IT IN MY MIND.

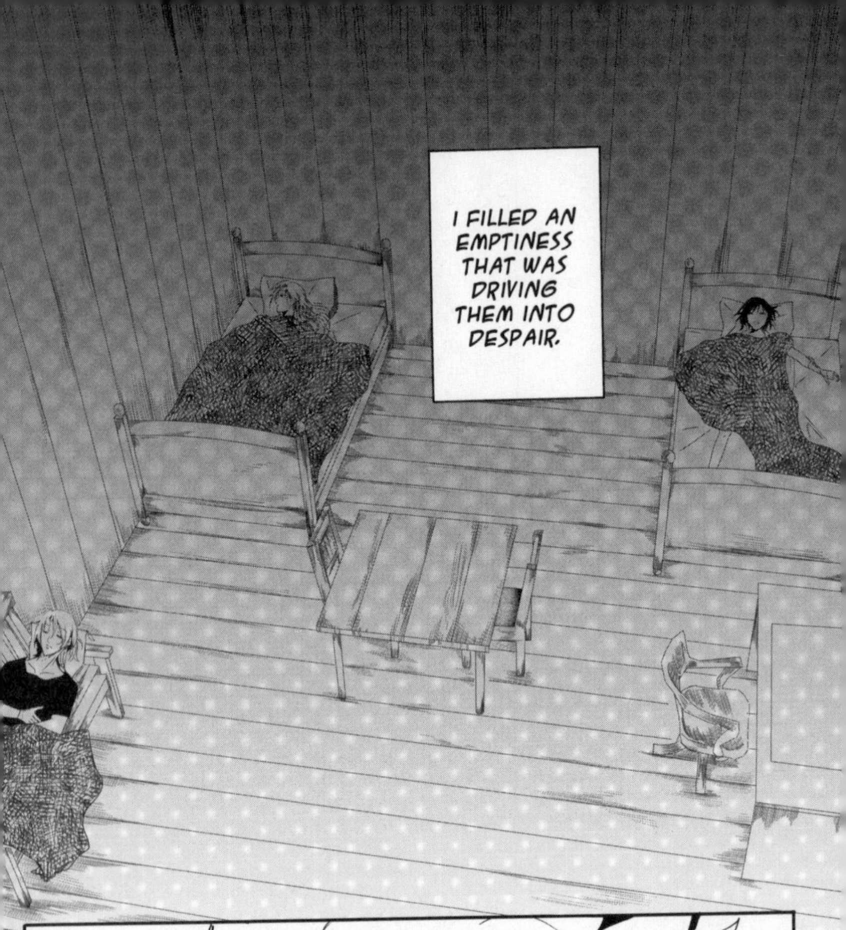
I FILLED AN EMPTINESS THAT WAS DRIVING THEM INTO DESPAIR.

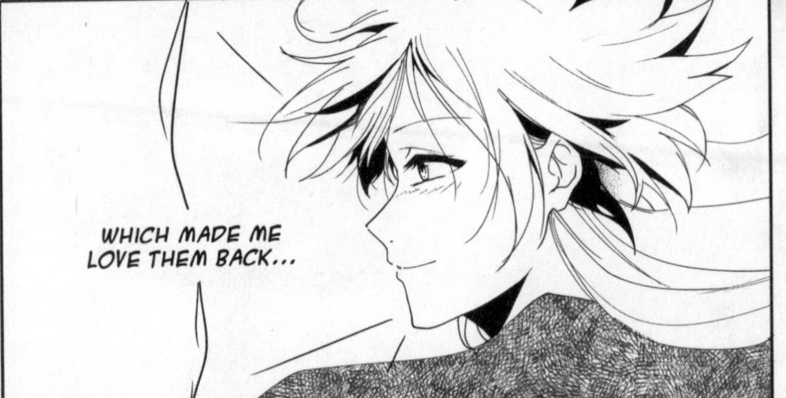
WHICH MADE ME LOVE THEM BACK...

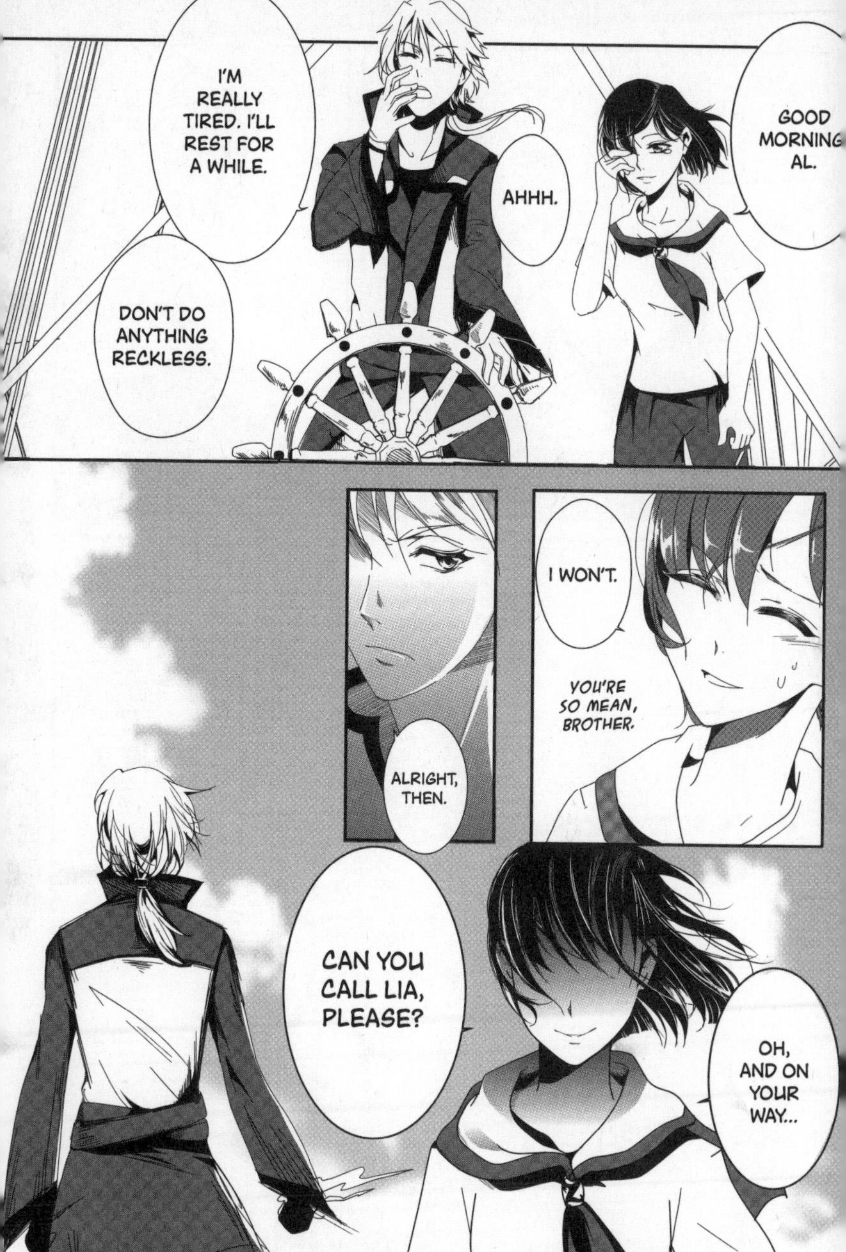
GOOD MORNING AL.
AHHH.
I'M REALLY TIRED. I'LL REST FOR A WHILE.
DON'T DO ANYTHING RECKLESS.
I WON'T.
YOU'RE SO MEAN, BROTHER.
ALRIGHT, THEN.
OH, AND ON YOUR WAY...
CAN YOU CALL LIA, PLEASE?

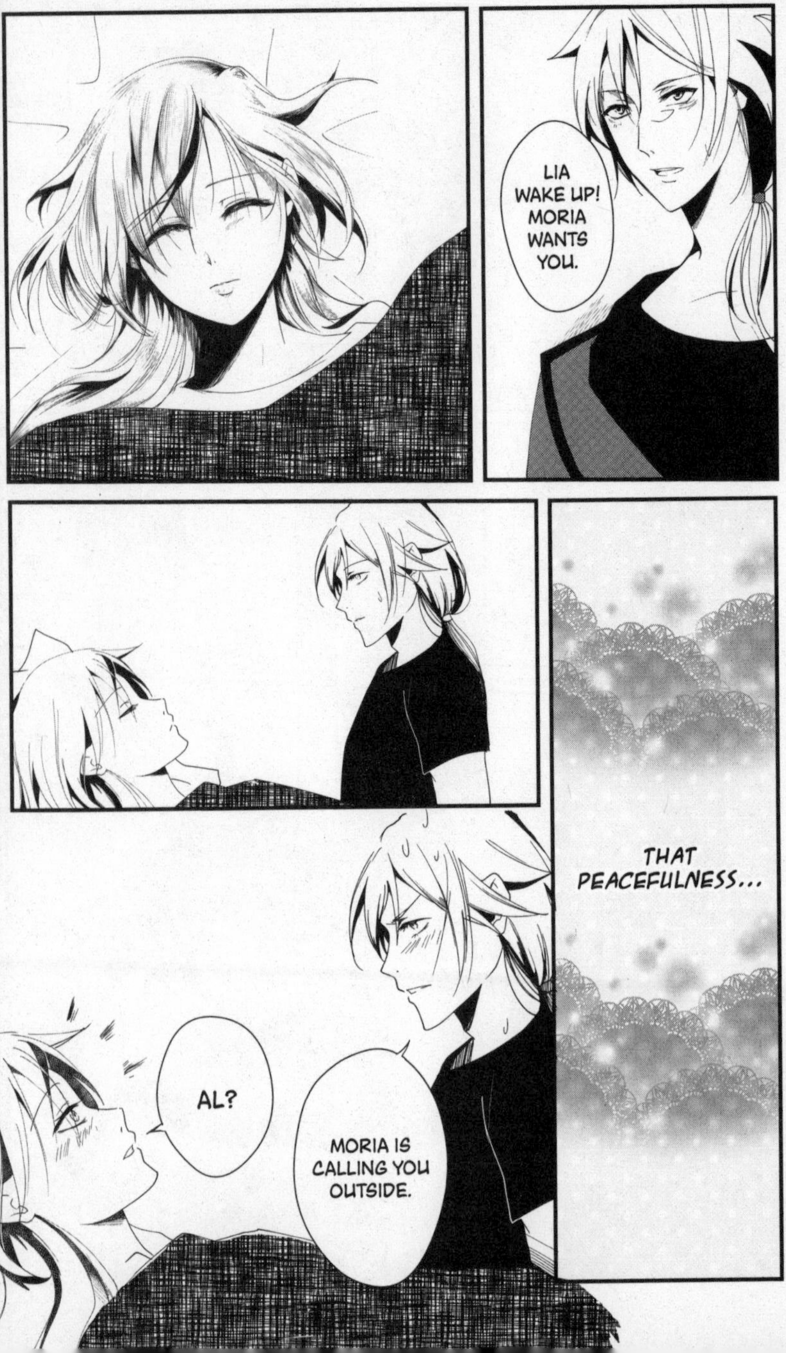
LIA WAKE UP! MORIA WANTS YOU.
THAT PEACEFULNESS...
AL?
MORIA IS CALLING YOU OUTSIDE.

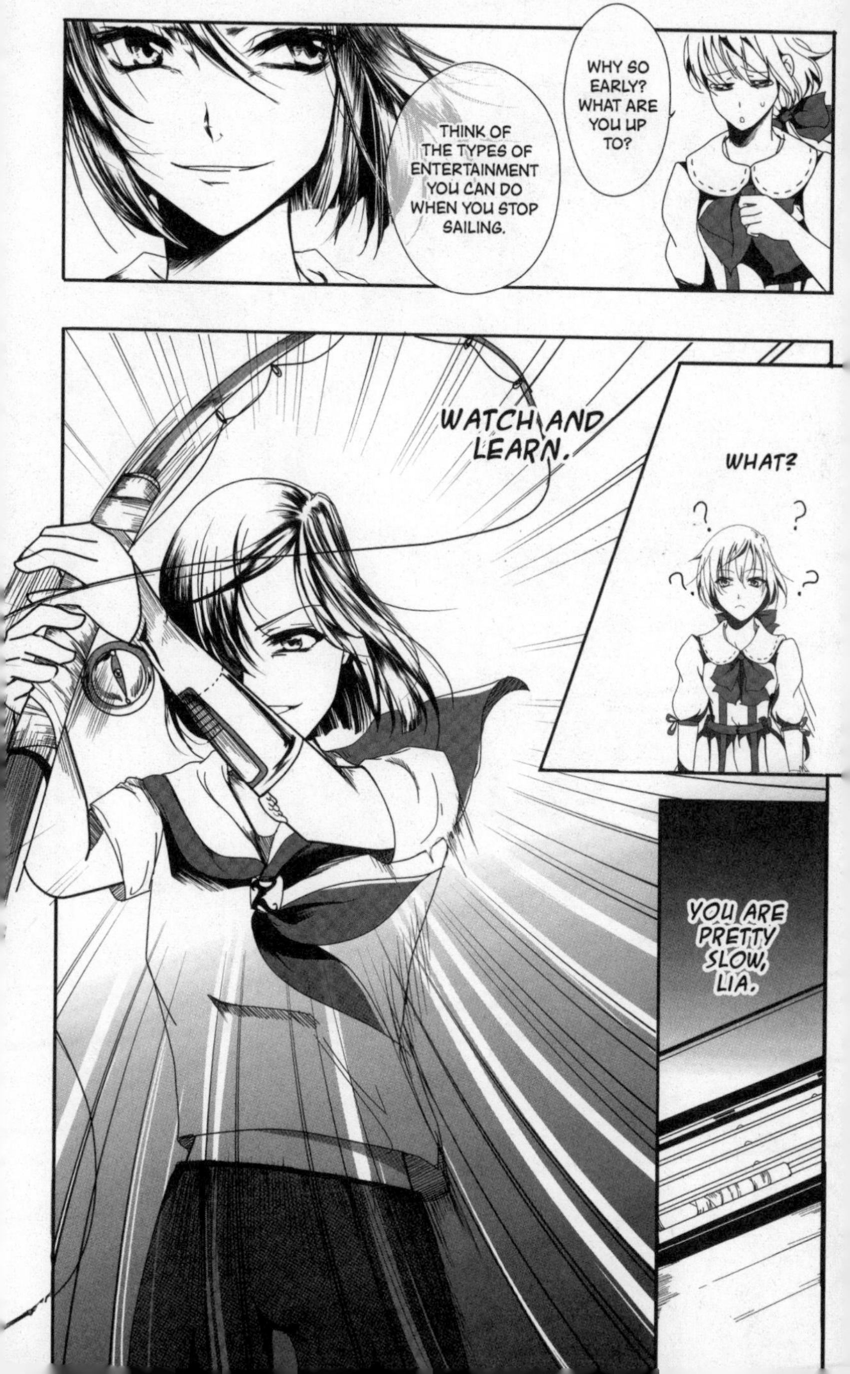
WHY SO EARLY? WHAT ARE YOU UP TO?
THINK OF THE TYPES OF ENTERTAINMENT YOU CAN DO WHEN YOU STOP SAILING.
WHAT?
YOU ARE PRETTY SLOW, LIA.
WATCH AND LEARN.

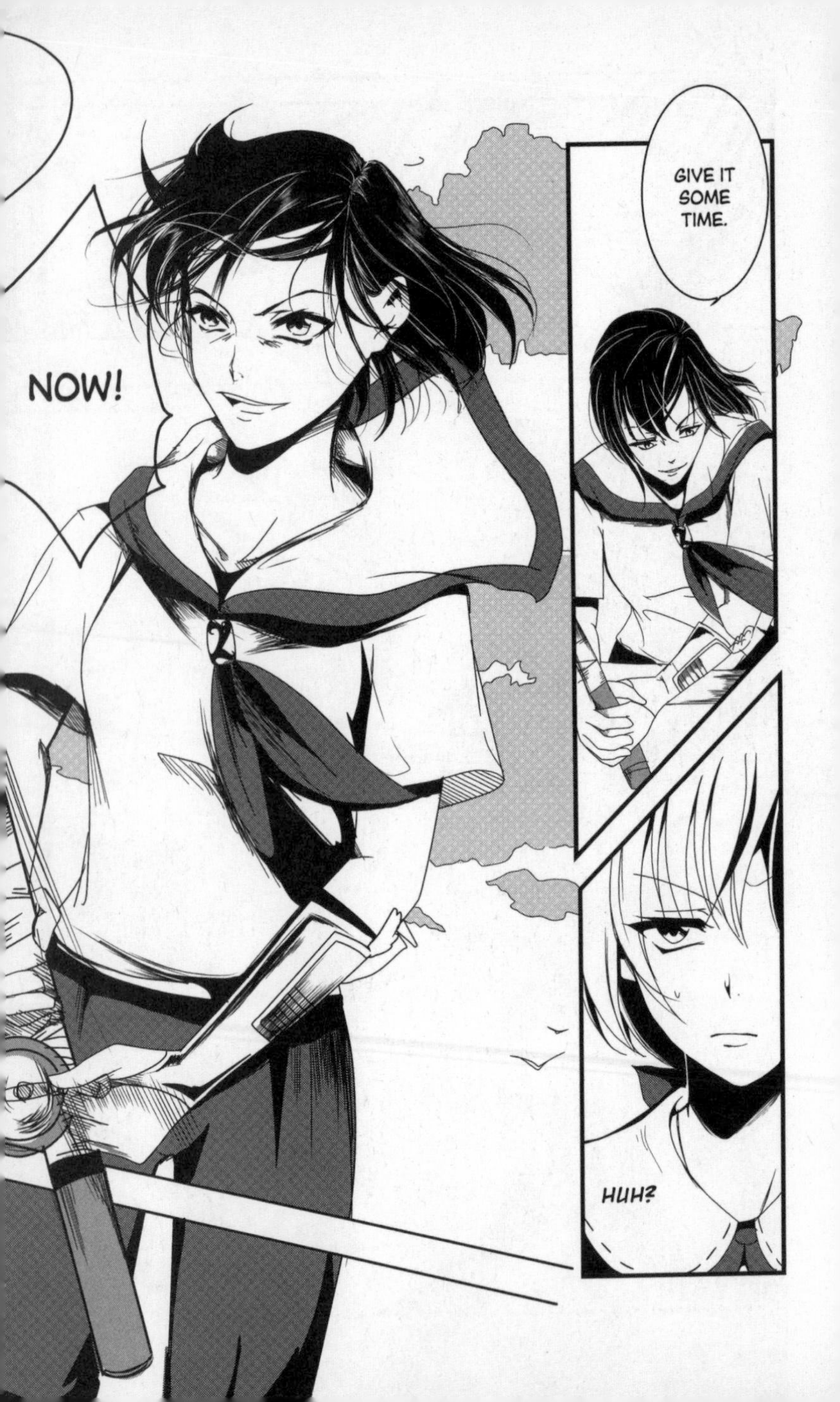
GIVE IT SOME TIME.
HUH?
NOW!

READ THIS WAY

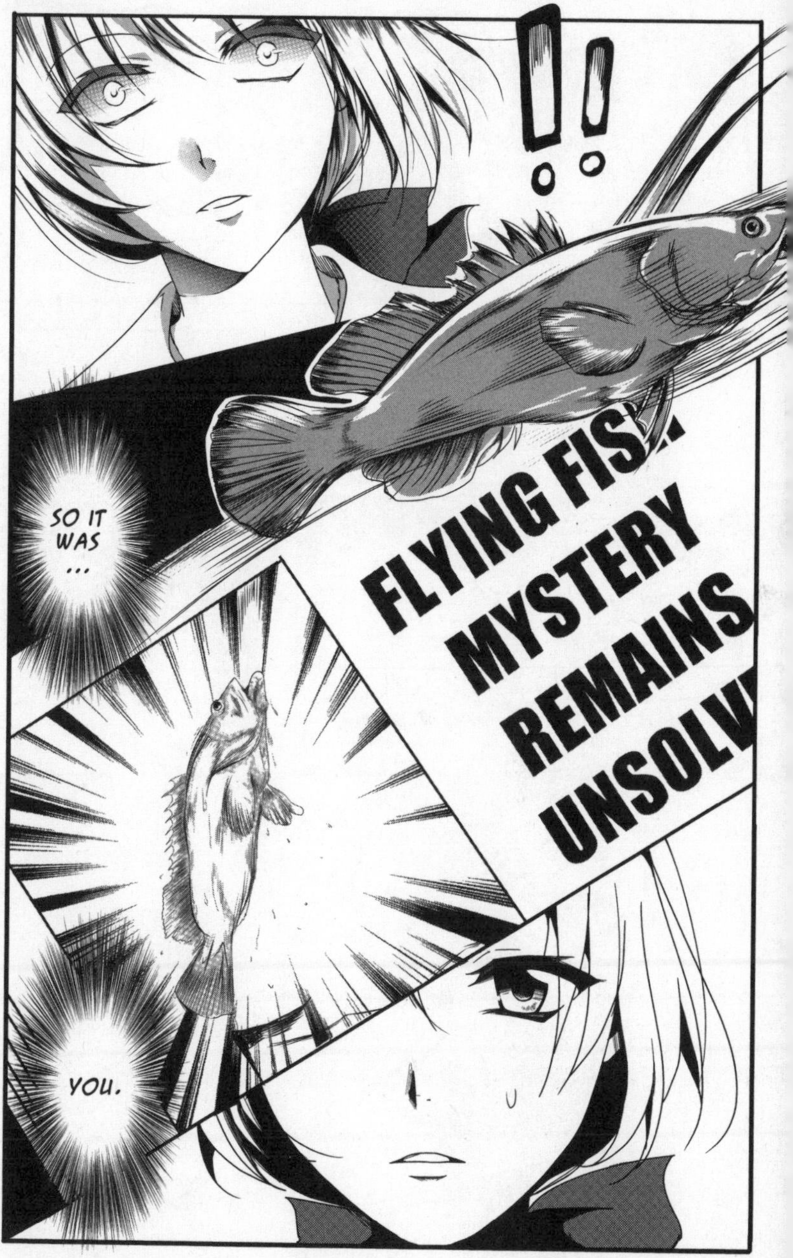

!!
FLYING FIS
MYSTERY
REMAINS
UNSOLV
SO IT WAS ...
YOU.

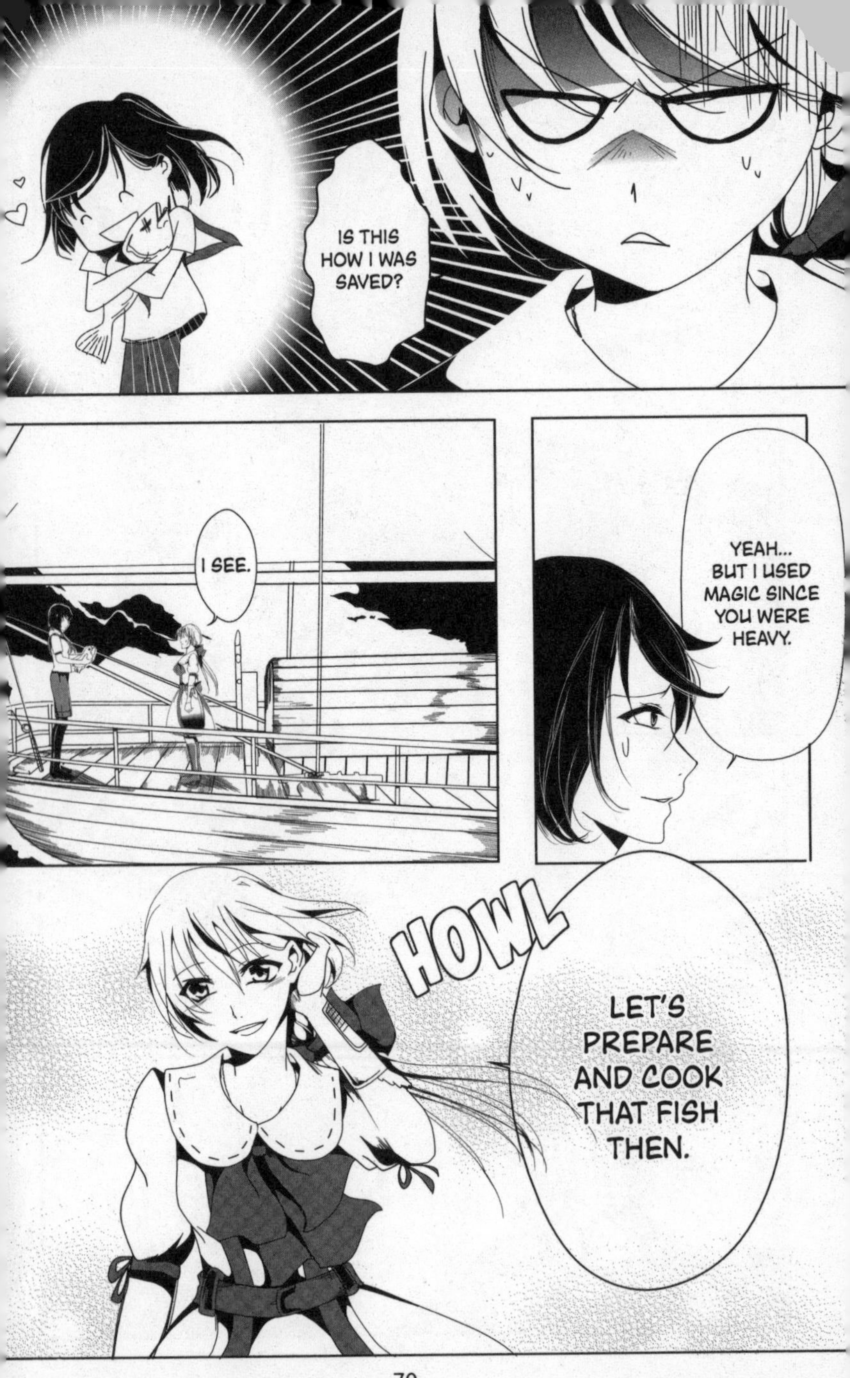

IS THIS HOW I WAS SAVED?
YEAH... BUT I USED MAGIC SINCE YOU WERE HEAVY.
I SEE.
LET'S PREPARE AND COOK THAT FISH THEN.
HOWL

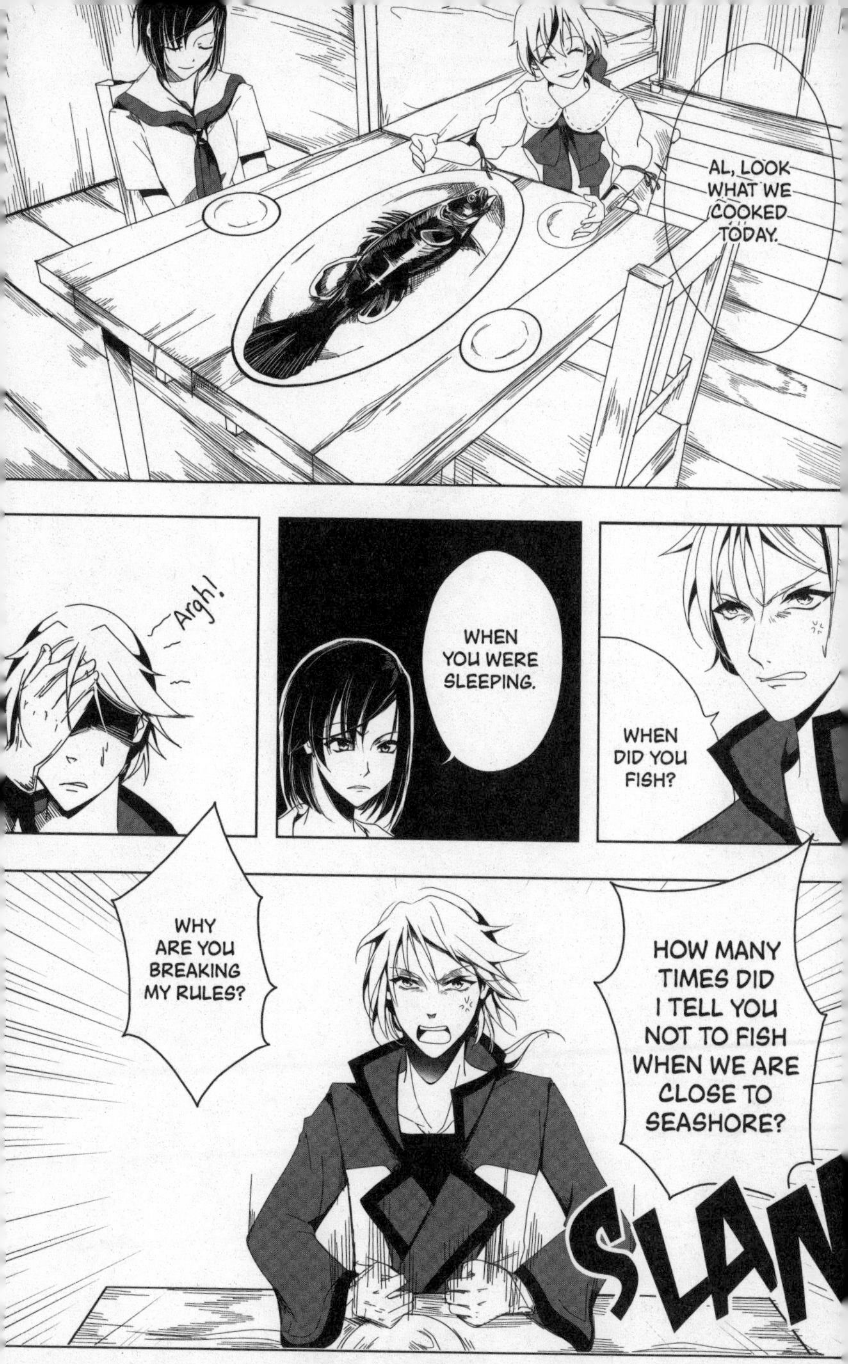
AL, LOOK WHAT WE COOKED TODAY.
WHEN DID YOU FISH?
WHEN YOU WERE SLEEPING.
Argh!
HOW MANY TIMES DID I TELL YOU NOT TO FISH WHEN WE ARE CLOSE TO SEASHORE?
WHY ARE YOU BREAKING MY RULES?

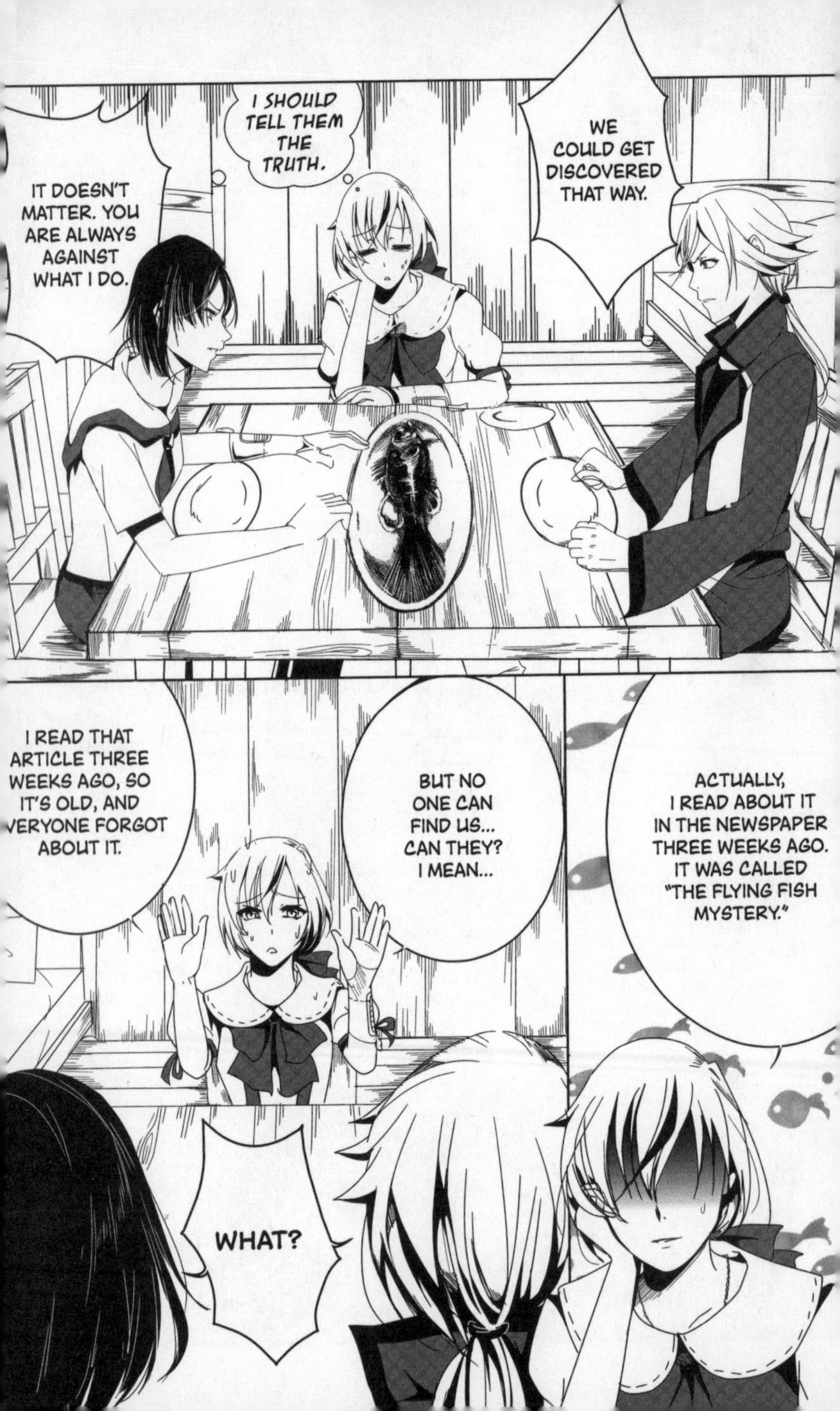
WE COULD GET DISCOVERED THAT WAY.
I SHOULD TELL THEM THE TRUTH.
IT DOESN'T MATTER. YOU ARE ALWAYS AGAINST WHAT I DO.
ACTUALLY, I READ ABOUT IT IN THE NEWSPAPER THREE WEEKS AGO. IT WAS CALLED "THE FLYING FISH MYSTERY."
BUT NO ONE CAN FIND US... CAN THEY? I MEAN...
I READ THAT ARTICLE THREE WEEKS AGO, SO IT'S OLD, AND VERYONE FORGOT ABOUT IT.
WHAT?

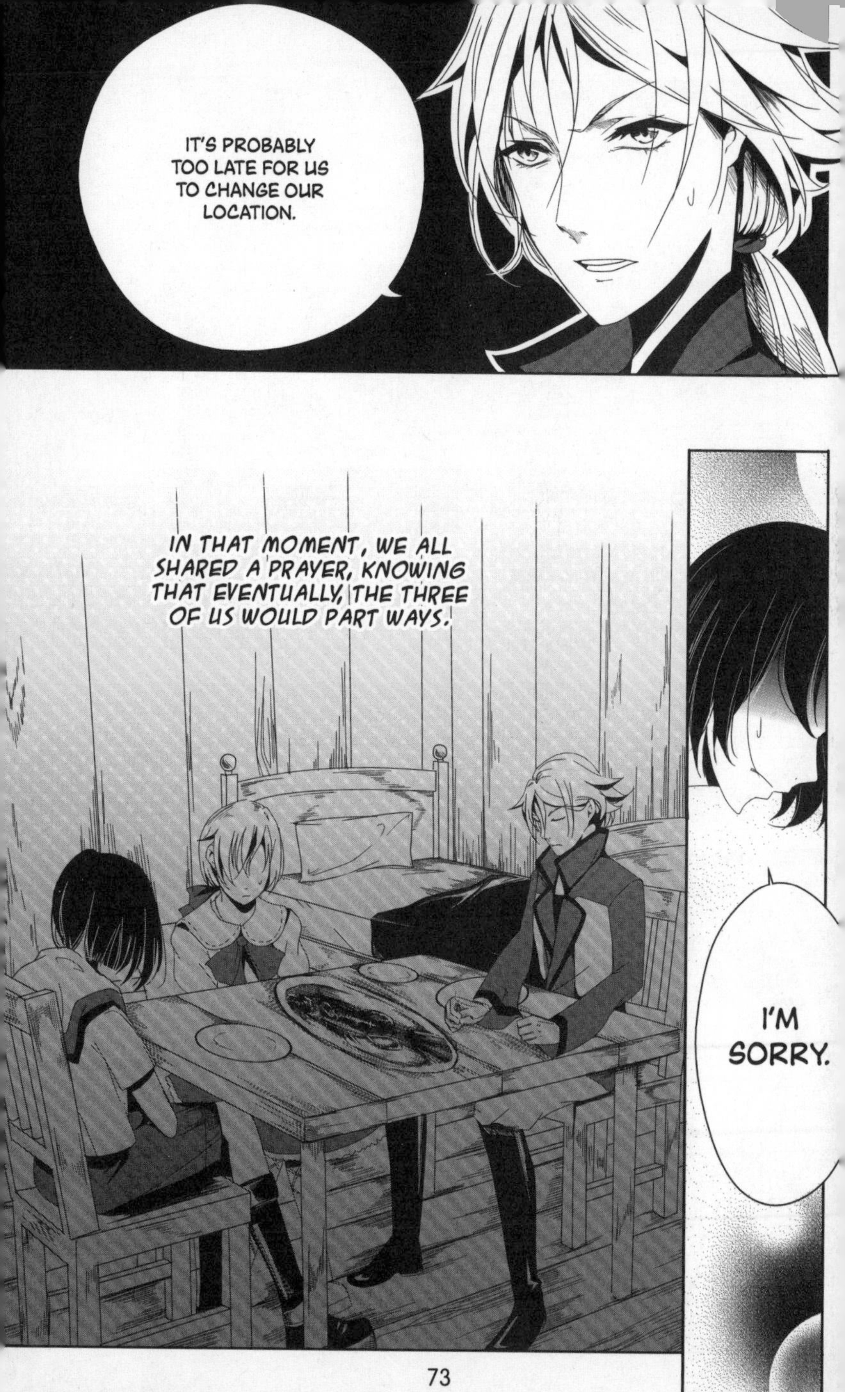
IT'S PROBABLY TOO LATE FOR US TO CHANGE OUR LOCATION.
I'M SORRY.
IN THAT MOMENT, WE ALL SHARED A PRAYER, KNOWING THAT EVENTUALLY, THE THREE OF US WOULD PART WAYS.

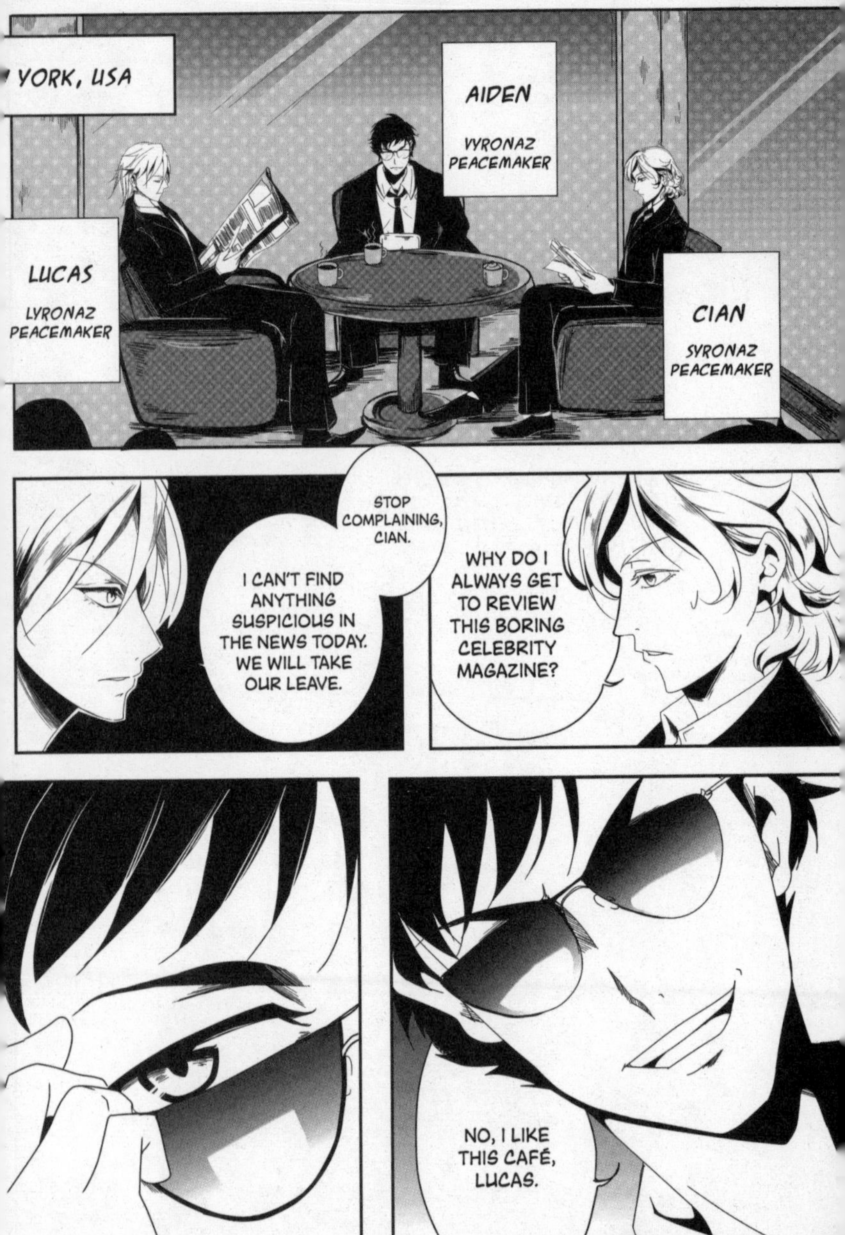
YORK, USA
AIDEN
VYRONAZ PEACEMAKER
CIAN
SYRONAZ PEACEMAKER
LUCAS
LYRONAZ PEACEMAKER
WHY DO I ALWAYS GET TO REVIEW THIS BORING CELEBRITY MAGAZINE?
STOP COMPLAINING, CIAN.
I CAN'T FIND ANYTHING SUSPICIOUS IN THE NEWS TODAY. WE WILL TAKE OUR LEAVE.
NO, I LIKE THIS CAFÉ, LUCAS.

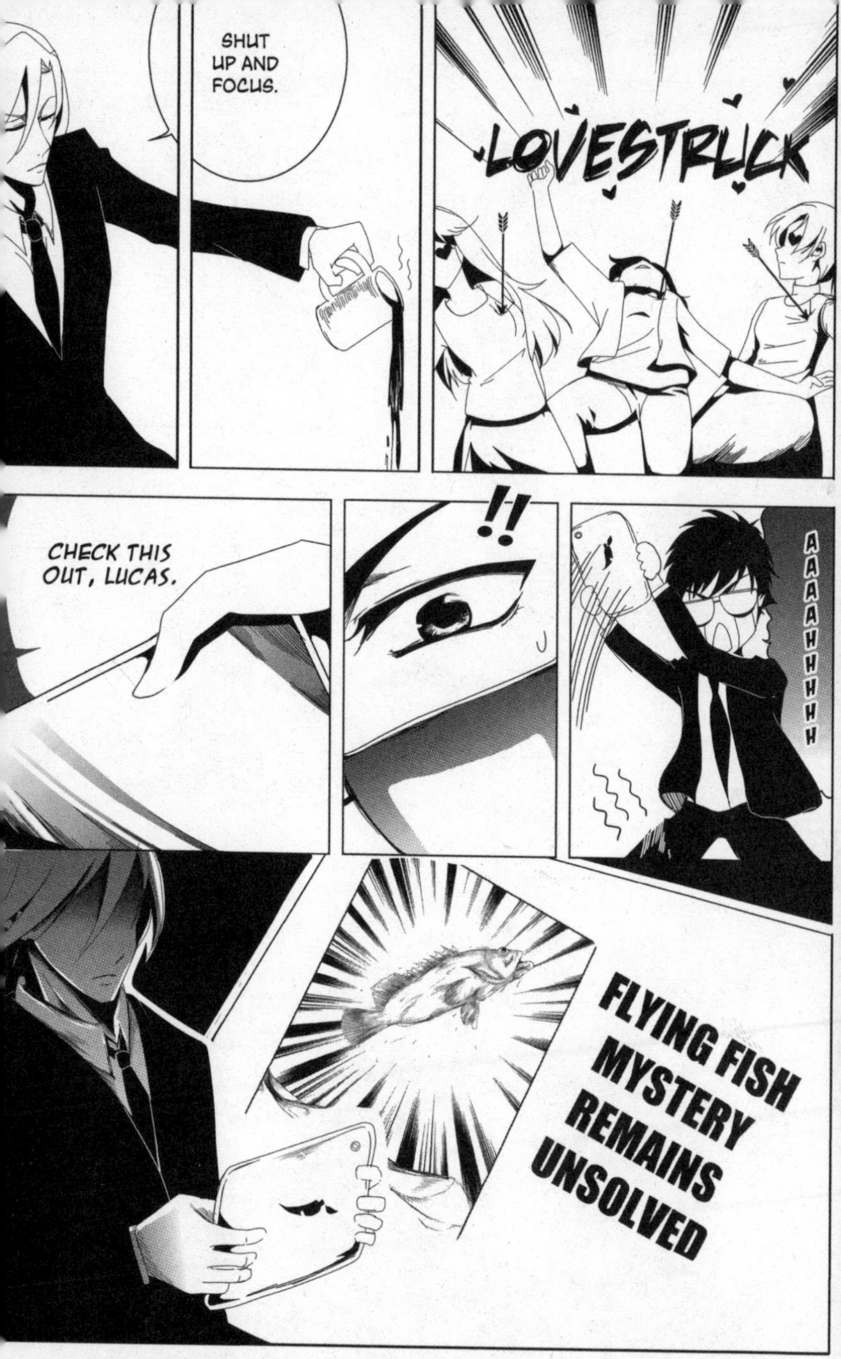
LOVESTRUCK
SHUT UP AND FOCUS.
AAAAHHHHH
!!
CHECK THIS OUT, LUCAS.
FLYING FISH MYSTERY REMAINS UNSOLVED

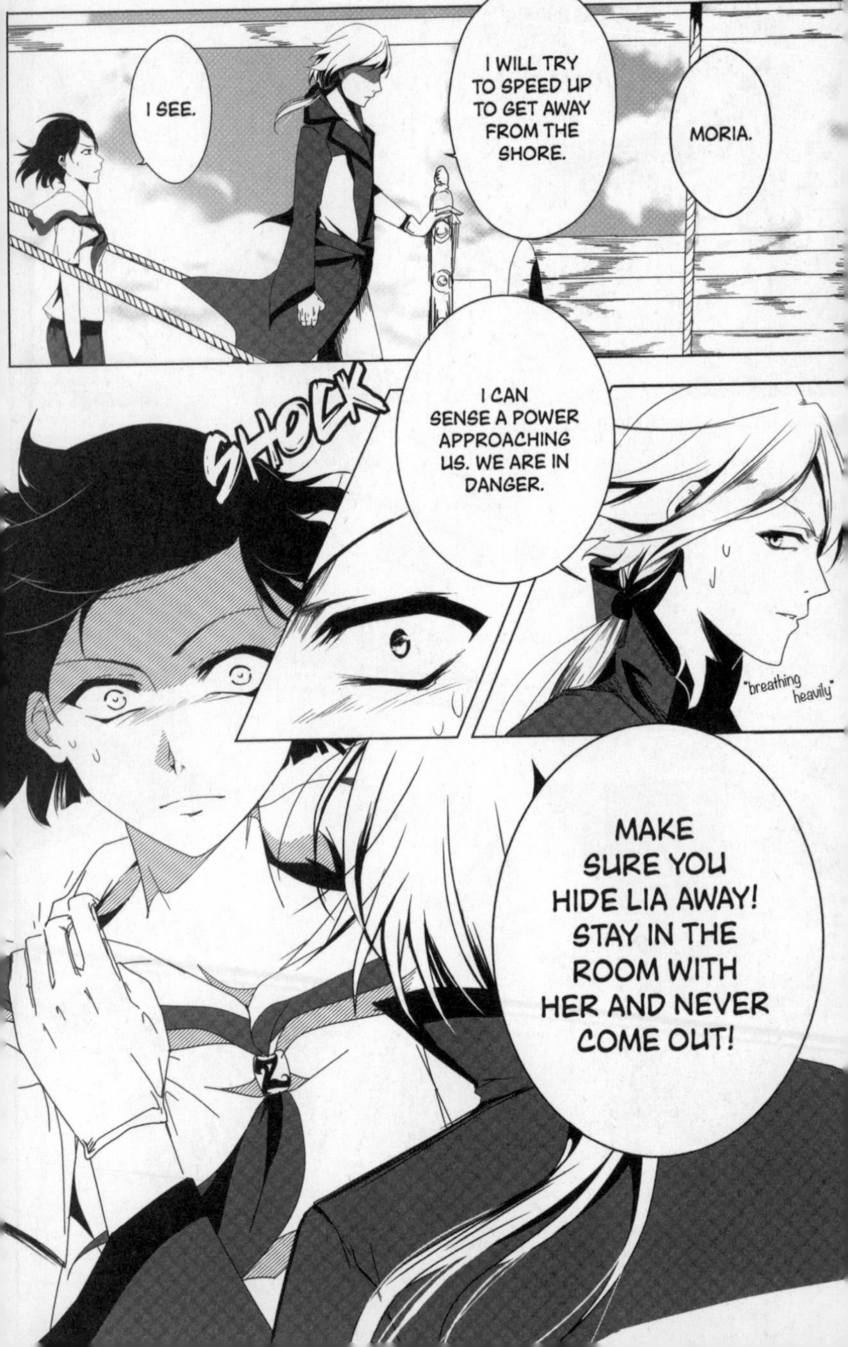
MORIA.
I WILL TRY TO SPEED UP TO GET AWAY FROM THE SHORE.
I SEE.
I CAN SENSE A POWER APPROACHING US. WE ARE IN DANGER.
breathing heavily
SHOCK
MAKE SURE YOU HIDE LIA AWAY! STAY IN THE ROOM WITH HER AND NEVER COME OUT!

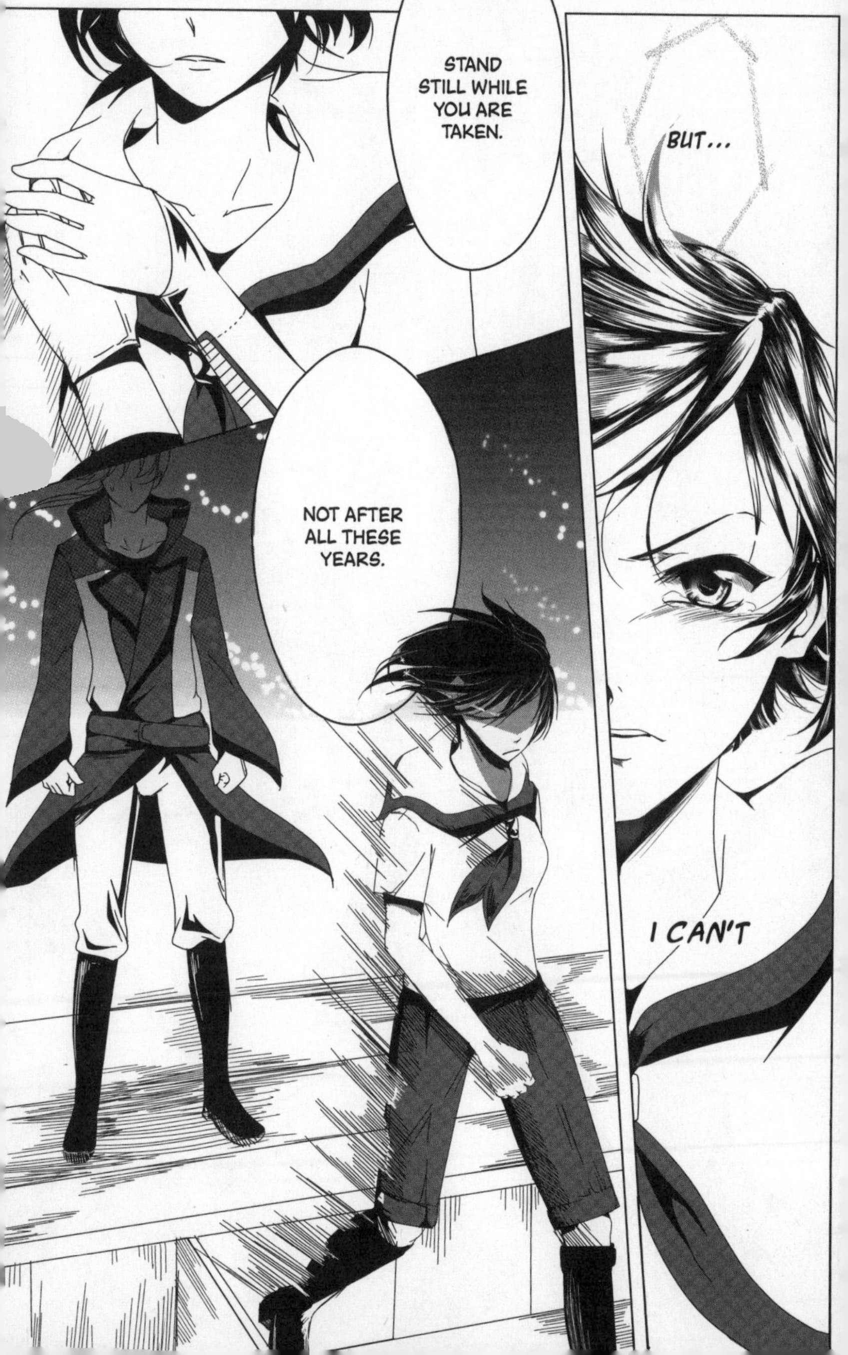
BUT...
I CAN'T
STAND STILL WHILE YOU ARE TAKEN.
NOT AFTER ALL THESE YEARS.

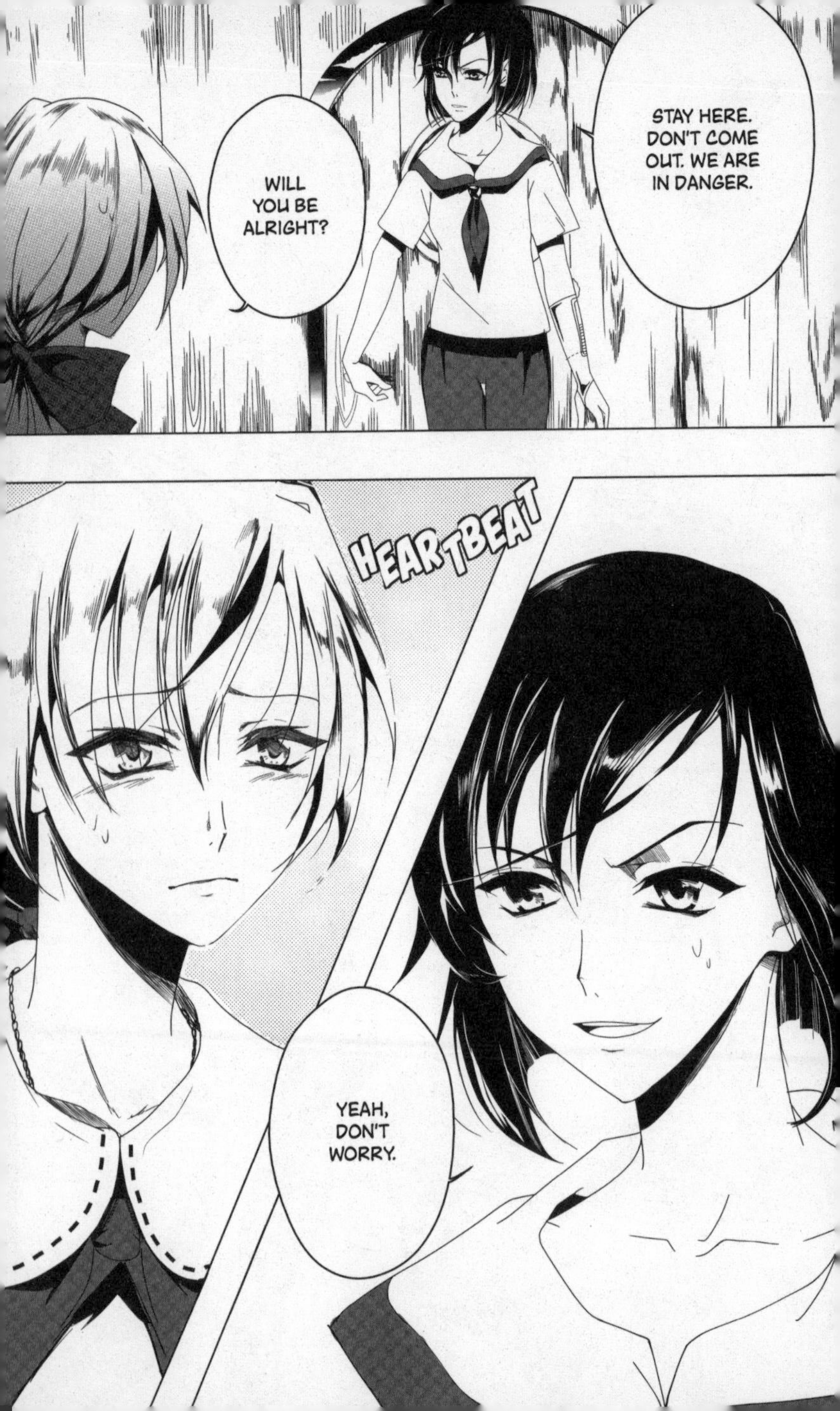
STAY HERE. DON'T COME OUT. WE ARE IN DANGER.
WILL YOU BE ALRIGHT?
HEARTBEAT
YEAH, DON'T WORRY.

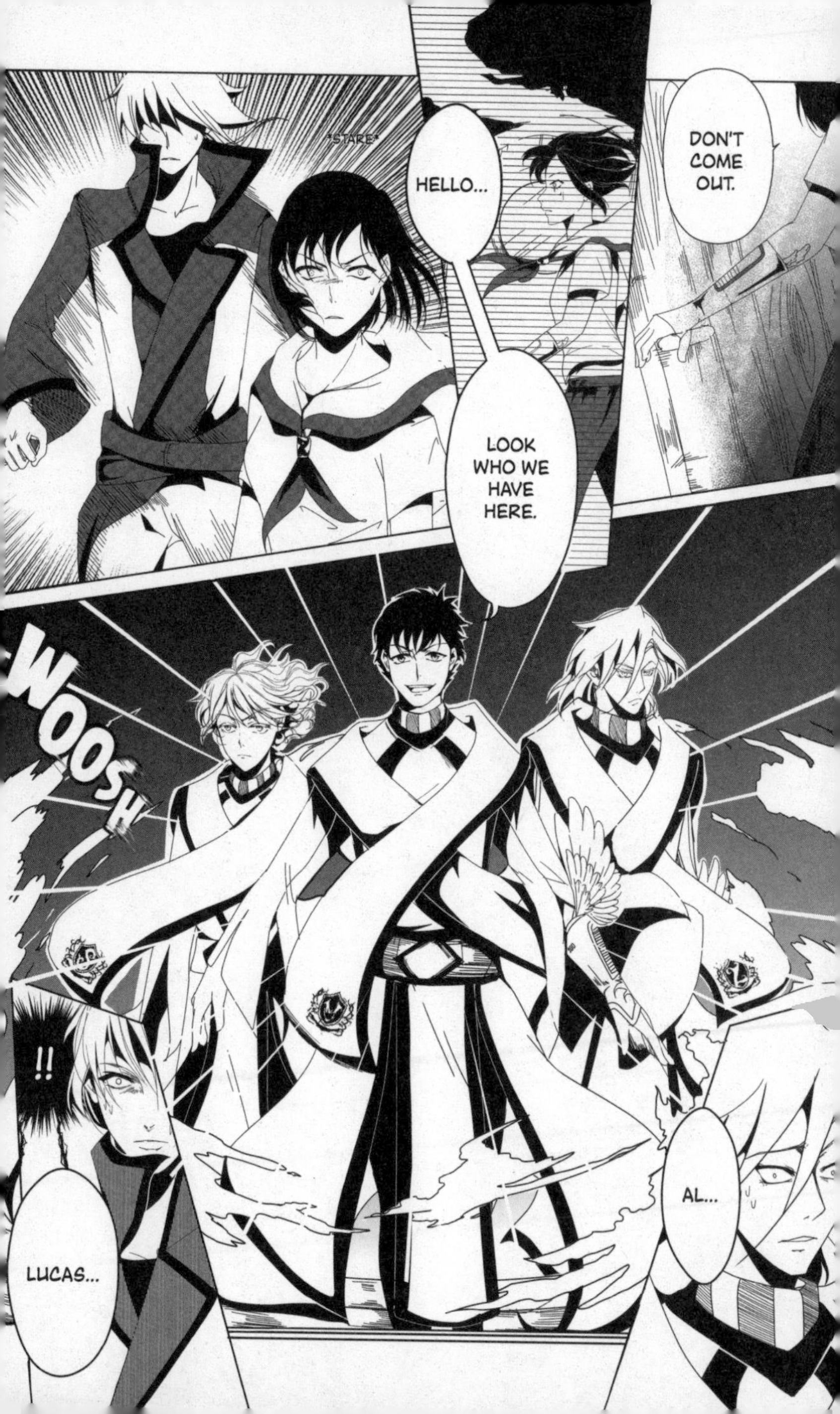
DON'T COME OUT.
HELLO...
LOOK WHO WE HAVE HERE.
STARE
WOOSH
AL...
!!
LUCAS...

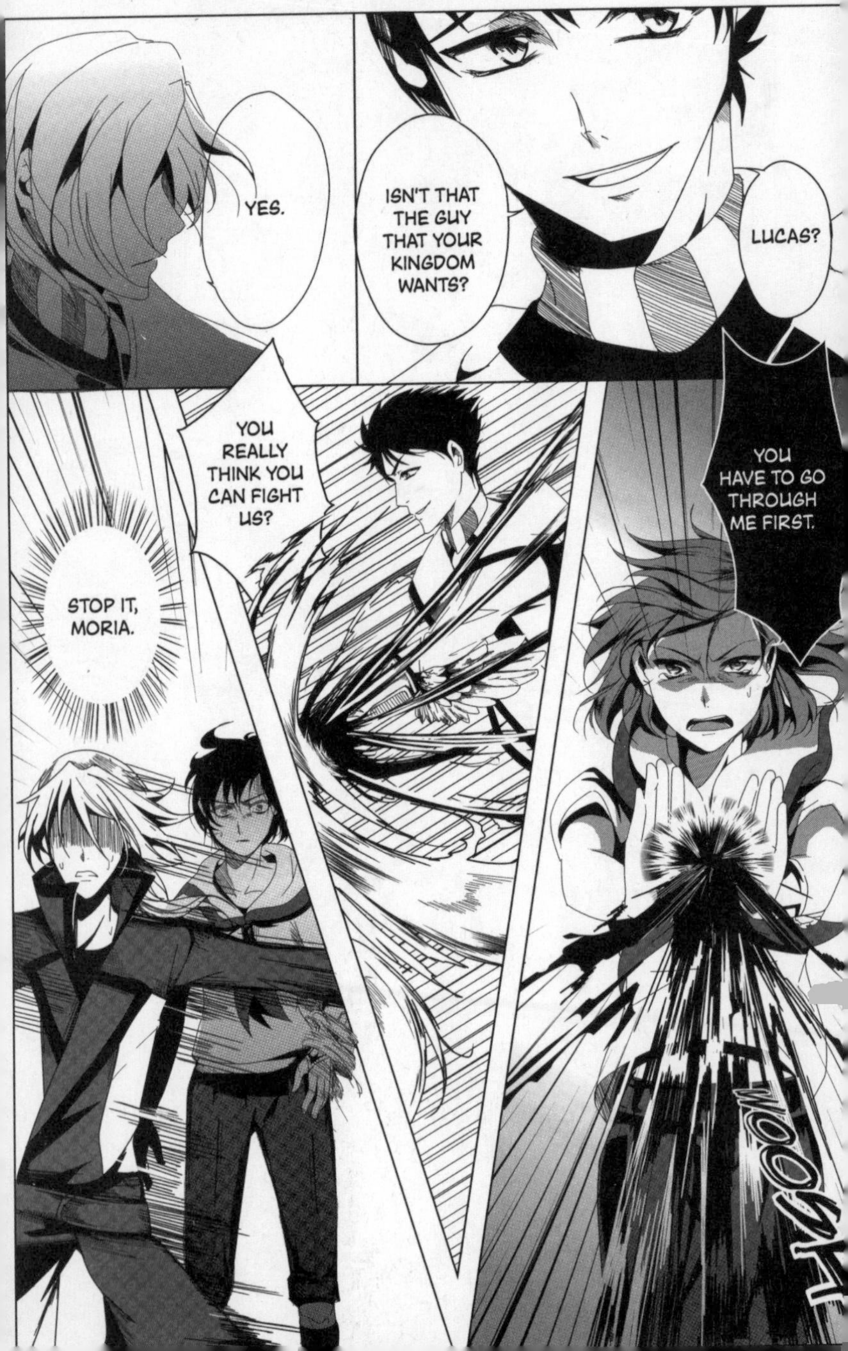
LUCAS?
ISN'T THAT THE GUY THAT YOUR KINGDOM WANTS?
YES.
YOU HAVE TO GO THROUGH ME FIRST.
WHOOSH
YOU REALLY THINK YOU CAN FIGHT US?
STOP IT, MORIA.

READ THIS WAY

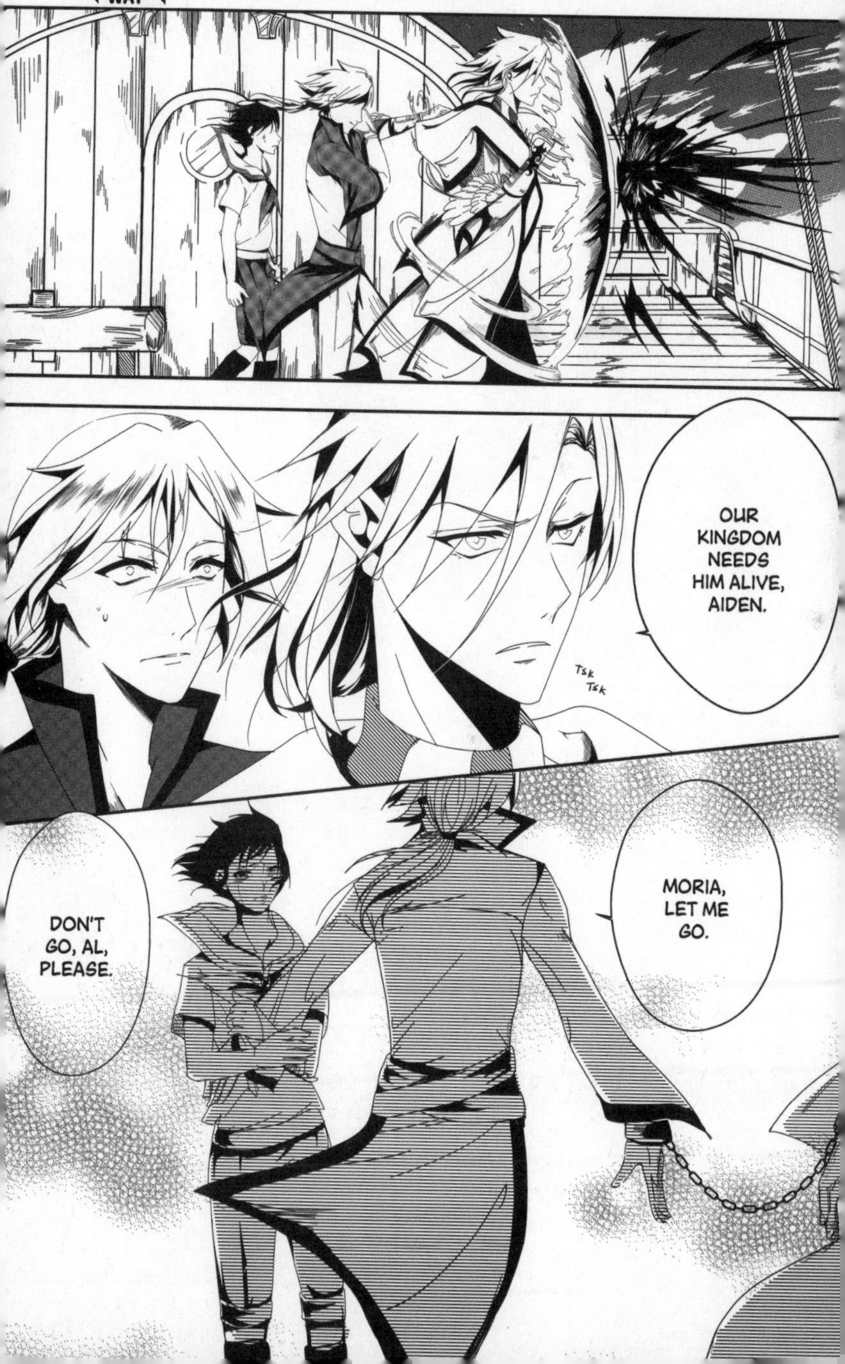
OUR KINGDOM NEEDS HIM ALIVE, AIDEN.
TSK TSK
MORIA, LET ME GO.
DON'T GO, AL, PLEASE.

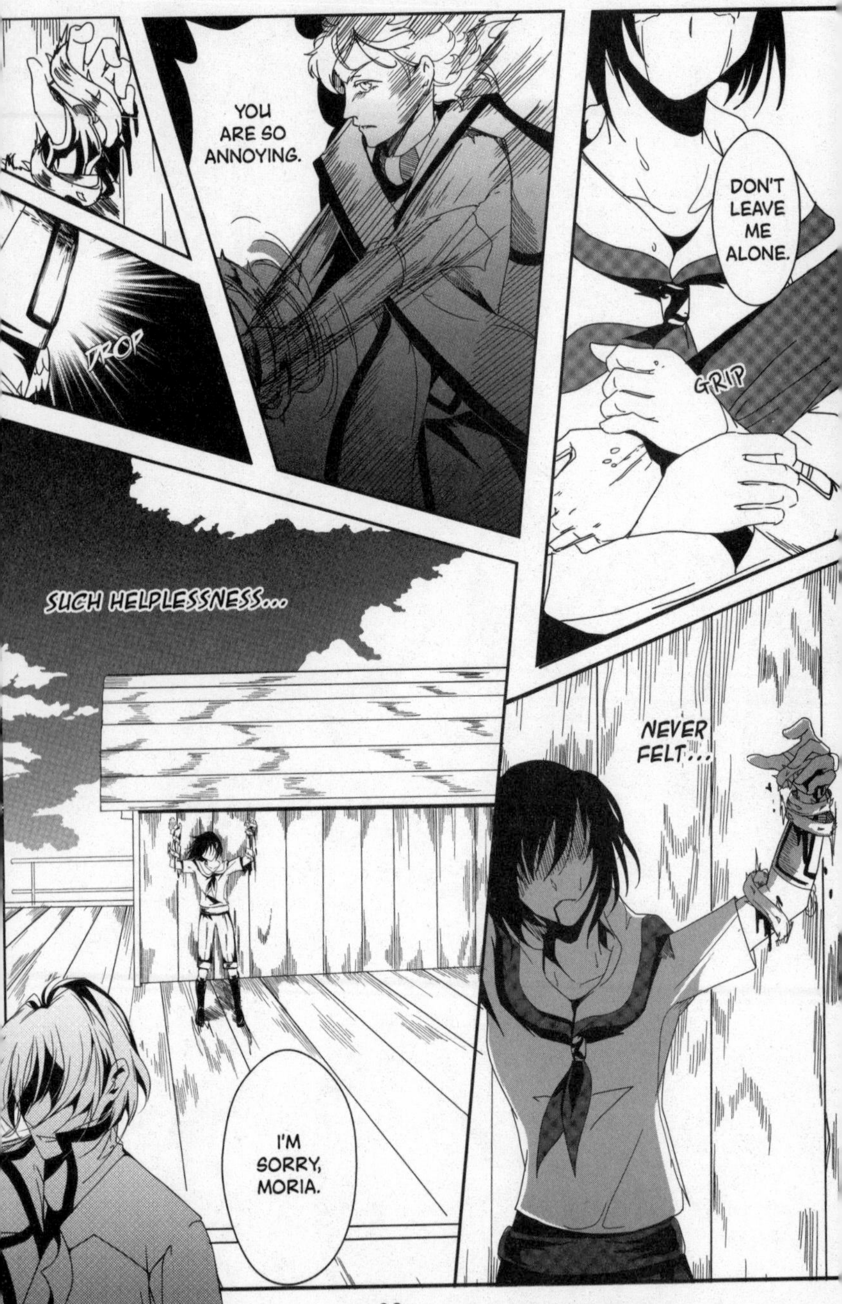
DON'T LEAVE ME ALONE.
GRIP
YOU ARE SO ANNOYING.
DROP
NEVER FELT...
SUCH HELPLESSNESS...
I'M SORRY, MORIA.

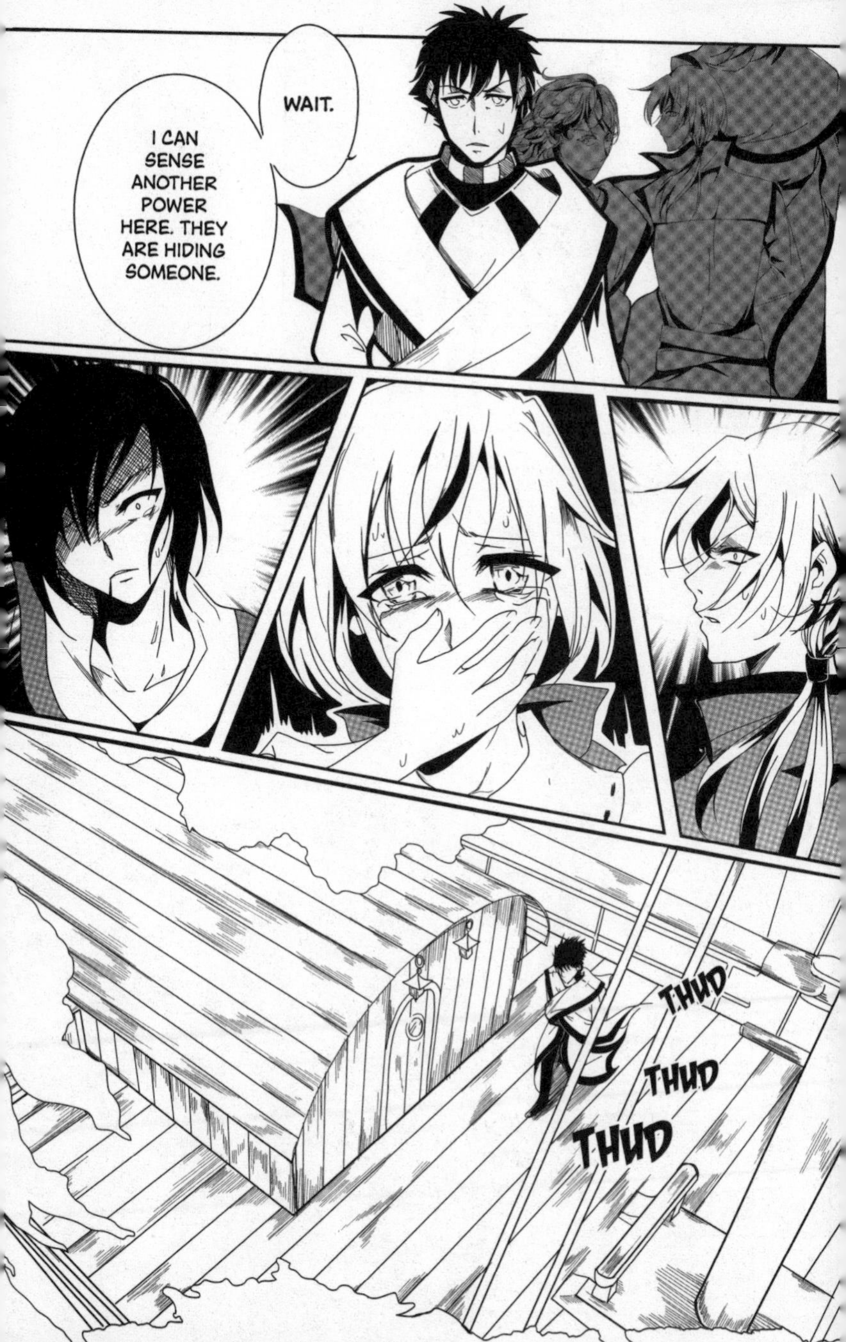
WAIT.
I CAN SENSE ANOTHER POWER HERE. THEY ARE HIDING SOMEONE.
THUD
THUD
THUD

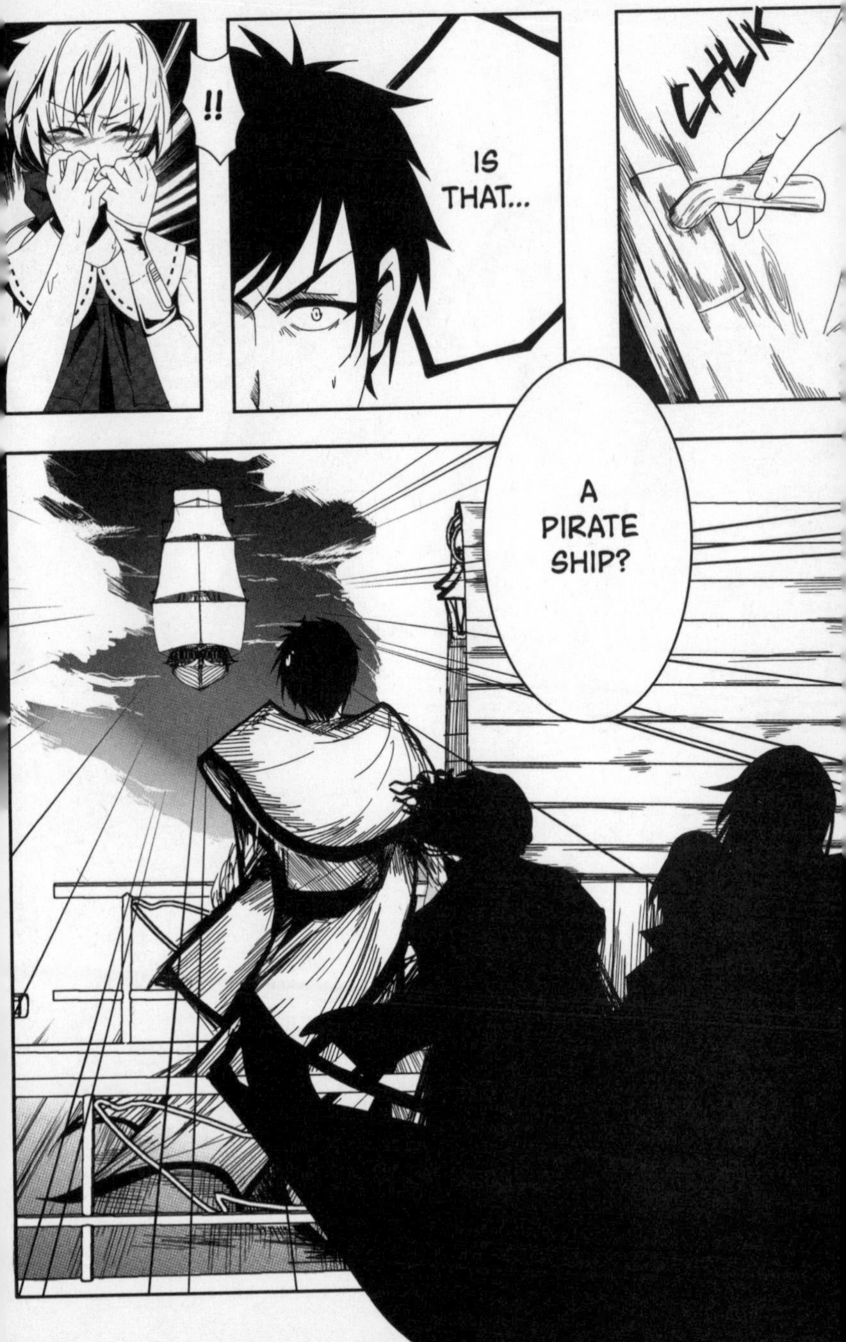
CHLIK
IS THAT...
!!
A PIRATE SHIP?

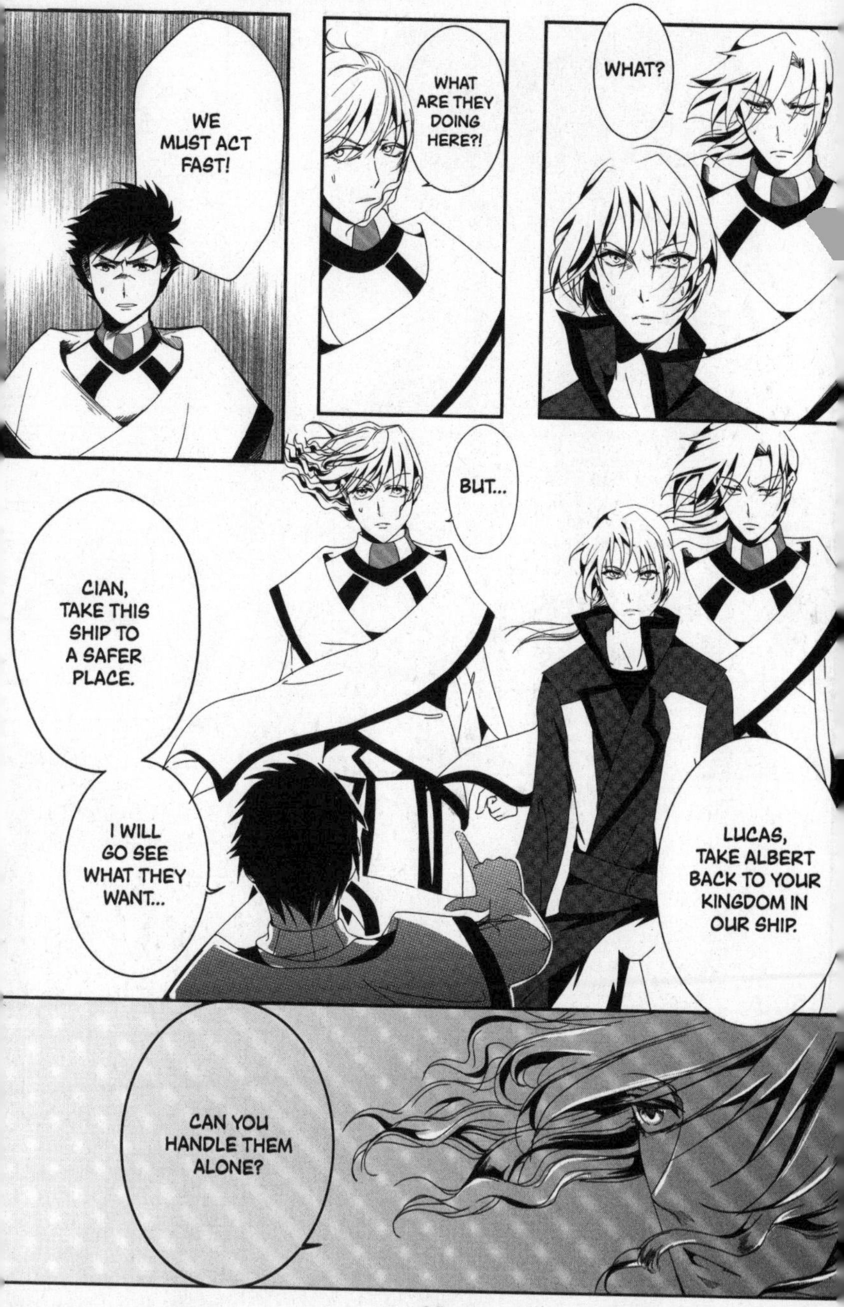
WHAT?
WHAT ARE THEY DOING HERE?!
WE MUST ACT FAST!
BUT...
CIAN, TAKE THIS SHIP TO A SAFER PLACE.
I WILL GO SEE WHAT THEY WANT...
LUCAS, TAKE ALBERT BACK TO YOUR KINGDOM IN OUR SHIP.
CAN YOU HANDLE THEM ALONE?

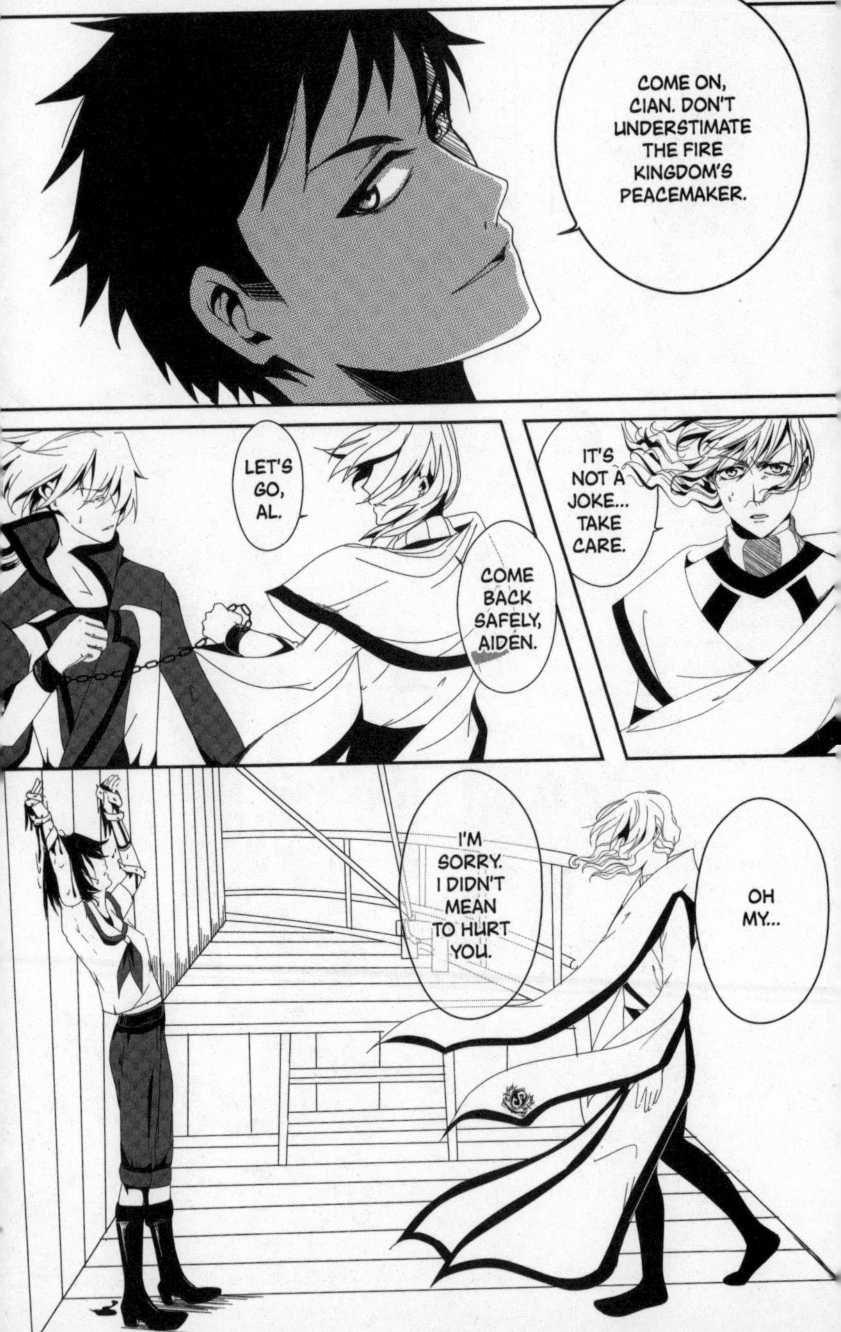

COME ON, CIAN. DON'T UNDERSTIMATE THE FIRE KINGDOM'S PEACEMAKER.
IT'S NOT A JOKE... TAKE CARE.
COME BACK SAFELY, AIDEN.
LET'S GO, AL.
OH MY...
I'M SORRY. I DIDN'T MEAN TO HURT YOU.

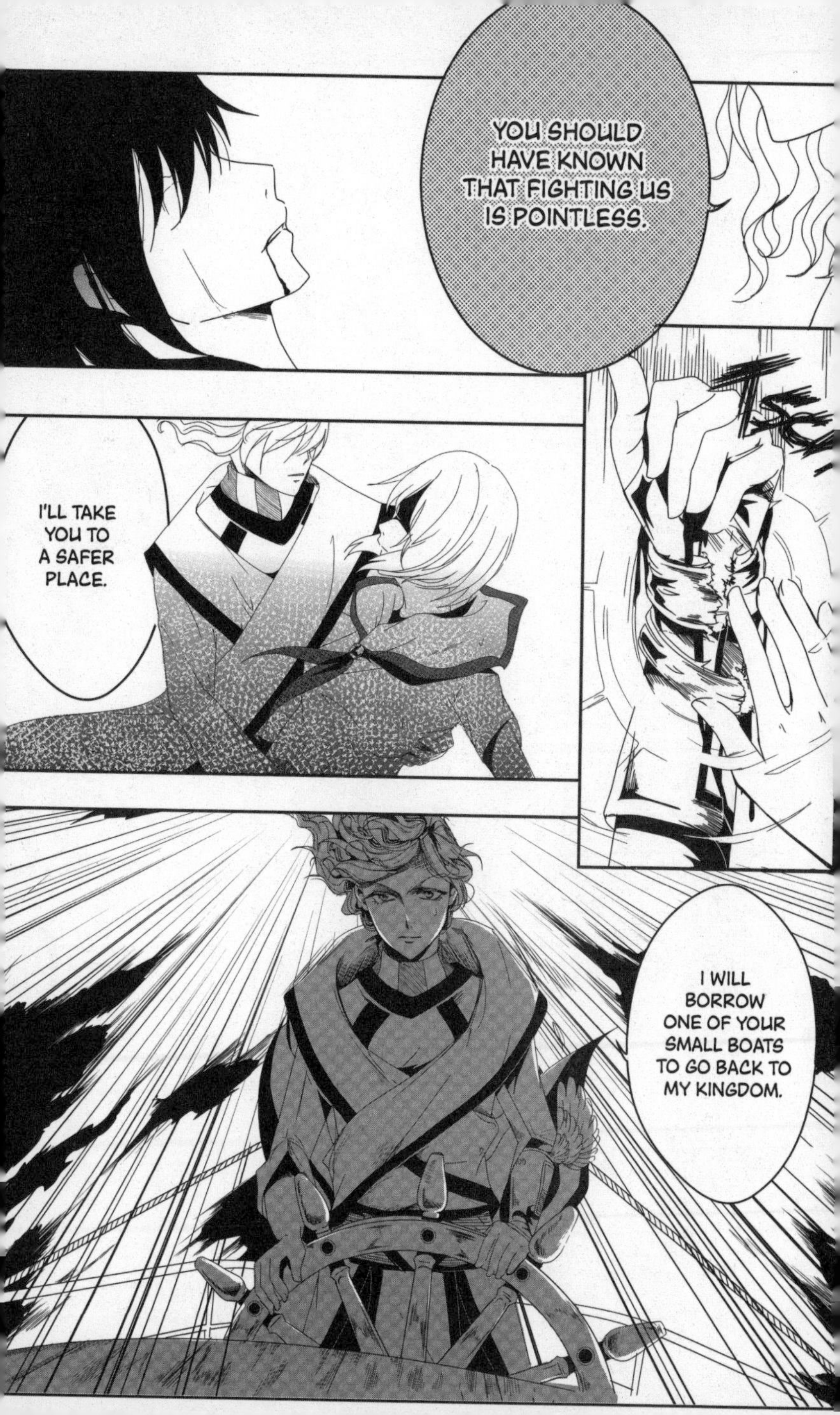
YOU SHOULD HAVE KNOWN THAT FIGHTING US IS POINTLESS.
I'LL TAKE YOU TO A SAFER PLACE.
I WILL BORROW ONE OF YOUR SMALL BOATS TO GO BACK TO MY KINGDOM.

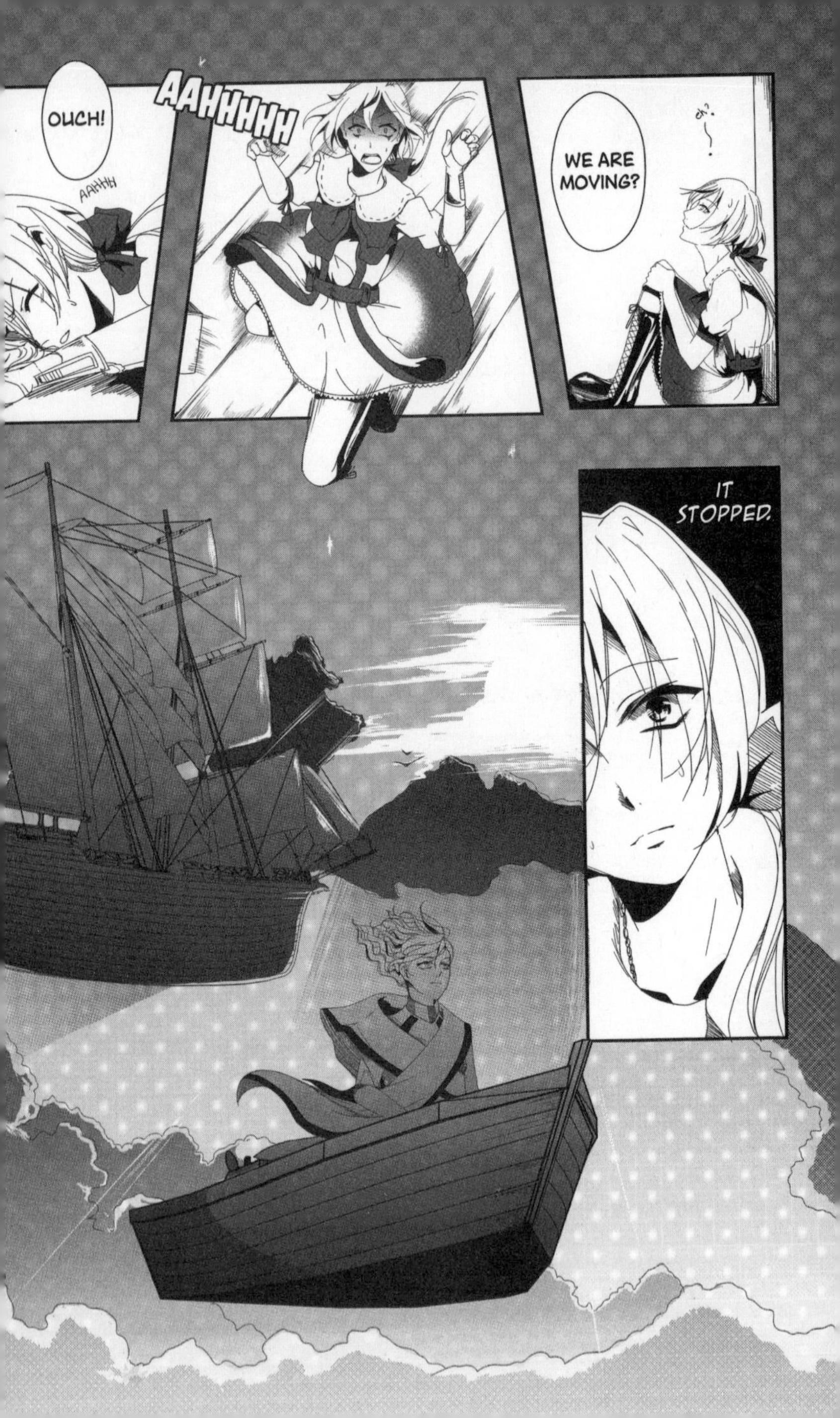
WE ARE MOVING?
AAHHHHH
OUCH!
IT STOPPED.

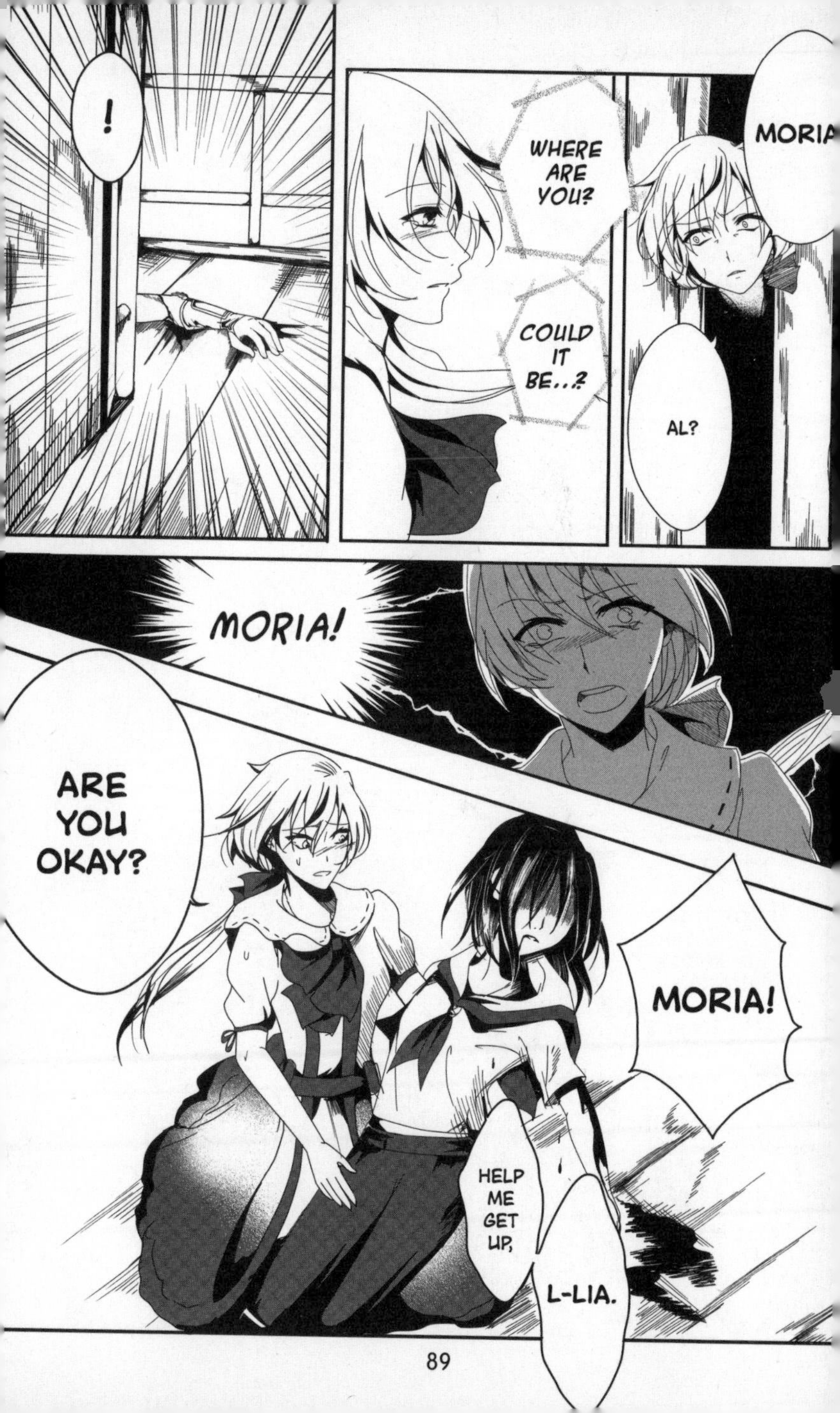
MORIA
AL?
WHERE ARE YOU?
COULD IT BE...?
!
MORIA!
MORIA!
HELP ME GET UP,
L-LIA.
ARE YOU OKAY?

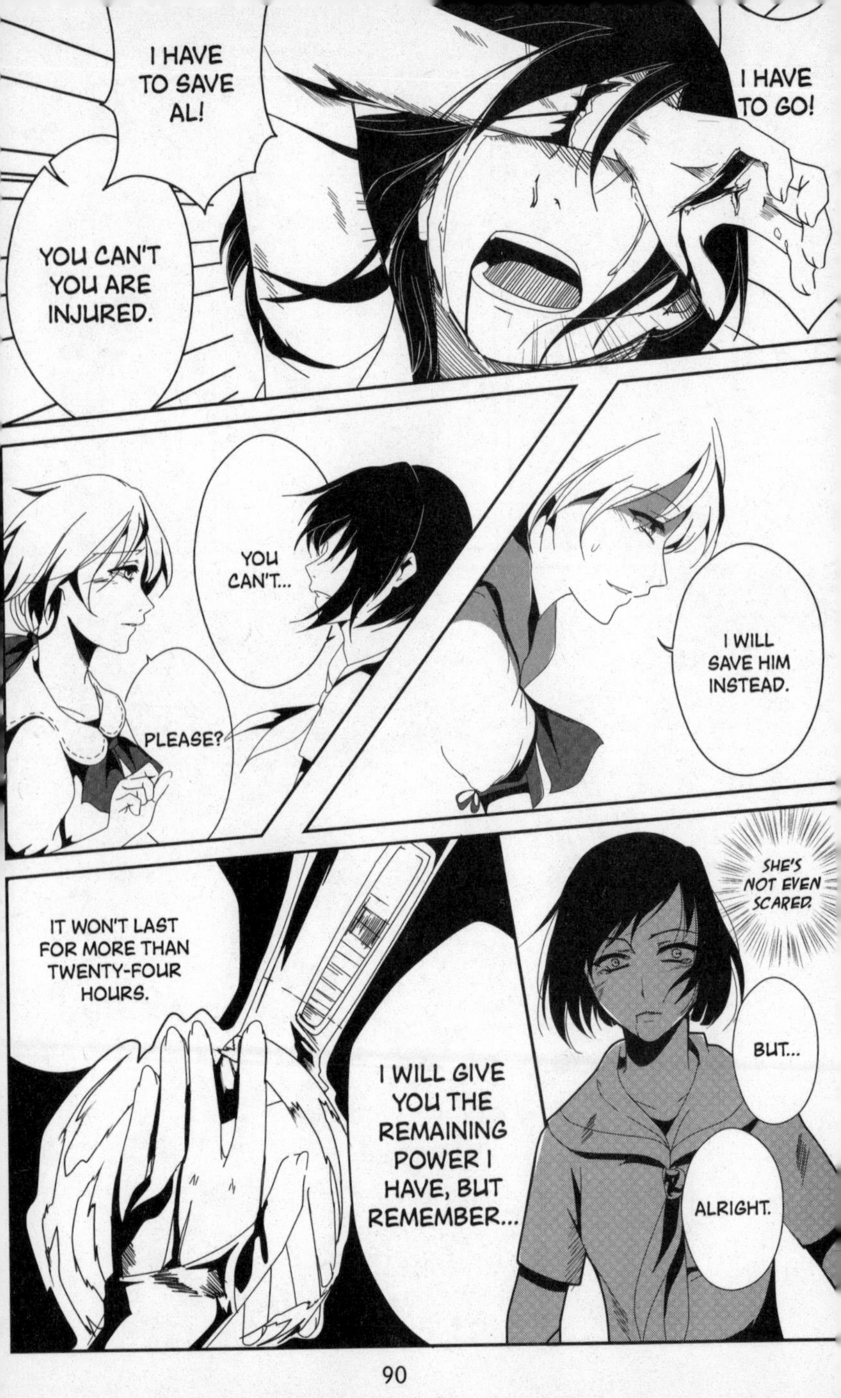
I HAVE TO GO!
I HAVE TO SAVE AL!
YOU CAN'T YOU ARE INJURED.
I WILL SAVE HIM INSTEAD.
YOU CAN'T...
PLEASE?
SHE'S NOT EVEN SCARED.
BUT...
ALRIGHT.
I WILL GIVE YOU THE REMAINING POWER I HAVE, BUT REMEMBER...
IT WON'T LAST FOR MORE THAN TWENTY-FOUR HOURS.

READ THIS WAY

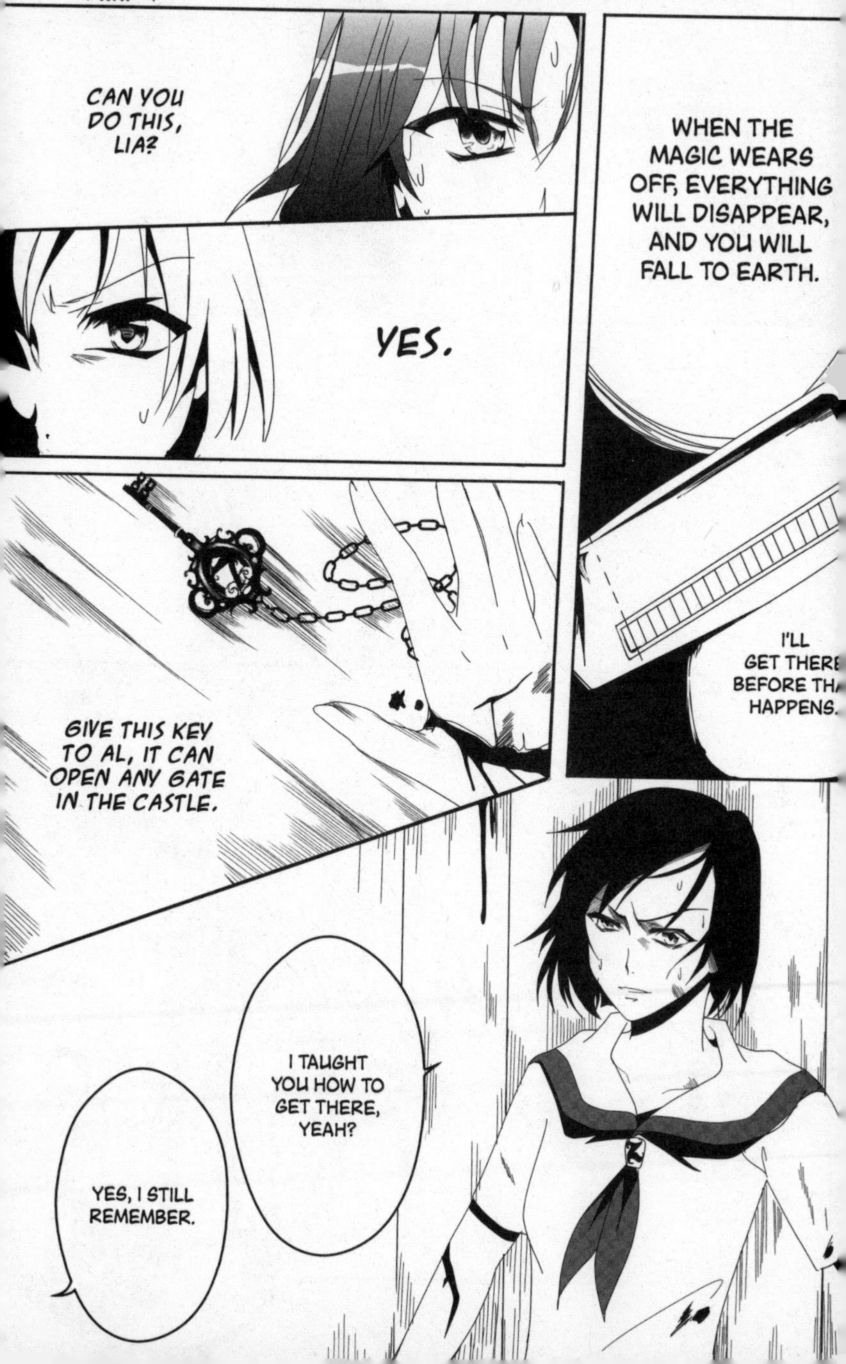
WHEN THE MAGIC WEARS OFF, EVERYTHING WILL DISAPPEAR, AND YOU WILL FALL TO EARTH.
I'LL GET THERE BEFORE THA HAPPENS.
CAN YOU DO THIS, LIA?
YES.
GIVE THIS KEY TO AL, IT CAN OPEN ANY GATE IN THE CASTLE.
I TAUGHT YOU HOW TO GET THERE, YEAH?
YES, I STILL REMEMBER.

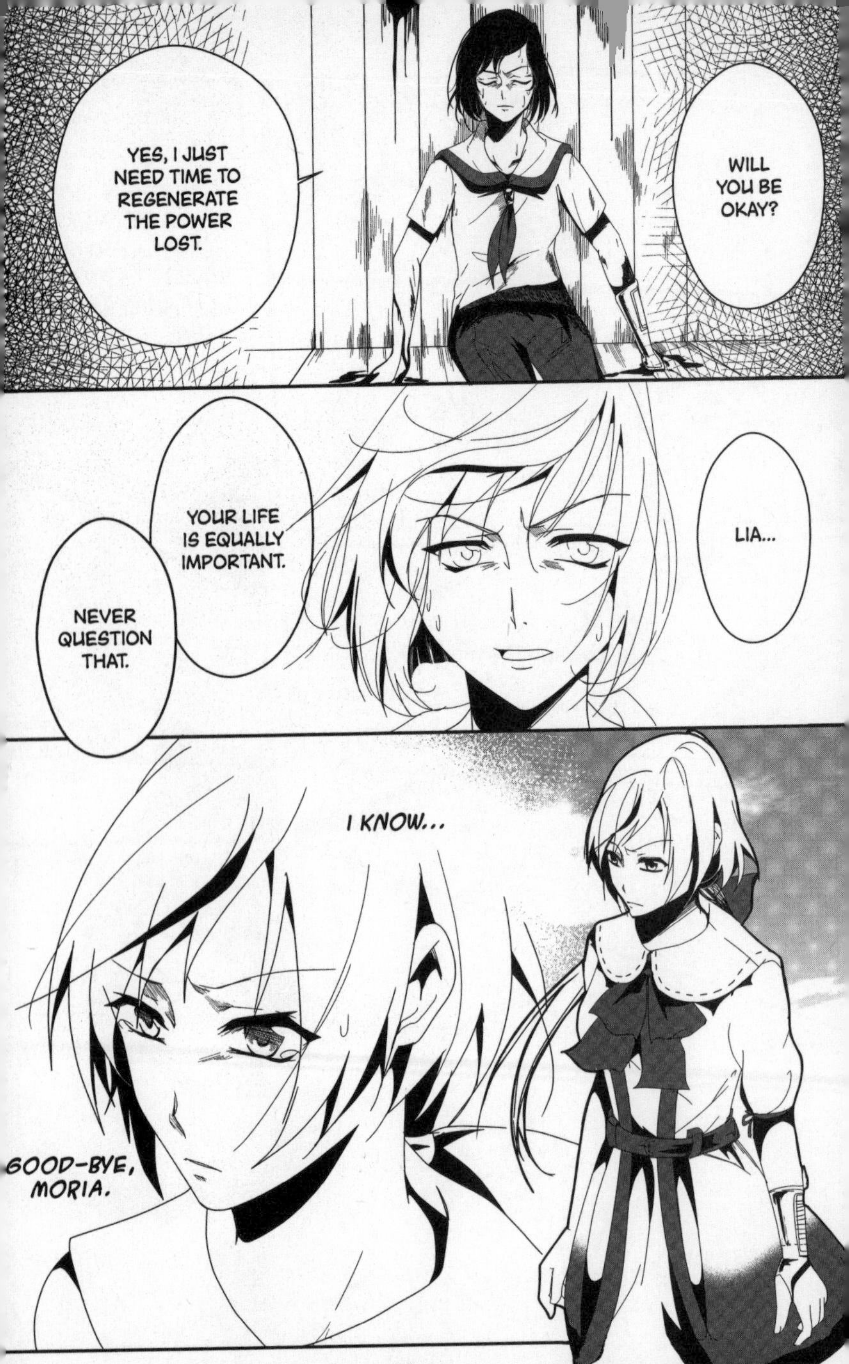
WILL YOU BE OKAY?
YES, I JUST NEED TIME TO REGENERATE THE POWER LOST.
LIA...
YOUR LIFE IS EQUALLY IMPORTANT.
NEVER QUESTION THAT.
I KNOW...
GOOD-BYE, MORIA.

CHAPTER 4

A JOURNEY TO FIND THE TRUTH

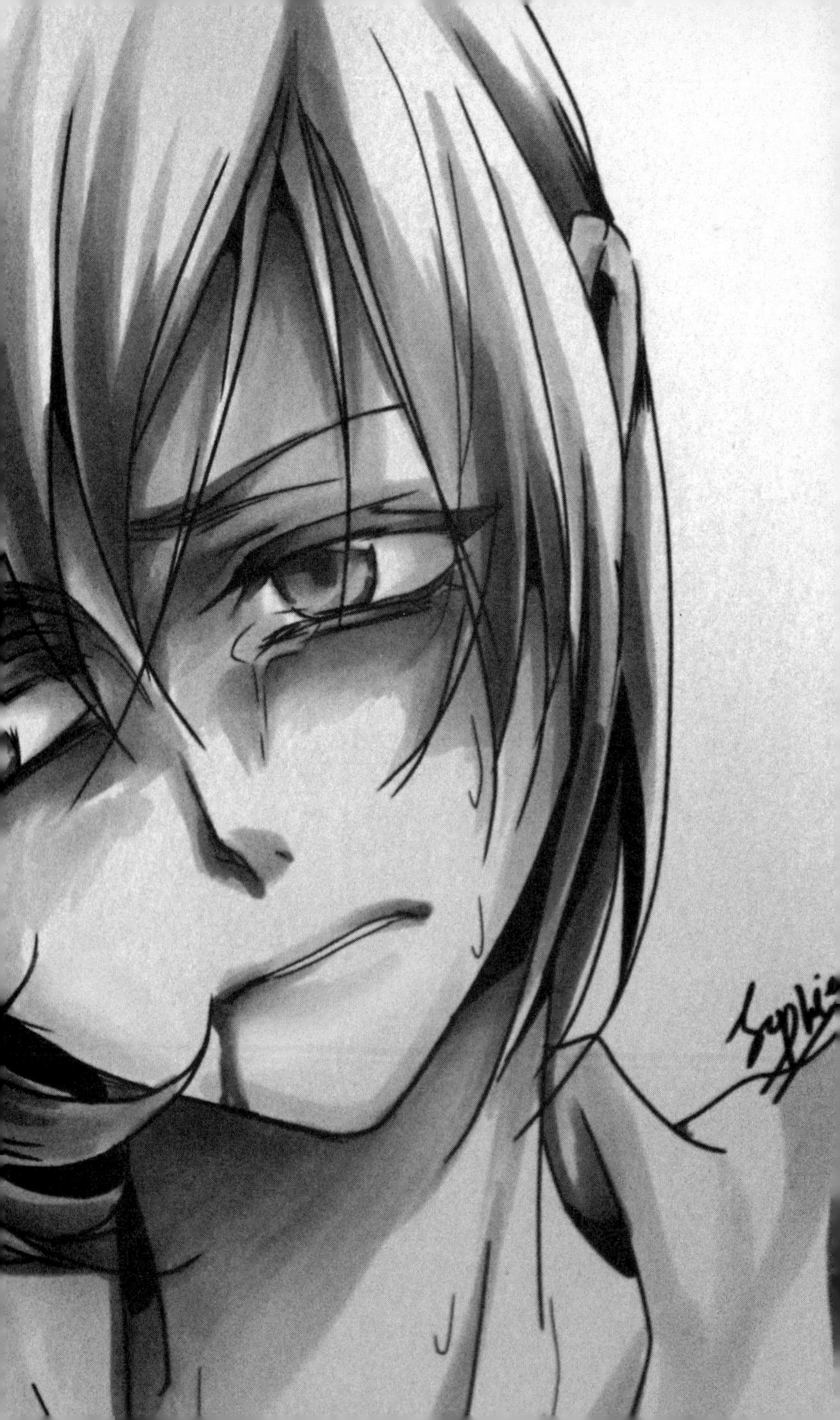

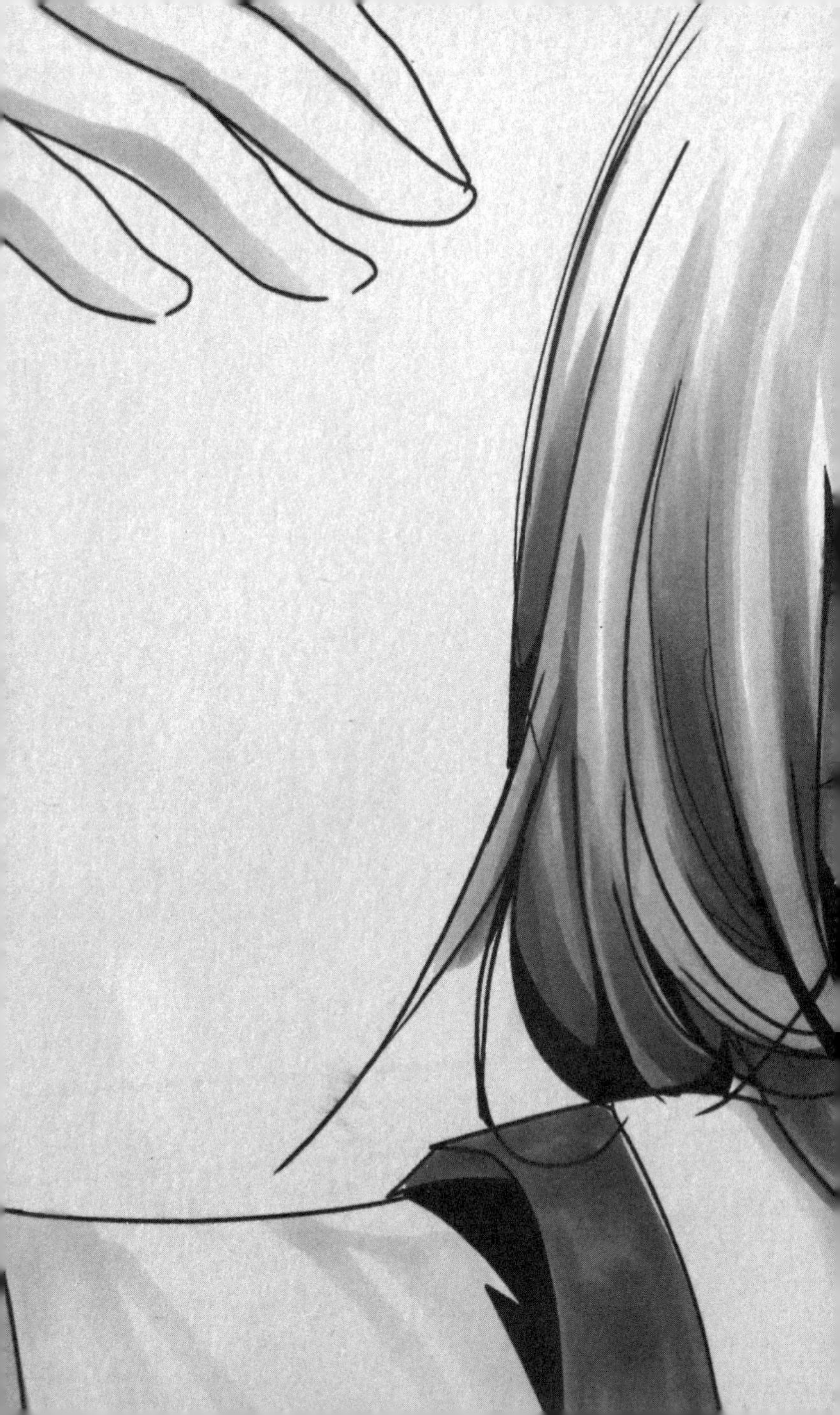

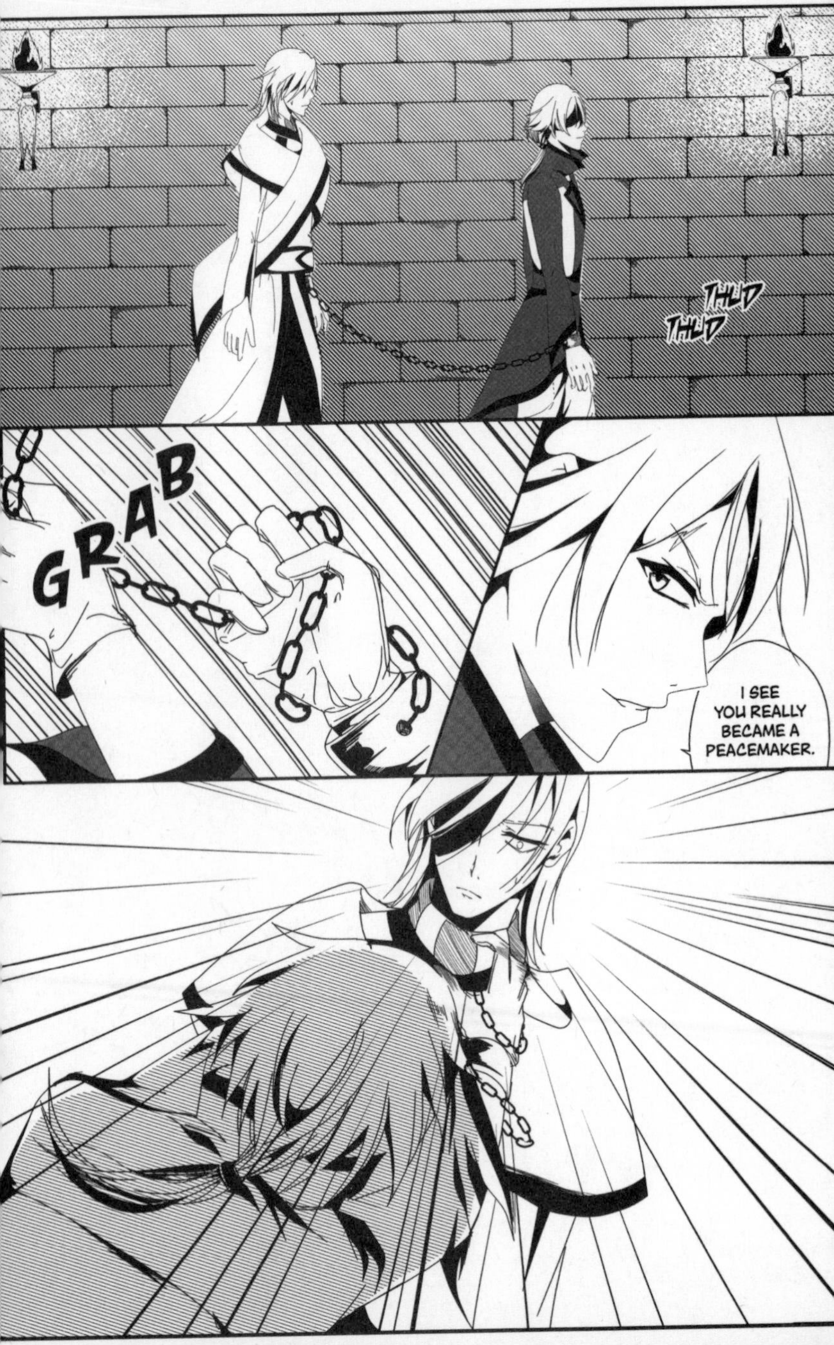
THUD
THUD
I SEE YOU REALLY BECAME A PEACEMAKER.
GRAB

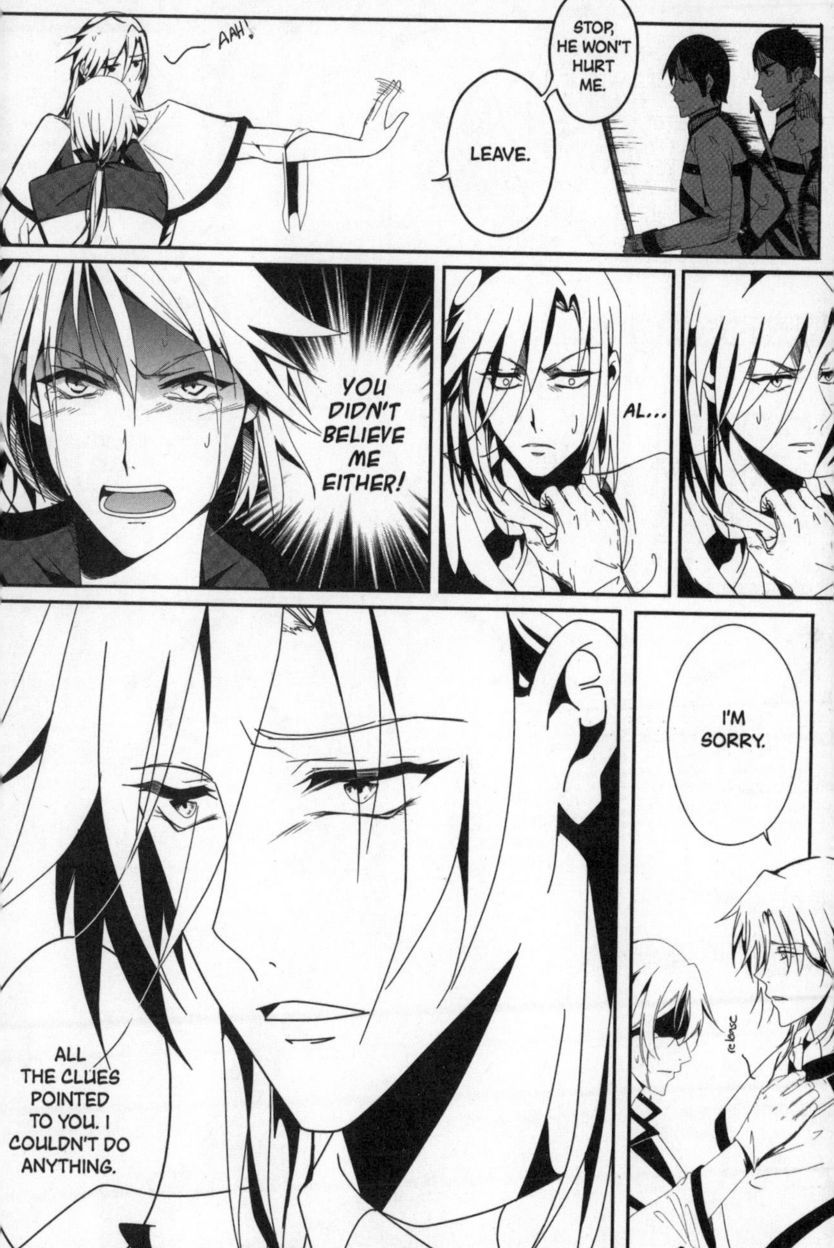
STOP, HE WON'T HURT ME.
LEAVE.
AAH!
AL...
YOU DIDN'T BELIEVE ME EITHER!
I'M SORRY.
release
ALL THE CLUES POINTED TO YOU. I COULDN'T DO ANYTHING.

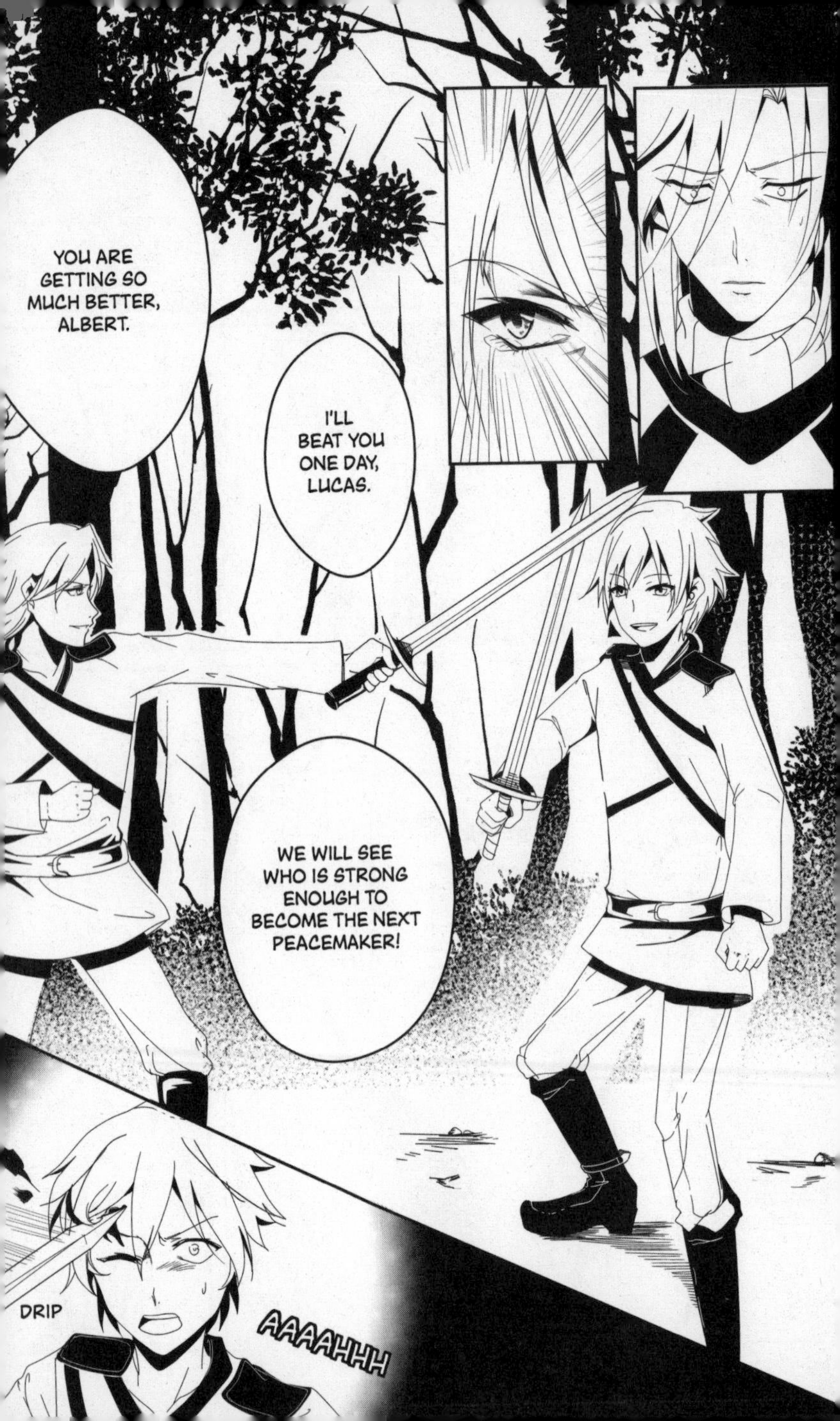
YOU ARE GETTING SO MUCH BETTER, ALBERT.
I'LL BEAT YOU ONE DAY, LUCAS.
WE WILL SEE WHO IS STRONG ENOUGH TO BECOME THE NEXT PEACEMAKER!
AAAAHHH
DRIP

READ THIS WAY

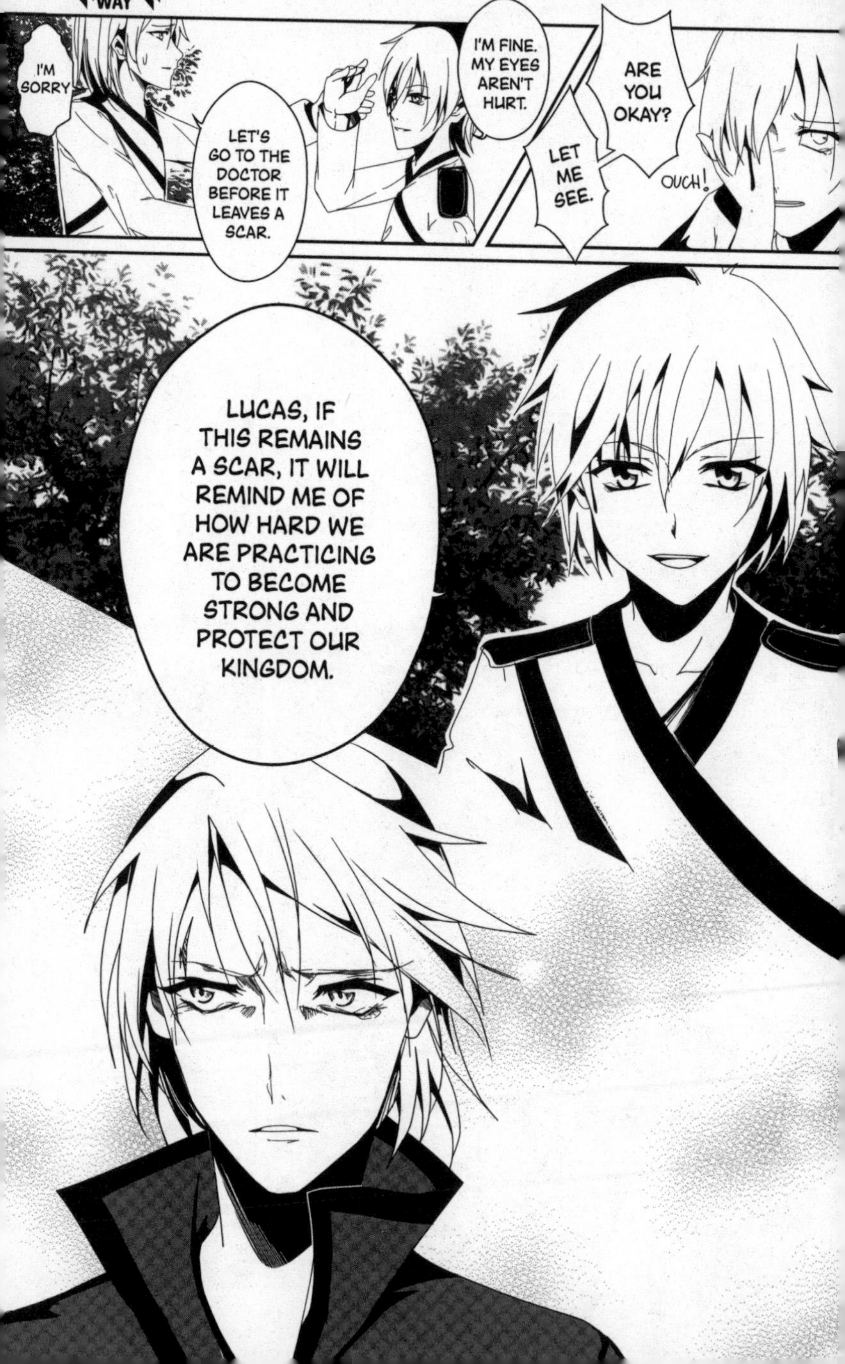
ARE YOU OKAY?
OUCH!
LET ME SEE.
I'M FINE. MY EYES AREN'T HURT.
LET'S GO TO THE DOCTOR BEFORE IT LEAVES A SCAR.
I'M SORRY
LUCAS, IF THIS REMAINS A SCAR, IT WILL REMIND ME OF HOW HARD WE ARE PRACTICING TO BECOME STRONG AND PROTECT OUR KINGDOM.

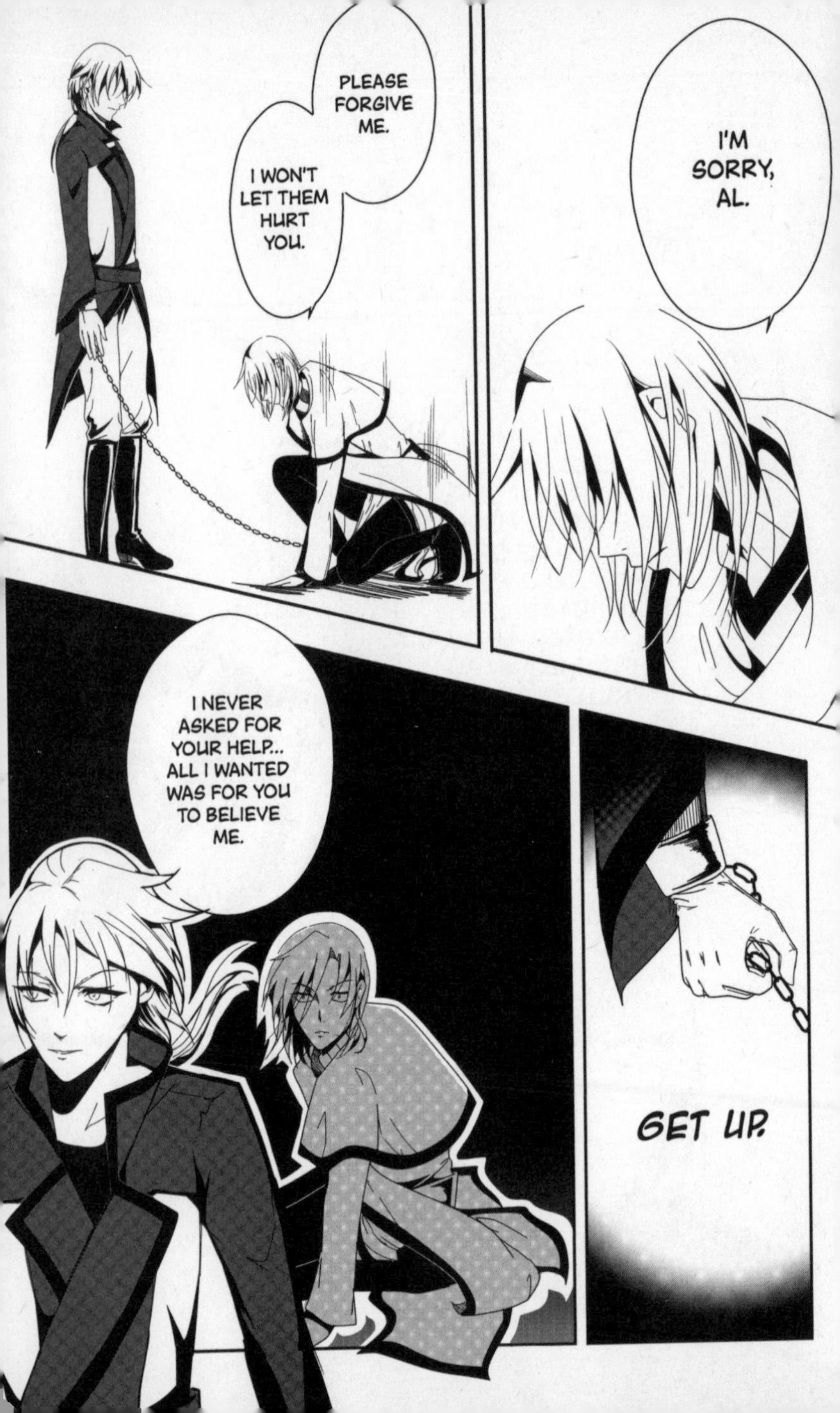
I'M SORRY, AL.
PLEASE FORGIVE ME.
I WON'T LET THEM HURT YOU.
GET UP.
I NEVER ASKED FOR YOUR HELP... ALL I WANTED WAS FOR YOU TO BELIEVE ME.

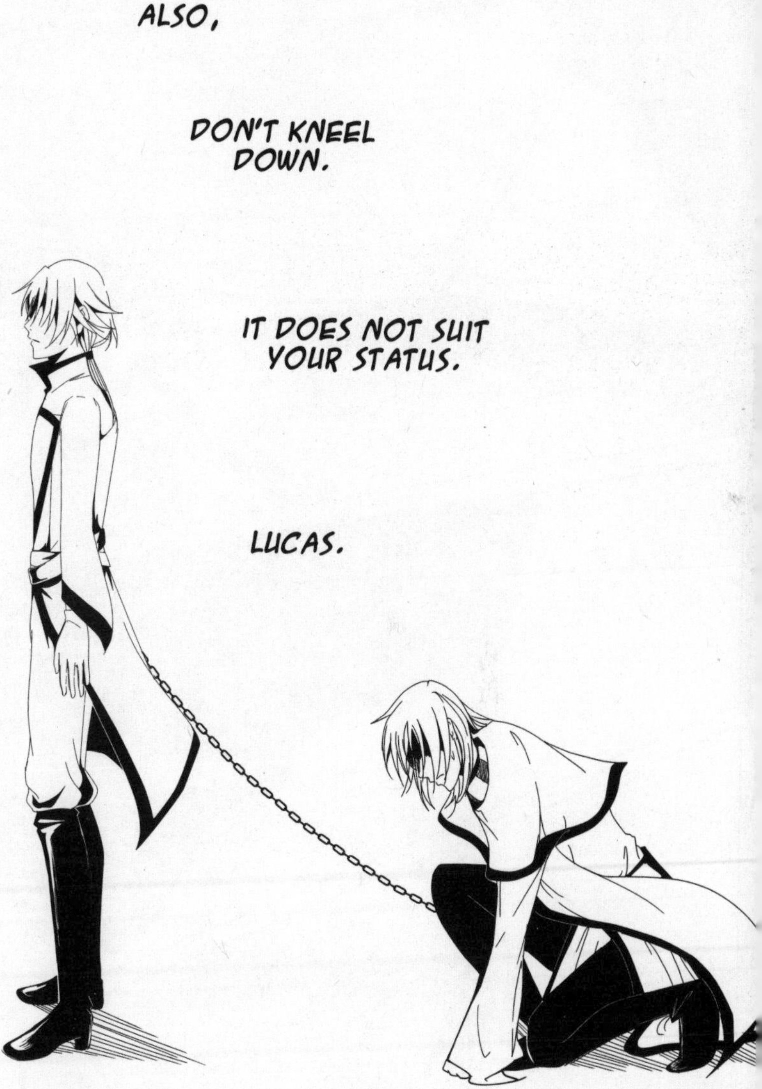
ALSO,
DON'T KNEEL DOWN.
IT DOES NOT SUIT YOUR STATUS.
LUCAS.

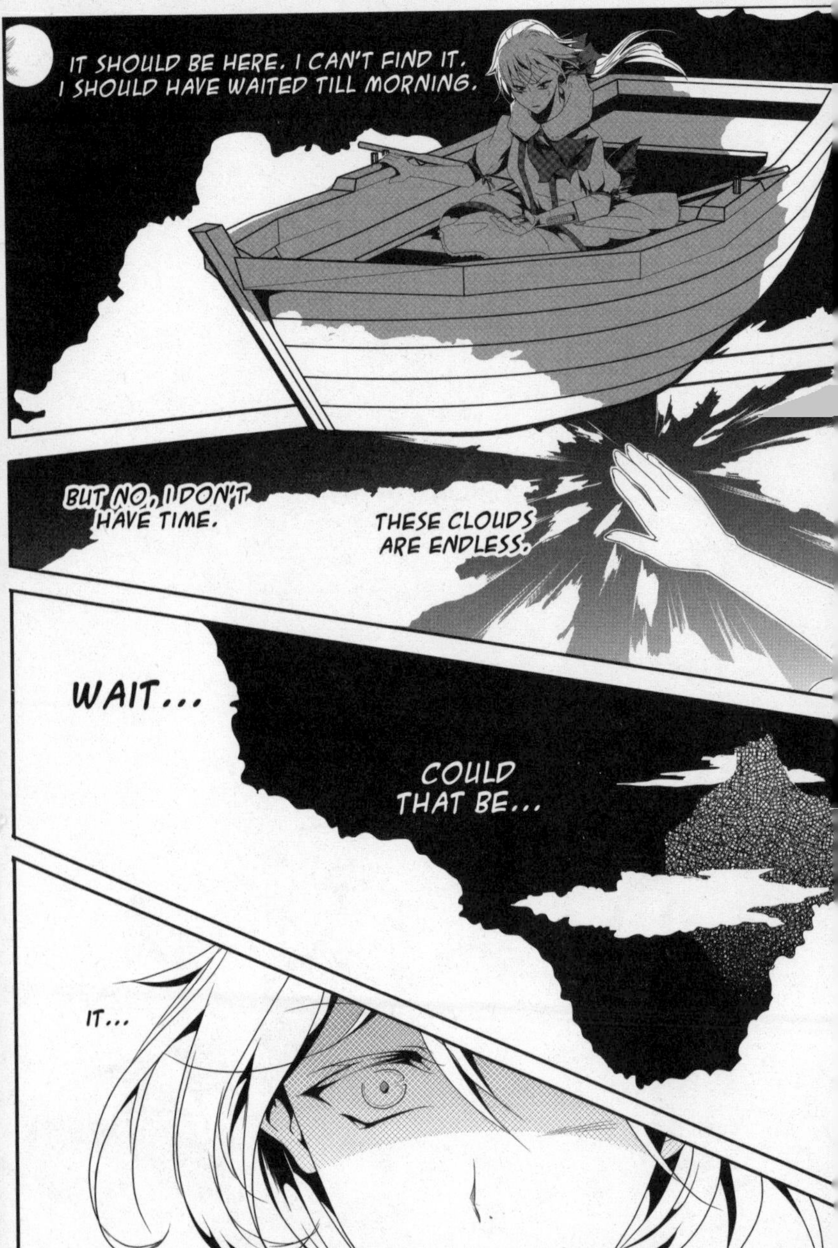
IT SHOULD BE HERE. I CAN'T FIND IT. I SHOULD HAVE WAITED TILL MORNING.
THESE CLOUDS ARE ENDLESS.
BUT NO, I DON'T HAVE TIME.
COULD THAT BE...
WAIT...
IT...

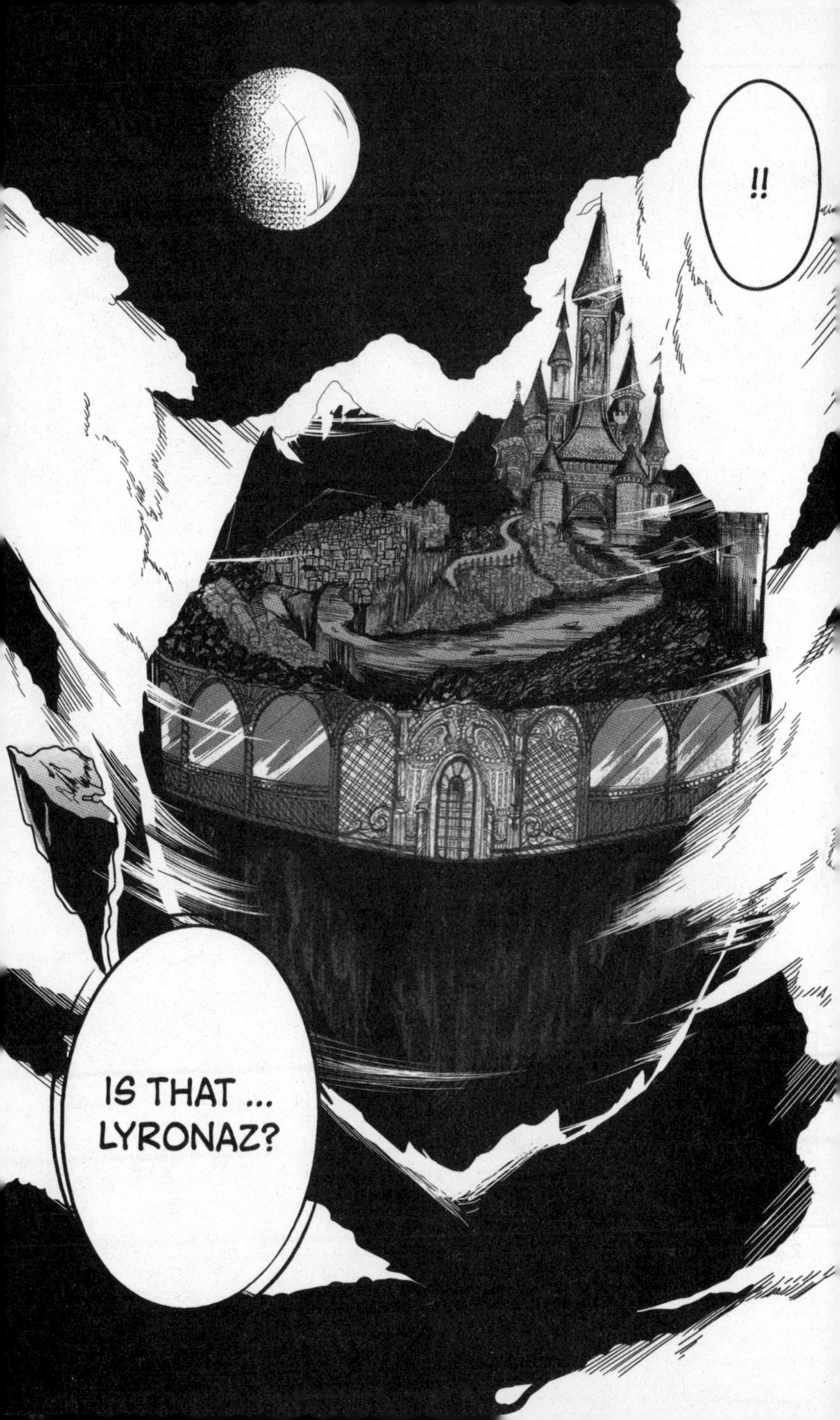
!!
IS THAT ... LYRONAZ?

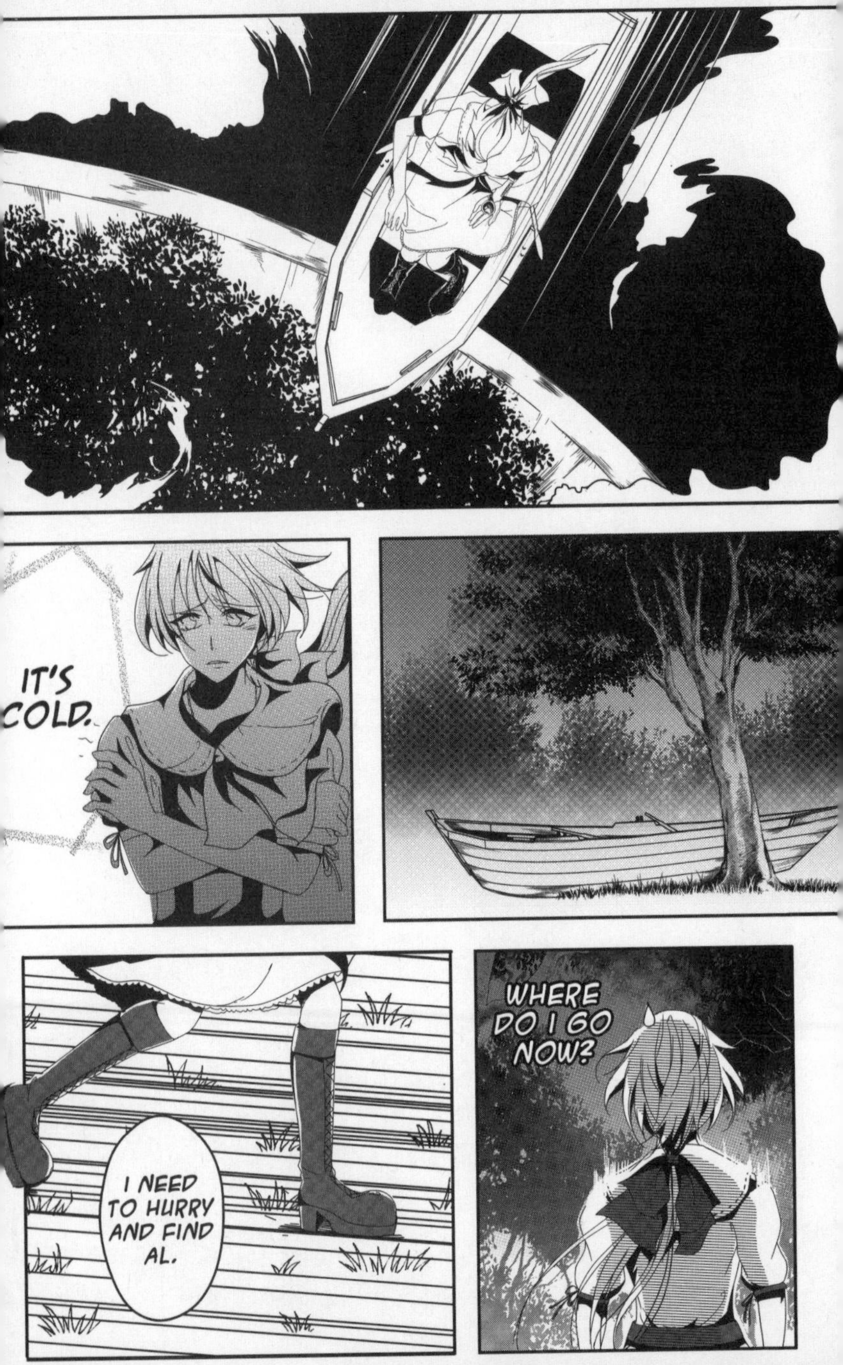
IT'S COLD.
WHERE DO I GO NOW?
I NEED TO HURRY AND FIND AL.

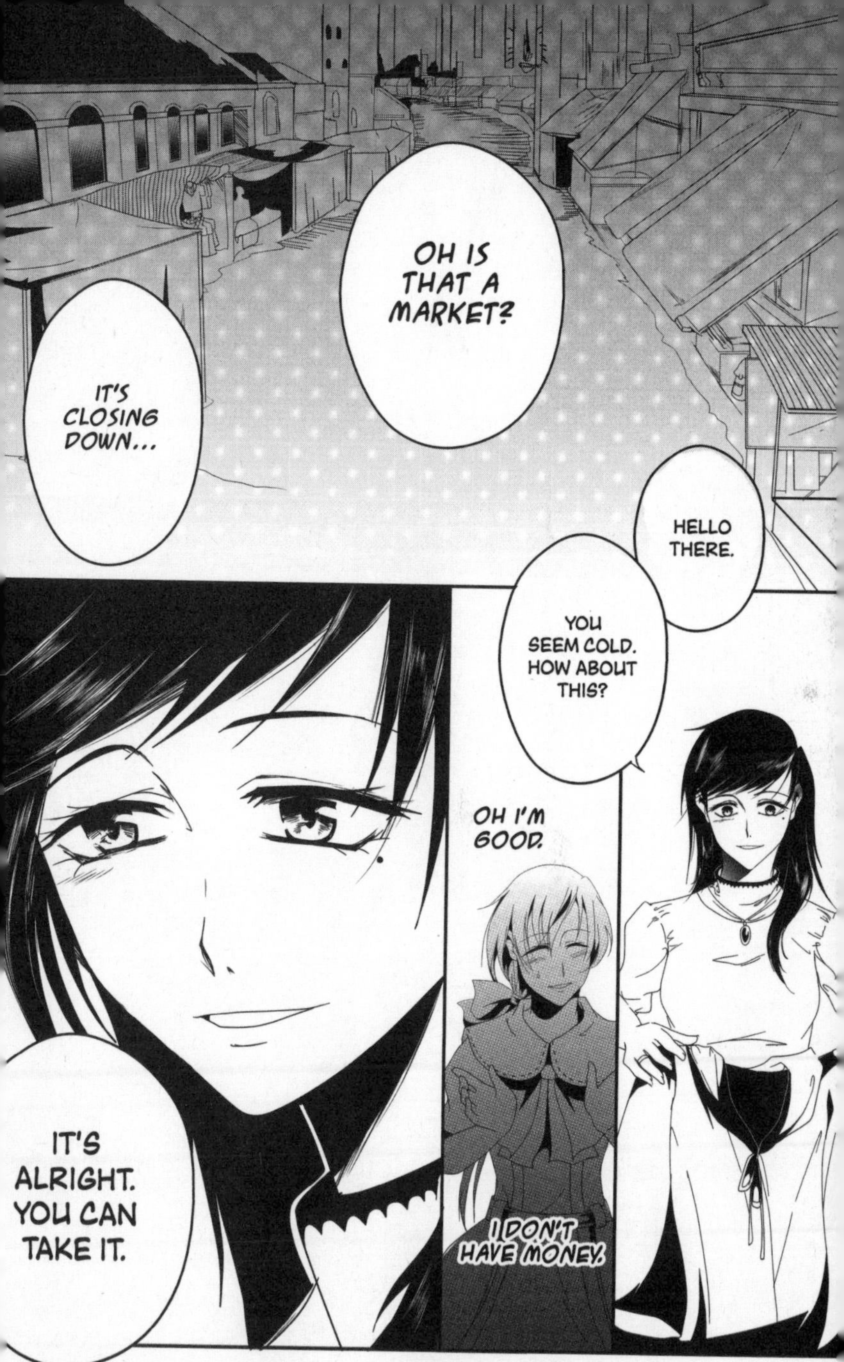
OH IS THAT A MARKET?
IT'S CLOSING DOWN...
HELLO THERE.
YOU SEEM COLD. HOW ABOUT THIS?
OH I'M GOOD.
I DON'T HAVE MONEY.
IT'S ALRIGHT. YOU CAN TAKE IT.

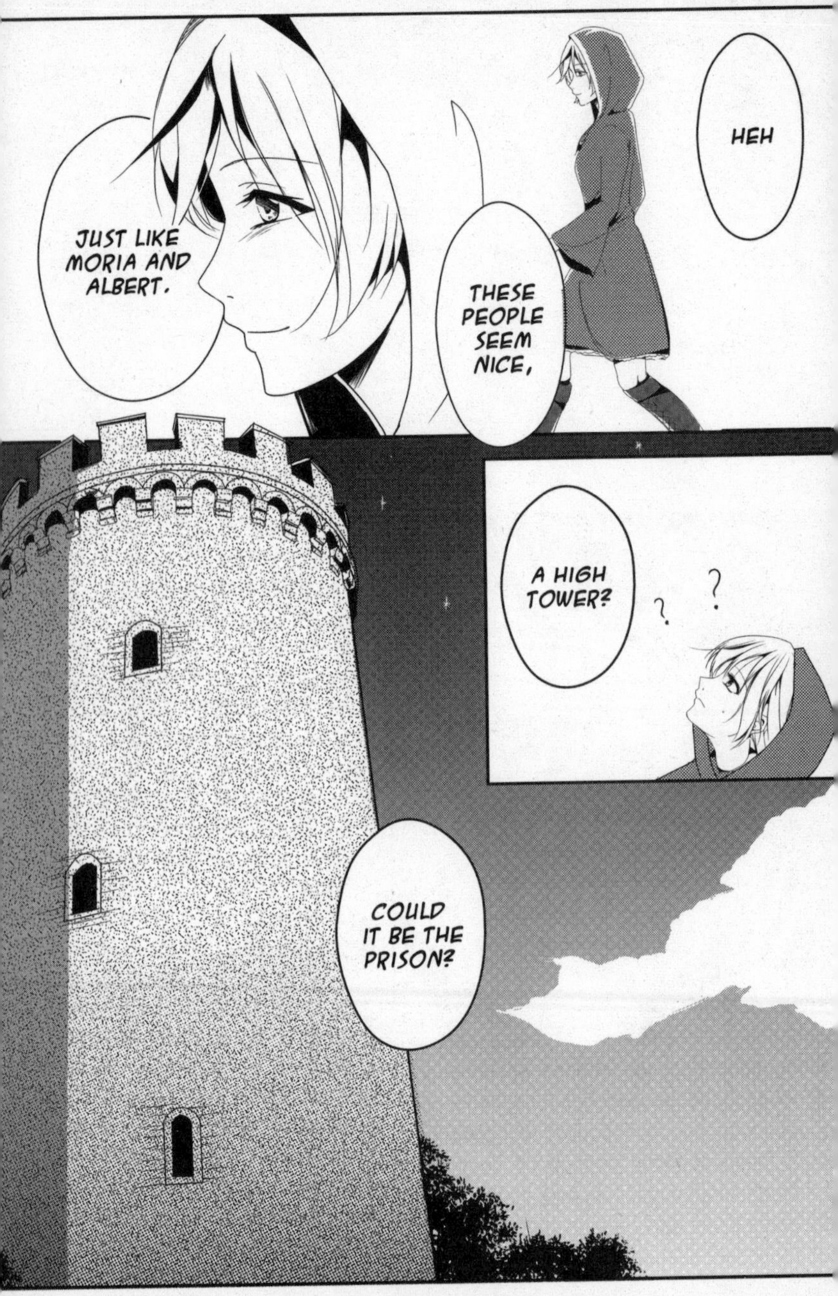
HEH
THESE PEOPLE SEEM NICE,
JUST LIKE MORIA AND ALBERT.
A HIGH TOWER?
? ?
COULD IT BE THE PRISON?

READ THIS WAY

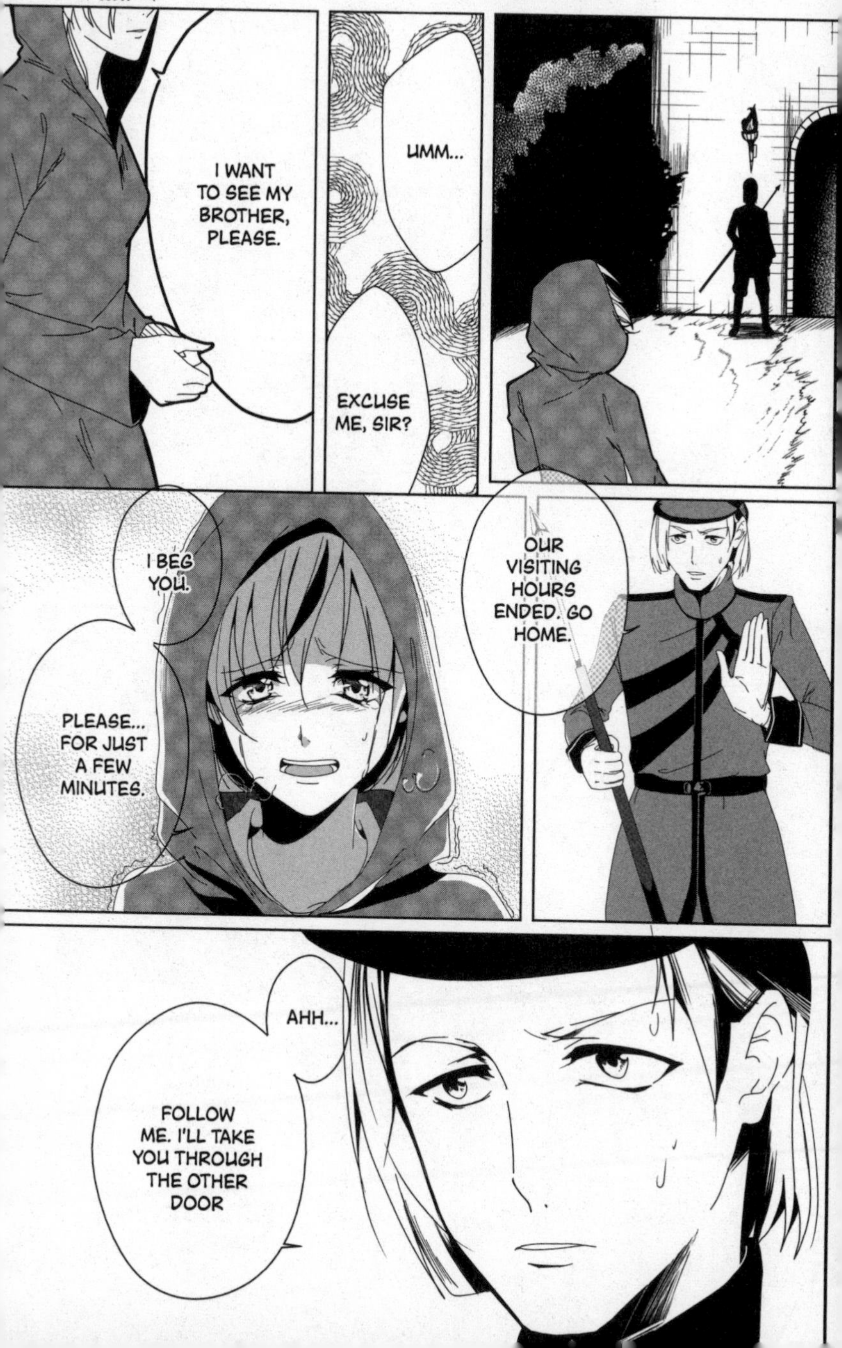
UMM...
EXCUSE ME, SIR?
I WANT TO SEE MY BROTHER, PLEASE.
OUR VISITING HOURS ENDED. GO HOME.
I BEG YOU.
PLEASE... FOR JUST A FEW MINUTES.
AHH...
FOLLOW ME. I'LL TAKE YOU THROUGH THE OTHER DOOR

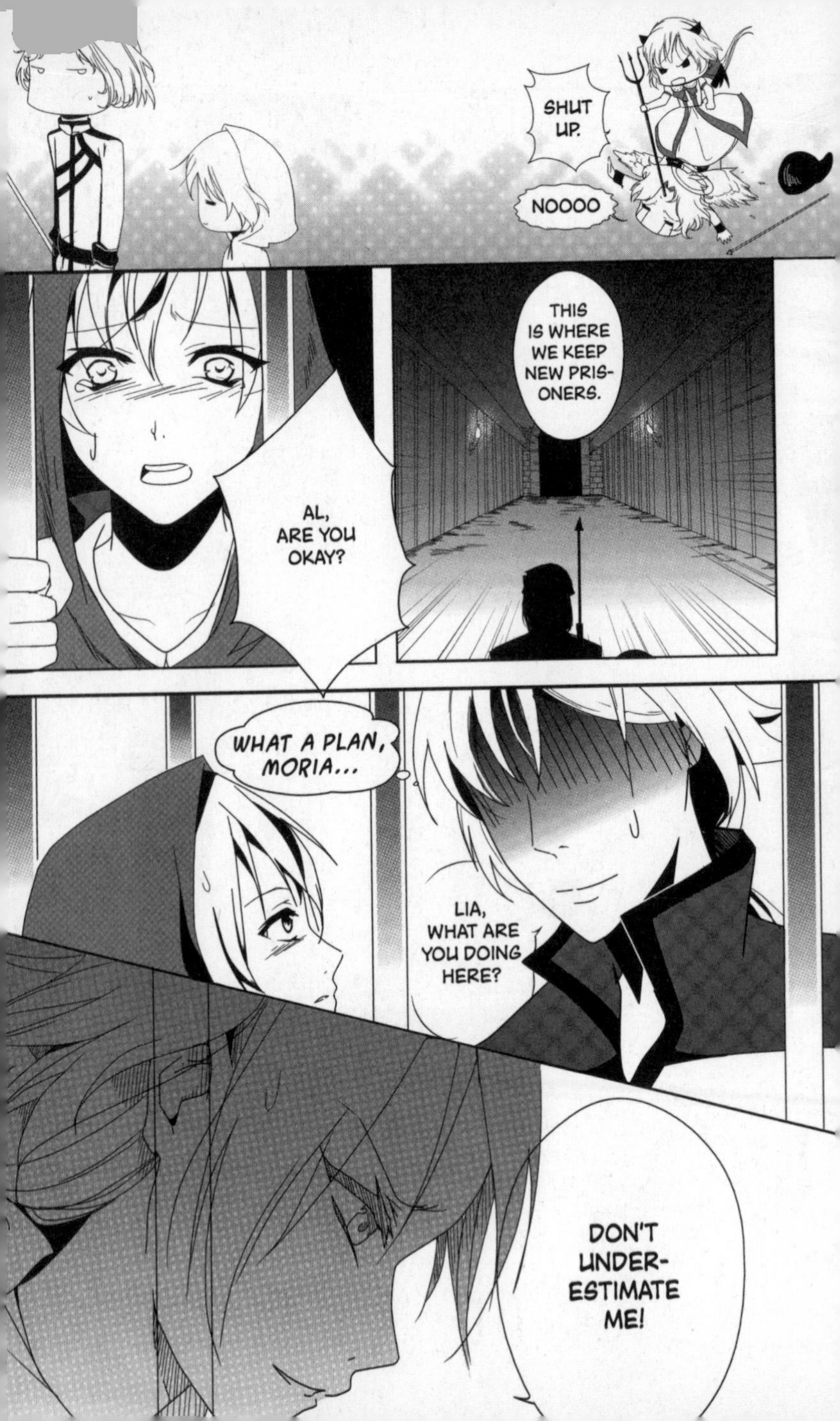
SHUT UP.
NOOOO
THIS IS WHERE WE KEEP NEW PRISONERS.
AL, ARE YOU OKAY?
WHAT A PLAN, MORIA...
LIA, WHAT ARE YOU DOING HERE?
DON'T UNDER-ESTIMATE ME!

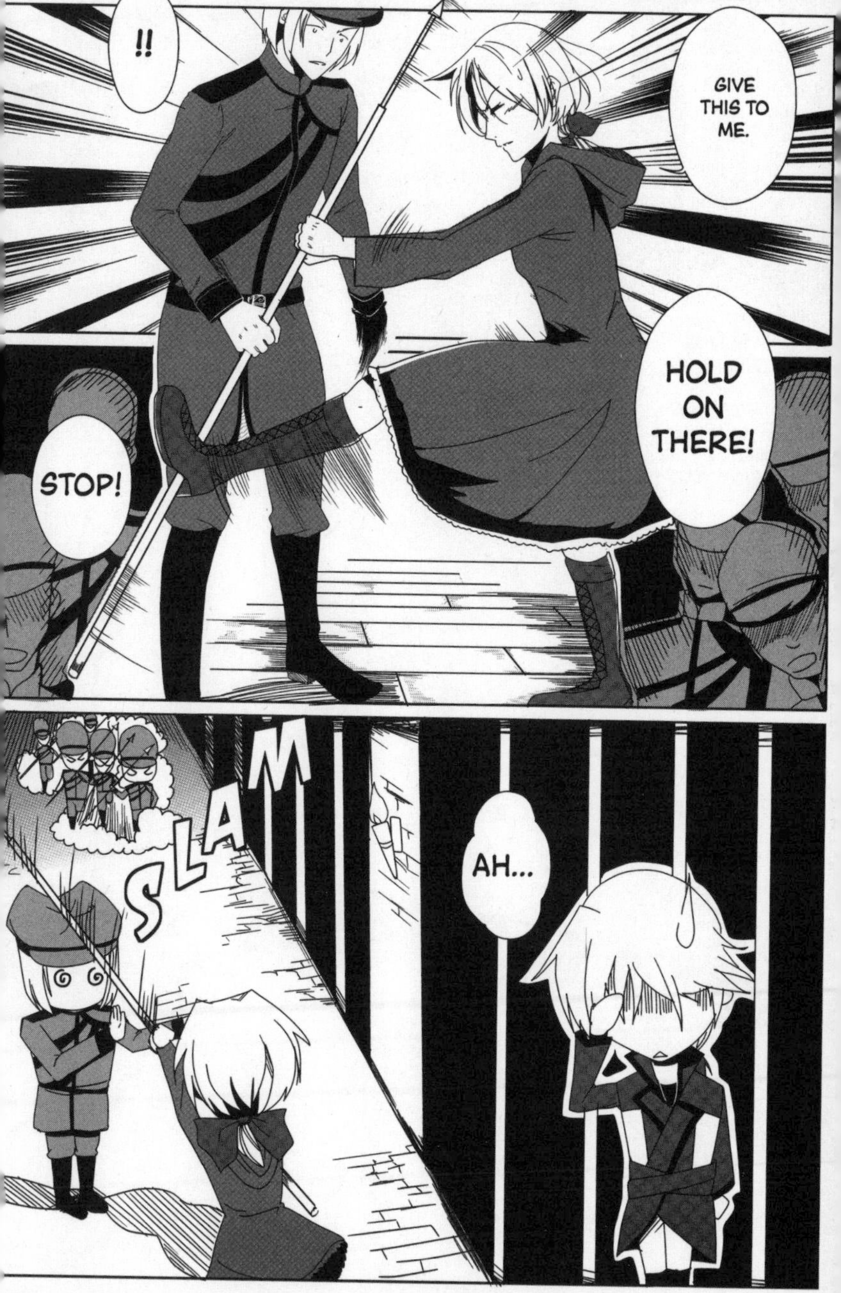
GIVE THIS TO ME.
!!
HOLD ON THERE!
STOP!
AH...
SLAM

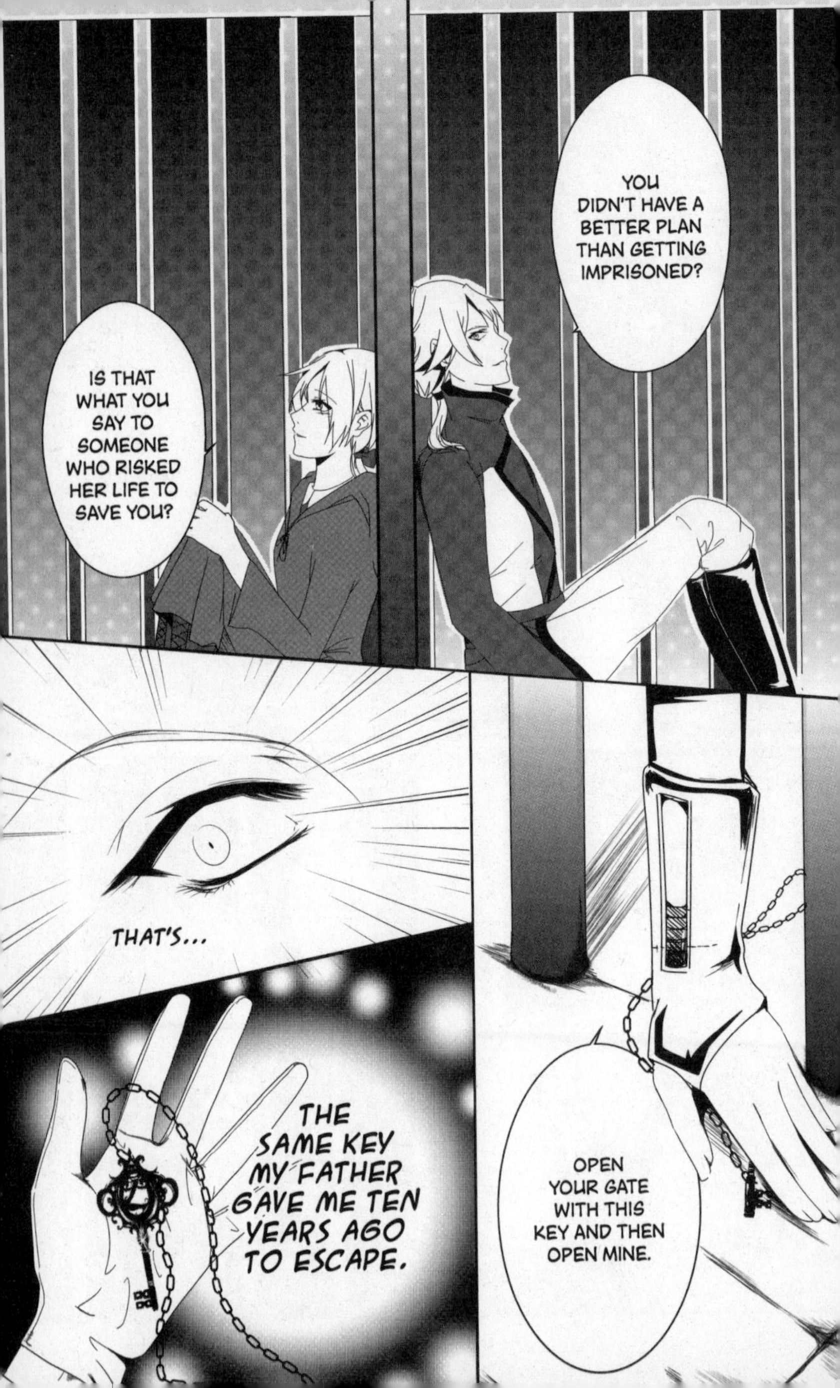
YOU DIDN'T HAVE A BETTER PLAN THAN GETTING IMPRISONED?
IS THAT WHAT YOU SAY TO SOMEONE WHO RISKED HER LIFE TO SAVE YOU?
OPEN YOUR GATE WITH THIS KEY AND THEN OPEN MINE.
THAT'S...
THE SAME KEY MY FATHER GAVE ME TEN YEARS AGO TO ESCAPE.

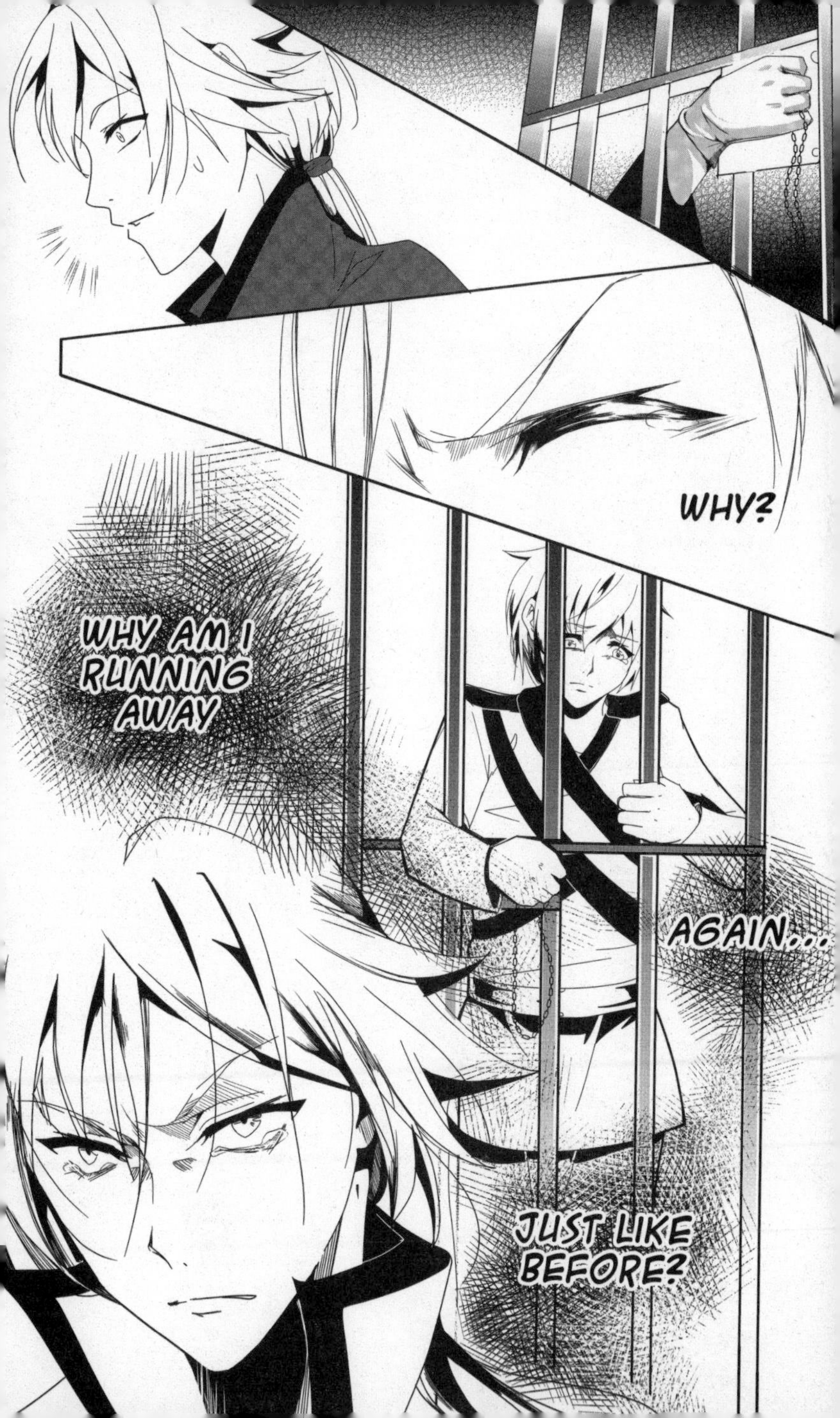
WHY?
WHY AM I RUNNING AWAY
AGAIN...
JUST LIKE BEFORE?

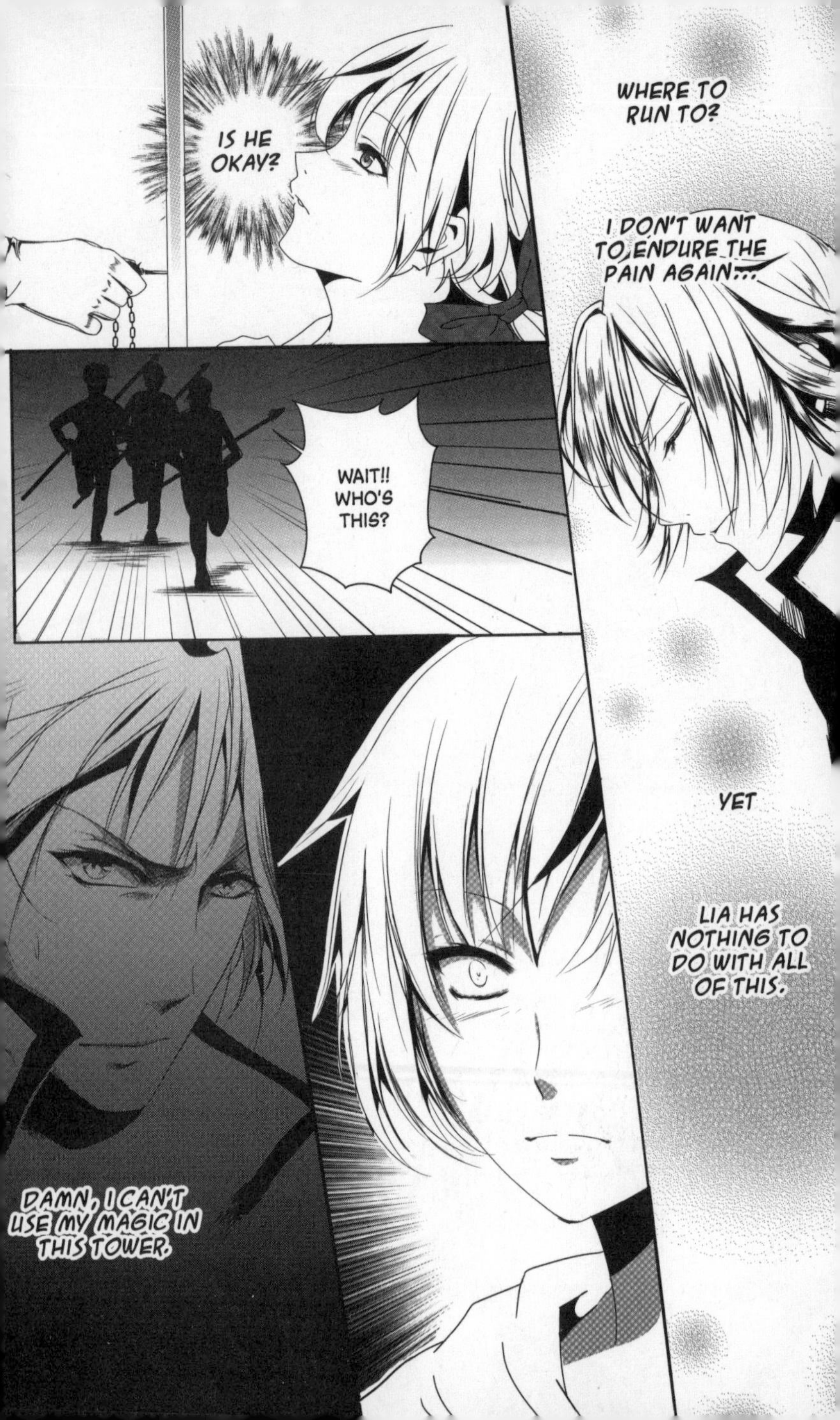
WHERE TO RUN TO?
I DON'T WANT TO ENDURE THE PAIN AGAIN...
YET
LIA HAS NOTHING TO DO WITH ALL OF THIS.
IS HE OKAY?
WAIT!! WHO'S THIS?
DAMN, I CAN'T USE MY MAGIC IN THIS TOWER.

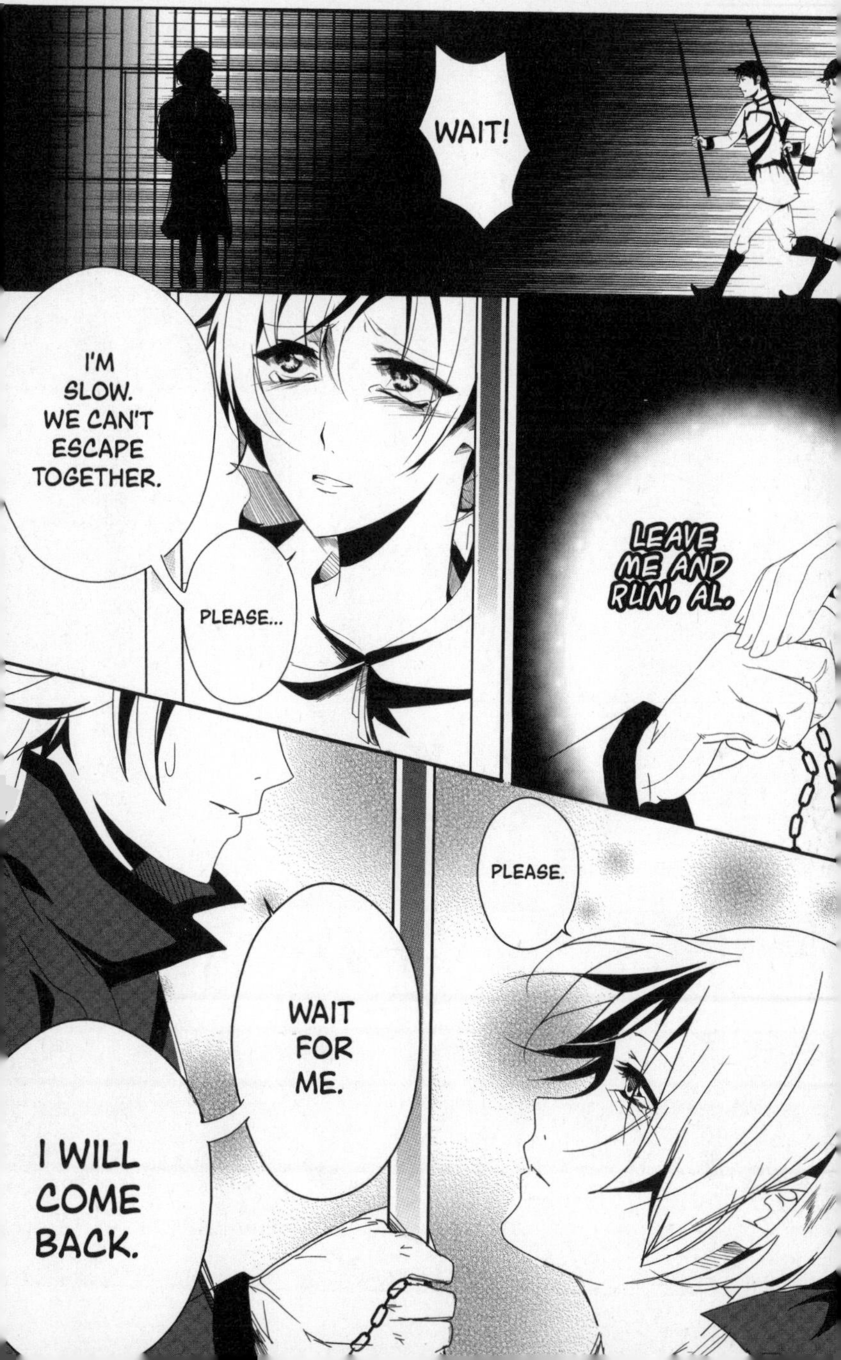
WAIT!
LEAVE ME AND RUN, AL.
I'M SLOW. WE CAN'T ESCAPE TOGETHER.
PLEASE...
PLEASE.
WAIT FOR ME.
I WILL COME BACK.

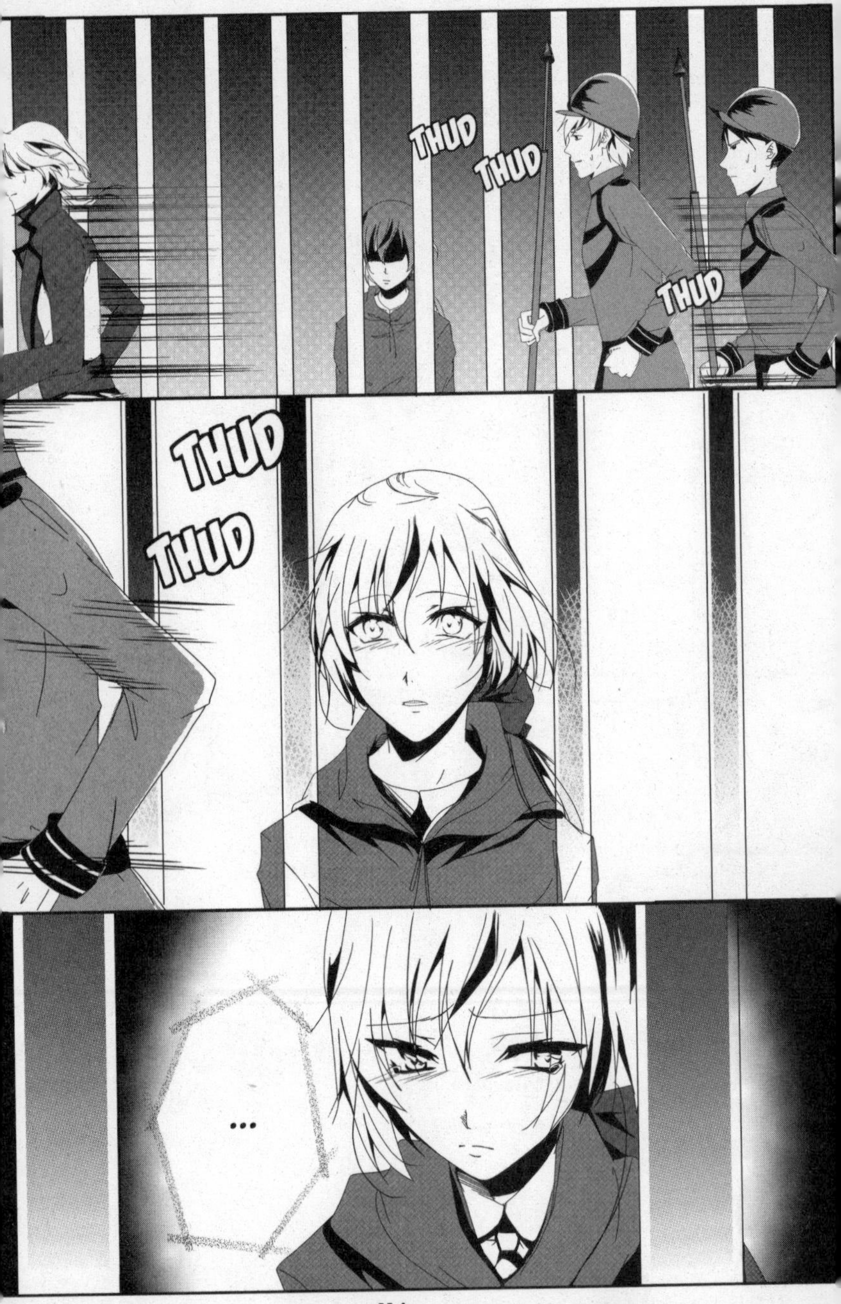
THUD
THUD
THUD
THUD
THUD
...

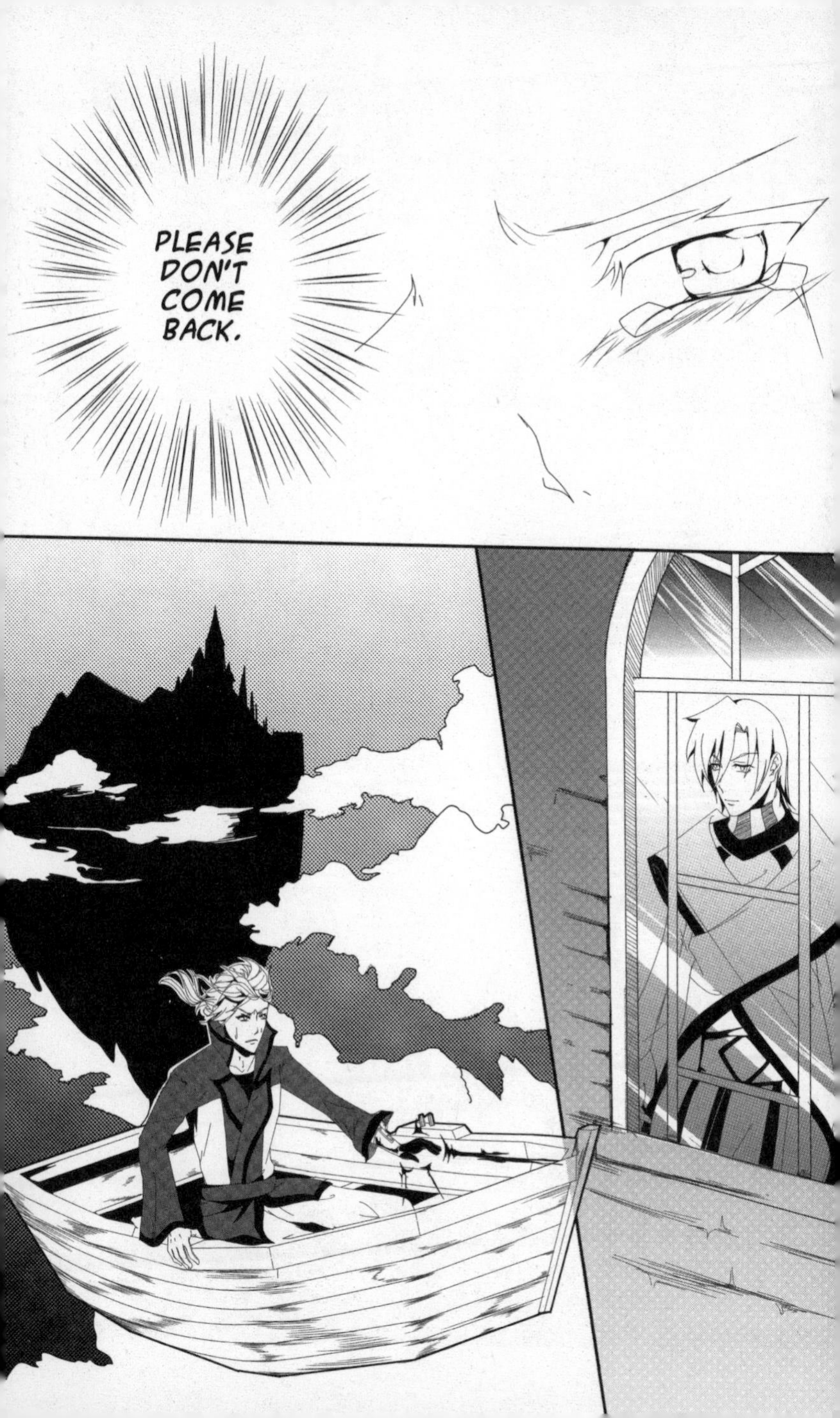
PLEASE DON'T COME BACK.

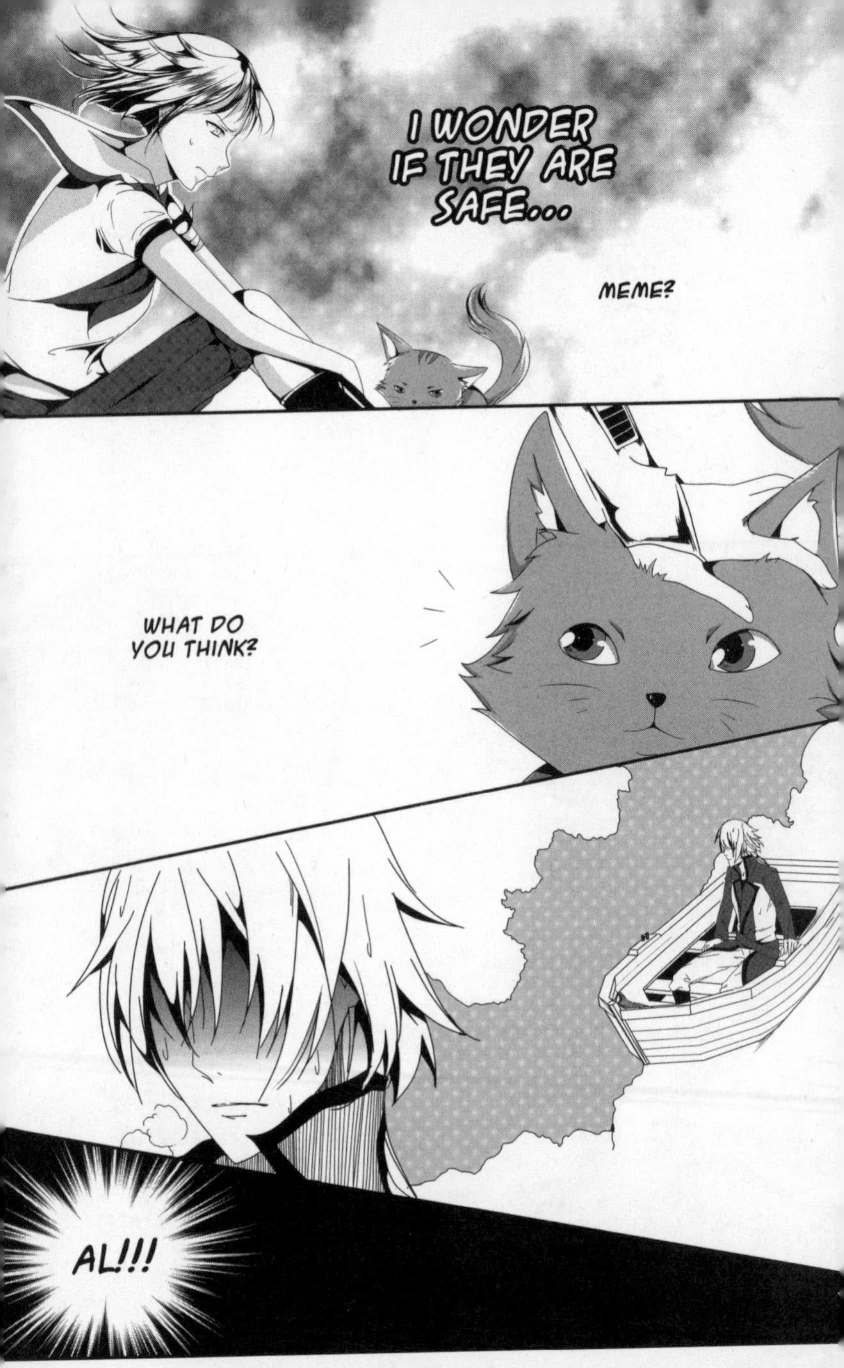
I WONDER IF THEY ARE SAFE...
MEME?
WHAT DO YOU THINK?
AL!!!

READ THIS WAY

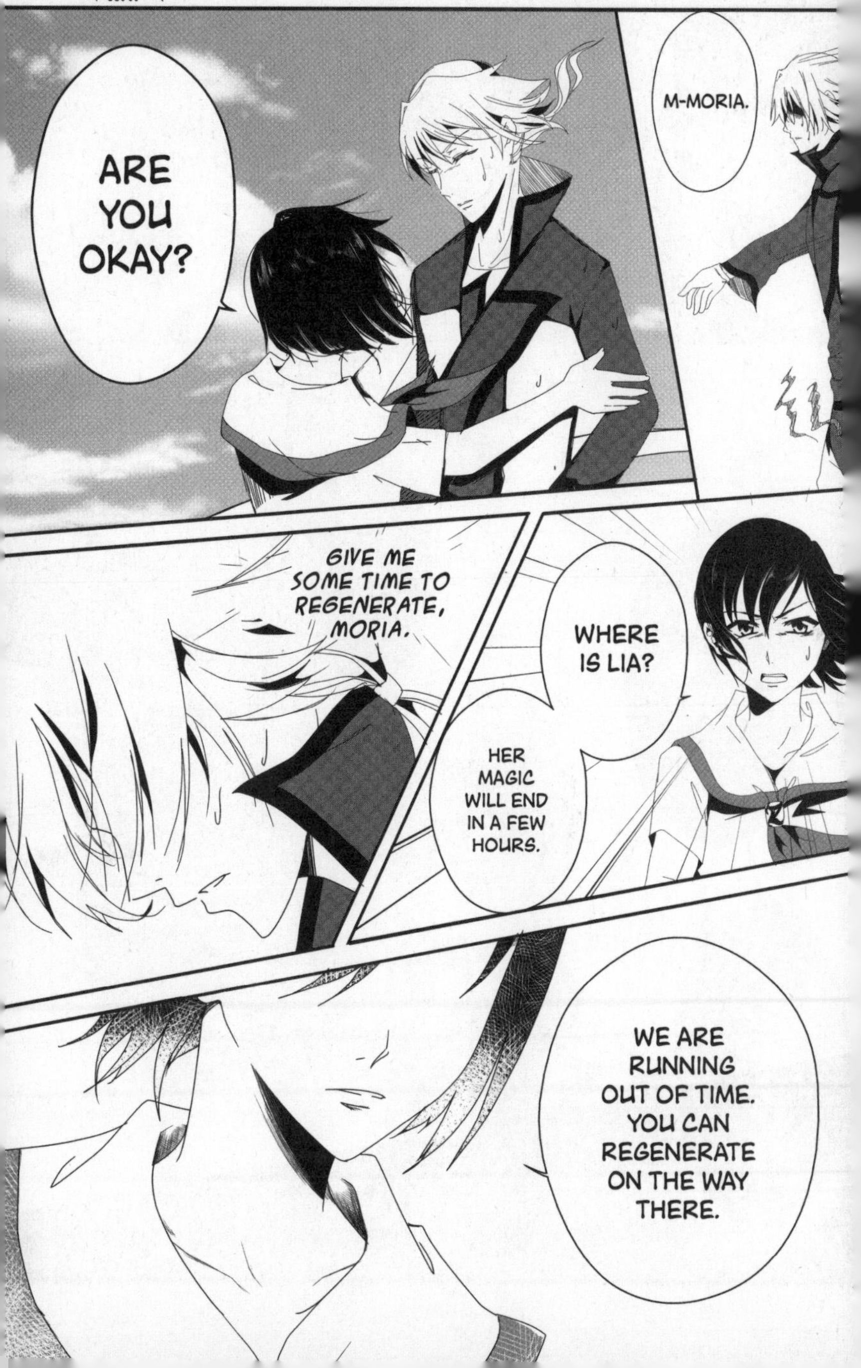
M-MORIA.
ARE YOU OKAY?
WHERE IS LIA?
HER MAGIC WILL END IN A FEW HOURS.
GIVE ME SOME TIME TO REGENERATE, MORIA.
WE ARE RUNNING OUT OF TIME. YOU CAN REGENERATE ON THE WAY THERE.

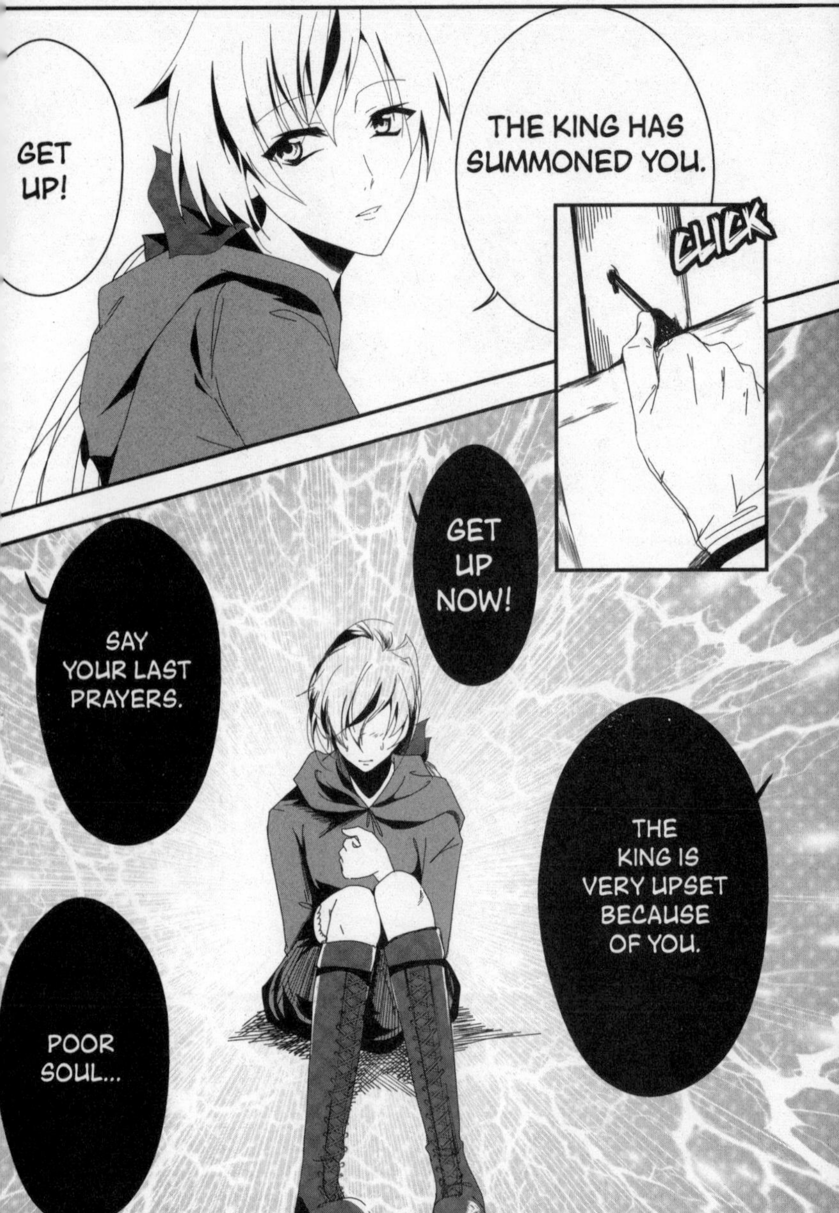
THE KING HAS SUMMONED YOU.
GET UP!
CLICK
GET UP NOW!
THE KING IS VERY UPSET BECAUSE OF YOU.
SAY YOUR LAST PRAYERS.
POOR SOUL...

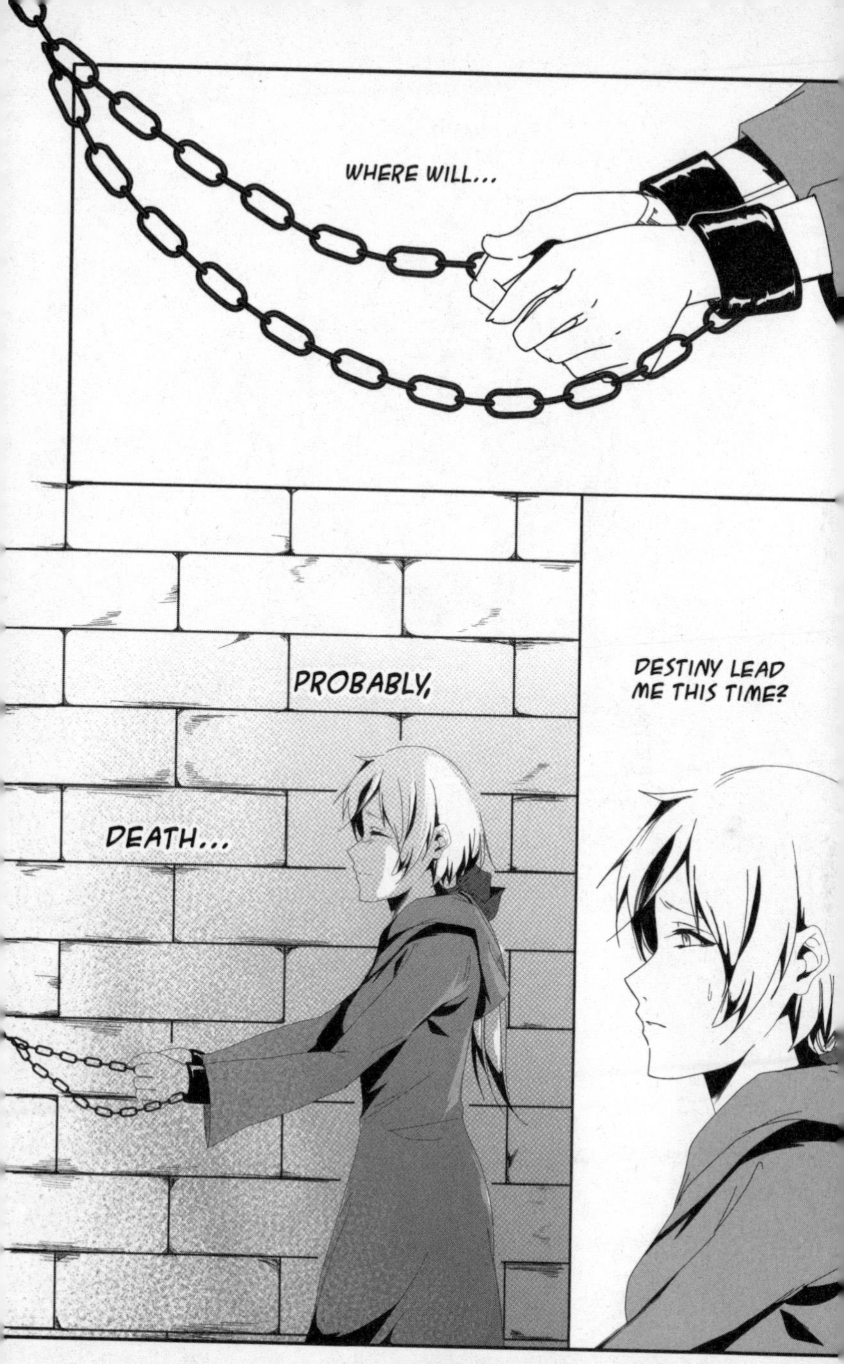
WHERE WILL...
DESTINY LEAD ME THIS TIME?
PROBABLY,
DEATH...

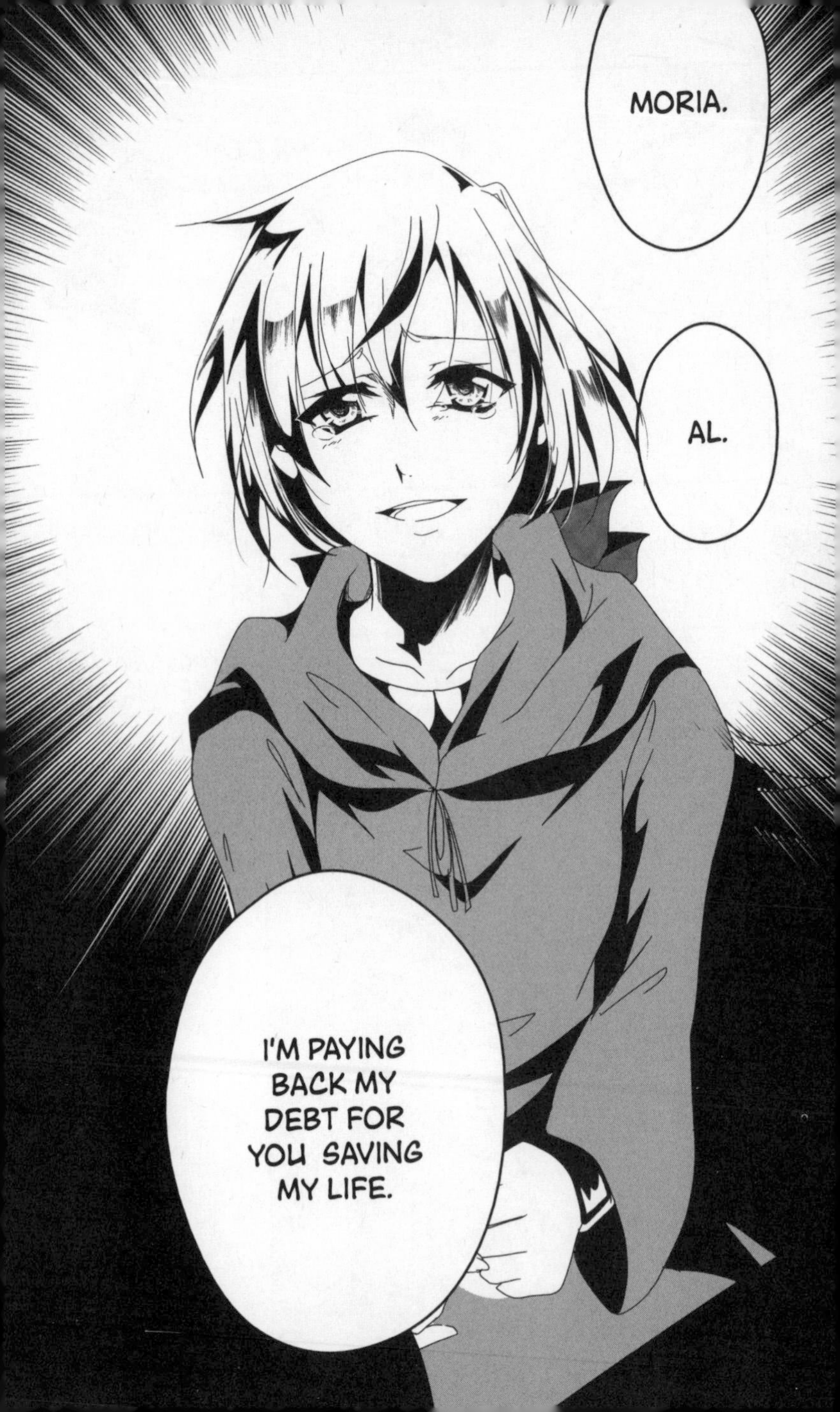
MORIA.
AL.
I'M PAYING BACK MY DEBT FOR YOU SAVING MY LIFE.

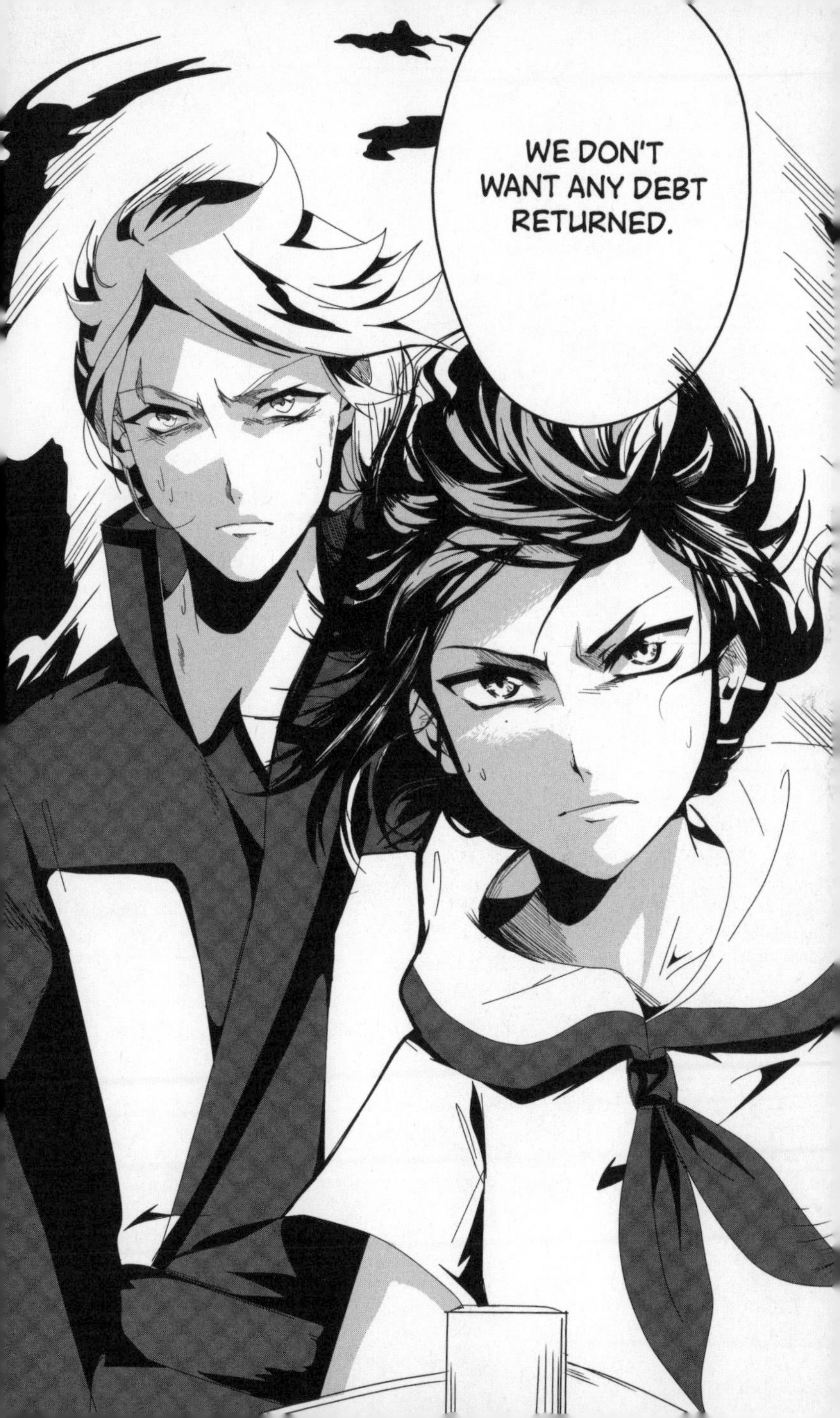
WE DON'T WANT ANY DEBT RETURNED.

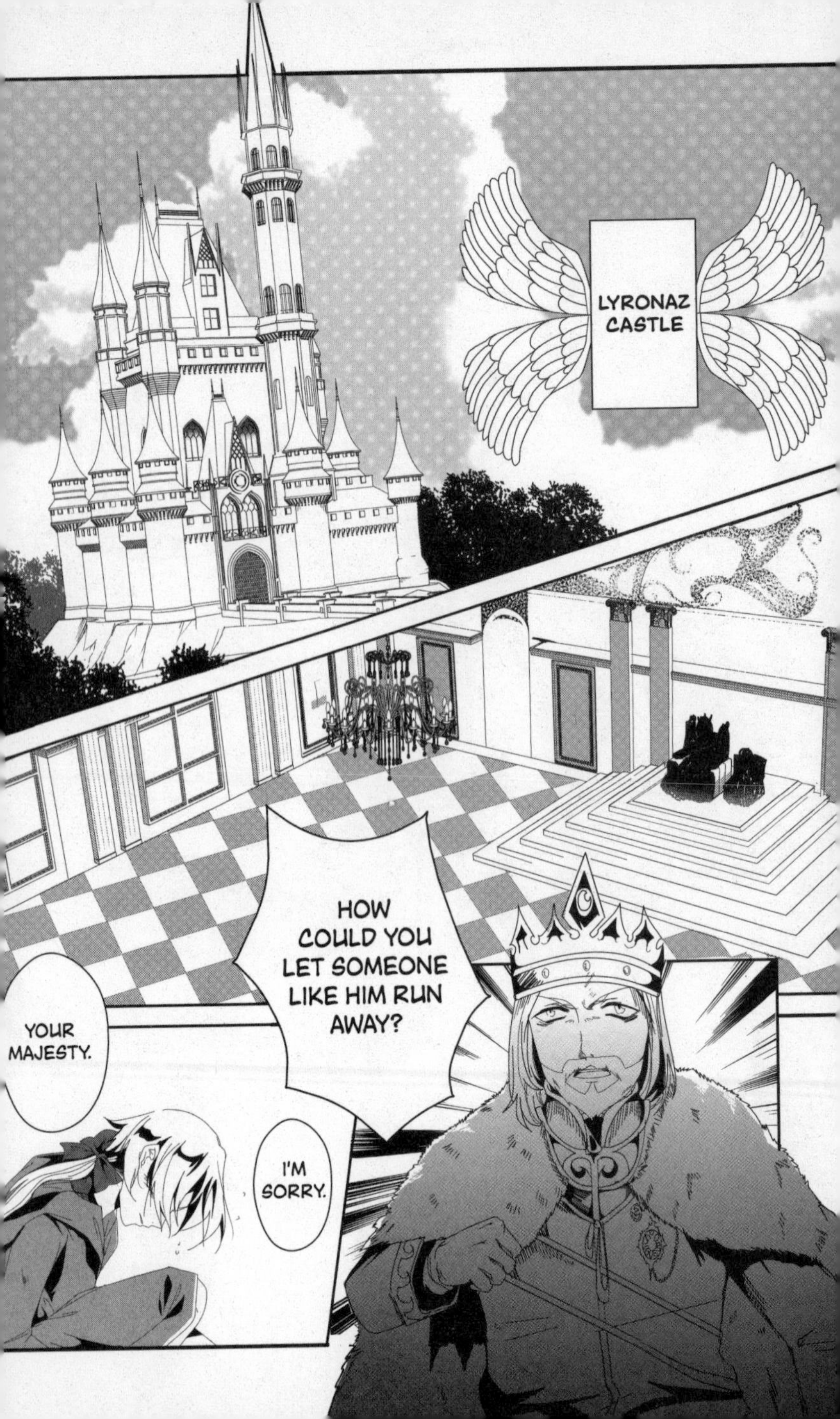
LYRONAZ CASTLE
HOW COULD YOU LET SOMEONE LIKE HIM RUN AWAY?
YOUR MAJESTY.
I'M SORRY.

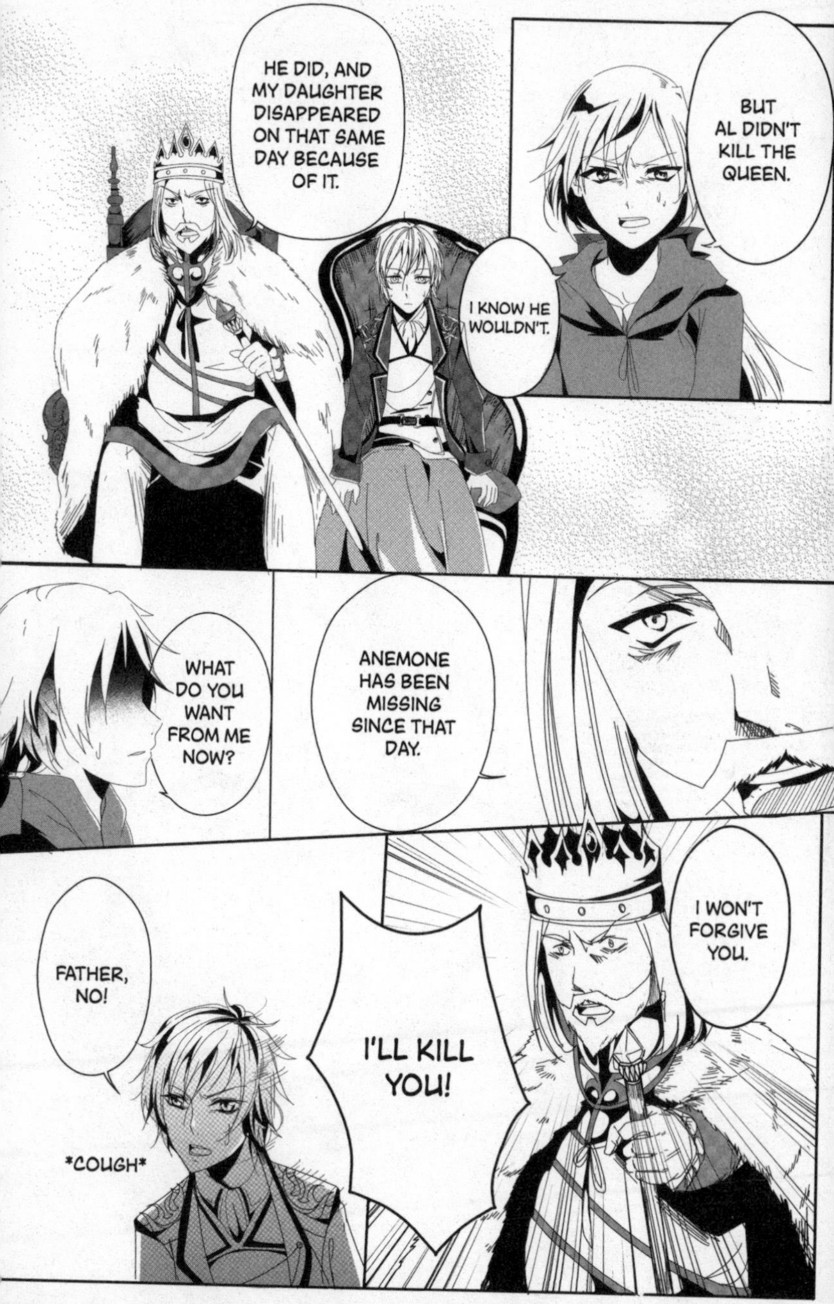
BUT AL DIDN'T KILL THE QUEEN.
I KNOW HE WOULDN'T.
HE DID, AND MY DAUGHTER DISAPPEARED ON THAT SAME DAY BECAUSE OF IT.
ANEMONE HAS BEEN MISSING SINCE THAT DAY.
WHAT DO YOU WANT FROM ME NOW?
I WON'T FORGIVE YOU.
I'LL KILL YOU!
FATHER, NO!
COUGH

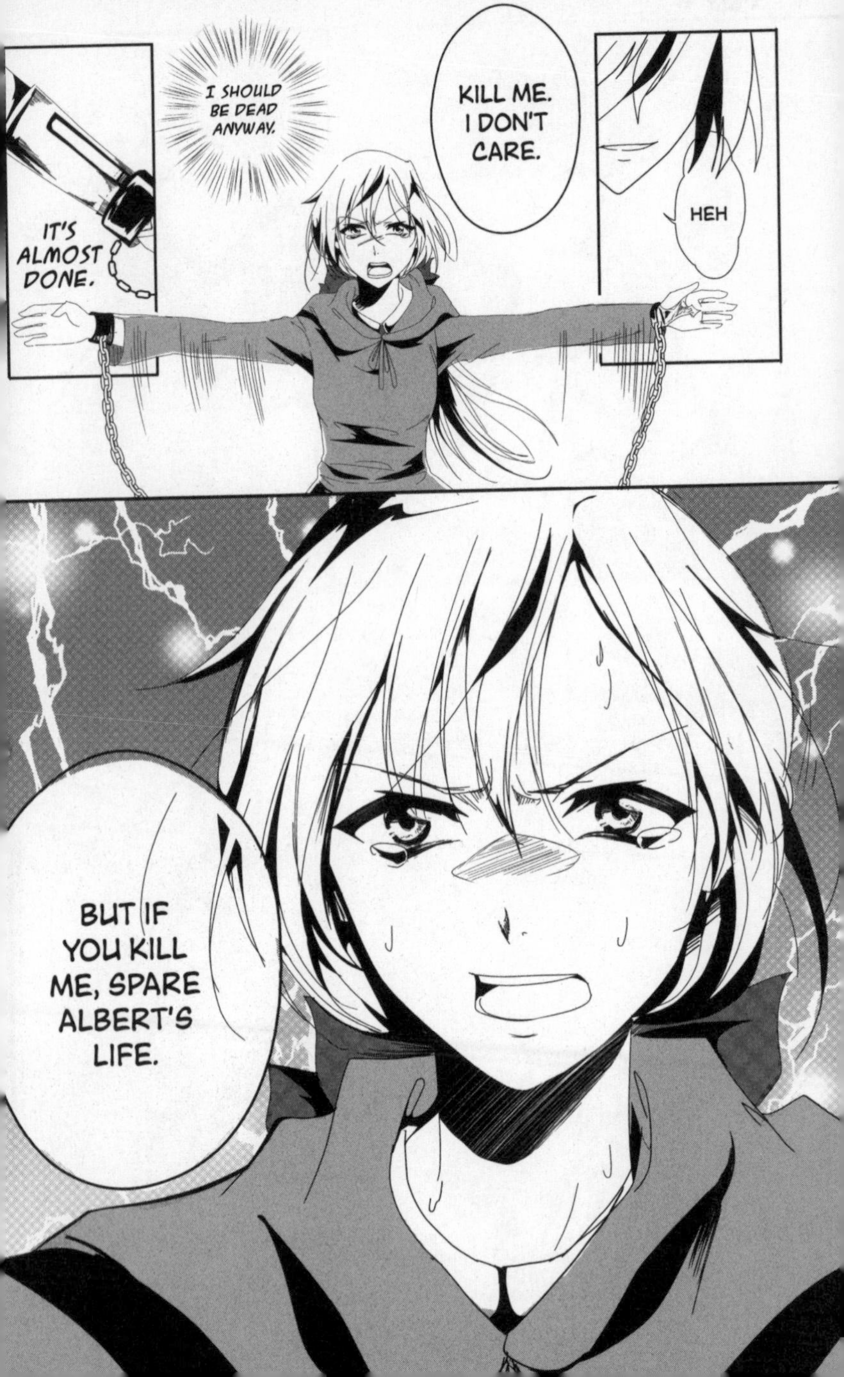
HEH
KILL ME. I DON'T CARE.
I SHOULD BE DEAD ANYWAY.
IT'S ALMOST DONE.
BUT IF YOU KILL ME, SPARE ALBERT'S LIFE.

READ THIS WAY

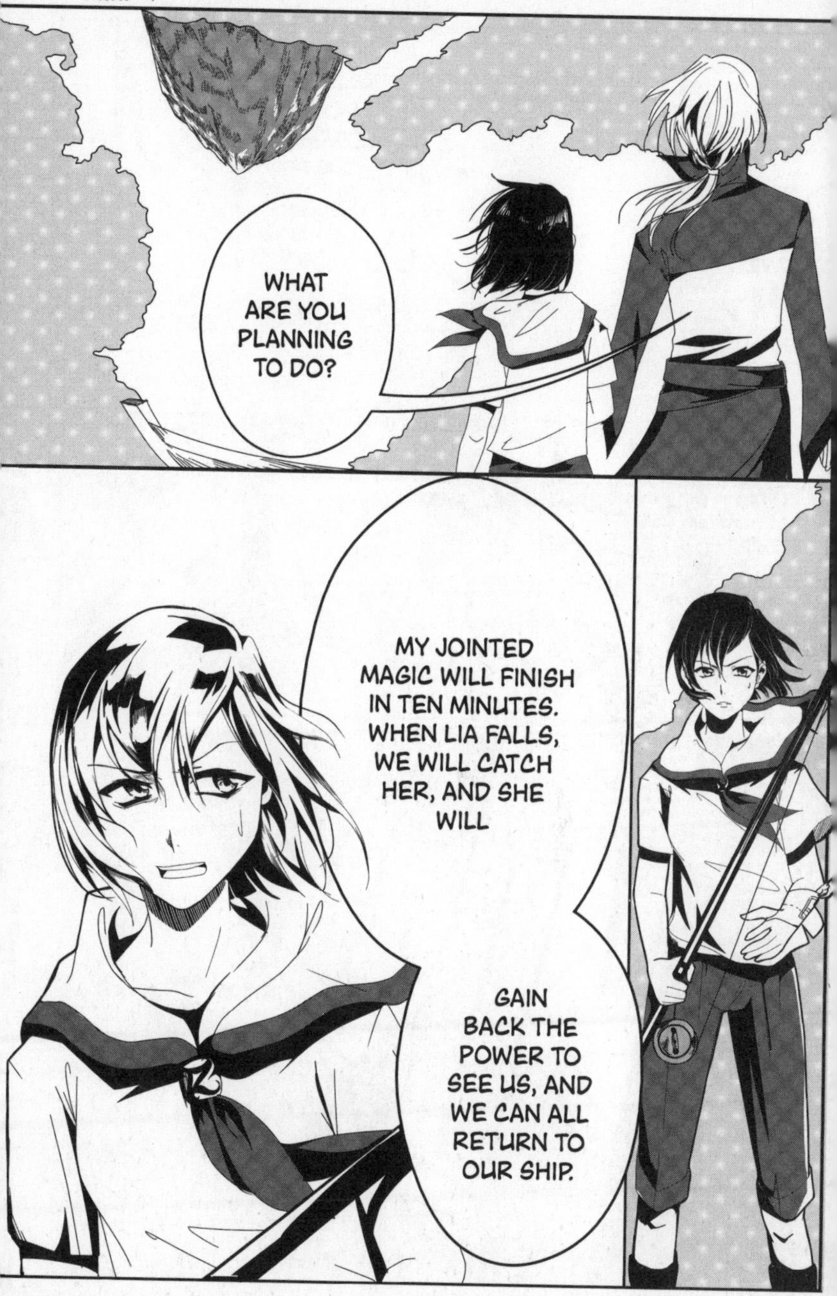
WHAT ARE YOU PLANNING TO DO?
MY JOINTED MAGIC WILL FINISH IN TEN MINUTES. WHEN LIA FALLS, WE WILL CATCH HER, AND SHE WILL
GAIN BACK THE POWER TO SEE US, AND WE CAN ALL RETURN TO OUR SHIP.

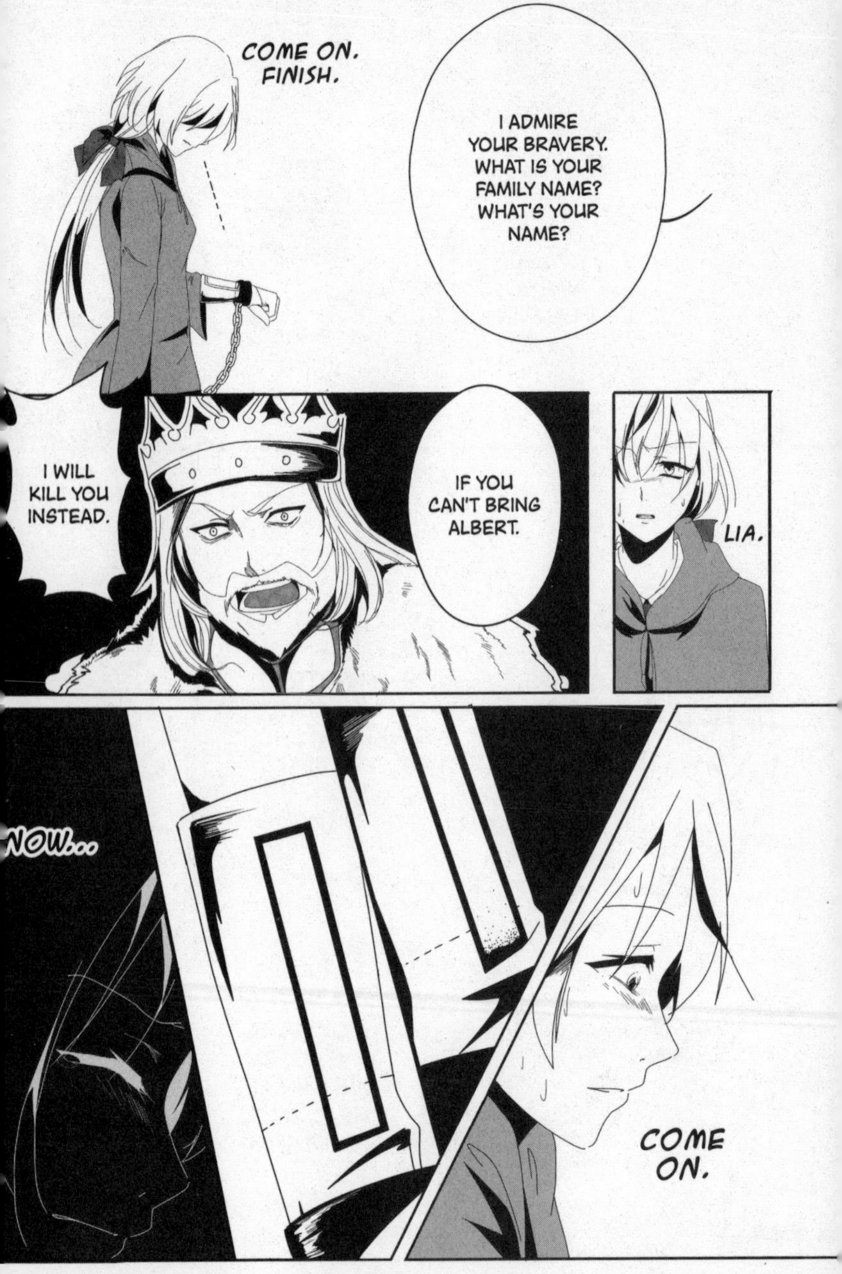
I ADMIRE YOUR BRAVERY. WHAT IS YOUR FAMILY NAME? WHAT'S YOUR NAME?
COME ON. FINISH.
LIA.
IF YOU CAN'T BRING ALBERT.
I WILL KILL YOU INSTEAD.
COME ON.
NOW...

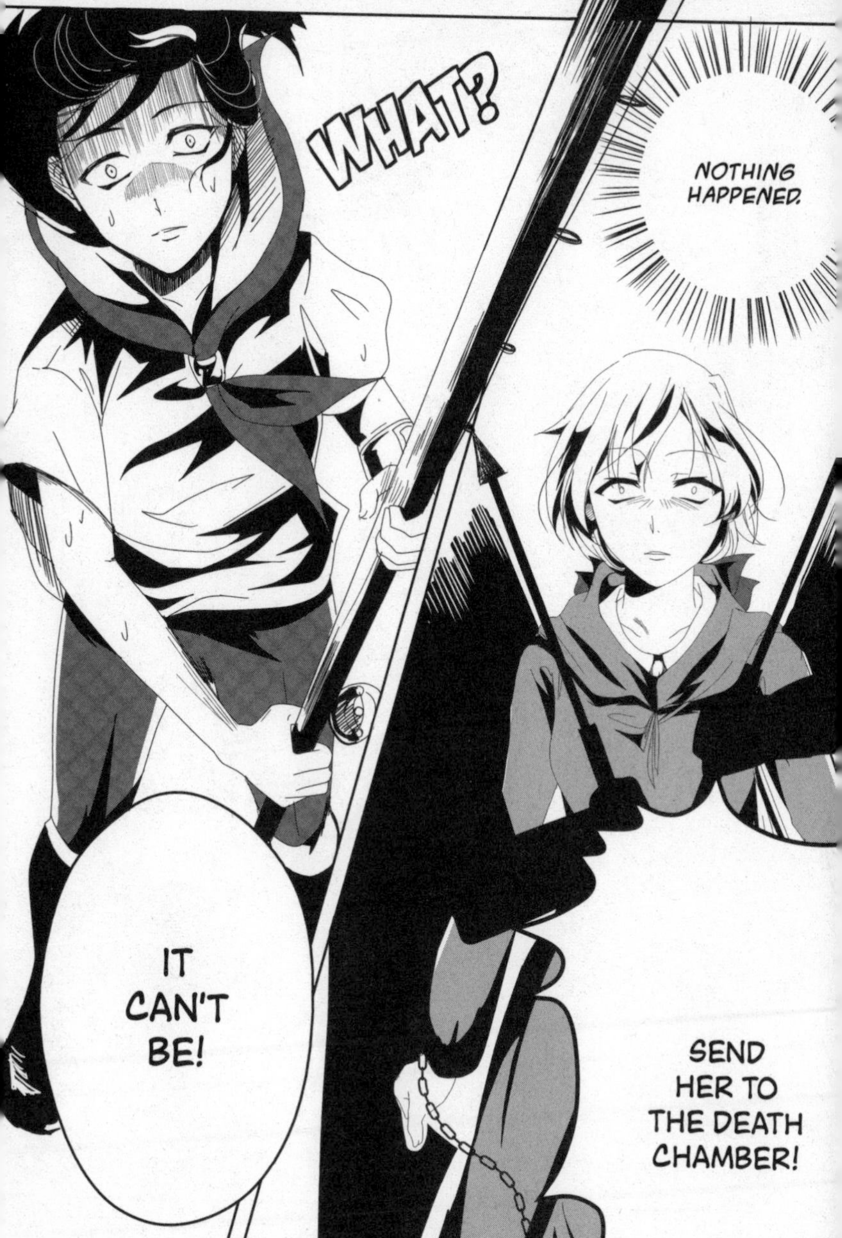
NOTHING HAPPENED.
SEND HER TO THE DEATH CHAMBER!
WHAT?
IT CAN'T BE!

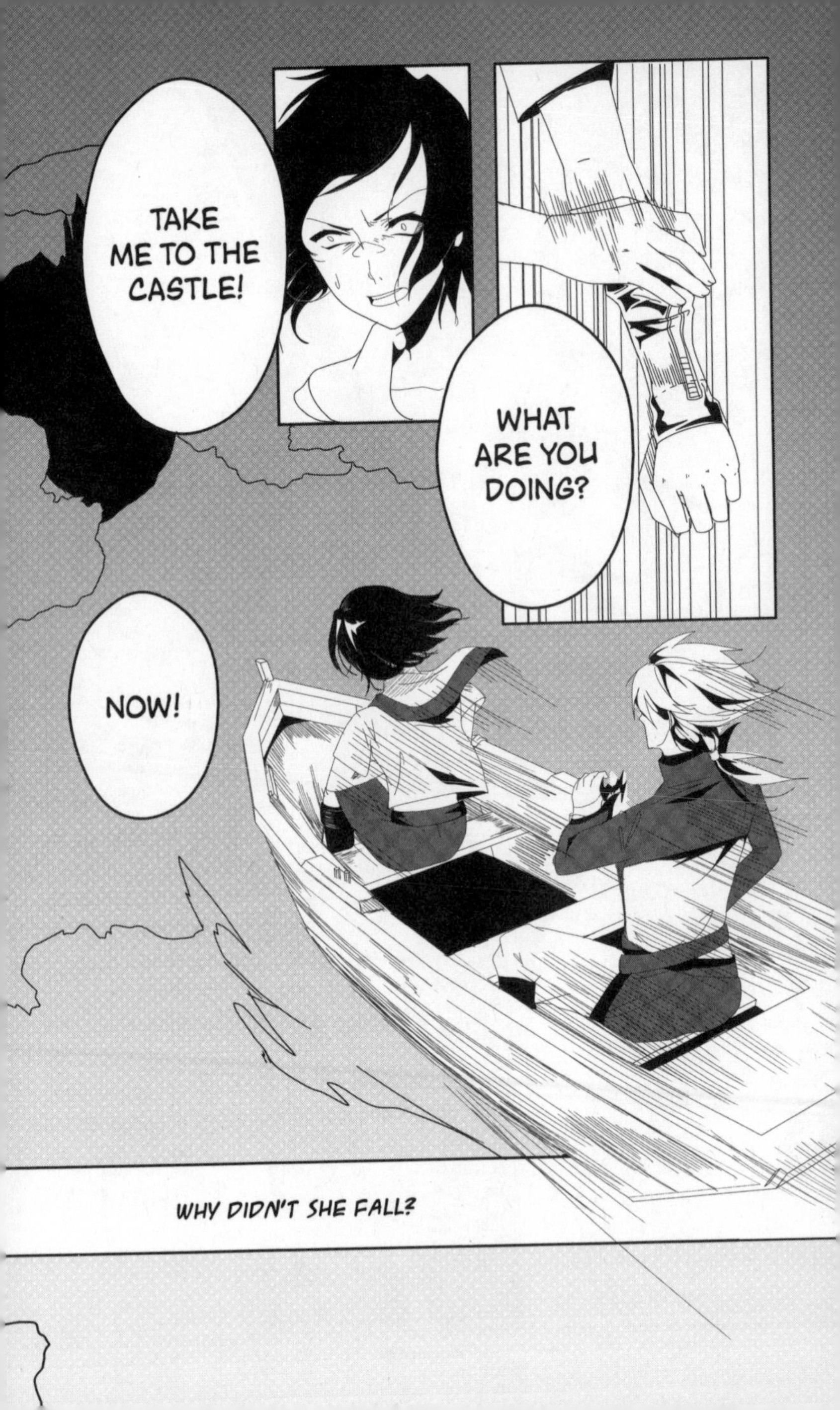
WHAT ARE YOU DOING?
TAKE ME TO THE CASTLE!
NOW!
WHY DIDN'T SHE FALL?

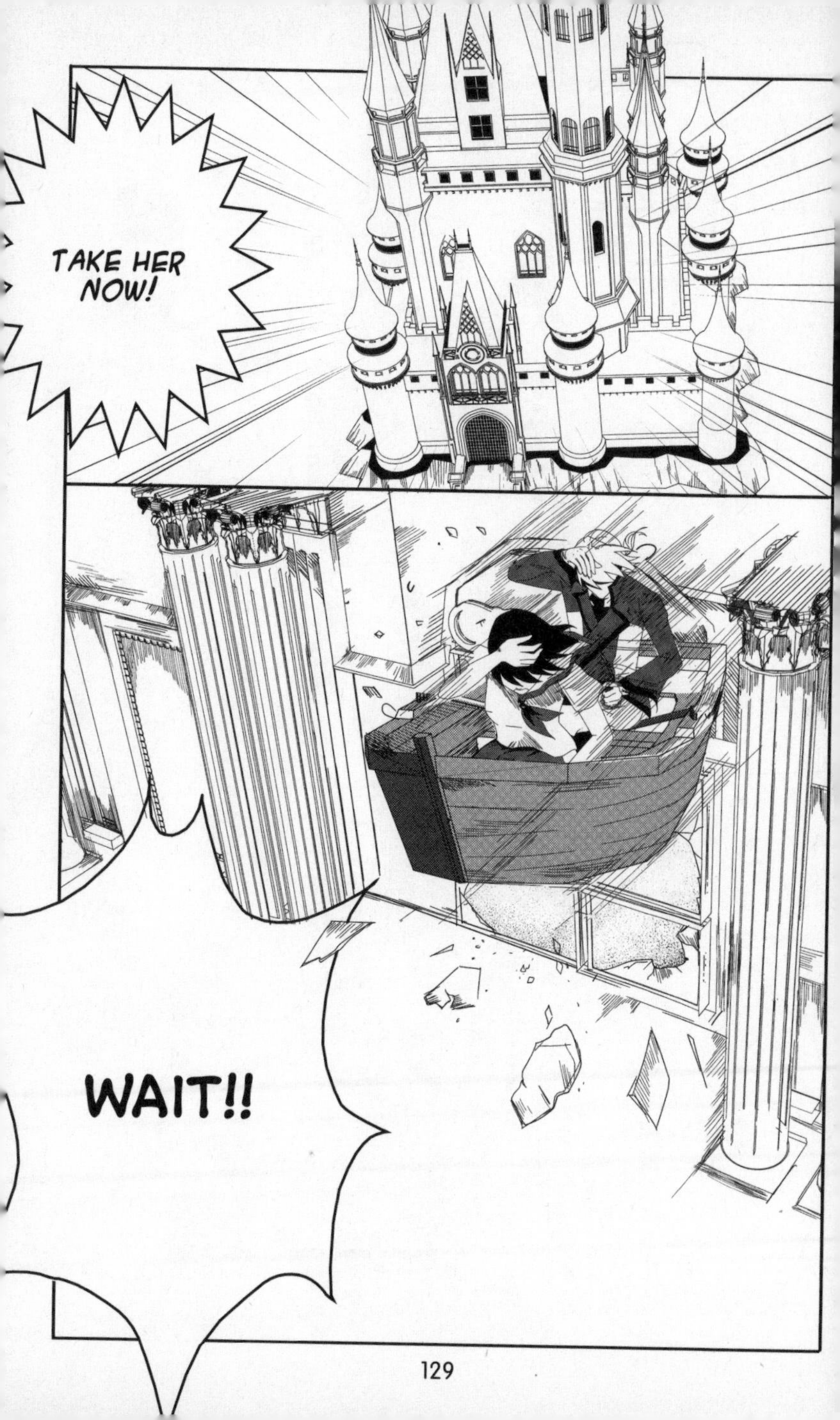
TAKE HER NOW!
WAIT!!

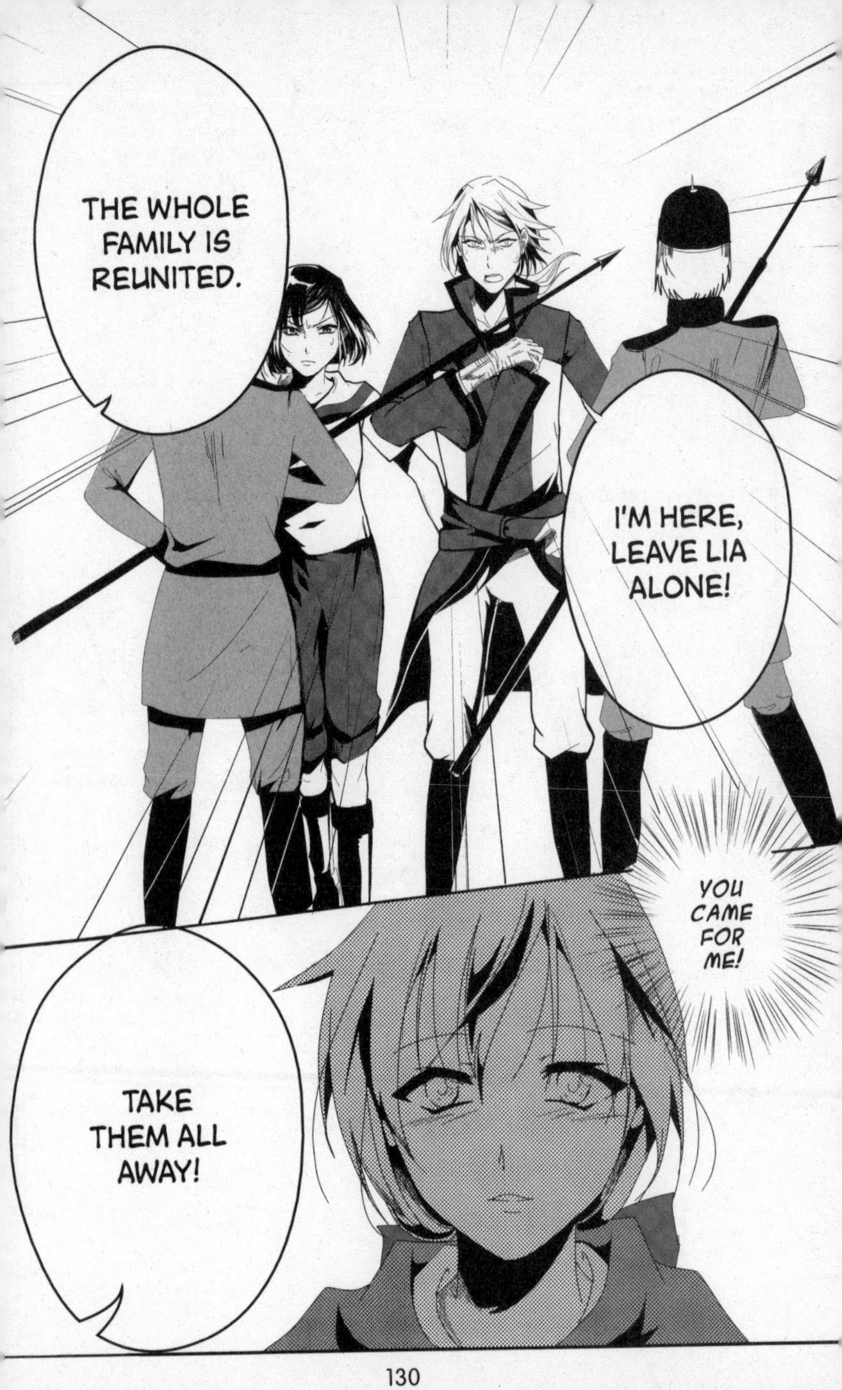
THE WHOLE FAMILY IS REUNITED.
I'M HERE, LEAVE LIA ALONE!
YOU CAME FOR ME!
TAKE THEM ALL AWAY!

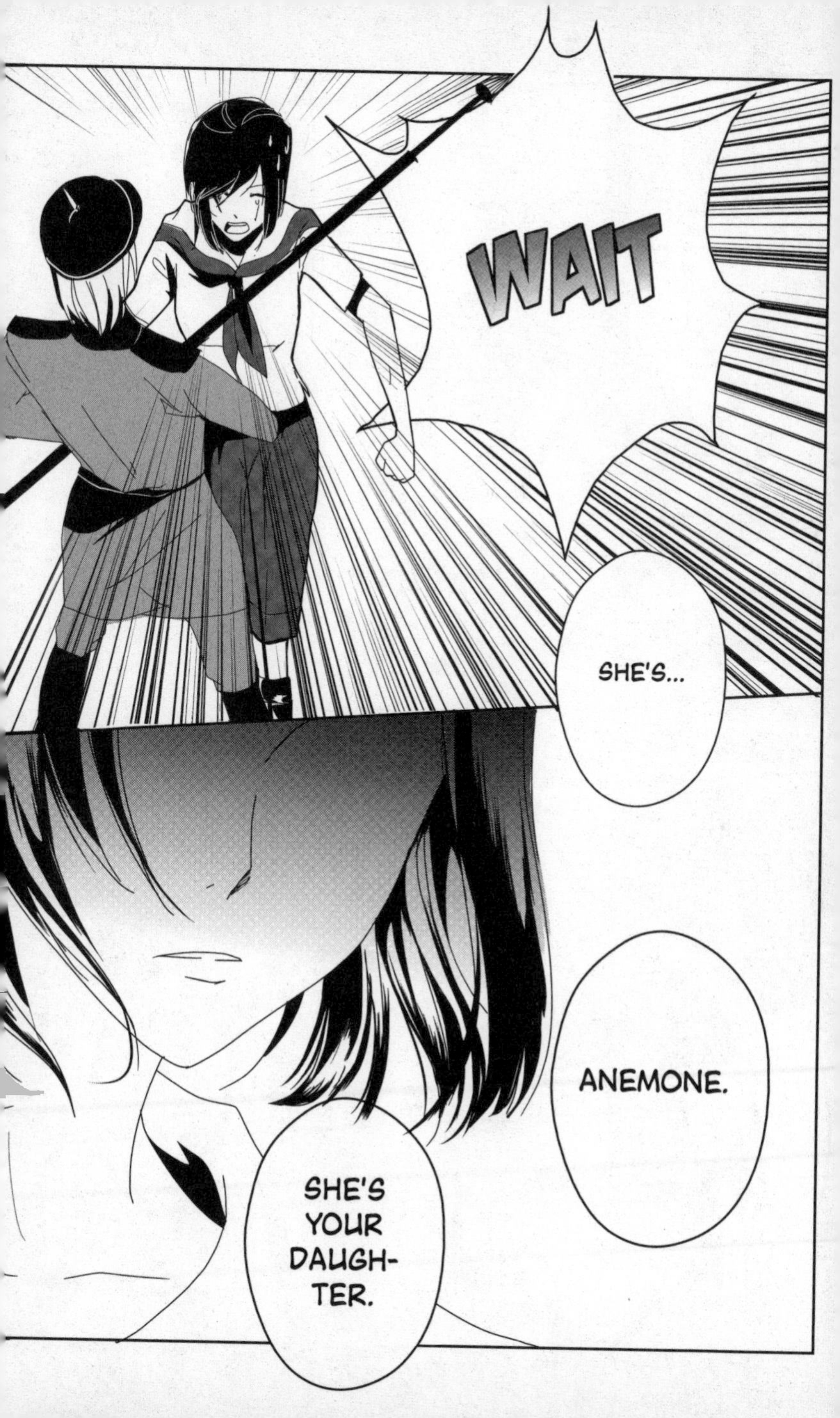
WAIT
SHE'S...
ANEMONE.
SHE'S YOUR DAUGH-TER.

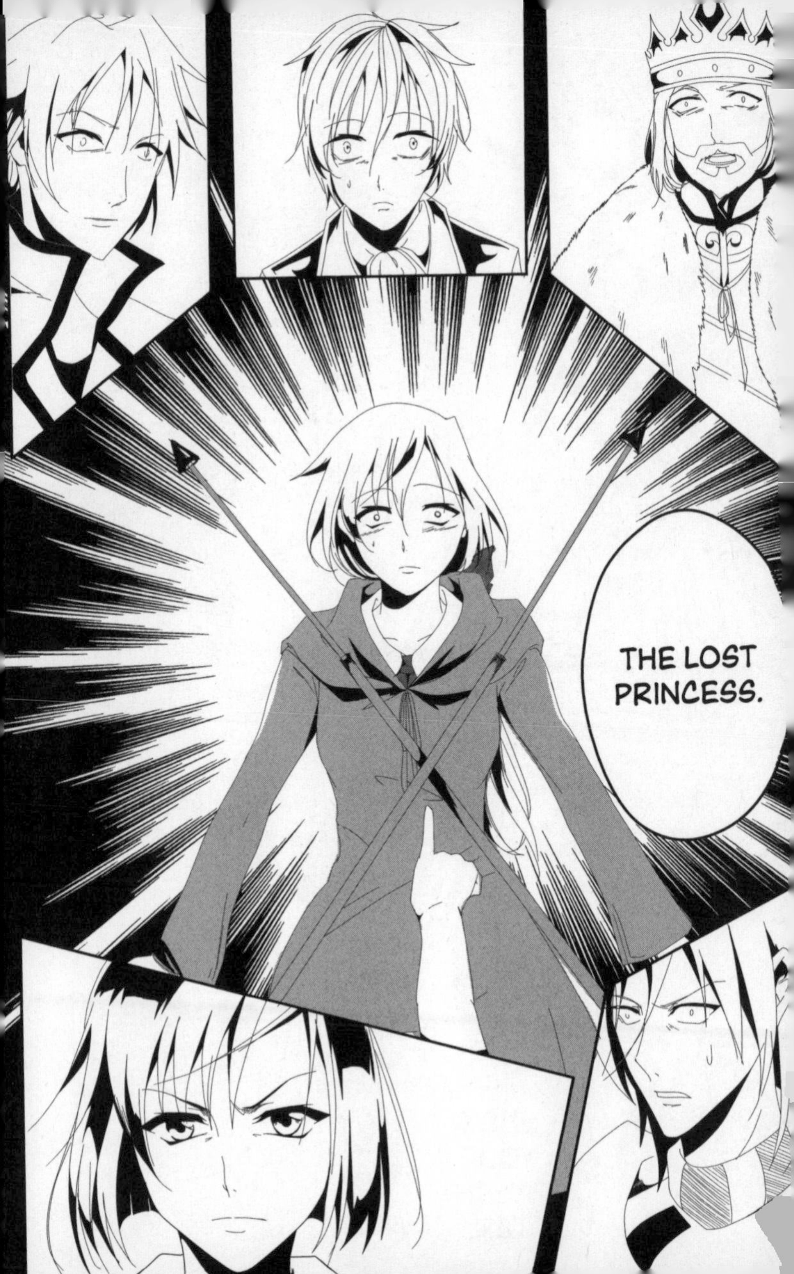
THE LOST PRINCESS.

READ THIS WAY

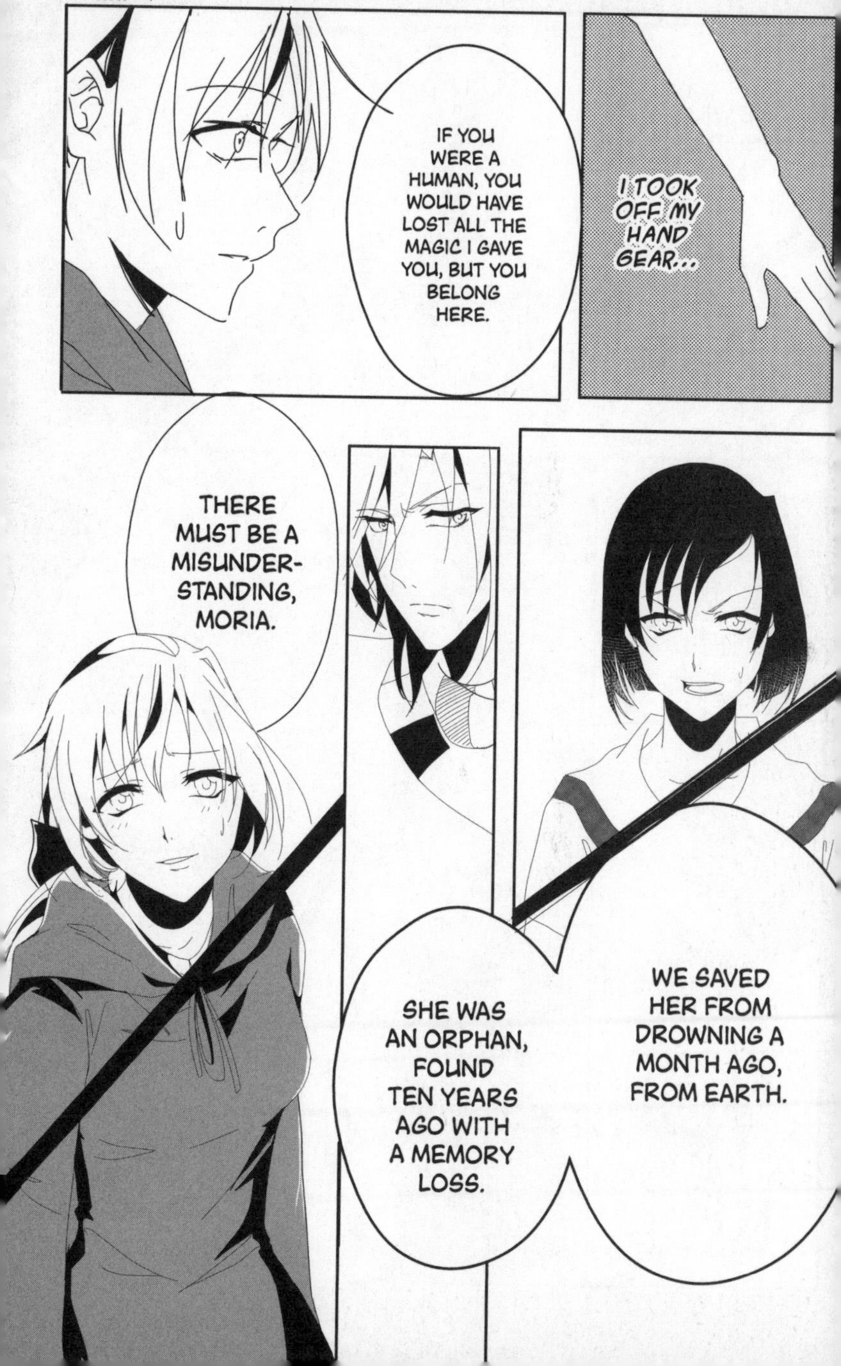

I TOOK OFF MY HAND GEAR...
IF YOU WERE A HUMAN, YOU WOULD HAVE LOST ALL THE MAGIC I GAVE YOU, BUT YOU BELONG HERE.
WE SAVED HER FROM DROWNING A MONTH AGO, FROM EARTH.
SHE WAS AN ORPHAN, FOUND TEN YEARS AGO WITH A MEMORY LOSS.
THERE MUST BE A MISUNDER-STANDING, MORIA.

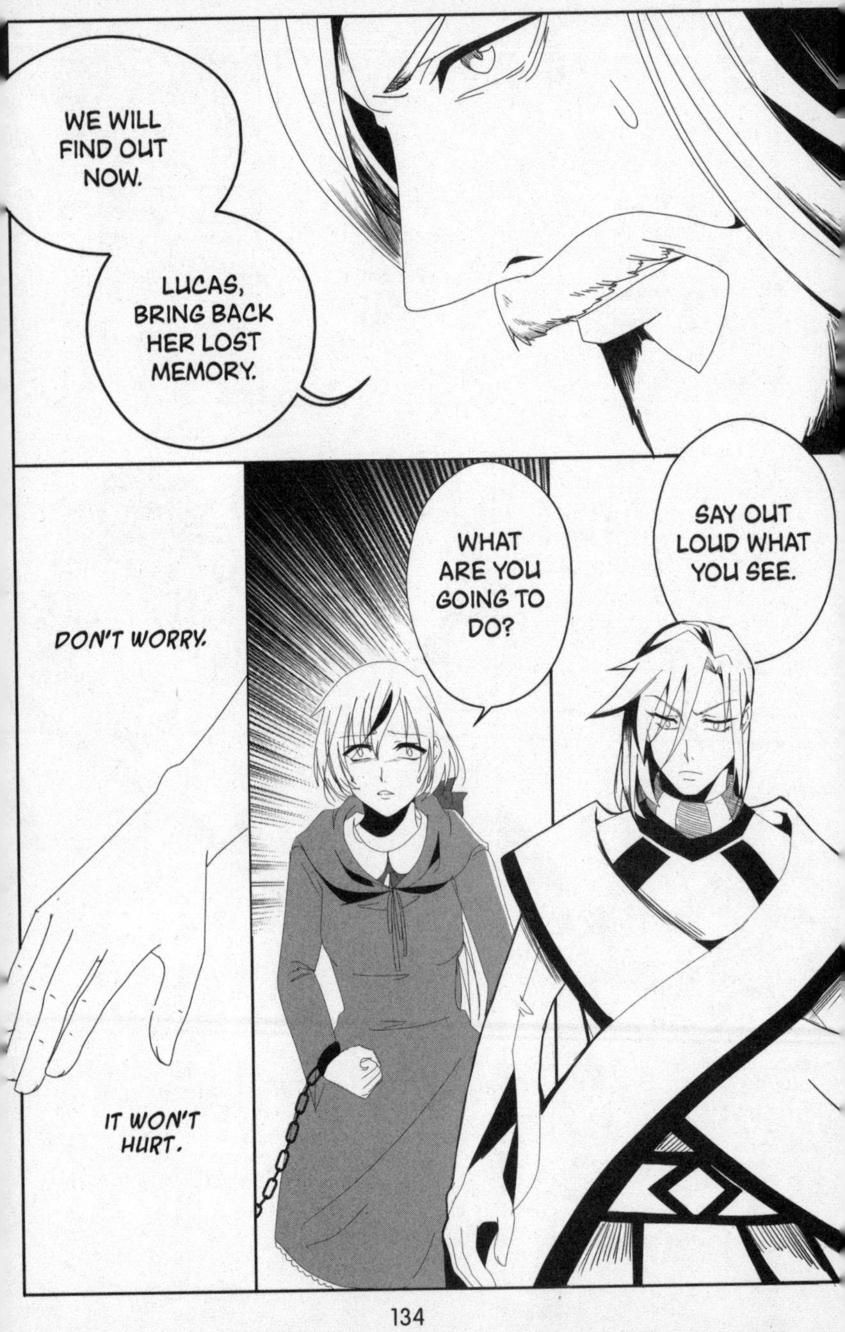
WE WILL FIND OUT NOW.
LUCAS, BRING BACK HER LOST MEMORY.
SAY OUT LOUD WHAT YOU SEE.
WHAT ARE YOU GOING TO DO?
DON'T WORRY.
IT WON'T HURT.

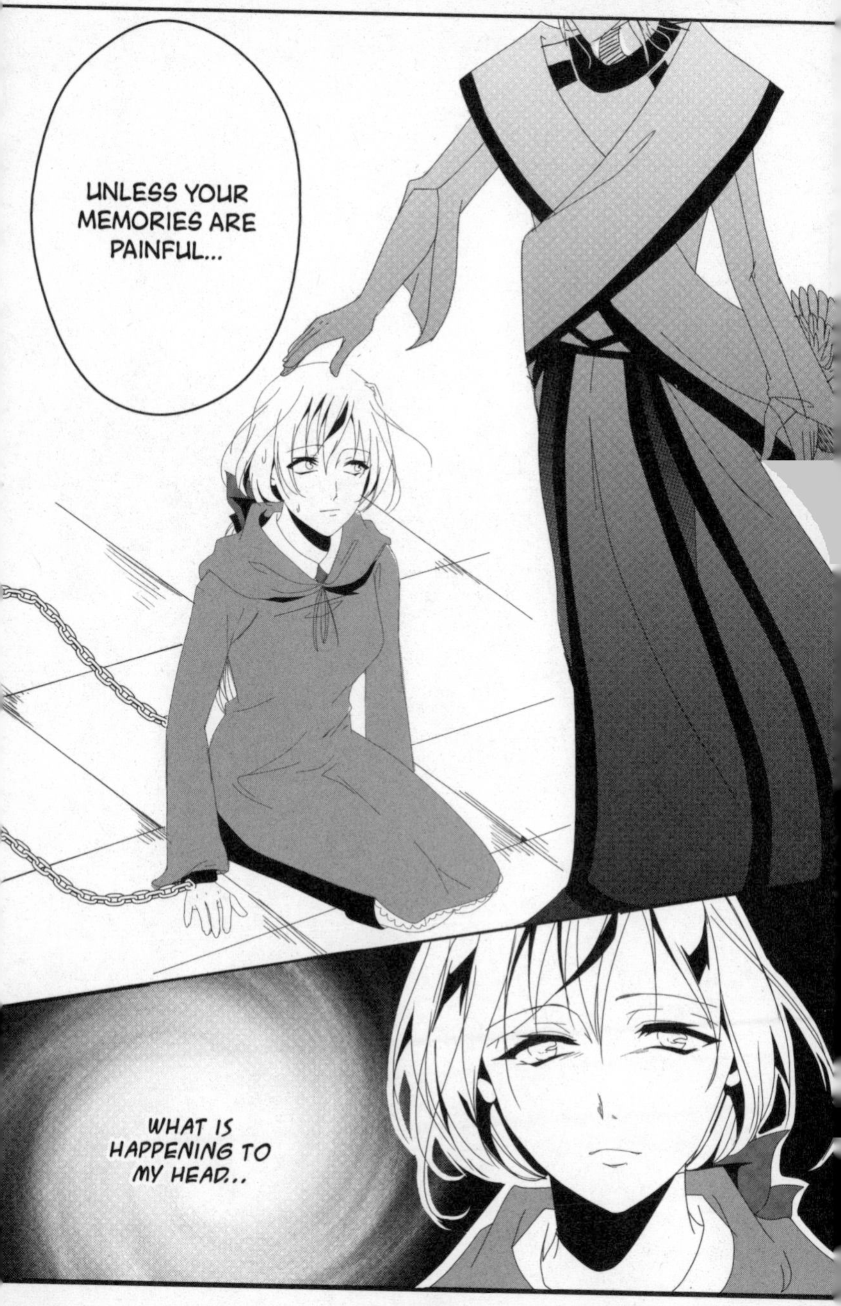
UNLESS YOUR MEMORIES ARE PAINFUL...
WHAT IS HAPPENING TO MY HEAD...

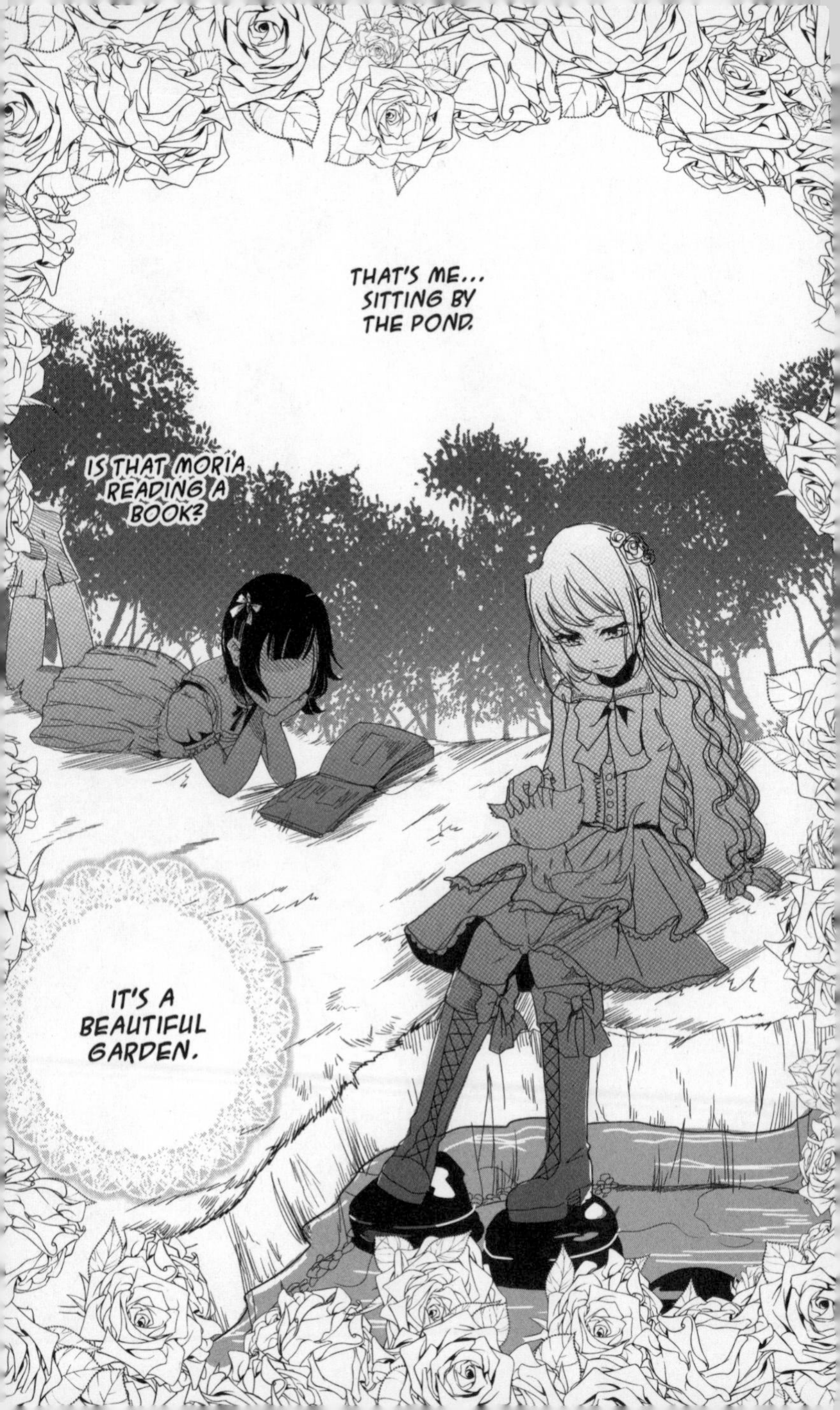
THAT'S ME... SITTING BY THE POND.
IS THAT MORIA READING A BOOK?
IT'S A BEAUTIFUL GARDEN.

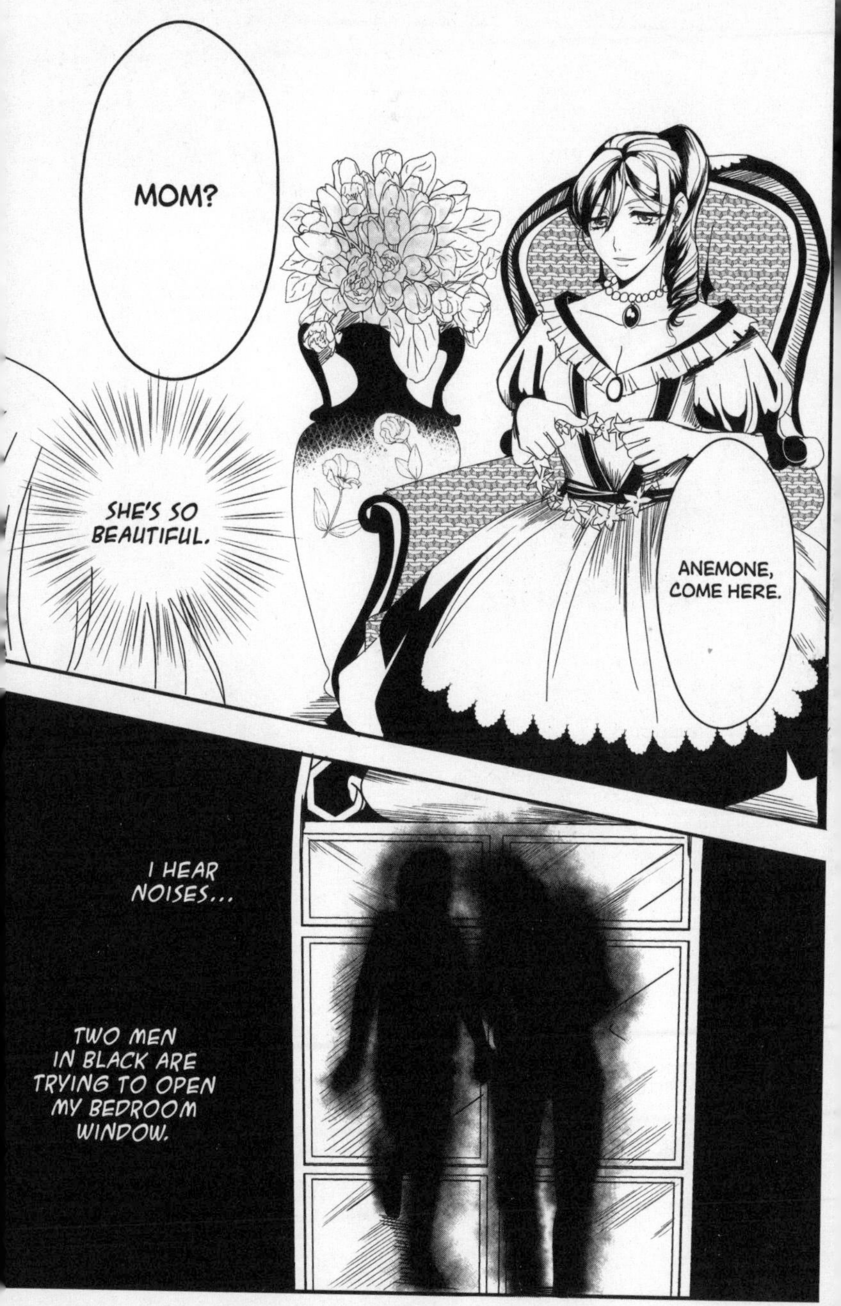
ANEMONE, COME HERE.
MOM?
SHE'S SO BEAUTIFUL.
I HEAR NOISES...
TWO MEN IN BLACK ARE TRYING TO OPEN MY BEDROOM WINDOW.

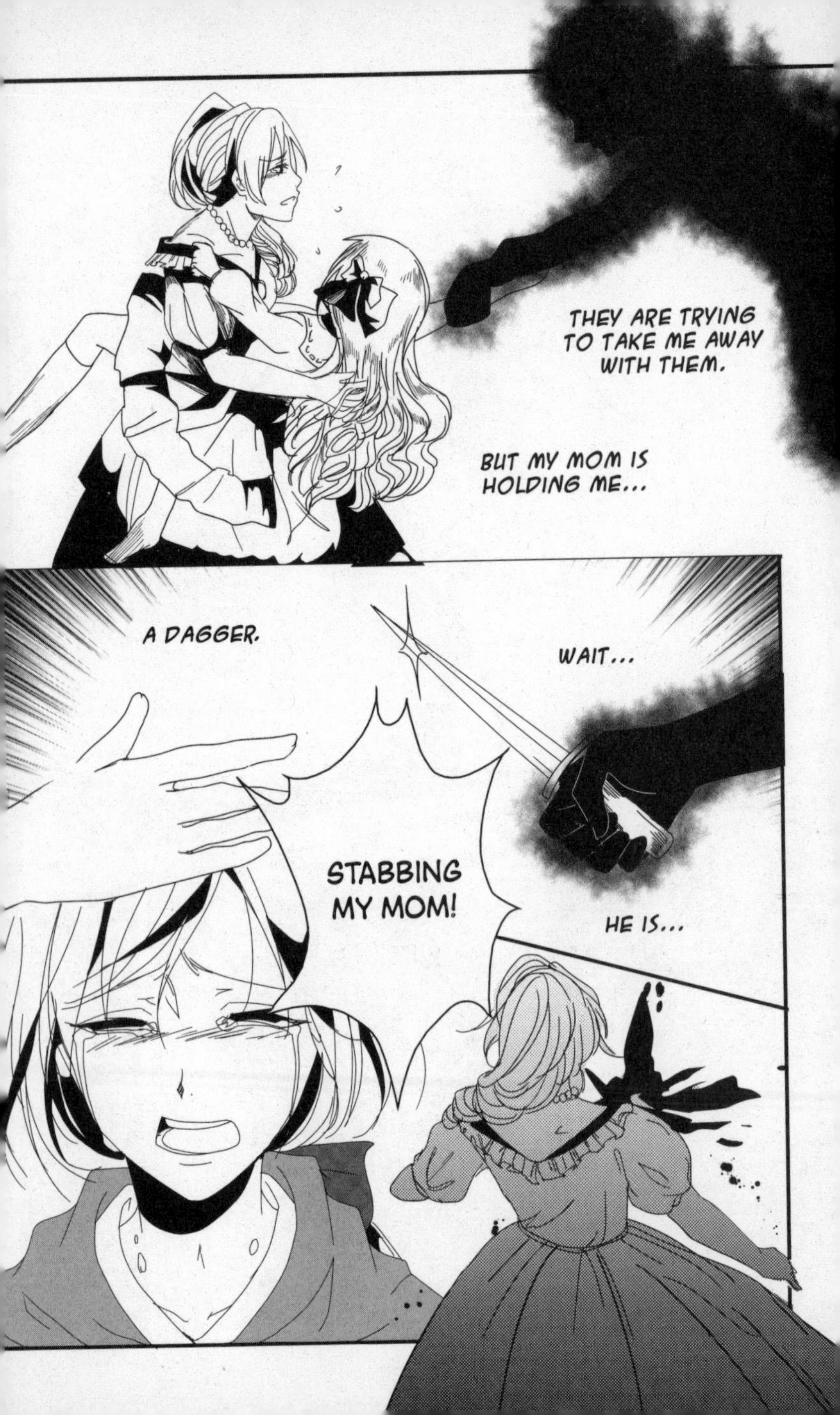
THEY ARE TRYING TO TAKE ME AWAY WITH THEM.
BUT MY MOM IS HOLDING ME...
WAIT...
A DAGGER.
HE IS...
STABBING MY MOM!

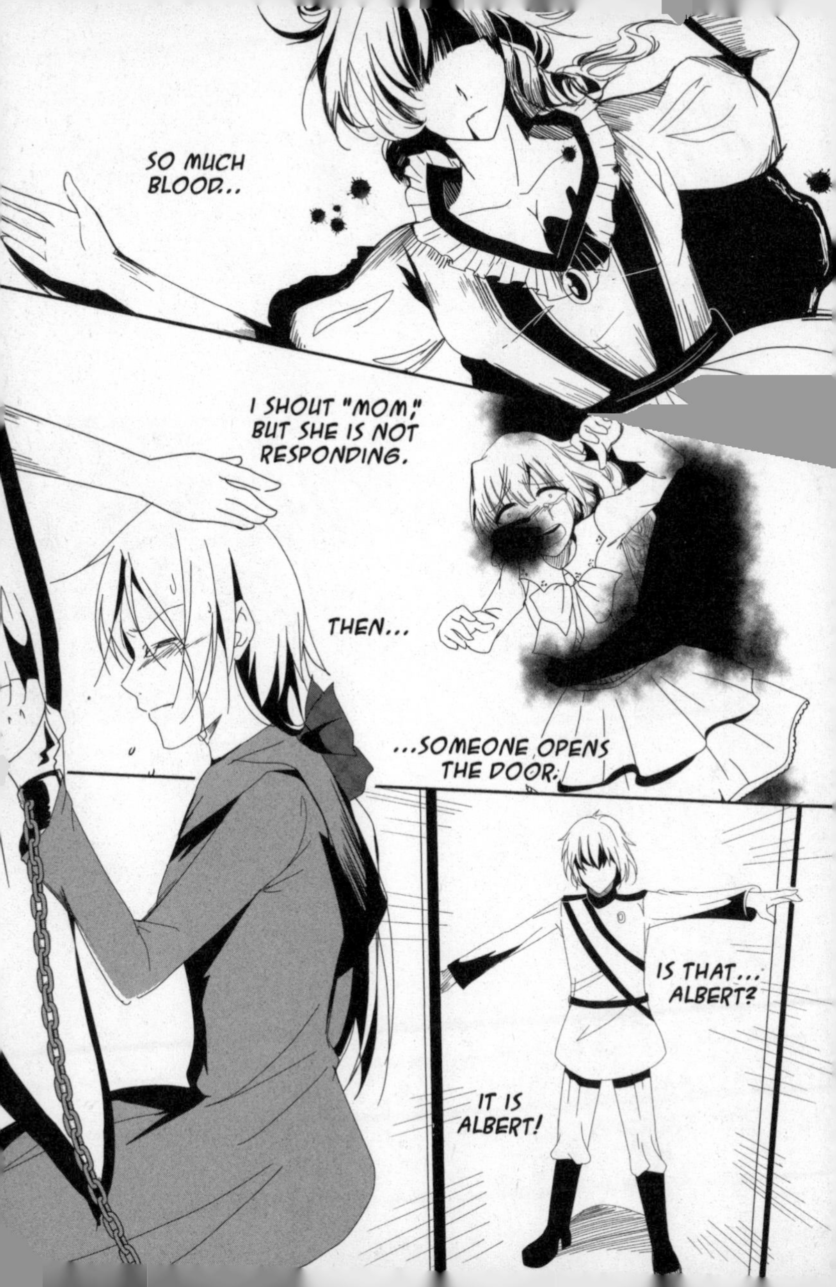
SO MUCH BLOOD...
I SHOUT "MOM," BUT SHE IS NOT RESPONDING.
THEN...
...SOMEONE OPENS THE DOOR.
IS THAT... ALBERT?
IT IS ALBERT!

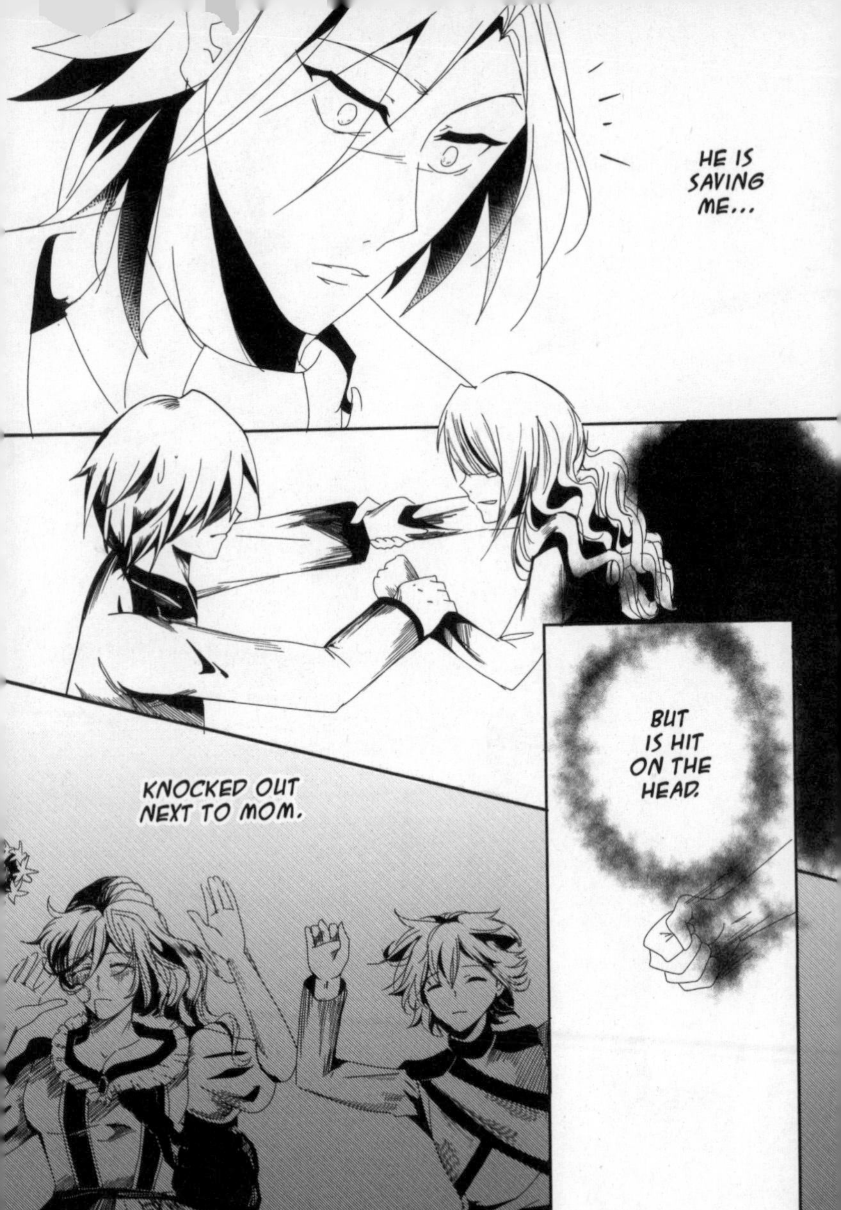
HE IS SAVING ME...
BUT IS HIT ON THE HEAD.
KNOCKED OUT NEXT TO MOM.

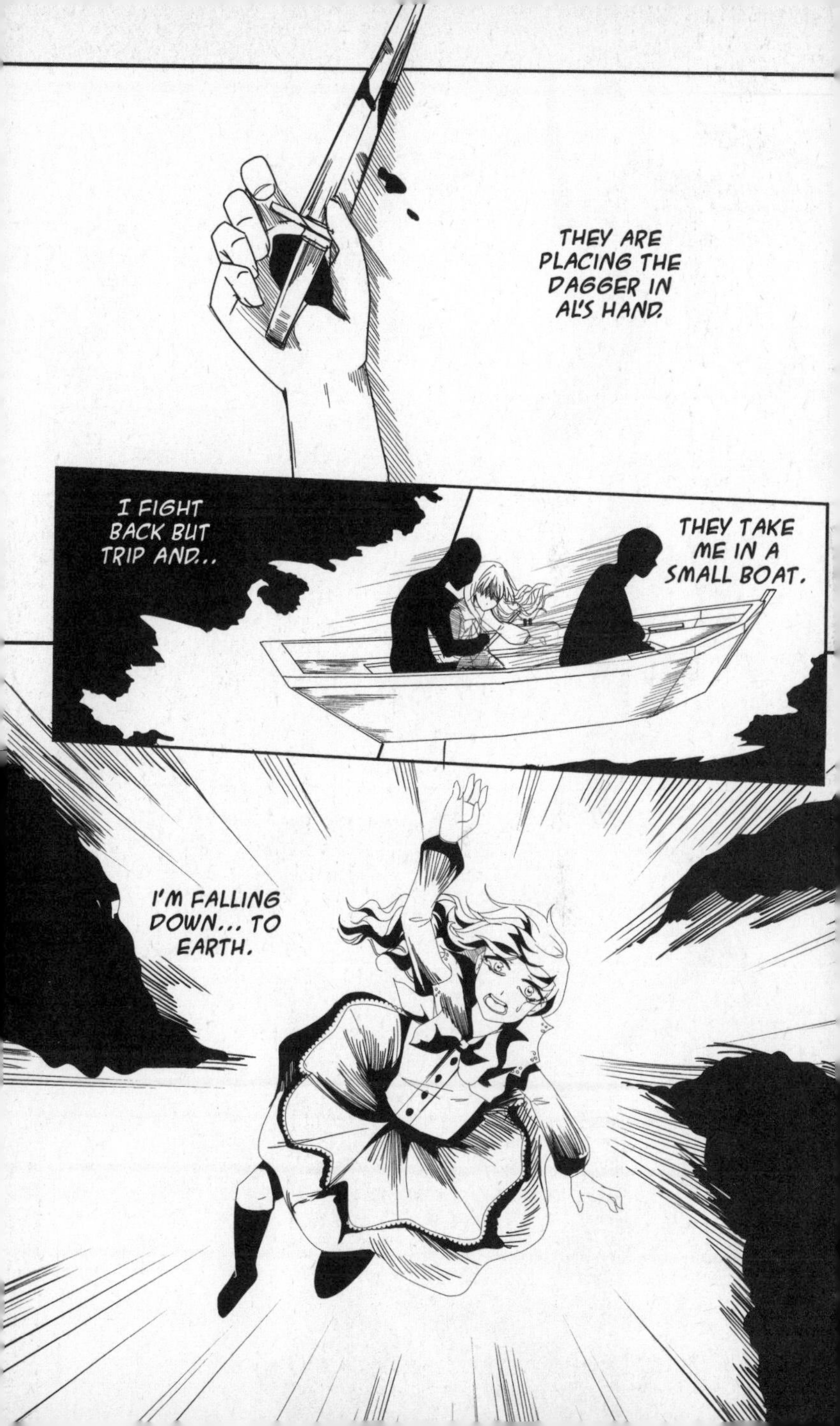
THEY ARE PLACING THE DAGGER IN AL'S HAND.
THEY TAKE ME IN A SMALL BOAT.
I FIGHT BACK BUT TRIP AND...
I'M FALLING DOWN... TO EARTH.

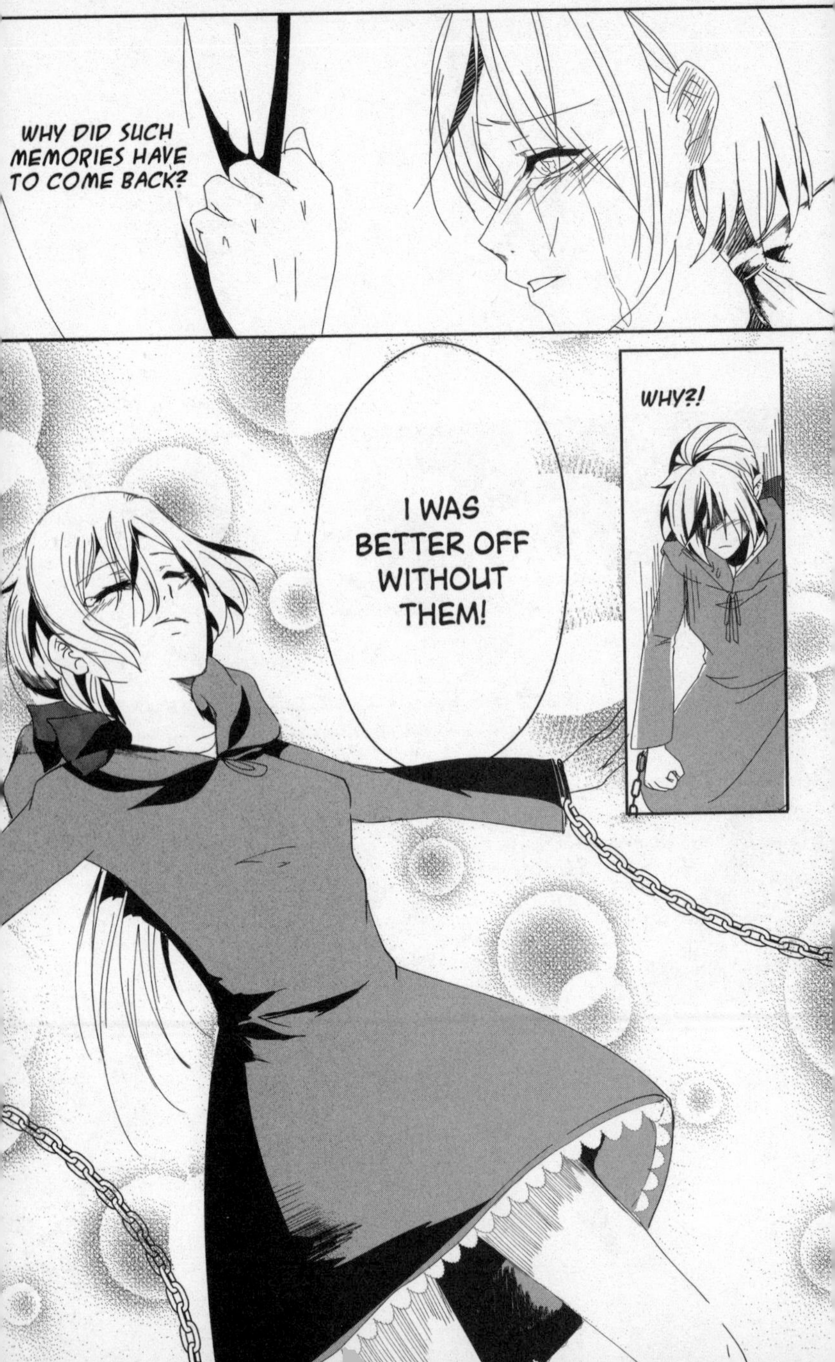
WHY DID SUCH MEMORIES HAVE TO COME BACK?
WHY?!
I WAS BETTER OFF WITHOUT THEM!

I'M SORRY FOR WHAT HAPPENED TO ALL OF US.

I'M SORRY, AL, FOR WHAT YOU HAD TO GO THROUGH BECAUSE OF ME.

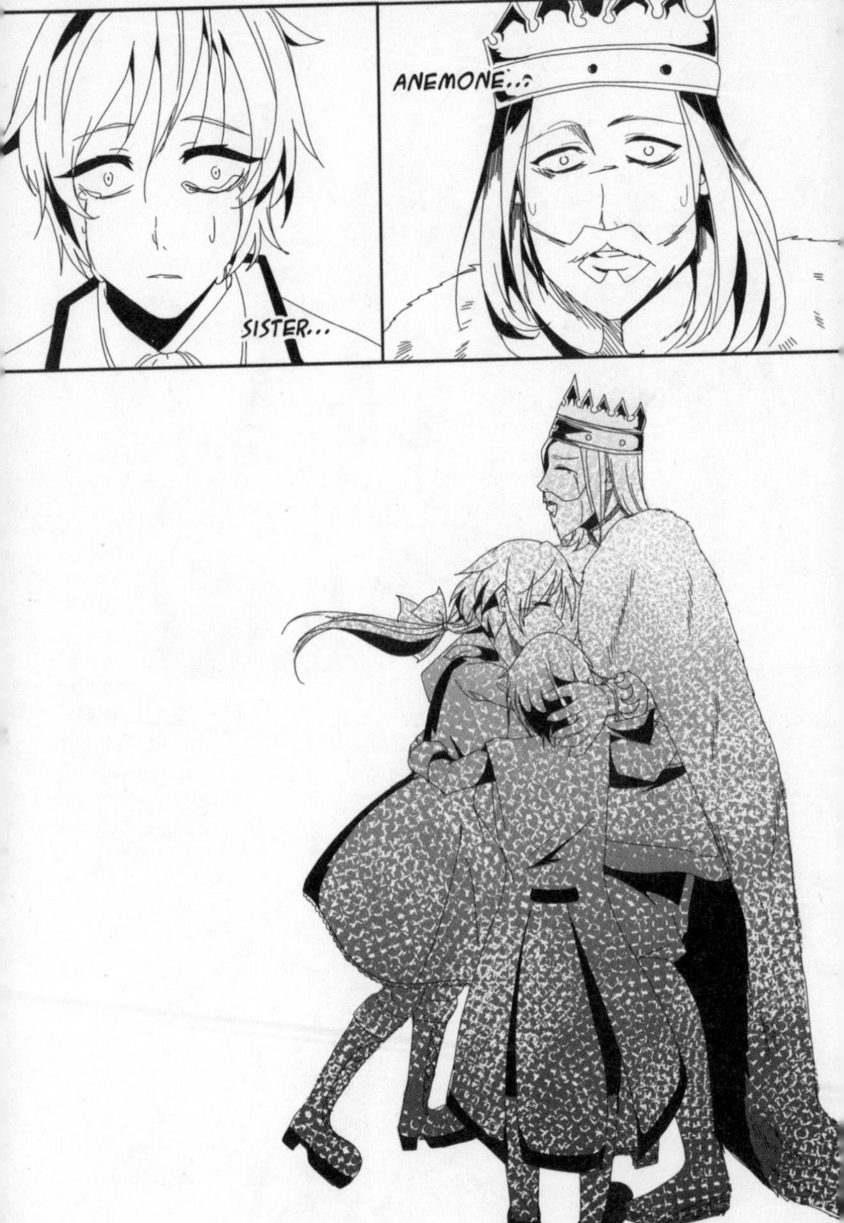
ANEMONE...?
SISTER...

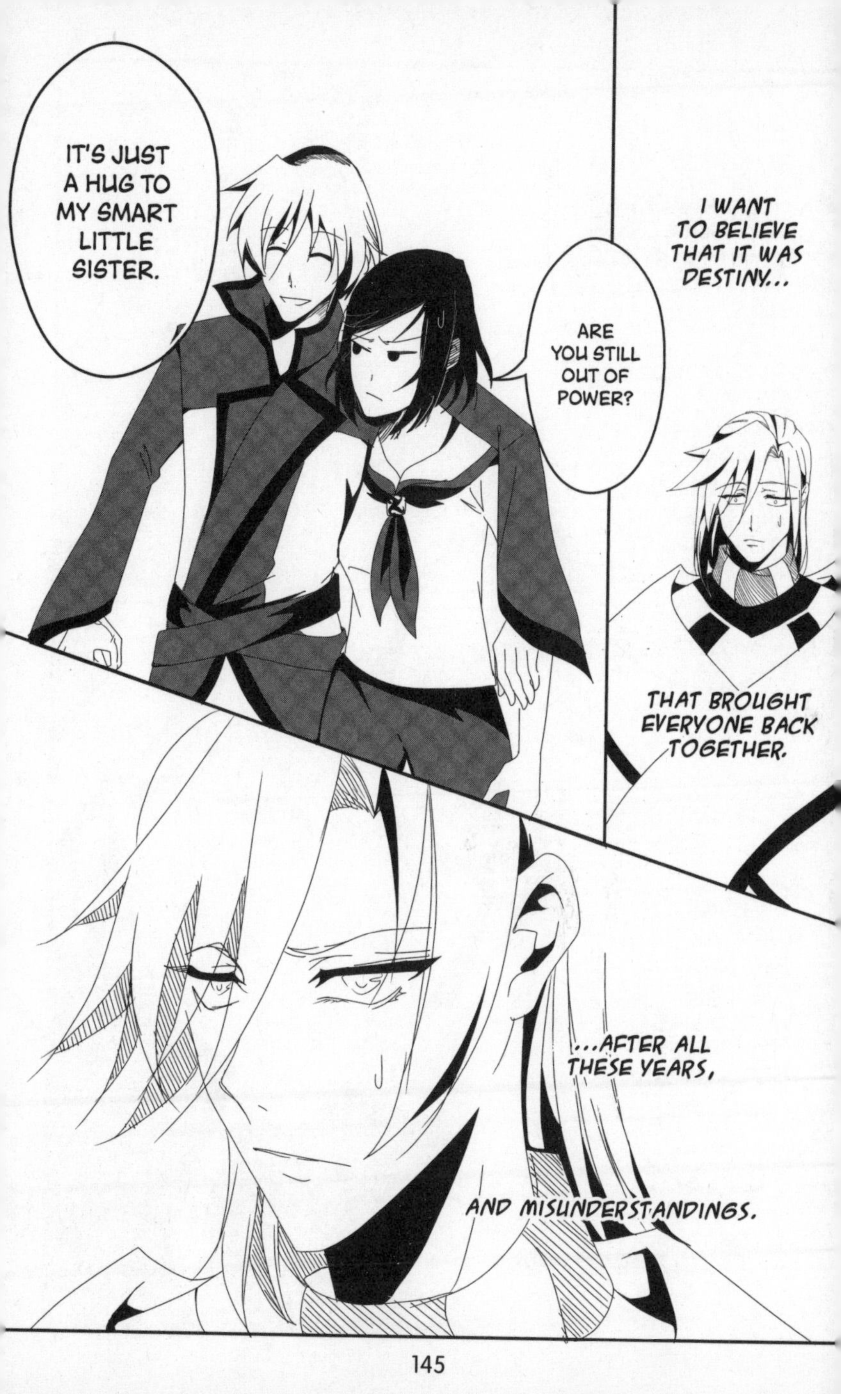
I WANT TO BELIEVE THAT IT WAS DESTINY...
THAT BROUGHT EVERYONE BACK TOGETHER.
ARE YOU STILL OUT OF POWER?
IT'S JUST A HUG TO MY SMART LITTLE SISTER.
...AFTER ALL THESE YEARS,
AND MISUNDERSTANDINGS.

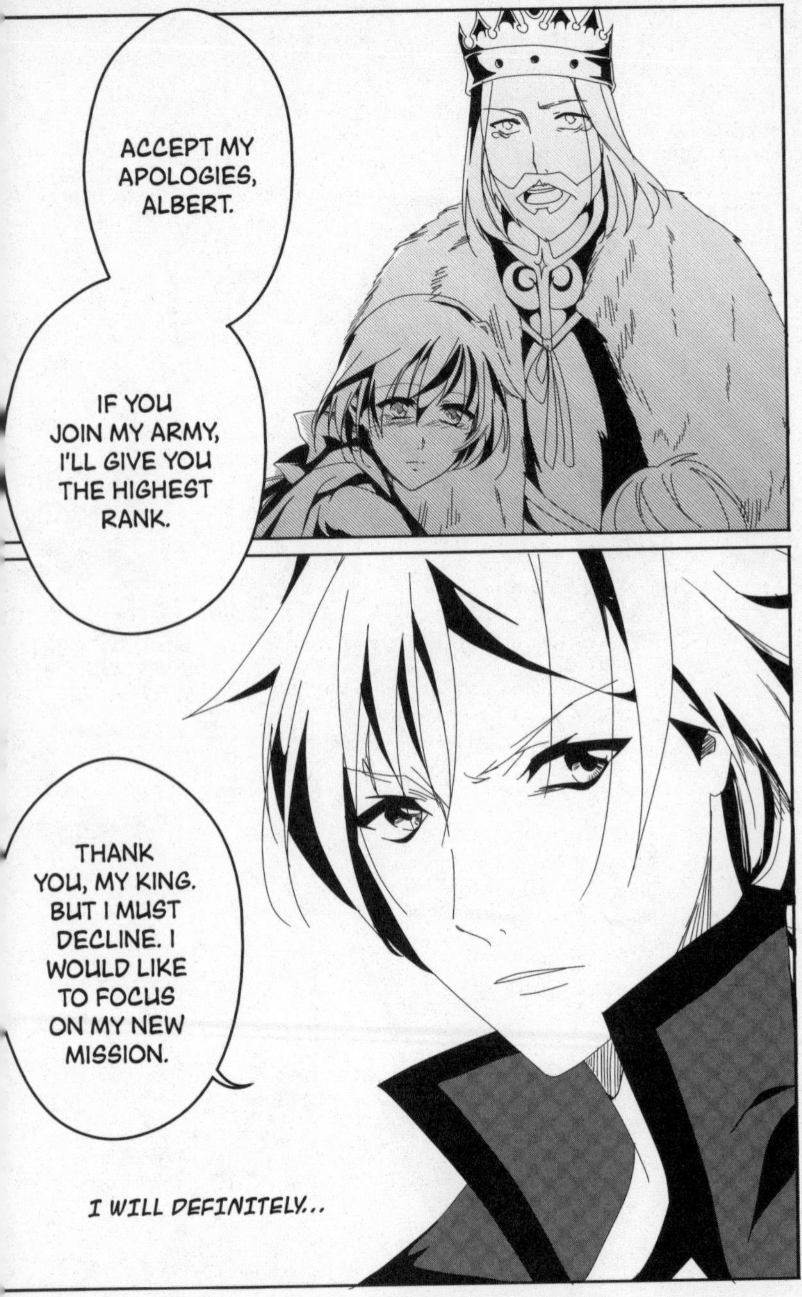
ACCEPT MY APOLOGIES, ALBERT.
IF YOU JOIN MY ARMY, I'LL GIVE YOU THE HIGHEST RANK.
THANK YOU, MY KING. BUT I MUST DECLINE. I WOULD LIKE TO FOCUS ON MY NEW MISSION.
I WILL DEFINITELY...

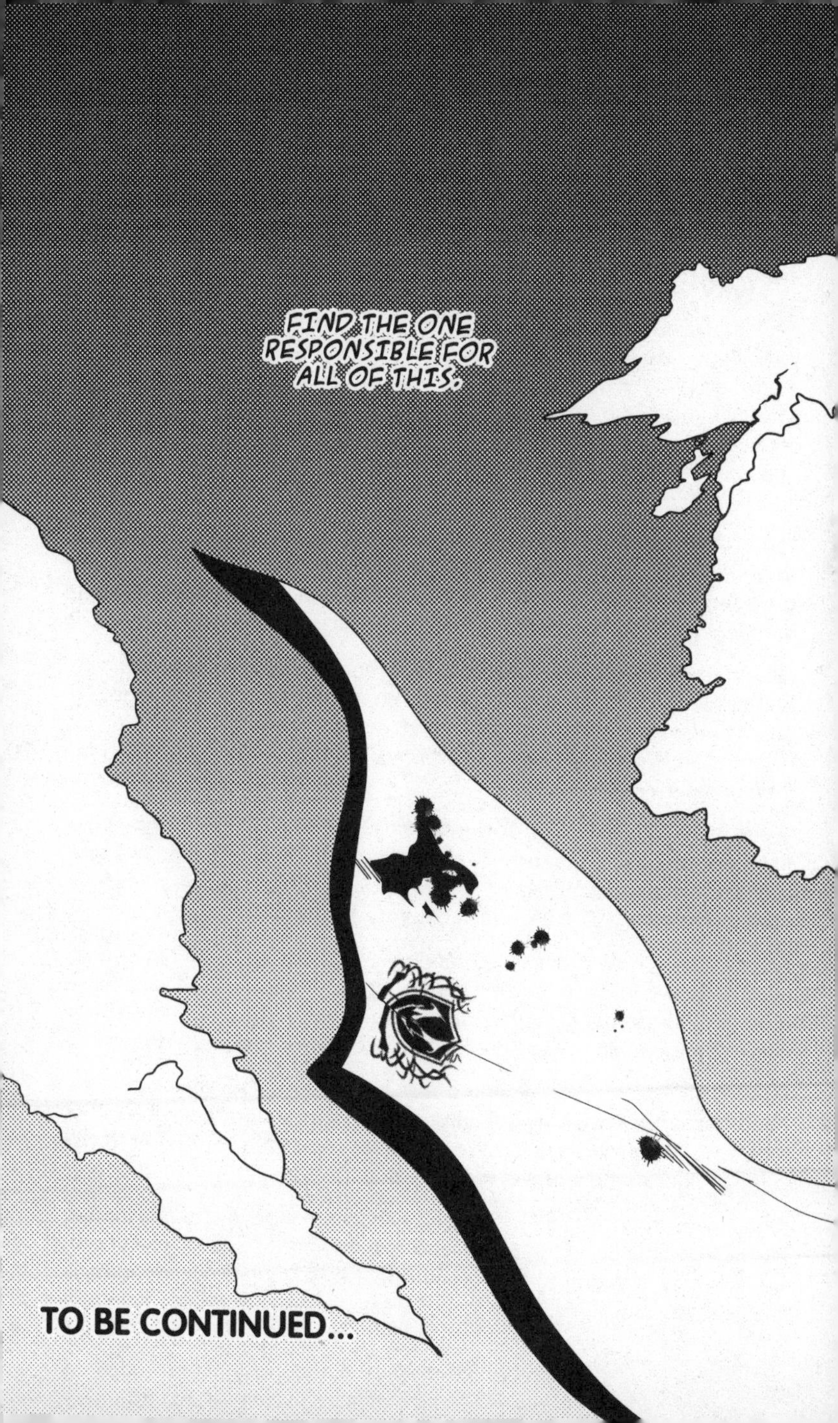
FIND THE ONE RESPONSIBLE FOR ALL OF THIS.
TO BE CONTINUED...

Ocean of Secrets

interview with Sophie-chan!!

TOKYOPOP: "Ocean of Secrets" is quite impressive for a debut manga - how did you finesse your artwork to get to this point?

Well...I have repeated chapter 1 three times! It sounds crazy but that's how motivated I was about getting better. I started the whole Ocean of Secrets project 7 years ago, I was still learning how to draw and can show you some old designs of Lia. I kept developing the story as I grew up and as I became more experienced... I always say this, I'm glad I never gave up on it!

TOKYOPOP: Lia's story really feels a lot like a longing for something forgotten, something deep inside but unknown to her. Do you have a personal connection with her? Have you gone through this type of emotional journey yourself?

I heard from some of my fans that Lia resembles a bit of my personality. I never planned for this, it just naturally happened. I have a happy family and never experienced Lia's emotional settings but I can relate to her desire to find where she belongs, which is something I was searching for throughout my journey.

TOKYOPOP: We feel a lot of classic shojo elements in the story - from the balance between innocence and maturity to an unrequited love that seems always within reach yet unreachable. Did you read a lot of shojo manga growing up? If so, which are your favorites?

I was a big fan of Shojo-styled Manga. My characters had big sparkly eyes and cute faces, but I then developed my style which I found more appealing to a larger group of readers especially for the Ocean of Secrets. Some of my favorite works were Fruits Basket, D.N.Angel and Nana.

TOKYOPOP: Of course, we find it fascinating how you grew up in the Middle East but somehow got bitten by the manga bug. Can you tell us a bit what it was like to discover and enjoy manga in your hometown? Is it popular amongst others too?

When I was in the Middle East, I'd only known Manga in a digital format. I travelled to the UK in 2006 and I still remember that feeling when I saw a huge aisle of Manga books. During that time, Manga wasn't famous where I lived, but some of my friends were into it which doubled the fun!

Nowadays, Manga books are in every major bookstore, worldwide. Along with the luxury of online shopping these days, it's waaaay easier to enjoy Manga than it was 10 years ago.

TOKYOPOP: While "Ocean of Secrets" has a solid shojo underpinning, it also has moments of almost shonen-like adventure. Were you aware of this when you wrote the story?

Yes, and I enjoyed drawing these Shonen scenes! The story appears to be shojo at first but it gets closer to Shonen as it progresses. The 2nd volume features a male main character and there will be more and more fighting scenes. Part of me, I believe, wants to show that although it's a female protagonist, it doesn't necessarily have to be shojo. There is no harm in integrating styles and making the story more dynamic.

TOKYOPOP: Besides continuing "Ocean of Secrets", do you have other stories and characters in mind for the future? Or are you focused on this world?

I'm focused on "Ocean of Secrets" since there will be multiple sub-stories that will feel like stepping-stones in the line of progressing my Manga. Each Up-coming volume will focus on a new character and how they are linked to the Ocean of Secrets universe.

TOKYOPOP: You have a tremendously popular YouTube channel teaching others about drawing manga - and even have published your own "how-to-draw" book. How did you get into the area of teaching others?

When I started YouTube, I never meant for it to be educational. I wasn't that good to teach Manga, but then after I got a little better I posted a tutorial and my channel was getting more attention. My fans were very supportive and that was the best way to support them back, help them get better at drawing! If it wasn't for that enormous support maybe I wouldn't have self-published my Manga or took it to this level of seriousness. I owe my success to them and I will do my best to inspire them to achieve their dreams.

TOKYOPOP: What's your advice to aspiring manga artists who either follow you on YouTube, social media or are fans of your work?

I always advise my followers to stay motivated and never give up. It sounds superficial but that's all you need. If YOU like drawing, and you KEEP drawing, you WILL get better with time. There will be plenty of opportunities to expand your knowledge and enhance your skills. Use them all! Always be open to new ideas and technologies and remember that you are uniquely different! You can achieve whatever you set your mind to.

Character Designs - LIA

ere are some variations of LIA that were created for concepts. Many of these
re older designs with different styles, including more extreme shojo versions.

WOAH!!!

Lia

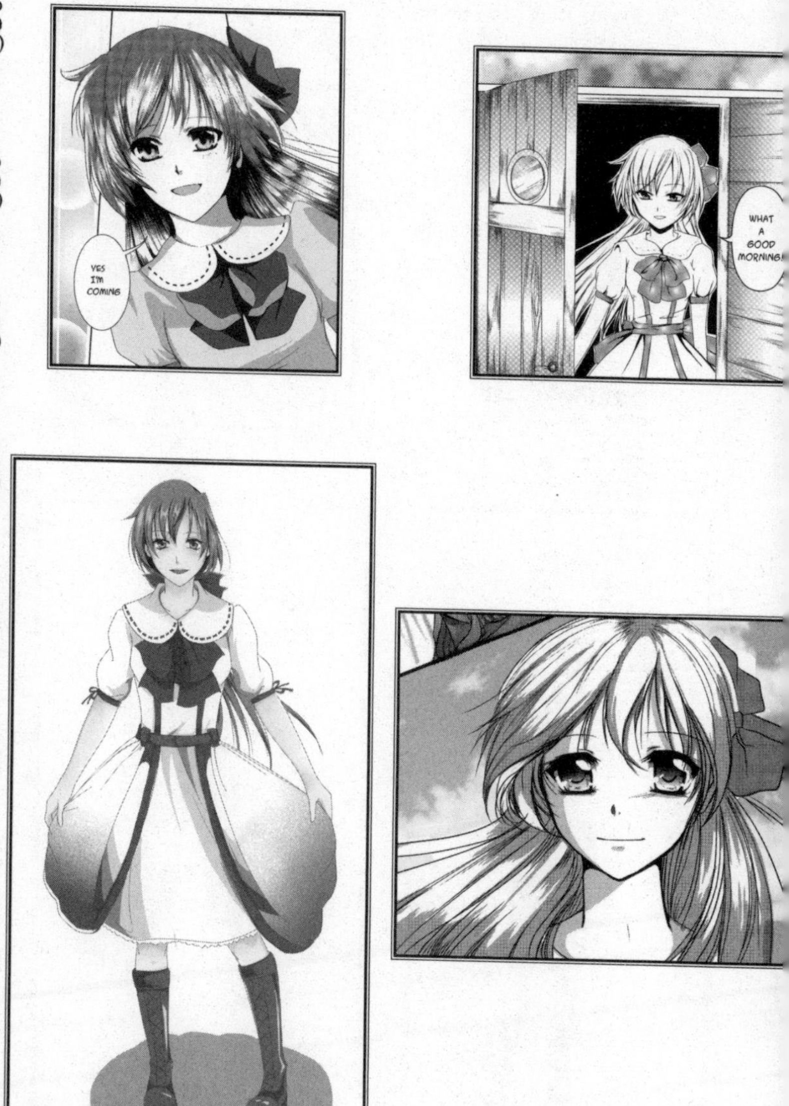
WHAT A GOOD MORNING!
YES I'M COMING

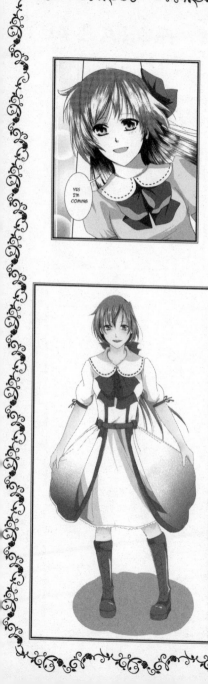

Character Designs - MORIA & AL

Moria and Al also went through deviations along the way to finding their true selves. Please enjoy these older concepts.

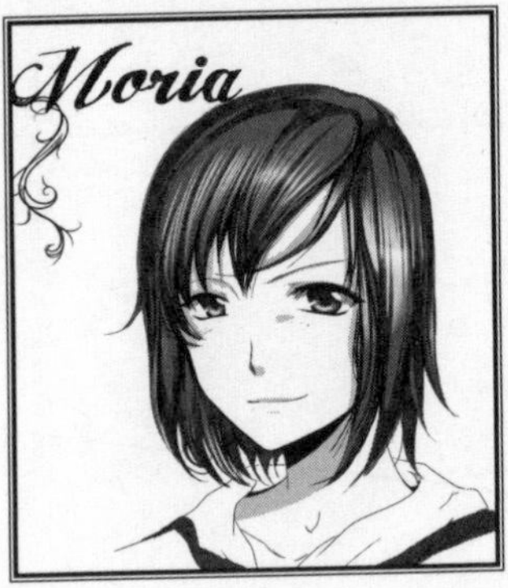
Moria

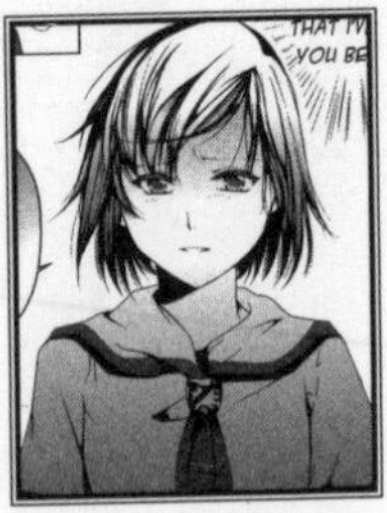

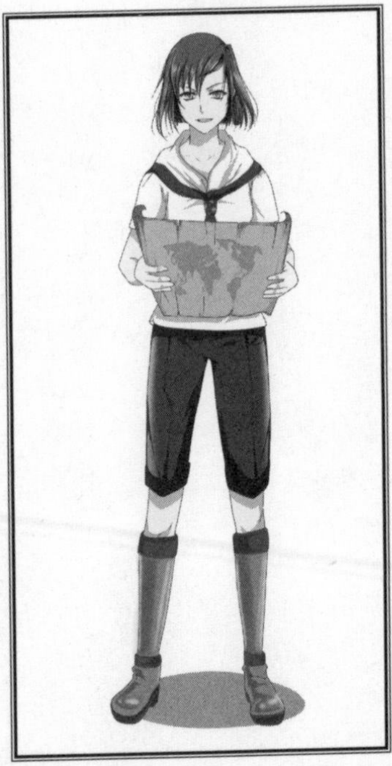

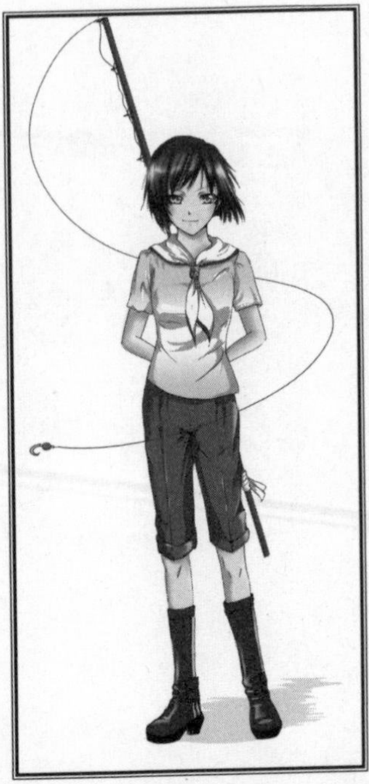

Albert

Chibis

Who doesn't love chibis? Here are a few fun chibis for you to enjoy!

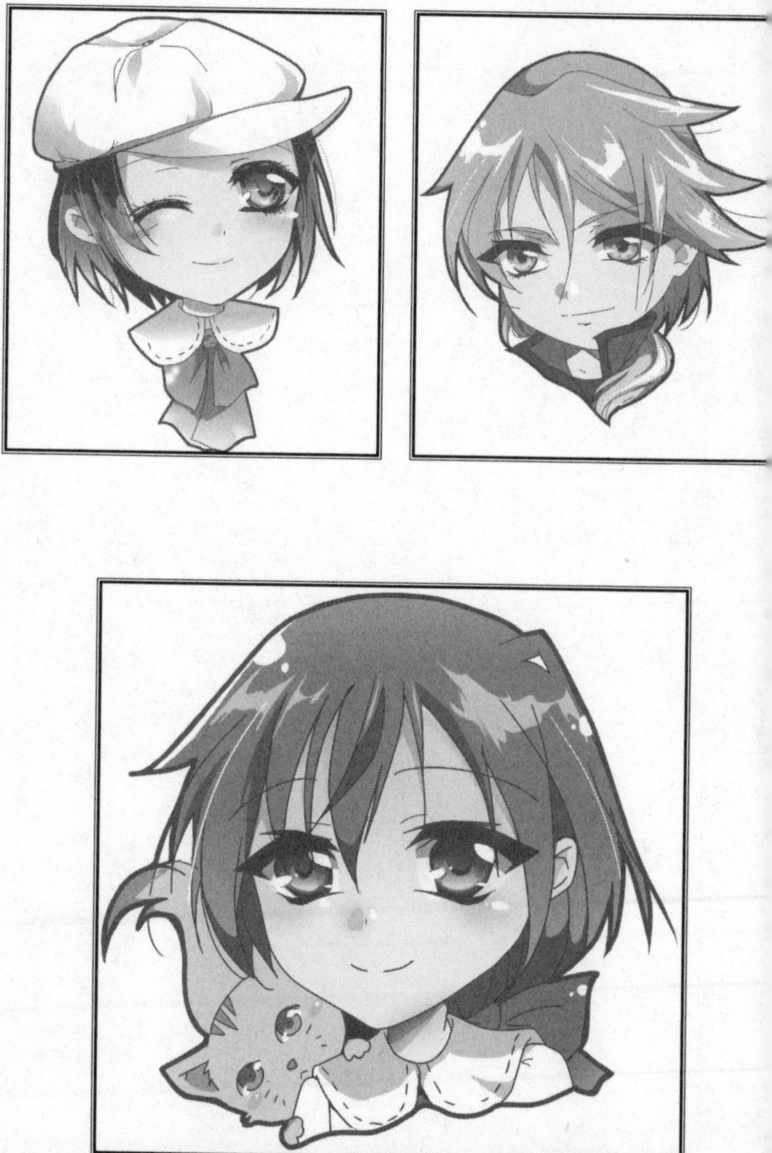

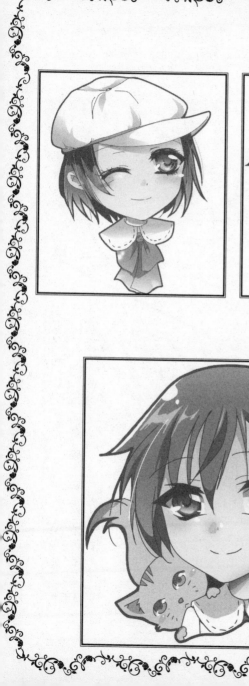

Old Pages

Learning how to construct manga pages isn't easy - see some of the previous attempts made along the way.

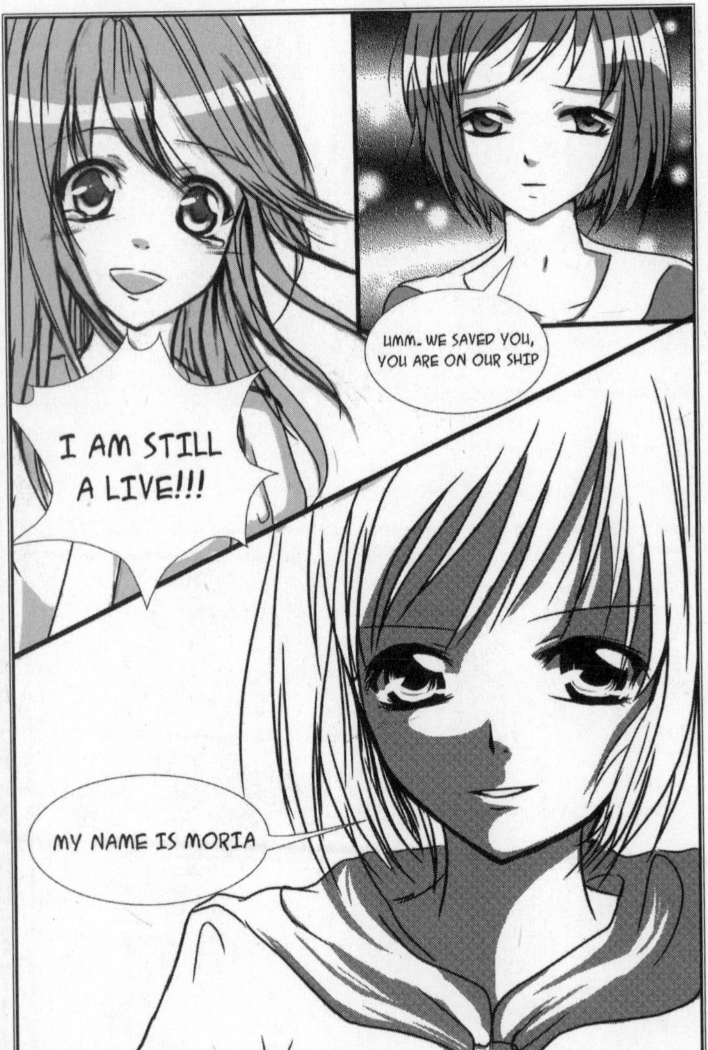
UMM.. WE SAVED YOU, YOU ARE ON OUR SHIP
I AM STILL A LIVE!!!
MY NAME IS MORIA

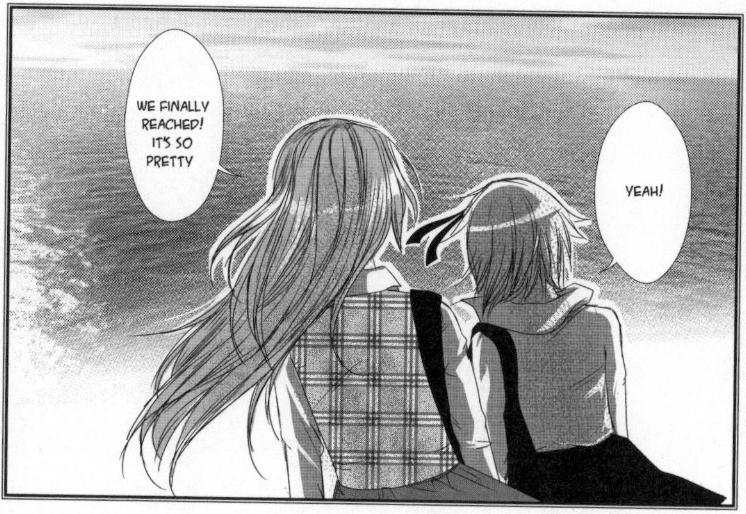
WE FINALLY REACHED! IT'S SO PRETTY
YEAH!
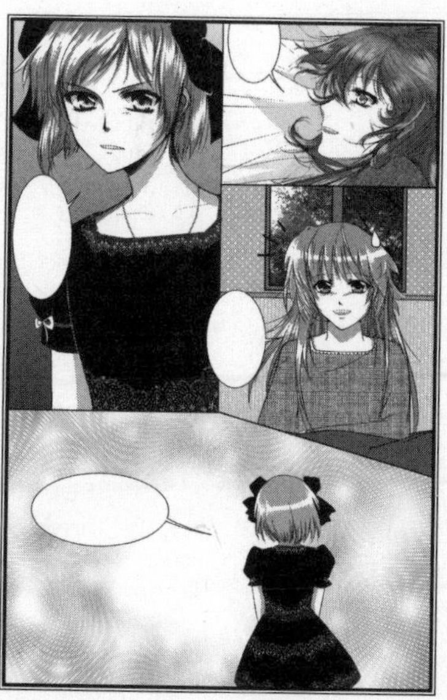
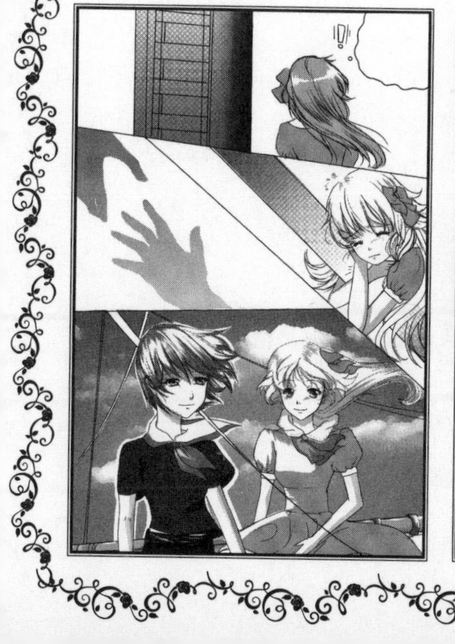
!

New Character In Volume 2 - RAI !!

I have pictured Rai in my mind so many times before sketching him. I wanted the brave/confident look that is similar to Moria and the same humbleness that Lia portrayed. He's not similar to any of them though – you'll find out how distinct his personality is in the next volume. I sketched him in the half armor costume since he looks much cooler that way!

–Sophie-chan

In the next volume of

Ocean of Secrets

On a flight back home, geology student Rai catches a glimpse of Lyronaz. Determined to find an explanation to what he saw, Rai begins an intensive search to find the mysterious floating kingdom. Meanwhile in Lyronaz, Moria discovers her father's involvement in the Queen's murder and finds out why Princess Aneome was kidnapped.

As pirates prepare to destroy the land, the three kingdoms prepare for war. What does Anemone hold that is so precious to the pirates? Will the three kingdoms unite and conquer the dark powers of magic that the pirates possess? Find out in Volume 2 of *Ocean of Secrets*!!

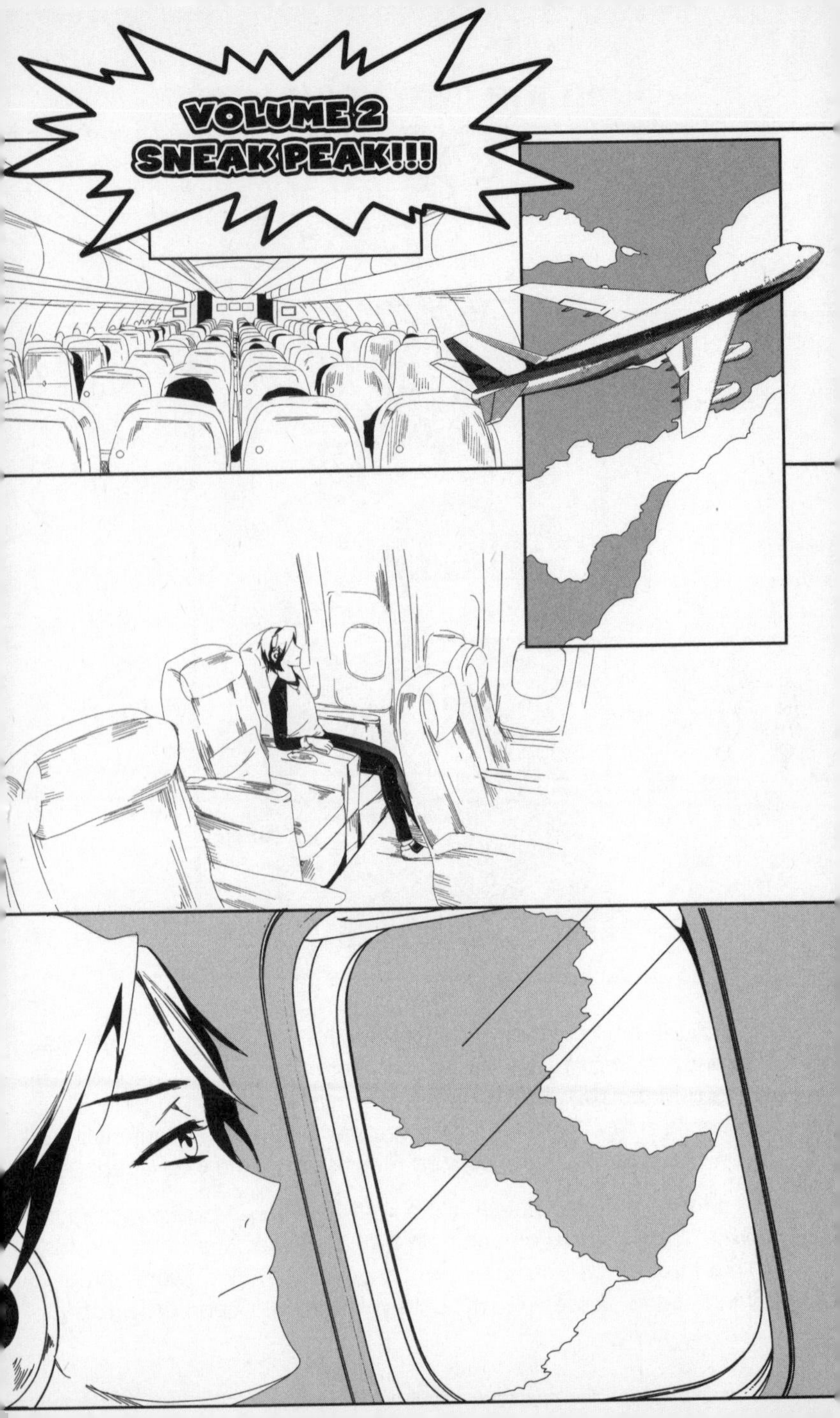
VOLUME 2
SNEAK PEAK!!!

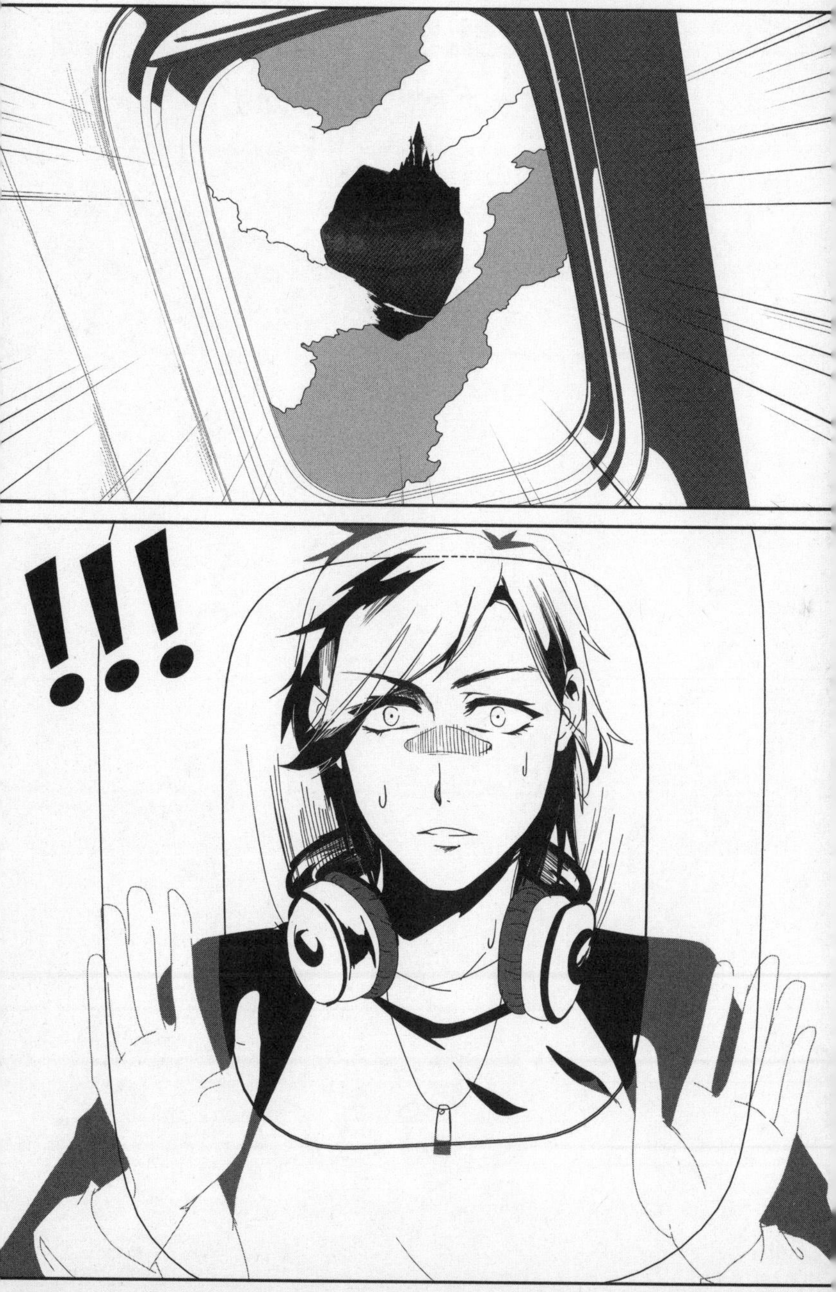
!!!

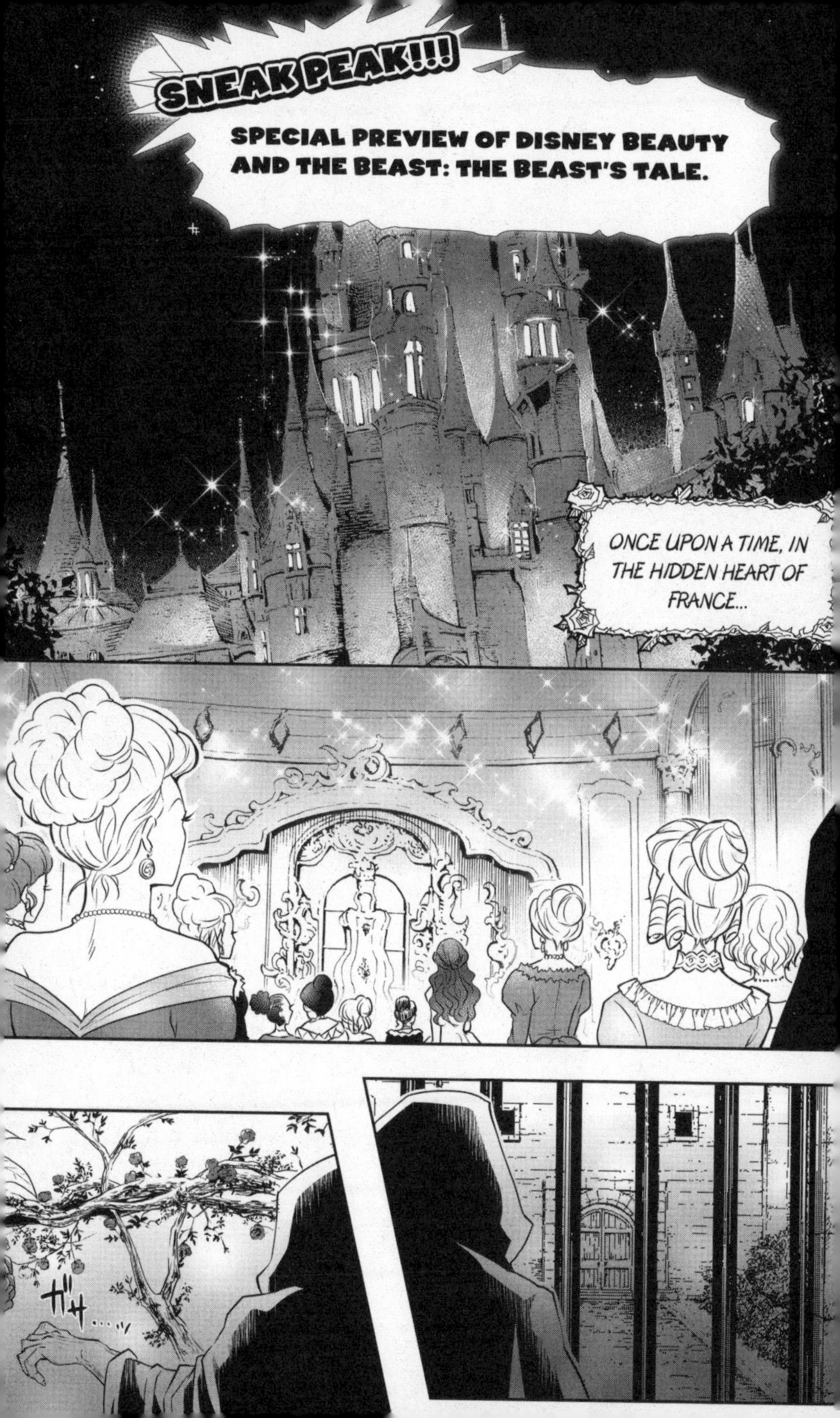
SNEAK PEAK!!!
SPECIAL PREVIEW OF DISNEY BEAUTY AND THE BEAST: THE BEAST'S TALE.
ONCE UPON A TIME, IN THE HIDDEN HEART OF FRANCE...
ガサ...ッ

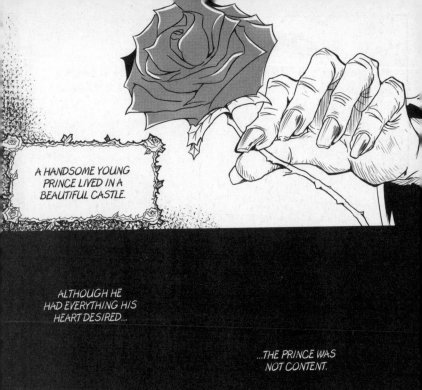

A HANDSOME YOUNG PRINCE LIVED IN A BEAUTIFUL CASTLE.

ALTHOUGH HE HAD EVERYTHING HIS HEART DESIRED...

...THE PRINCE WAS NOT CONTENT.

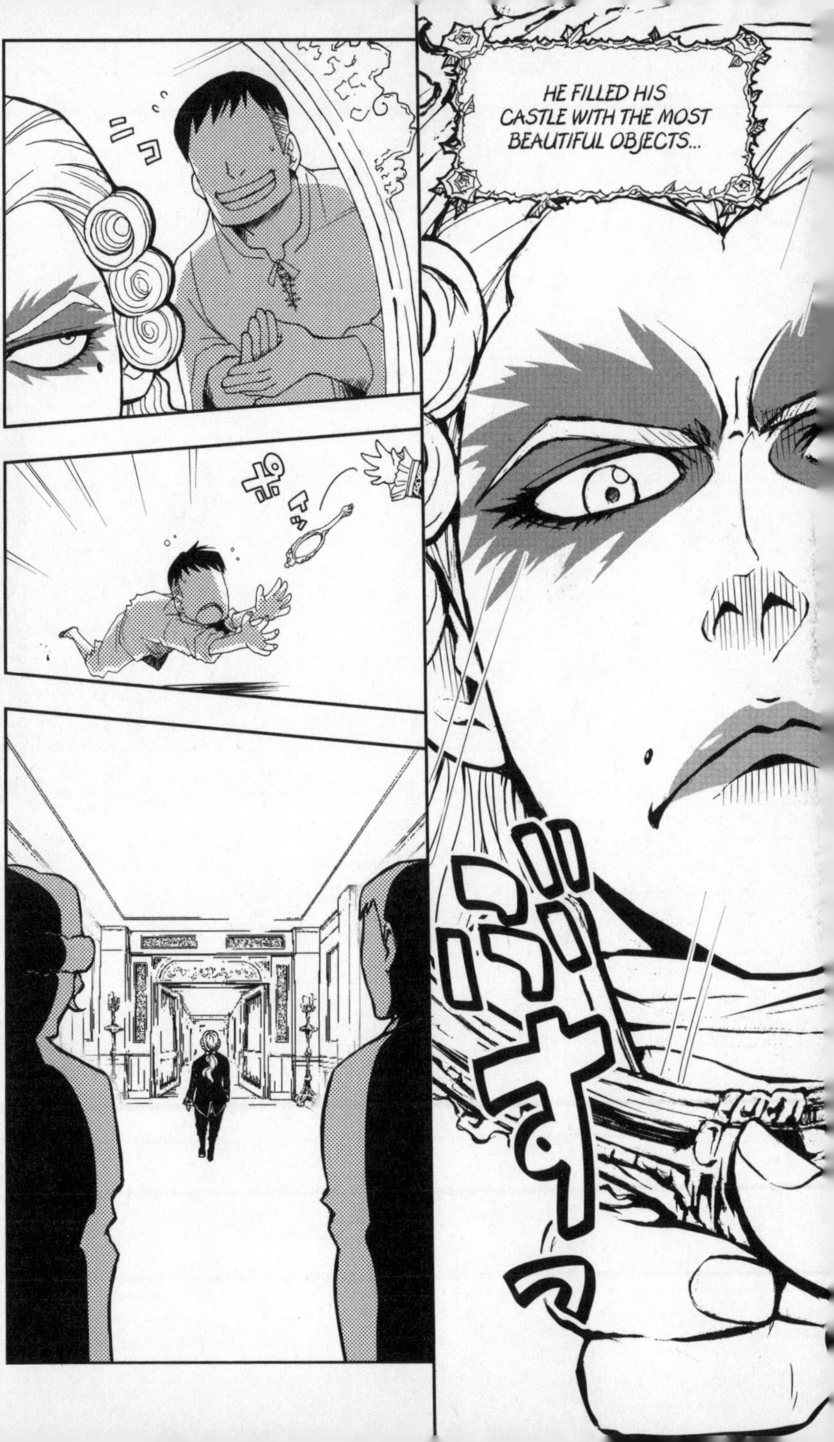
HE FILLED HIS CASTLE WITH THE MOST BEAUTIFUL OBJECTS...
ニコ

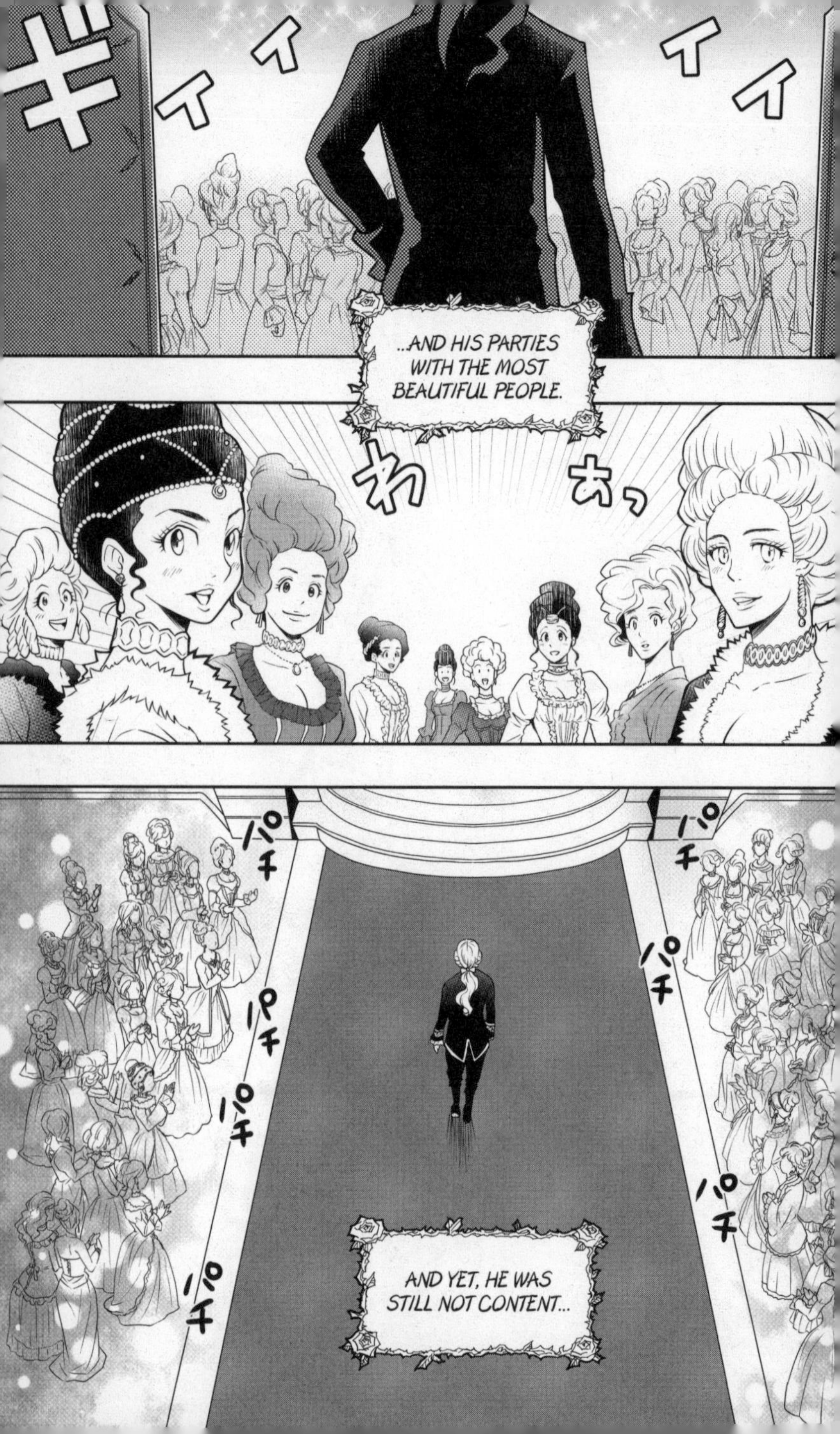
ギィィ
イイ
...AND HIS PARTIES WITH THE MOST BEAUTIFUL PEOPLE.
わあっ
パチ
パチ
パチ
パチ
パチ
パチ
パチ
AND YET, HE WAS STILL NOT CONTENT...

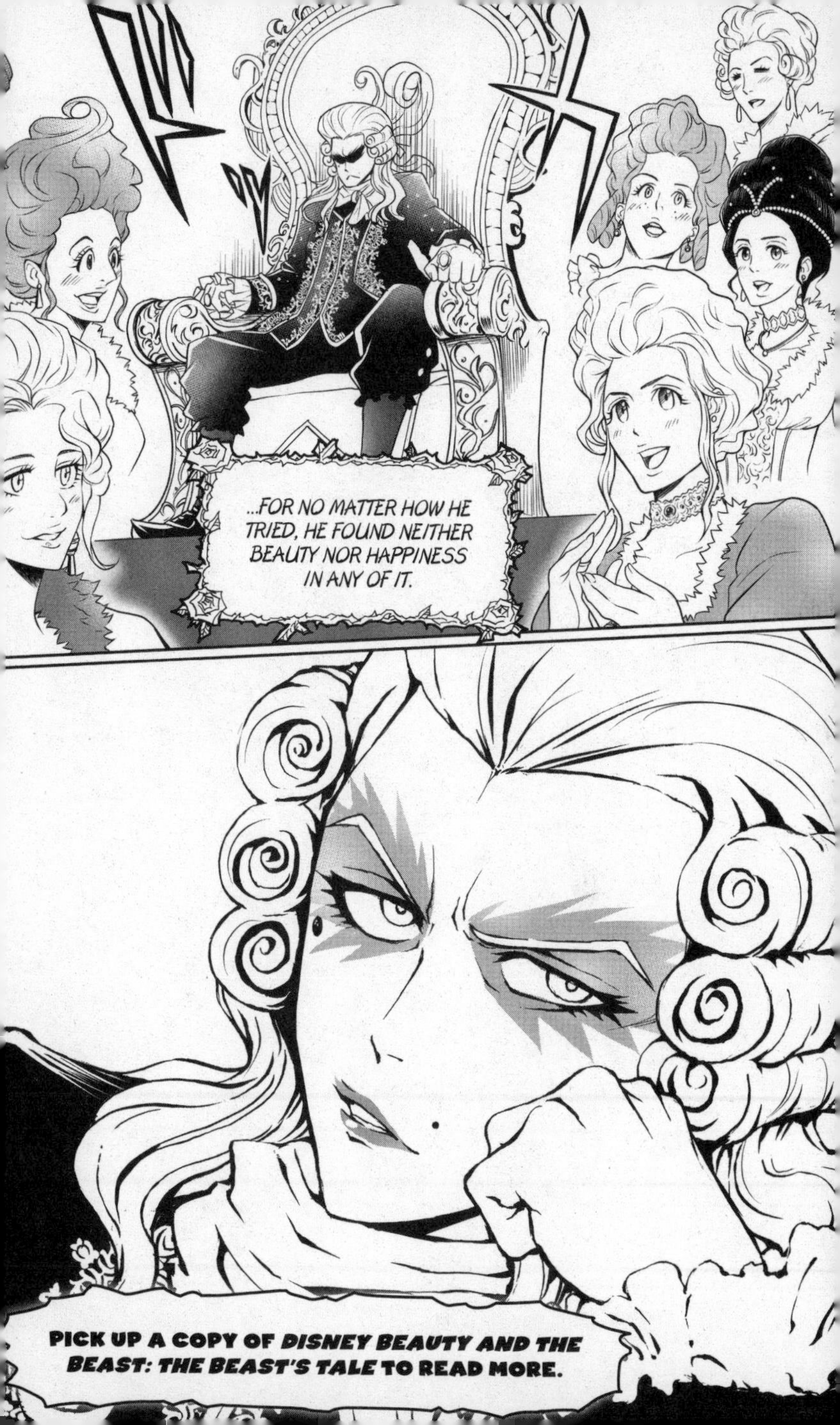
...FOR NO MATTER HOW HE TRIED, HE FOUND NEITHER BEAUTY NOR HAPPINESS IN ANY OF IT.
PICK UP A COPY OF *DISNEY BEAUTY AND THE BEAST: THE BEAST'S TALE* TO READ MORE.

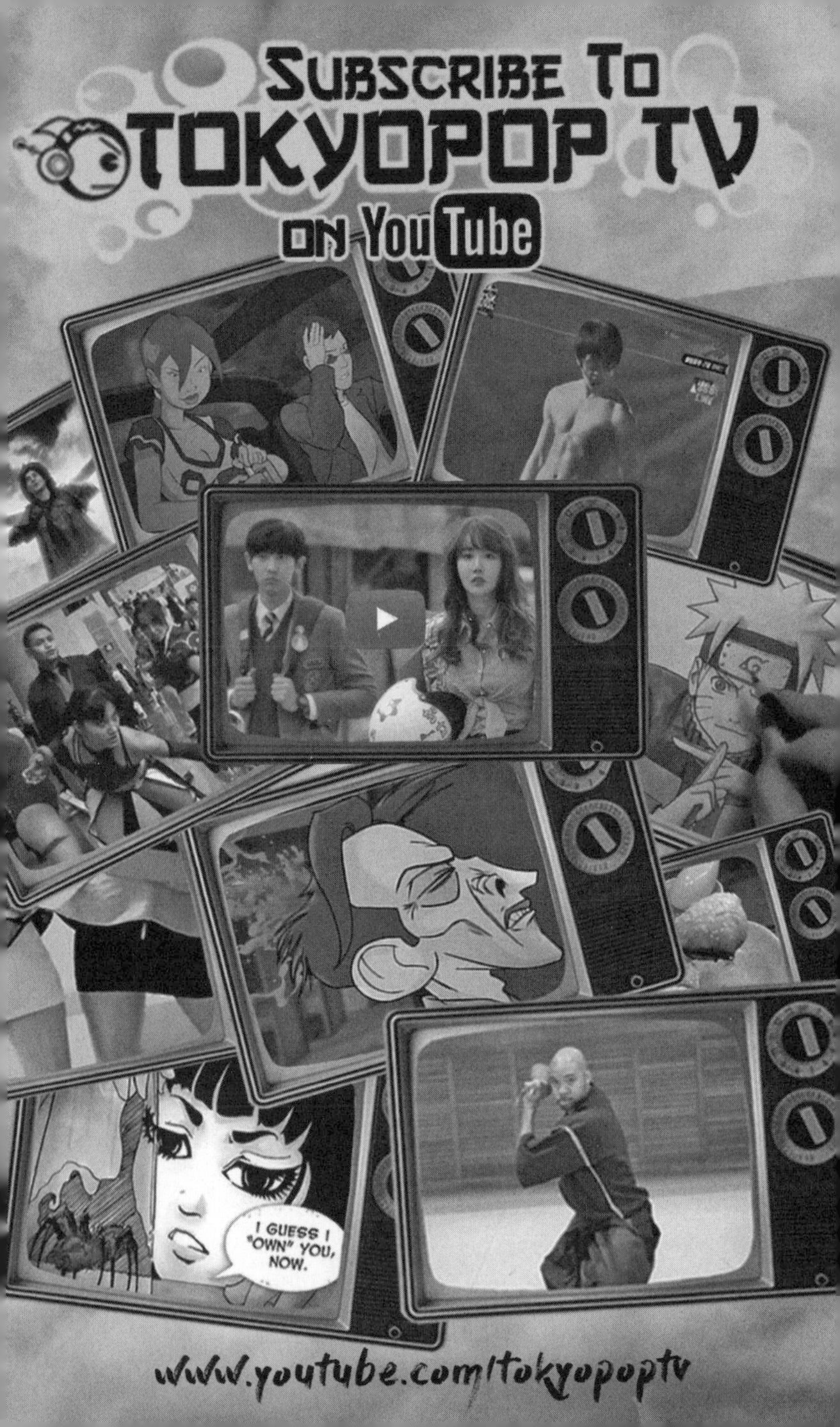
SUBSCRIBE TO
TOKYOPOP TV
ON YouTube
I GUESS I "OWN" YOU, NOW.
www.youtube.com/tokyopoptv

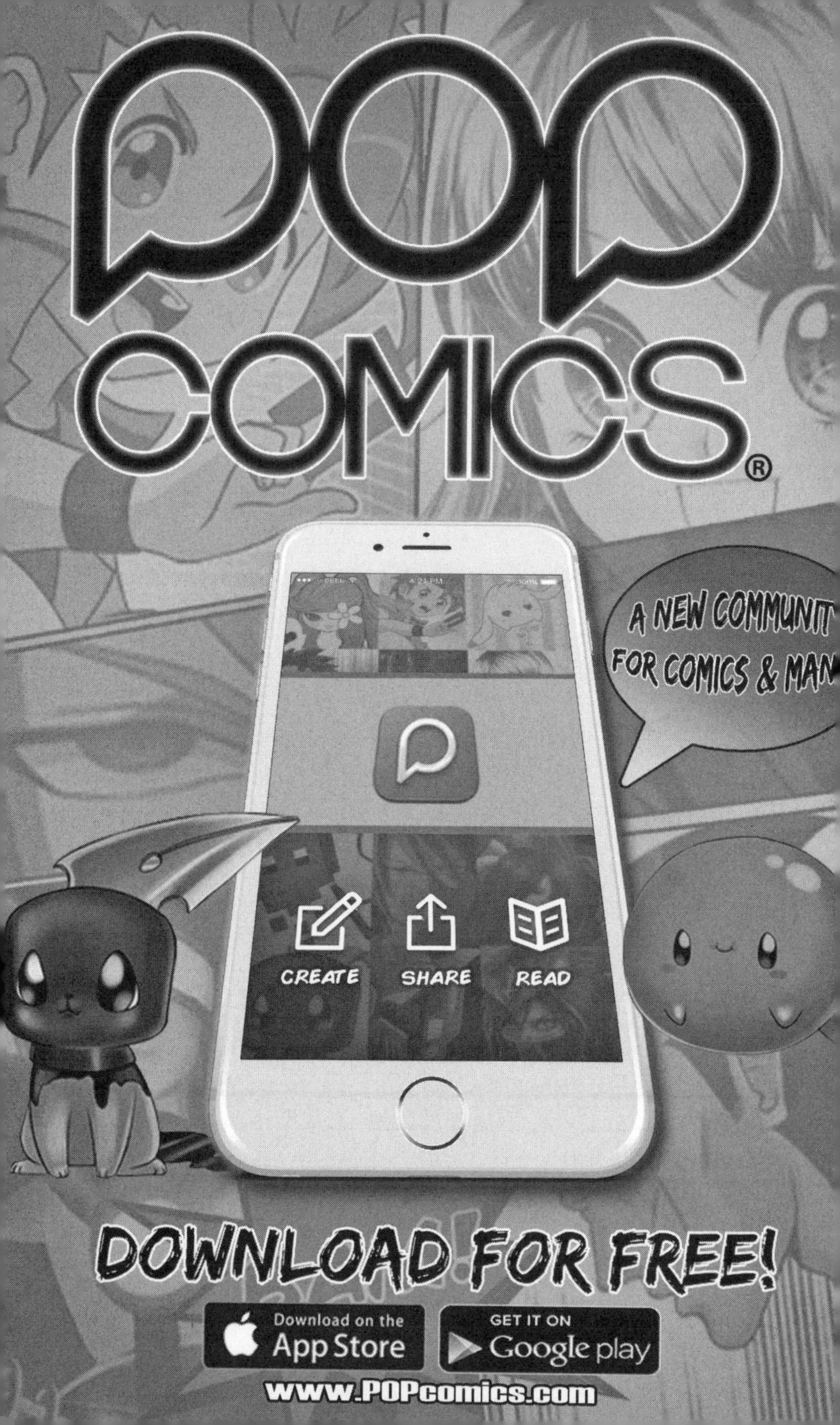

POP COMICS®
A NEW COMMUNIT
FOR COMICS & MAN
CREATE
SHARE
READ
DOWNLOAD FOR FREE!
Download on the App Store
GET IT ON Google play
www.POPcomics.com

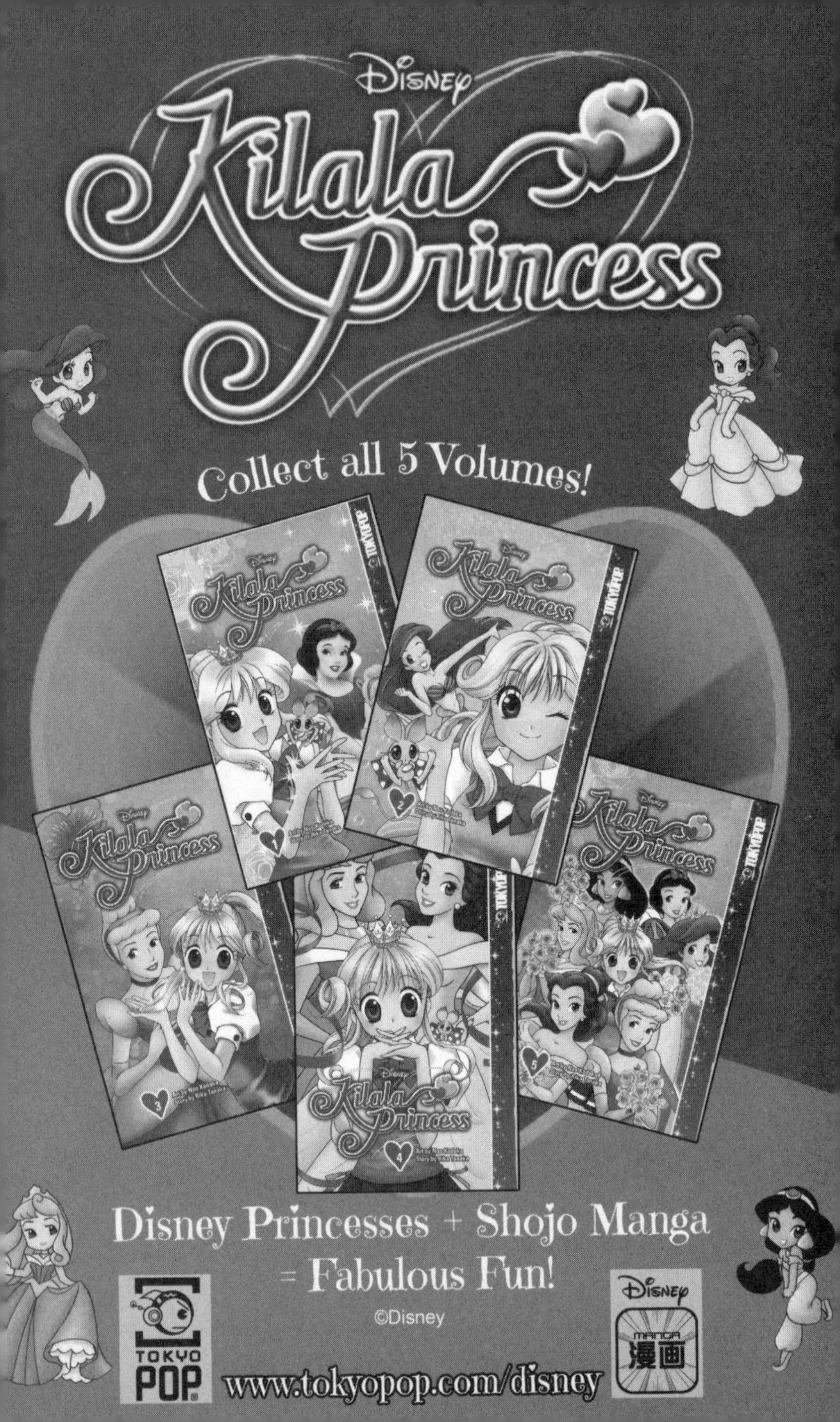
Disney
Kilala Princess
Collect all 5 Volumes!
Disney Princesses + Shojo Manga
= Fabulous Fun!
©Disney
TOKYO POP
www.tokyopop.com/disney
Disney
MANGA
漫画

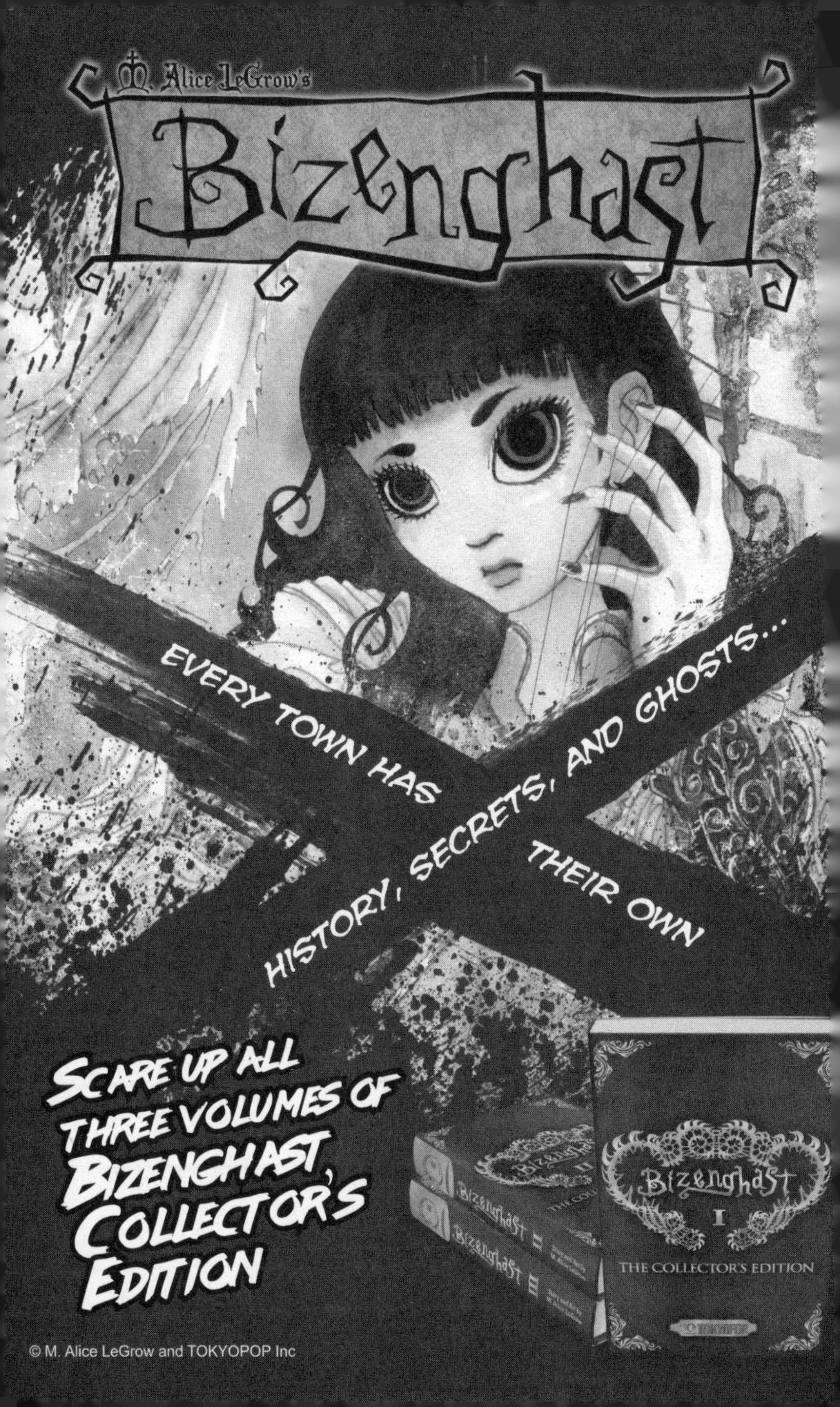
M. Alice LeGrow's
Bizenghast
EVERY TOWN HAS HISTORY, SECRETS, AND GHOSTS... THEIR OWN
SCARE UP ALL THREE VOLUMES OF BIZENGHAST, COLLECTOR'S EDITION
Bizenghast I
THE COLLECTOR'S EDITION
TOKYOPOP

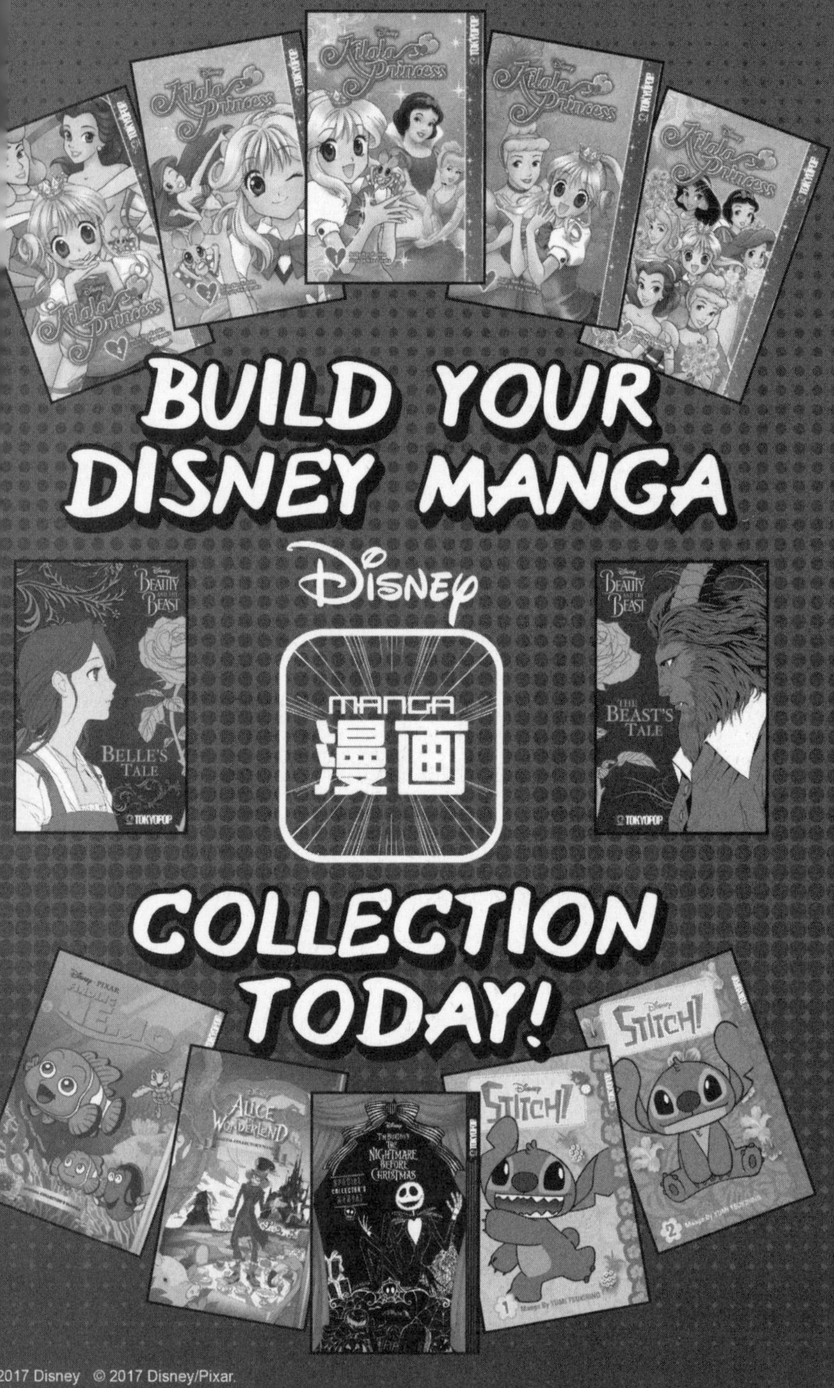
BUILD YOUR DISNEY MANGA
Disney
MANGA
漫画
COLLECTION TODAY!
Kilala Princess
Beauty and the Beast
Belle's Tale
The Beast's Tale
TOKYOPOP
Alice in Wonderland
The Nightmare Before Christmas
Stitch!

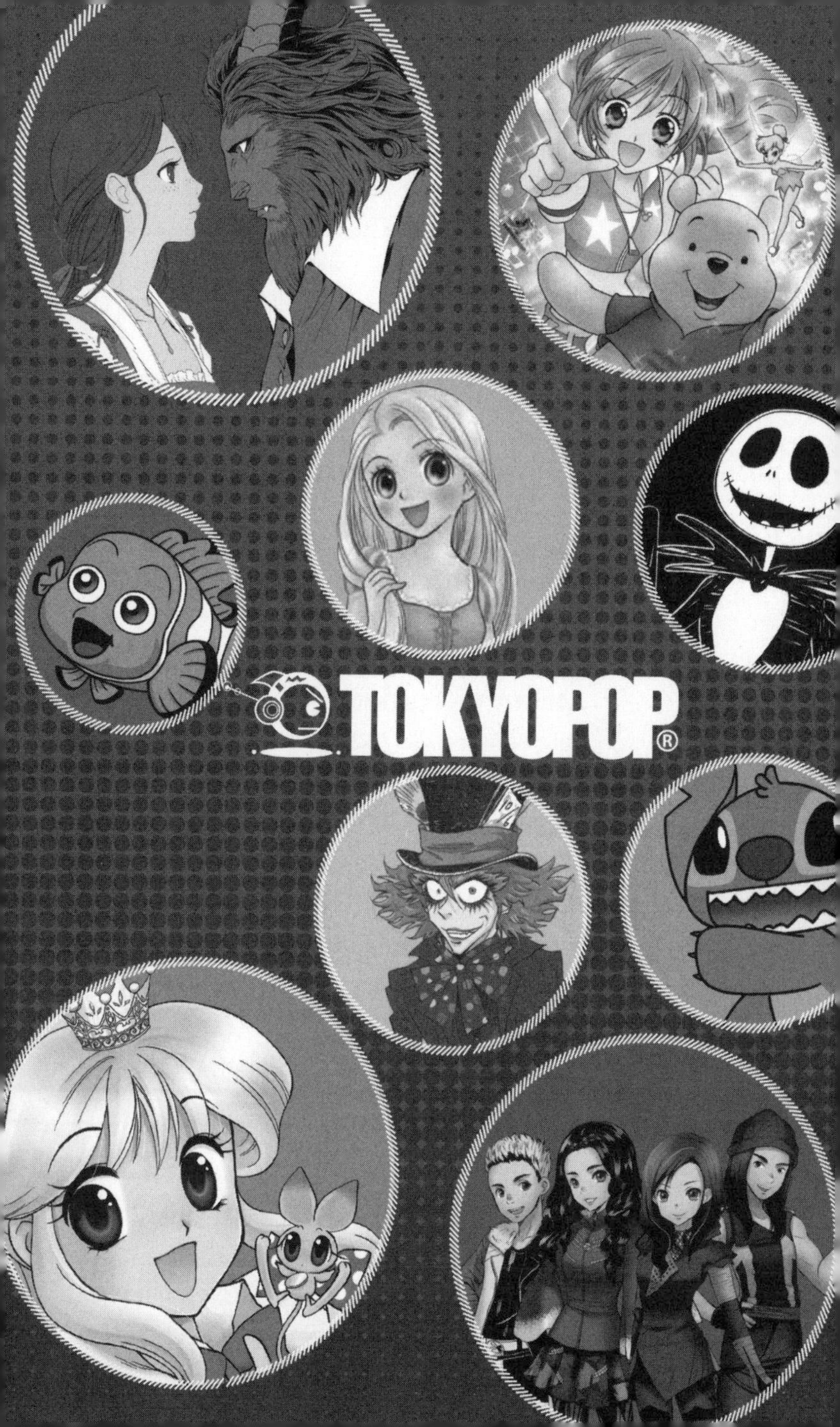
TOKYOPOP®

ABOUT THE AUTHOR:

Sophie-chan (Safa Al-Ani), a self-taught manga artist, born December 1990 in Iraq, gained a following by posting drawing videos on her YouTube channel titled "sophiechan90" with over 30 Million views.

She began drawing and writing stories when she was 7 years old, determined to reach her goal of having her own manga series/anime adaption.

Although Sophie's educational background is in engineering, she continued inspiring artists to follow their dreams no matter where their studies lead them to. Sophie first self-published her graphic novel "The Ocean of Secrets", a full volume manga, in April 2015. Later in November 2015, Sophie created "manga Workshop characters", a how-to-draw book published by IMPACT.

Sophie appeared in several comic conventions such as Middle East Film and Comic Con, New York Comic Con and Anime North. Sophie held several school workshops and a fund-raiser contest for the Syrian Refugees in 2016.